OCEANS OF GRACE

RACHEL MARIE SERIES
BOOK TEN

DAVID B. SMITH

D1446309

Copyright 2020
Waldo Publishing
San Bernardino, California

CAST OF CHARACTERS

If you're reading *Oceans of Grace* as a stand-alone adventure, here's a brief primer on the main characters in Pranom's new Bangkok world.

Khemkaeng and Rachel Marie Chairsurivirat
She's one of the central players, a hugely popular sixth-grade teacher at BCS. Her husband is the school's VP and converted to Christianity as a result of his friendship with Rachel Marie.

Miles and Sue Carington
Sue is this thriving Asian school's leader and can-do miracle worker. Her husband is an Aussie doctor who loves the 1,300 adorable kids at BCS.

Gino and Natty Carington
Gino is Miles's son, miraculously cured of leukemia and now United Christian Church's associate pastor. He married Khemkaeng's youngest sister Nattaporn.

Benjie and Chloe Cey
Benjie is the school's mischief-loving chemistry teacher and resident Brit. He stunned all of Thailand by landing the beautiful volleyball superstar Chloe as his bride.

Noah and Ratana Charoenkul
BCS's music teacher is a long-haired wonder who came out from California for a televised music competition. He's half-Thai and successfully wooed "Dr. Ratana," the contest's winner in the debut season.

Charles and Audrey Jennings
Audrey came out to BKK for hip-replacement surgery, got drafted at BCS, and decided to stay. Her husband teaches at a Christian college on the outskirts of the city.

Ethan and Vasana Gray
He's the gray-haired rocker embraced by United Christian Church in Bangkok after the tragic passing of his wife. He soon fell in love with Vasana, a university professor in Phuket, and now ministers in that tropical paradise.

ONE

There's nothing so sweet as a grad-level math problem that fills up a whole page with impressive scribbles and cross-cancelled exponents (fractional, no less), and layered GCFs. And then you peek in the back of the book. *Are you kidding? I got it!!* I'd just done a doozy, one of those two-paragraph horrors at the genius tail end of the section. And maybe it was the Mountain Dew rushing through my capillaries, but my bits of Galois Theory were working for me, and when I peered at the answer guide, there it was. *Eighty-two pi divided by 15.*

Half-grinning to myself, I slid my phone out of my purse and thumbed in a text to Mom. *You should see the stinker I just did. Took half an hour, but I got it right. See u at 10. P.*

My cell dinged less than twenty seconds later. Just a happy-face emoji and the cryptic reply: LMLD.

I know, I know. "Like Mom, Like Daughter." Samantha the Actuarist has a degree in math as well; in fact, most of my university friends rag on me for my lack of imagination in picking a career path. "Some stereotypes are actually true," grumbles Leanne, who generally sat in suffering silence next to me during multivariable calc lectures. "Asian ladies are brilliant at math without hardly trying."

That wasn't exactly accurate. Okay, I was still nursing my 4.0 GPA with less than seven weeks before graduation. And my scores on Canvas, the college's Learning Management System, were hovering at 99.2%. But that came from pure Bangkok perspiration. My math achievements don't just tumble out of a papaya tree. More nights than not, Dad shuffles into my bedroom, earbuds dangling around his neck, and gives me a kiss atop my head. "G'night, genius. Don't stay up too late using all my electricity."

"Good night, Daddy."

And it's always the same. "Sure glad I found you, sweet cakes."

"Me too."

Dad's an unreformed rocker who still looks the part. Shaggy hair, beard, posters of the Eagles and Rolling Stones plastered up on his studio walls, along with a massive blow-up of his one and only recording project which he pulled off two years after bringing me over to America. Thinking about it now made me smile, and I spun my phone's music library over to my favorite Tommy Daggett praise song. *One more problem and I'm heading out.*

It was a luscious evening here in Portland. Peering out through the massive glass windows on the other side of eight rows of reference books I could make out the inky outlines of stately trees poking up into the moonlight. I love our campus: modern with clean architectural lines, but all the main buildings done in brick. I don't know how the campus custodial department does it; I guess around midnight they probably attack the place with a vengeance, armed with rolling trash carts. But every morning at 8:53 when I wheel into Lot F, the vast lawns are spotless green rectangles. Leaves raked up; soda cups from the nearby delis tossed into trash receptacles.

Exercise #109 stymied me for the moment; I stared blankly at the diagram, trying to claw a mental hole in the barricade. When in doubt, sip more Dew, so I did that. I reviewed recent theorems and felt my math pulse brighten. *Aha. That might work . . .*

I was halfway through setting it up, tracing out a schematic of the problem and penciling in the variables. Just then my chair jiggled and I looked up, startled. "Oh! It's you."

"Hey." Logan glanced around, but of course, by 9:30 the upper levels of a university library have mostly cleared out.

He moved in for the perfunctory kiss and I tried to not betray my trepidation. Most guys expect a hello kiss, which isn't an unreasonable ask. It wasn't Logan's fault I always felt that imperceptible squeeze in my gut whenever duty called. But I brushed my lips against his stubbly cheek. "I didn't think I'd see you."

"Well, I had a lady want a test drive, but then when it came right down to it her husband said forget it, too much, going all-electric's not worth the extra seven grand on the invoice. They stormed out and I didn't figure any more customers coming by this time of night."

I nodded absently, trying to decide if I wanted to make him wait while I soldiered through this last math exercise. Sighing, I flipped my notebook closed.

"I didn't mean to make you cut off your work. Go ahead and finish."

"It's okay." I tugged my backpack up from the floor and stuffed my massive tome inside, wedging my sheaf of notes in next to it. "It would take twenty minutes to do and I need to get on the freeway."

Logan grinned. "I'll walk you out."

We clumped down the two flights of stairs together, my heels clicking on the metal guards on each step. I spotted Gwen at the main reference desk, an angular African-American girl I know from my one aborted semester in the campus dorm. She spotted me and gave a half-hearted wave. "Hey, Pranom."

I swerved a bit closer. "How soon are you off?"

"At ten."

"Okay." I managed a grin. "I'll see you at graduation if not before."

Her smile dimmed. "Huh uh. I messed up my transcripts. Got to take two more classes this summer. So much for Guided Pathways, thanks for nothing, guidance counselor."

"Bummer."

Shrug. "It is what it is."

The colloquialism stayed with me as I followed Logan up the sidewalk toward the student parking lot. *It is what it is.* In Thai, I guess we'd say *mai bhen rai*: it doesn't matter. It was odd, I mused, how even after a full decade here in Oregon, living my decidedly American life with Tommy and Samantha and my siblings, Paloma and Tommy Junior, way down deep in my soul I was still a twiggy Thai girl.

Logan gallantly reached across me and plucked my backpack loose. "Ahem. Allow me, beautiful."

I forced a smile and tried to relax as we held hands and walked together through the indigo corridors guarded by foliage. *He's a guy. Hold his hand. Don't sweat something so innocent.*

And really, I didn't mind holding Logan Johnson's hand. I didn't mind going to movies with him. I didn't mind our meals at Taco Bell. I just didn't think this was a romance that was ever going to go anywhere beyond *I'll have a chalupa and two bean burritos, red, hold the onions, hang on I got a coupon.*

We approached my beat-up Saturn and I fished in my jeans pocket for the key fob, my mind restlessly rehearsing the why of my edgy pessimism. Young Mr. Johnson was an okay guy, but really, we had nothing in common except for his admitted penchant for Asian chicks. He was all-Portland white, fair-weather Trail-blazers fan, nominal Christian who only came to church when I guilted him into it. He had some sort of community college certificate, but had drifted into a three-quarters sales schedule at the local Toyota dealership, devoting most of his weekends to surfing and Comic-Con events anywhere in the Pacific Northwest. After three months of dating, he'd dutifully learned to say *sawatdee* and *kaw todt* (sorry), and that's it. I had plenty deeper cosmological conversations with my baby brother and that's the truth.

I pulled out onto the Interstate, tucking myself into the lazy row of red taillights and squinting at the approaching green offramp signs. *Holy moly, I really have to get my eyes rechecked*, I grumbled inwardly. I'd gotten my prescription upgraded just this past Christmas; my lenses were approaching Coke-bottle thickness, and I was edging ever closer to the front seats of classrooms, trying to make out my professors' scribbles. *Sigh.* A scant twenty-three years old and already my vision was faltering.

My mind went back to Logan and my inescapable diffidence. I wondered if this clueless man had any idea how far out on the periphery of my emotions he lived. I let him hover there, occupying a small space, for no reason other than the reality that I hadn't figured out a nice way to cut him loose. I didn't generally break up with guys because it just never got that far. *And why is that?*

Some lady on KOPB was going on about endangered seals and how the station relied on the support of listeners like me. I muted the volume and allowed my mind to drift, balancing the nice things with the other ones. On the surface, I had the sweetest gig a lady could imagine. Tommy and Samantha were nothing but generous and caring. They had embraced me as a seventh-grader, adopted me into their hearts and lavished me with unconditional love. We lived our cocooned life in Portland prosperity. Mom was now pulling down six figures at her old firm and my dad was a perennially juvenile Mr. Silly at Evergreen Christian Academy, teasing the kids and freaking out the school board with his gospel remakes of Beyoncé hits. We vacationed in Hawaii every Christmas and Dad was already scheduling a shopping trip for his baby's new car the moment the university band finished with "Pomp and Circumstance."

On my own branch of the family tree was that 4.0 GPA and a glittering future in the world of math academia. I was about to get handed a sheepskin for my master's degree and then field what I presumed should be a flurry of teaching offers. I expected Dad could score me a gig at his place, but it's always nice to look around, fuzzy vision or no.

The NPR lady went into full pledge-drive mode and I jabbed at the off button, still reflecting on my resumé and overall life experience. Musical talent: just okay. Church: ours is awesome, even though I sometimes shudder at my dad's corny antics leading the praise band. I team-teach a class of six-year-olds, and actually enjoy that, even though my own doubts and theological resentments are always bubbling just below the surface. But I hide that pretty well. You know—the inscrutable Asian face.

My exit came up and I nudged the Saturn over to the right, the quiet *tick tick tick* of the turn signal punctuating the silence all around me here on a 10 p.m. freeway. All the baubles on my family tree couldn't paper over the fact that inside, I was desperately unhappy a lot of the time. Cheerful moments, giggling at jokes, satisfaction at acing a test, were all gauzy flickers at best. My fractured relationship with Mr. Logan John-son was just one more in a long line of *threes* and *fours*, men I tolerated but never could love. My suitors scored in low single digits and the intensity never got higher than *three* either. After a few halfhearted dates, one way or another, things always drifted away and I found myself standing alone on the beach, chilly Pacific currents biting at my ankles.

And yeah, I had an adopted mother who knew the score. I tried to confide in Samantha; I really did. But you can only tell your replacement American mom so much.

My junior year of high school I'd spent eight months in weekly counseling sessions. And I guess it helped some. My therapist gave me visualization exercises to do; she encouraged me to pound the sofa cushions and scream. Let it all hang out. Yeah, right. Lady, you have no idea what that would look like.

I saw our house come into view, third from the corner, Dad's studio lights still on. And after pulling into place behind his SUV, I turned off the engine and simply sat there for several long minutes, wishing I could cry but knowing it wouldn't help. No stream of tears, no Bible verses, no group hugs from the Daggett family, could undo what had happened to me way back before.

Because I'm Pranom Niratpattanasai. Oh, it says Daggett on my Oregon driver's license, but in my core I'm still a fragile Thai girl from Bangkok Christian School.

And little Miss Pranom spent four neon-drenched months in the sex trade at the infamous Pussycat Club in downtown Pattaya Beach.

When I was thirteen years old.

TWO

It was a splashy weekend, typical Oregon gray, and I huddled under the blue comforter, content to be serenaded by the raindrops. Out in the hallway I could hear Tommy Jr. banging one of his toy trucks against the vertical rails on the bannister. "Shut up out there; I'm trying to sleep," I called out, trying to feign irritation.

He nudged my doorway open and stood there in his drooping Batman pajamas. "Hey."

"Hey back." I squinted at him. "Ever hear of knocking?"

"Oh. Sorry. I thought you said 'come in.'"

"You did not think it. 'Cause I didn't say it."

It was impossible to nurture a feud against my little brother, though; he's really the sweetest kid in the universe. "Get over here."

He nudged his dump truck out of harm's way and shuffled in, climbing onto the bottom corner of my bed. "Did you sleep okay?"

"I guess." He rubbed some sleep out of his eyes. "'But when there was thunder, I kept waking up."

"Wow. I didn't hear it."

"It was way loud."

Mentioning thunder gave me a bit of math inspiration. "I've got a cool guessing game for you."

"What?" His face revealed mild interest.

"Well, last night you heard thunder. Did you see lightning too?"

Tommy tried to think. "Um . . . I think just one time."

"Okay. The next time it rains and you see some lightning, right away start counting: 'One Mississippi, two Mississippi' and like that."

"How come?"

"Well, look. See, wherever there's a thunderstorm, there's both lightning and thunder. They happen at the same time. But because light travels way faster than sound, we see the lightning, like, right away. But then the sound takes longer to get to us."

"So?"

"So here's the deal. For every five 'Mississippis' you count, that means the storm's a mile away."

"No way."

"Yep."

He seemed impressed. "So what if you saw way big lightning"–he concocted his own spatial creation of electrical sizzle, waving his arms around in jagged sheets and adding sound effects: *peow! peow! peow!*–"and then did 'One Mississippi, two Mississippi,' and then heard it?"

"I guess that'd be about half a mile," I told him. "Five makes a mile, so two is, like, a half. Little less.

It'd be like the storm was down at that Wendy's Dad likes."

He nestled close to me and leaned his head against my shoulder. "Your bed's nicer than mine."

"How come?"

"I dunno. I like your room. Here in the corner."

He was right about that. Dad had splurged and extended himself by getting us a plush two-story house with two extra bedrooms in it. I staked my claim to a cheerful corner with my own cozy bathroom suite and a walk-in closet. And my queen mattress really is a sink-in-and-go-*aaah* wonder.

"So," I teased. "What are you buying me for graduation?"

"Nothing."

"Nothing!" I pretended indignation. "Some brother. I'm getting my master's degree in math, I've helped you all year with your arithmetic homework, and you're buying me a big old nothing?"

"Sorry." He sniffed. "I wouldn't know what to get you."

"Well, I can give you a list," I offered expansively. "There's tons of stuff I want."

"That's Daddy's job."

"I guess." I pretended to sag. "Well, if things are going to be like that, then go away. Leave me alone so I can sleep some more."

"Can't I stay in here?"

I heaved a comic sigh. "Oh, all right. I don't know why I treat you so nice."

He giggled and burrowed under the covers with me. "No snoring," I admonished. "And this is just for ten minutes. Otherwise we'll be late for church."

Amazingly, the kid was asleep in less than sixty seconds. I felt the soft *hoosh* of his breathing as it nudged against the silk collar of my pajamas. Not really meaning to, I bent my face forward and laid down a small row of kisses against his bushy eyebrow. *He and Dad sure got the facial vegetation.*

A few minutes later I extricated myself and padded down the hall. Paloma was perched on her bed and I could hear the digital squawks coming from her iPad. "What game's that?"

She grinned. "Don't even know. These monkeys throw rocks at a tree and you score points. I've played it four times and haven't got to the second level yet."

"You going to take your shower now?"

"Already did."

I grinned. "Just wanted to make sure there was still some hot water."

"I think so."

Back in my own bathroom, I peeled off my things and let the steamy water envelop me, idly looking down at my own curves and female bits. Really, nothing looked that much different from, well, *you know when.* Even as a bare seventh-grader, or what Thai folks call *Matthayom* One, I already had enough of a shape and hair-down-there, my uncle had no problem pushing me into the sordid world of girlie bars and "short-time" bargains. But a decade later, of course, I'd filled out into a more sturdy 135 pounds. Five foot five, the same long straight hair as all other Thai women. Good smile, good skin, good teeth. I pushed my mind away from the Asian pitfalls and examined my face in the vanity mirror affixed to the shower wall. I'd missed a spot of my shampoo and ducked back into the hot stream, resolved to keep my mind away from ancient wounds.

Mom generally outdid herself on the breakfast just before church, maybe a way to keep her brood happy in God's service. She was still in her bathrobe, humming to herself as she hovered over the stove. "Hey, sweetheart." She set the fry pan down, giving the omelet a tiny shake, and padded over to embrace me. "Sleep all right?"

"Sure."

"Your eggs'll be up in twenty-five seconds."

"Thanks, Mom."

It made Dad immensely proud to have me and Paloma around; he bragged incessantly about his three lovely ladies. Really, despite my inner travails, my parents are kind of awesome and I can't think what else they might ever have done to ease my transition to American life. He breezed in wearing shorts and a Beatles "Let It Be" T-shirt, his tummy jiggling beneath the stretched-out fabric. "Hey, hey, Pranom Baby."

"Hi, Dad."

He looked on covetously as Mom slid the omelet onto my plate. "How come that's not for me?"

"'Cause we've got you on a no-cheese regimen," she retorted with a grin. "So leave your daughter be."

"That kid eats nothing but pop tarts and McFlurrys and never gains an ounce of fat," he grumbled. "Bangkok DNA is such an unfair tilt of the playing field."

"Don't want to hear it," my mom responded, coming over and planting a kiss on the top of his unkempt mop of hair.

We spent an irreverent hour in the first-grade kid division, Tommy Jr. as my designated helper amid a throng of maybe fifteen squirmy sinners. The Bible adventure of the day was where four guys lugged their invalid friend over to see Jesus, then let him down through a hole they clawed in the roof. It would have been hilarious to actually reenact such a colorful anecdote, and I suggested that to the kids, peering up at the asbestos roof tiles. "If it weren't raining, we'd try it," I teased, and the boys all hopped to their feet, volunteering to be the guy in the elevator bed.

"You're not afraid your buds here would drop you on your noggin?" I teased one.

He shot daggers at his friends, then relaxed. "It's okay. 'Cause Jesus could make me well from that too!"

"Ah. Good point."

After church Dad was stuck on some conference call with two of his peers at the school, so Mom offered to drive us home. "Unless you want to, honey." She dangled the keys in front of Paloma.

"For sure? With the whole family along?"

Dad covered his phone for a moment. "Yeah, Sam, you trying to kill the entire Daggett clan in one fiery collision?"

"Daddy!" Paloma slapped his forearm, then seized the keys from Mom. "Who wants shotgun?"

Being the oldest, I agreed to serve as her sidekick and watched nervously as my sister eased us out of the church parking lot. "The freeway onramp's on the left side here," I reminded her. "Better scoot over one lane."

"Oh yeah. Thanks."

"Mirrors," I admonished, feeling very much the adult nag.

Halfway home I was just feeling my on-high-alert muscles relax when my cell phone did its soft *brrrr*. I glanced down at the text screen. "Wow," I called out.

"Aunt Rachel."

"That's news." Mom poked her head between the bucket seats. "What's my cousin want now? A Cody Bellinger jersey?" Our family was always guffawing about how Aunt Rachel was such a diehard Dodger fan while being stuck in Thailand where the time zone warp made most baseball games inaccessible even over the Internet.

"Just says: *Watch for incoming video with huge pitch. SAY YES!!*"

"Uh oh. I don't like the sound of that," Dad quipped. "Your auntie's bright ideas generally involve selling a house and moving to Siam."

Samantha rested her head against his shoulder. "And finding a sexy man to marry."

"There is that," he agreed. Then to me: "In that case, go ahead and take her call."

"She just says a video's on its way."

"Good luck getting that to transmit," he said. "T-Mobile's been terrible lately. I tried to send BCS a music file back in February; the silly thing didn't go through for almost three days."

To our surprise a Fed Ex truck was just pulling up at the curb as we arrived at home. The driver was a roly-poly Hispanic guy who could have been Dad's twin in the body-shape department. "Which one of you is Pranom?" He stumbled slightly over the Bangkok-flavored name.

"That's me."

"This just came." He glanced admiringly at the postage markings. "From a long ways off, looks like."

I scrawled my signature on his digital reader and tore the envelope open right in front of my family.

"What is it?"

There was a silver wafer in its own plastic case. "Looks like Aunt Rachel decided to send me a hard copy."

"Well, let's go in and fire it up," Dad declared. "Now she's got me curious as well."

Mom tugged him toward the front door. "It's Pranom's business." She tossed me a pointed look. "Unless she wants us involved."

I felt a subconscious urge to hold the DVD wafer close to my chest. Partly because I'm a 23-year-old college student, but also because anything floating toward me from Bangkok waters reactivates those old land mines.

"Can I watch it?" Tommy started following me up the stairs.

"Come on, you guys," I remonstrated. "Let me see what it is first." For a fleeting moment I thought about inviting Paloma into the inner sanctum; even though she's six years younger than I am, we've been super close since the pivotal week at Pattaya Beach. But for now I sensed a need to keep everybody at arm's length. Going into my room I shut the door and pulled my laptop over to my bed, angling the screen to get the clearest picture. It took a couple minutes to calibrate the settings; the DVD seemed to have a sort of Asian code lock on it, but after pressing the menu key several times, the picture sprang to life.

It was Rachel Marie and Khemkaeng, and they were sitting together inside one of the BCS classrooms. I saw just the corner of a Thai flag dangling down into the frame, and at first I honestly thought I was seeing Missie Stone's original *Prathom* Six classroom where I initially met this amazing American import. But as my adopted aunt began speaking, the camera panned out wide and I could tell they were shooting in part of the high school section over in the other wing. There were posters on the wall with intricate physics equations and my mathematically trained eye spotted a leftover calc formula someone had left on the whiteboard just behind the two presenters.

"Hi, sweetie," Aunt Rachel sang out. "I know this is a surprise, but something massively huge and exciting and wonderful and . . ." Her list of superlatives began to wane, but all at once she burst into giggles. "Your dad would say it this way: 'Stupendous with durian pie on top.'"

I grinned in spite of myself. That did sound like Mr. Thomas Daggett, king of jokesters.

"Anyway, this is what's going on," she went on. "See, when your mom ran out on us, which was just totally, like, irresponsible and flighty, just to marry this rock-and-roll vagabond named Tommy Something-or-other . . ."

Khemkaeng, smiling, tried to get his wife back on track. "I know, I know," she went on. "No more kidding around 'cause this is important. But look, sweetie, see, our high-end math teacher is Tong Inn. Mr. Kugasang, the *Matthayom* kids call him. Anyway, he and his family decided to move up to Chiang Mai. There's a pretty big Christian school up there now, and his brother and sister live in that area. So all at once we're without somebody to teaching little things like Calculus One. Calculus Two. Trig. I'd do it, but then 135 seniors would all fail their university entrance exams."

I was in a mild state of shock, barely comprehending what Mom's cousin was proposing. But with all her kidding around, I guess Uncle Khemkaeng decided he was going to have to step in and give this pitch some kind of coherence. "This is so true, Pranom," he asserted. "We realize you are finishing your studies in mathematics. You are very accomplished; we know this. And since you are already contemplating a career in teaching, why not come home and serve right here where your Christian life began?"

Part of me wanted to hit the pause button and clutch my skull to keep my brain from exploding, but I swallowed hard and let the video continue. My aunt gestured around the *Matthayom* classroom. "You'd be right here," she explained. "This room would be your personal kingdom. You'd have . . . what is it, Khemkaeng? Three classes a day."

My adopted uncle interjected that in the high school, student took their upper-level math on a block schedule, meeting just twice weekly in double-period segments. "We have Calc I and II," he reiterated. "Two sections of pre-calc; this class is a lot of fun and most students do very well. Also trigonometry."

There was an abrupt video jump-cut, and all at once I was looking at the cheerful face of Sue Baines. I remembered she had come out to BCS just around the time "Mr. Daggett" and I were heading stateside for his marriage to Samantha. "Hi, Pranom," she called out, getting up from behind her principal's desk. "I just want to add my vote to that of your very nice relatives out here. We've got this opening, and somehow we feel like you could come out here and be a wonderful part of our team. We have a lot of fun; the staff is unified; kids are giving their hearts to Jesus." Her smile seemed to spread and almost outgrow her face. "And look. Your Aunt Rachel is a superstar teacher for us here at BCS. Everybody knows it. When your mom was here, she was a superstar too. The whole school said so. 'Missie Kidd is number one.' Now we have Khemkaeng's sister Natty teaching in *Prathom* Three. All over campus, folks know she's great. Parents are just enthralled with her. So we keep saying to ourselves, 'Hey, this is a family where the DNA is just rocking good.'"

I don't suppose Miss Baines–check that, "Mrs. Carington"–had stopped to edit her pitch regarding DNA. Because in terms of chromosomes and bloodlines, my own chart lined up with a nondescript Thai man named Anuman Niratpattanasai, who, as far as I knew, was still in lockdown, a fifteen-year prison bust for drug charges and conspiracy to commit fraud in the tourism business. But it was equally true that growing up under Samantha Daggett's generous wing, and getting endless home tutoring in high school statistics, meant I had absorbed at least some nurtured advantages.

The DVD camera took me on a jerky down-the-stairs-and-across-the-quad tour through the dining commons, out to the flagpole where I still remember standing in a row with my friends, all clad in our maroon-and-white uniforms, singing our Thai national anthem with gusto. Over to the athletic courts where I once beat Missie Stone, now my adopted aunt, in a game of badminton. There was another abrupt jump, and all at once I was peering at the face of a man I didn't recognize.

"Greetings, Miss Pranom," he sang out, and his voice seemed to carry some exotic Aussie flavor. "I'm Pastor Gino, and I have got to say this: man, it would be amazing and wonderful if you could come and help us out here at Bangkok Christian School. Your dad was here before my time, but BCS folks still talk about Mr. Daggett and how his piano-playing and the way he taught choir . . . well, he gave the Body of Christ a lovely and lasting boost. If you could feel like Jesus was calling you to this beautiful land, well, actually, still *your* land, I know our Lord would use you in a special and super-anointed way. Take a look at this."

There was some decent footage of a song service; the camera did close-ups of a long-haired guy jamming on a guitar, and I remember emails from Aunt Rachel about Noah and his wife, the lady who won some big music contest on TV. Then the camera scooted down a hallway, the motion jerky, and I could tell whoever was filming wasn't always remembering to hit the pause button. There was maybe a minute in one of the kid rooms, and I grinned as some Thai kids gaped up at a felt board looking almost identical with what I'd been using less than an hour earlier right here in Portland.

Suddenly we were back in Aunt Rachel's classroom. "It's me again. I know it's a bunch of stuff to think and pray about. But I have one more really nice campaign speech from a friend of yours." A moment later some more footage came up and I could tell I was suddenly off-campus.

An absolutely gorgeous Thai woman was sitting behind a teakwood desk; her blouse was expensive silk and I could tell this lady didn't just go to any hairdresser's in a strip mall. She leaned forward, and as she began to speak I suddenly gasped and my hands flew to my mouth.

"Hi, Pranom," she began, speaking in our shared

Thai language, and all at once a million memories rushed at me. "Do you remember me? My name is Vuthisit, and we always sat by each other in Missie Stone's classroom."

"No way," I murmured. That entire year in *Prathom* Six, we had been inseparable friends, sharing sleepovers and gossiping about the boys we liked. When my mom died so suddenly, Vuthisit and her parents had been enormously helpful, bringing my dad carry-out food from favorite restaurants. Two weeks after the funeral, Dad and I had escaped Bangkok and enjoyed a week of recovery at a Hua Hin condo this pretty girl's parents had booked for us.

My friend from so long ago began speaking in a warm, almost intimate way about what all happened "after you left BCS." I wondered vaguely if Vuthisit had any idea of the horrors that phrase entailed, but she went on quickly. "I finished my schooling at BCS and was so happy when *Kuhn* Khemkaeng encouraged me to be a Christian. Now my husband and I attend church at UCC; it is so wonderful! We are very happy there." She gestured at the quiet elegance surrounding her. "I have such a good job in a bank, Pranom. And all because BCS was a great blessing, teaching me so well. I hope you can come to Bangkok! We could be friends again. And also, I feel sure you would be as good a teacher as Missie Stone! She says to me that now she is like your auntie. Not really auntie, but the cousin of Missie Kidd. It is all the same, you see! Please pray to God about coming to BCS, and if so, I know we will be just as close in friendship as ever before." This stunning beauty paused for a moment, gave me an inviting smile, then a little wave as the camera image blinked off.

THREE

Mom and I could see the faintest glistening outline of Mount Hood as we stacked our plates high with waffles; I emptied a veritable swimming pool of syrup onto mine. "That's obscene," she grinned, nibbling on a tater tot.

One of the Radisson buffet waitresses led us over to a secluded table near the picture window. "Pretty nice view here," she encouraged. "Will this be okay?"

"It's perfect," Mom assured her. "Thanks."

"Enjoy, ladies."

"I still don't get why we're having breakfast in a hotel lobby," I told her. "I mean, it's awesome. But pretty plush."

"There's a method to my madness. But I'm starving. Let me get at least this first waffle into my tum."

It was always our custom to say a blessing, and we held hands across the plates and silverware. "Thank you, Lord, for my amazing children," Mom prayed. "Now we're here to think through this proposal about Thailand. Jesus, we don't know the future; we just have our human ideas about what's the best thing to do. So please guide Pranom as she thinks about where she wants to spend this coming year. In your name, amen."

Despite my ongoing jitters, it was always comforting hearing my parents in communion with Jesus. I grinned in relief, then took a sip of my orange juice. "So what's the Radisson Hotel got to do with all this?"

She seemed surprised. "I thought you knew. Way back when, right when Auntie Rachel was about to get married, all of us were staying in a Radisson. Not this one, but up in Seattle. And it was in a restaurant exactly like this one where John Garvey and this pastor friend of his from California pitched me the idea of putting my Portland life on hold and trying out a semester at BCS."

I'd heard the story a dozen times, of course, but mentally replayed it now as I swabbed my waffle pieces in the pool of syrup. "Of course, that worked out awesome for you. You met Dad, fell in love, I crashed the party . . ."

"Oh, stop it. You did not. I fell in love with him and you all at the same time."

I flushed gratefully. "What was it like, though, when you first got there? Were you scared?"

She didn't hold back. "Tremendously so. A couple times, I hate to tell you, I cried myself to sleep. Like: 'What have I done?'"

There were a couple of realities tilting in her favor, and I reminded her of them. "Look, though. Weren't you, like, twenty-eight years old?"

"Something like that. I'd have to do the math."

"Okay. Plus you had Paloma along."

Mom nodded, nudging around the pile of strawberries and then picking one to spear with her fork. "If you go," she warned, "you won't be eating very many of these for a while."

"Yeah. But trading strawberries in for mangoes: that's an okay deal."

"Sure is."

We bounced around among the pros and cons, and I felt like one of those silver pinballs banging into the digital posts while the score climbed. It would certainly be an amazing adventure. I figured I'd do an okay job teaching the *Matthayom* students, and in a way someone like me would offer BCS the best of both worlds. The students would have a fully Thai peer instructor to admire and emulate. Plus I'd show up with, if I say so myself, perfect linguistic skills. Having come to Portland as a tender eighth-grader, I'd worked diligently with my adopted parents until I spoke accent-free English.

"You'd be amazing," Mom conceded, and as she spoke I couldn't be sure if she was rooting for me to want to hop on the plane or burrow into her arms and say no way using baby talk.

"But . . ."

She sighed heavily, and almost teared up. "Yeah. I know, honey. There's a big, ugly 'but' in the way. I thought of that the minute your Auntie Rachel said hi."

I'd invited Tommy and Samantha to watch the DVD with me, so I was fully aware of their own angst about my emotional reserves. What would it be like for me to again walk the streets of a city where I had been so cruelly betrayed?

"I don't know," I admitted now, as I took careful

bites of my berry yogurt. "Bangkok was actually okay. It was going down to Pattaya. That's what killed me."

"You think the school, and church, and riding city buses, and just, you know, *daily life* . . . that'd be all right?"

"I don't know, Mom. Even just here in Portland, I'm okay for months at a time, and then something weird sets me off and I just crawl under the covers and bawl for an hour."

"Really?"

Mom, you really have no idea, do you? And I didn't blame her for that. A 23-year-old girl just cannot put into words what the hell of that godawful go-go bar was really like. I'd never explained the half of it, and they didn't ask.

"You could do this," Mom said all at once, reaching for her mug of coffee.

"What?"

I waited, trying to imagine how she must have felt a decade earlier: same plate of devoured hotcakes, empty coffee cup, the Radisson's carefully imprinted breakfast invoice resting there amid the wadded-up cloth napkins–and knowing that this looming choice was a monumental fork in the road of life.

"Here's what I'm thinking. Dash out there for maybe ten days. Just see the sights, connect with your aunt. Eat mangoes; wander the halls of BCS. Maybe a preview trip would settle your mind on whether it's a good idea."

I chewed on my lip, thinking hard about whether I wanted to even let this possibility linger beyond today. I was a fleeting seven weeks away from my own unfurled adult existence. Fully credentialed, ready to be hired by any high school or community college. Home with Tommy and Samantha was materially comfortable, and they were stalwart spiritual pillars for the three of us kids. I wasn't eager to kick away so many advantages. "I guess. But hey. If I end up doing it, that's a whole extra plane ticket."

"Sure. But we've got the money."

I had a bunch of homework to get to, so Mom paid the bill and we headed out to the parking lot. The sun was glistening off the faraway snowdrifts of Mount Hood, and the flickers of white frosting centered in the Oregon sky were their own wordless reminder of just how different a school term in Bangkok would be.

The Daggett clan was in the nice habit of watching *Downton Abbey* reruns together every Sunday night, and this evening we spun through two DVD episodes instead of our usual one. "I shouldn't have done that," Paloma grumbled as we headed toward our bedrooms. "I still have five problems left in trig, and they really stink too."

I draped an arm around her. "Allow me."

We didn't usually collaborate on math; Paloma was naturally bright with her mom's DNA flowing out to the tip of her mechanical pencil. But I nudged her through the factoring of her assigned trig equations, reminding her to check for extraneous roots. "I always forget that," she confessed, sticking her lower lip out in a comic pout.

"Well, just make it a habit. Always ask yourself: 'Does this give me a zero denominator?' Or: 'Did I square both sides?' Anytime you say yes to either of those, you might have a phantom answer."

Paloma closed her book with a snap of satisfaction. "Are you really thinking about going to Bangkok next year?"

I twisted around on her bed, and pulled a corner of the quilt over my legs. "A little bit. Maybe thirty percent."

"It sounds amazing," she told me. "But holy cow, Pranom. I'd miss you so bad, I think I'd die."

I felt a lump in my throat at her confession. "Yeah. Me too."

We talked there in the dim lighting of our shared past-curfew sanctuary, just two bonded sisters: Thailand and Portland. I'd loved this kid ever since she sat on my lap listening as I read *The Cat in the Hat* stories to her right after my rescue, those long-ago moments bathed by the aura of her strawberry shampoo. Now here she was heading toward her senior year of high school, a drop-dead gorgeous blonde, sweet as sugar and with a heart of gold. *There's no way I can leave her,* I thought to myself, feeling my pulse flutter again.

The weird reality was this. My *Cat in the Hat* memories with Paloma went right back to that damned beach house at Pattaya, a scant six blocks away from the neon-sprayed dance bar where girls peeled off their bra tops and perspiring guys ogled them and fingered the stacks of baht in their pockets. And yet, here a decade later, my younger sister knew absolutely nothing about my private nightmare. Years ago, my adopted folks and I had pledged that we'd never reveal the gruesome saga to my siblings. When Tommy Junior showed up, we guarded his emotional virginity as well. Aunt Rachel and Uncle Khemkaeng had been sworn to secrecy, and up till now, the fortress had held.

So this Sunday night bonding was a carefully redacted unburdening of my heart. I wondered aloud how lonely a time such a mission assignment might be, so far away from Portland and my family. "Aunt Rachel's there," Paloma reminded.

"I know. But it's not the same."

We indulged in some girly giggling about guys, and I did my trademark *meh*. My sister laughed and flopped her head down into my lap. "You're so cute. I don't get why you go from one boyfriend to another. But maybe way down deep your soul craves a Thai guy." She peered up at me. "Think that's it?"

I sighed heavily. "I don't know what it is." *Sure I do, but we're not going there.* "Just haven't met the right man yet."

Paloma rolled over and peered up at my face through the semi-darkness. "The only bad thing would be this."

"What?"

"Well, Aunt Rachel went out, she found this awesome guy, and just look. She never came back. Then this other lady from the States chugged over there for some surgery of some kind, she said. She met a guy, got married off, and she stayed there too."

I guffawed, but it came out sounding hollow. "So you're saying what? After all of high school, and now university, and I haven't had a guy hang around for more than two months, I'm going to trip off to Bangkok and *marry* someone? You kidding me?"

"I'm just saying."

The clock crept past midnight, the scarlet digits scolding us, and still we huddled there among the quilts, knowing Mom and Dad and Tommy were all conked out, but that some pillars in our shared world needed realigning. The girl talk drifted over to church and God and stuff like that, and I admitted that even with our parents being so vibrantly born-again, I was still grappling with a lot of issues. "Hard to say what all it is," I hedged. *The understatement of the century.* "I mean, I believe God exists and all that. And that the stuff Jesus promises about being our Savior . . . sure. I guess. But somehow I've just kind of *watched* it all go by. Like a play, instead of being real."

Paloma looked puzzled and I tried to formulate my schizophrenic thoughts. "I've said to Jesus, 'I accept you.' I really have. And I guess I mean it. But then all kinds of times, it just stays in my head: 'No, you haven't. You're holding back.'"

My sister weighed that and then gave a careful shrug. "I wish I could help. It doesn't feel like that for me, but I sort of see what you mean." She fished around in her underwear drawer and located a two-inch stash of Saltine crackers with the packaging twisted in a halfhearted knot. "This is horribly wicked," she giggled. "Us snacking at one in the morning." She bit down on the first one and made a face. "Oh poo, these are stale. They taste like paper."

We chewed on them anyway, and the gossip turned to this new guy she was admiring in chemistry class. "He's been flirting with me during labs, but hasn't asked me to anything yet."

"Got a picture?"

"Well, you know, just kidding around." Paloma hopped off her bed and flipped her iPhone into action. "Hang on, hang on. Maybe I don't have it," she grumbled. Then: "Here it is. Don't laugh; he's way cuter than this shot."

I peered at the blurry image. "I can't see a thing 'cause my glasses are in my room. Be right back."

"Oh, it's not worth it."

"I'll be back in seven seconds."

The guy was decked out in a stained lab coat, and was kidding around, trying to affix safety goggles on Paloma as she teasingly ducked out to the way. "See? Cute, don't you think?

"I guess. If you go for that sort of sultry, muscle-toned, tan sort of gentleman."

Paloma reached over and plucked my glasses off my face. "Holy cow, these are thick. I didn't realize. You must be slowly going blind."

"Don't remind me."

With her digital bedside clock actually registering twenty past one in the morning, I reluctantly took charge of the moment. "We are going to bed. Right this minute."

"Okay."

"All right then." I offered her a hug, and felt a bit of drippiness pass between us. "I sure love you, kid."

"Me too. You're so awesome. That's for sure one way I know God is good and amazing. He snagged you into the Daggett family."

Back in my own bedroom, wrapped up in blankets and memories, I peered sans glasses at the moon-outlined shadows as they drifted across my ceiling. *Bangkok. A teaching gig at my old Christian school, right where Missie Stone used to perch up there on her teacher desk and read us those cheesy stories about Nicky and his pet raccoon. Could I possibly survive an entire school term fifteen time zones removed from Tommy and Samantha and Paloma and Tommy, Jr.?*

My mind sailed across the cold, heartless trillions of gallons of Pacific Ocean separating me from my former world. It was in an upstairs bedroom Over There, with disco music coming through the screen windows, where a sweet blond waif with a green toy froggy named Freddy curled up next to me, her strawberry curls tickling my cheek as we spooned together during those first few nights of recovery. It came back to me: our synchronized breathing and the sweet Seuss-y cadence as I read her the adventure of Thing One and Thing Two and helped my hoped-for little sister spell out the words. *Sweet Jesus, if you're up there at all, listen to me here! There's no way I can do a year in Bangkok without Paloma.*

It was almost two in the morning, but all at once I realized something that was insistently non-negotiable. I didn't hesitate. Pushing back my covers, I padded across the hallway and tapped an apologetic fingernail on her bedroom. It took a second, but her muffled voice came through the crack. "Hey, Pranom. What'd you forget?"

I walked in and sat down next to her, trying to fight back my emotions. "My God, are you crying?" she gasped.

"It's so dumb," I half-wailed. "But I just figured out something weird."

"What?"

"Look," I said. "And here's my bottom line. I'm not going to Thailand for next school year unless you come along with me."

FOUR

Well, that was for sure a keg of TNT blowing up the Daggett household. At first Mom was theatrically indignant, saying no way no how. Dad was fairly sure we were just kidding around, trying to sabotage the BCS offer. At one point in the discussion, he went into his studio, lugged out a nondescript trombone some band student had left behind. He managed a mournful sliding *mwaa mwaa* on it, effecting a funereal tone. "You girls have any idea how bereft your old man would be if you both ditched me?"

"It's only for ten months, Daddy," Paloma asserted. "Plus we could come home for Christmas break even."

Mom gave her a pointed look across the lasagna casserole. "Sweetie, it's your senior year of high school. Are you sure you want to spend it in Bangkok?"

I nudged her. "And it wouldn't be Miss Kappel this time. You'd have to actually do some schoolwork." Both of us had to keep in mind the surreal concept of me being the professor up front and having my oh-so-white-and-blond sibling sitting right there on the second row in a sea of Asian faces, smirking irreverently as she raised her hand and addressed me as "Miss Daggett" before tossing me some really smart-aleck calculus question.

"I'll give you a million years of detention if you try that," I warned. "You'll be down to Uncle Khemkaeng's office so fast your head will spin." Of course, threatening someone with a trip to see "Uncle" anybody is a defanged motivator.

After two hours of going round and round, Mom and Dad finally agreed we could pitch the counter-proposal to the BCS team. I drafted a cautious response and we all held our collective breaths. The response from Aunt Rachel was quick in coming. "Are you kidding? YES!!!! Sue says yes. Khemkaeng says yes. Fifty good-looking guys in *Matthayom* Six all say yes!" Paloma cackled for five minutes when she heard that, and we could literally see Mom's scowl hardening before our eyes.

Rachel Marie's return email continued with some interesting tidbits. *Here's some news. You ladies could park in #305, the same apartment where I first lived. What memories! What a heritage! If these walls could talk! Rent's gone up a little bit (but so has pay.) And by the way, this is awesome. Paloma, tell your folks you attending here would be on the house. No tuition.*

Tommy immediately doffed his Angels hat and tossed it into the overhead fan, where it got caught on the whirling blades, then sailed across the room and spanged against the picture window. "We're in!" he yodeled. "Free tuition! I'd send that kid to Sing Sing for a discount like that."

"You're hilarious," Mom scolded him. But she read through the long email again and then set it down with a sigh. "Yikes. It sure sounds like they want the both of you."

So we were literally all in. I couldn't believe my lurching pulse. "Professor Daggett!" First things first. I was amazed to find that Mom had actually stored away a pile of PowerPoint files she'd used when she taught calc at BCS way back when. "And I can have them?"

"No charge." This being a decade later, I scrolled through them and updated to the latest Microsoft version, which jiggled some of the pictures. "These are really pretty amazing, Mother dear," I teased as I tweaked the order. "I guess that Carington lady's right. You and Aunt Rachel were both kind of superstars."

"And don't you forget it."

There was one slightly messy detail to get through. It was actually Paloma's burden, but as the adopted big sister I agreed to share it. The Thursday night before graduation, we drove together through the business district of downtown Portland till we came to a nondescript Chinese restaurant close to the shore. Then cooled our heels through a texted apology and forty-minute wait before Brian walked in. You'd think a biological dad would be on time, but the Daggett family had always had a rather tenuous connection to my little sister's DNA contributor. Brian's actually not a sinister guy; he's one of those construction dudes who simply failed to ever grow up and cultivate a character. He and Mom divorced about six months before her own mission trip to Bangkok, and Brian gave a nonchalant wave of the hand over the idea of his own flesh and blood sailing nine time zones to the west and out of his life forever.

But we had an affable ninety minutes together over chow mein and spring rolls. "We shoulda kept in touch more," he apologized repeatedly to his daughter. "Baby, you've turned out so pretty! And you too, Pranom." I hadn't bumped into him more than perhaps three times in the past decade; he made it to my kid sister's eighth-grade graduation, and did a drop-in for one of her birthday parties. Sixteen, I think. You'd think a guy who'd flaked out on ten years of child support would have at least sprung for a new car. You know, a guilt gift. But no. Anyway, with his baby just months away from turning eighteen and stepping across the line of chromosomal connection once and for all, he was sanguine about our upcoming adventure.

"Well, you did it before; I bet you girls'll be great again." He displayed at least some interest in my brand new teaching career. "And this school has stuff like trigonometry?"

"Uh huh. Plus Calc One and Two, even."

We could both tell he didn't have the foggiest idea what sorts of math that entailed. "Pretty hard, I bet." He popped a fortune cookie in two and grinned. I got the impression he was envisioning me standing underneath a papaya tree scribbling times tables on a scratchy chalkboard as cobras darted around among the barefoot-and-naked urchins.

The waitress came by with our tab, and he fished some bills out of a tattered billfold. "Well, don't know if we'll rendezvous again before you ladies get on the plane," he said. Then to Paloma: "But look, honey. I know what a mess I made of things. 'Cause look at you. Just a real classy lady. And I missed out. But I'm proud of you. Have a wonderful time in Thailand, and I'll try and email and stuff when I can."

Paloma was quiet as we drove home. "You okay?"

She shrugged. "Sure. It's just so weird, though."

I was pretty sure I knew. "You mean, because this is your real dad, and yet you feel a thousand times closer to Tommy?"

She sighed, the sharp exhale bathed in confusion. "I know. How messed up is that? How can guys, you know, be with a woman? And then a baby shows up. And they don't care enough to work things out with the mom? And when girls like us luck out and move on to something way better, it's still like, well, honey, you're sure pretty. That's really nice. So yay for me, Mr. Sperm Donor."

That was actually funny in a morbid sort of way, and we shared a sisterly laugh. "Well, it's the same for me," I told her, carefully steering my words down the center divider. "My biological dad's over in Bangkok somewhere." *Oh yeah. She does know about him being in jail. It's Uncle Viroj we're keeping in the forever dungeon of silence.* So I added: "Probably making prison license plates for *tuk-tuks*." That got us to howling in unison, and the Saturn almost drifted into the next lane of traffic.

I was grateful for one Bangkok bonus. Signing up for such a distant adventure offered me a convenient offramp with Logan. "It was sweet spending time with you," I sort of lied during a shared coffee break the last week before graduation. "But this gig in Thailand was too good to pass up, and I just don't think I ought to tie you down for the whole next year."

He peered at me over the steaming brew. "Well, hey. I . . . um, I just wasn't in your class anyway. Plus all the God stuff you and your folks are into."

"Yeah." I brushed my hand against his cheek, feeling slightly ashamed of my standoffishness that had kept this decent soul spinning his wheels in the sand. "And I've got issues I never really put on the table. Until I get my head back on straight, I'm really not much use to a guy."

Another sip. "Don't talk stupid. You're incredibly beautiful." *Which missed the point, but oh well.*

He dropped me off at the house and I rested my head against his shoulder for a moment, forestalling an awkward goodbye at the front door. "I won't forget the really nice times we had."

"Good luck with teaching."

And that was that. I chanced to see him again at graduation; he threaded his way through the throngs and gave me a now-platonic hug, nodding carefully in my folks' direction before peeling away. Tommy was in high spirits, bribing total strangers to snap photos of the five Daggetts. He spotted a gray-haired professor ambling past in his doctoral robes. "Isn't that Dr. Chen?"

"Uh huh."

He beckoned my teacher to join us. "Pranom talks about you all the time! Come on and let me get a picture of the two of you."

My professor lit up. "Of course. Miss Daggett, please remind me again of your plans."

"Bangkok. But just for one term."

"Oh yes. Wonderful."

"You ever been to Thailand, professor?" Dad edged closer to frame a better shot.

"Unfortunately, no. I received my training in Beijing. Then USC," he added. "But did not travel to that part of Asia."

"It's pretty amazing. And my baby girl is going to light up all of Thailand with her great calculus skills. Thanks to you," he added.

"Very good. I am sure she will represent our university with great proficiency."

Two days before our flight, Mom got off work early and texted for me to meet her. *Just over on Beeline. At the McDonald's. See U soon. Love, Mom.*

It was just four blocks over, so I left my packing and hiked there through the August heat. She was waiting at a booth and handed me a fistful of dollars. "Get whatever you want, sweetheart."

Minutes later I plopped down with a Big Mac and a supersize fries. "No ice cream?" she teased.

"Yeah, but I didn't want it to melt."

We said a quick grace together, and then she explained. "It was right before our big adoption thing in Thailand. Way back when. And I took your little sister out to a McDonald's on some big road. Sukhumvit, I think."

I had a vague memory of the main arteries threading through Bangkok, so just nodded.

"Anyway, I remember like it was just last week. Paloma had a berry shake and fries. And then I kind of had to spill my guts out about the big transition. Tell her I'd fallen in love with Tommy and that he might end up being her stepdad. Which, of course, turned out really, really great." She smiled through eyes suddenly brimming with happy moisture.

I said nothing, a bit fretful about what might be next.

"Anyway, honey, you're heading back to a world

that is kind of home and is kind of also . . . well, hell, maybe. And I just want you to know how much I love and treasure you and hope that you'll allow Jesus to give you a brand new level of happiness in Bangkok."

I nodded, feeling a lump in my throat. "I know, Mom."

She stared down at her sandwich, and then back to me. Setting it down, she reached for my hand and gave a squeeze. "Sweetheart, you have been such an amazing gift to Tommy and to me. I love you as much as if I'd gone to the hospital and 'borned you myself.'"

It was a colloquialism I'd heard from her lips before, but now it seemed extra special. "Thanks, Mama." I almost never called her that, but somehow it came out that way.

"Anyway, listen, honey. That horrible thing that happened to you . . . it's real. I can't talk it away. Your daddy and I hoped we could erase it with our love, but of course, that's wishful thinking. You got hurt real bad and all the hugs in the universe can't undo the scars. But we do have the love of Jesus." Mom swallowed hard and her green eyes were on mine, unblinking. "We always say that Jesus is the Lamb that can take away sins. But I just hope and pray that for these next ten months, your faith in him will be enough to at least shield you from the . . . the . . ." She fumbled for a moment, then stumbled into this. ". . . The *soul-ache* that has to still assault you sometimes."

I weighed that. "I . . . sure. I mean, I get that, Mom. God's grace is sufficient. And I buy it. Whether it's enough or not, I don't know. I'll find out when I get there."

Mom's face softened. "Let me make a promise to

you. Okay?"

I nodded.

"Every single day you're serving the Lord in Bangkok," she told me, "Daddy and I will pray. We'll hold hands and we'll think of you and Paloma. We'll invite all of heaven's hosts to just stand by you. When good times comes, the angels will let the joy spill in. And if there are hurtful moments, or bad memories, we'll be praying that the Holy Spirit will soften those times of attack. I know they can't just be blown out to sea, but he'll give you strength enough for at least that day, that moment."

What she said made me think of Brian, and I told her so. She nodded, replaying, I'm sure, her own split-up and bank of bad memories. "Well, it took me an awfully long time to cooperate with heaven in coping with how my marriage exploded. I wasn't much good at forgiving, and that really held me back. But now, see, God really did bless me with a whole new life. Tommy's a godsend of a man. Paloma grew up to be a treasure. And you . . . dear God, Pranom. I don't think there's sixty minutes ever goes by where I don't whisper a prayer and say to my Jesus: 'You're so amazing to have given me this girl.'"

That made me smile at last. "Stop," I chided, half-teasing. "I'm going to start crying now."

"Don't do that." She pushed three dollar bills into my hand. "Go get a McFlurry, please. And I want two bites of it. Just two, swear to God."

FIVE

There was random turbulence on the endless leg between Portland and Manila, and the pilots opted to carry us high, high above the surging Pacific. I think we topped out at something close to 43,000 feet, just a pale dot in the empty black sky, and the buffeting mercifully subsided. Paloma got halfway through one of the Jack Reacher movies, but abruptly conked out, her head drooping over to my side and resting against the seat back. I fluffed her pillow into place and actually dropped a kiss on the crown of her head before returning to my own muddled thoughts.

I'm really going. Back to Bangkok. And Pattaya Beach. Are you kidding me? Why?

I'd thought several times during our packing ordeal that a girl can really only prepare in terms of suitcases and carefully stacked piles of blouses and panties. I had my stash of clothes; I had my master's degree in hand. I had Mom's PowerPoint files. I had a paid-up abode, the legendary #305 at Orchid Garden Apartments. And I had every confidence Uncle Khemkaeng and Aunt Rachel would see me through any temporal crises involving baht or BCS's Internet server or what days of the week we had faculty meetings.

It was *that other thing* I couldn't prepare for. That was a moral void to me. What would it feel like to walk the streets of my former world and face endless reminders of the sex-industry machine that had so ensnared me? Bangkok hadn't changed one whit in a decade; I was sure Patpong Road and *Soi* Cowboy still had the same clubs, the same weary pink neon, the same booming speakers with the disco beats to cover up the sorry reality that young girls' hearts were breaking.

Well, okay, I could stay away from those neighborhoods if I was diligent about it. The other good news: the City of Angels is also generously populated with, well, *angels*. There are places of beauty: churches and Buddhist *wats* and unselfish charities and millions of sweet, innocent folks. I hoped and prayed my little sister and I could navigate these next ten months by walling ourselves off from my ugly memories.

Even as I toughened up my spine, though, and aimed myself toward optimism there in Seat 44J, moonlight spilling in through the Plexiglass, I knew this overloaded jet plane was taking me into a battle zone. My own aunt was still teaching in *Prathom* 6C; her classroom was wall-to-wall kids, giggling boy-crazy girls, faces cute as cherubs, all trying on their first bras and having *Kuhn Mae* explain about sanitary pads. I was soon to encounter these prepubescent females day in and day out, their angelic voices floating through the national anthem each morning. I had no doubt they would endlessly accost me with teasing remarks about

"Auntie Rachel" and did I have a *fan* yet, did I want a Thai boyfriend, would I like to meet their big brother and on and on.

Paloma's unwatched movie came to an end, the endless crawl of credits grinding up the screen, white letters against the black background. I'd already loosened her headset so she could sleep unencumbered, and I heard the faint whisper of violins through the ear buds. I watched, my own reverie interrupted, as the entertainment menu came back on. I hit my sister's off button and the picture went dark.

For an extended moment I wondered about another thing. Could I spend this entire term rooming with Paloma—and never once confide my tragic tale? In Oregon I'd found a whole new life, brimming with Americana and wealth and iTunes, and it was a fairly simple thing to edit my story. But now we were hurtling toward Thailand at almost a thousand kilometers an hour. Would I be able to brush away both her questions and my own impulses to unburden myself? I was determined to protect my sweet sibling, and without meaning to, I breathed a prayer asking God to help me keep my cone of silence intact.

But my mumbled prayer fragments, some rote and others bracingly blunt, took me right to what was becoming my overriding reality, go-go bars notwith-standing. I was heading to Asia to work at a Christian school. But I wasn't at all confident that I actually *was* a Christian any longer. I didn't know if I meant what I said in my prayers. I wasn't sure if I believed all the Tommy Daggett platitudes about hey, Jesus is just so awesome. And the jury was way, way out on whether a loving God in heaven could tolerate even once, let alone *endlessly*, the injustice that had washed me away.

Outside my window there were midnight clouds gathering around the wings now, a committee of gray ghosts, the moonlight feebly trying to push through them and bounce off our silver walls. I could barely make out the three-quarter orb so far off in the distance. There were something like 425 other souls on board this great big bird, but at this moment, Paloma dead to the world, my family four time zones to the east and rapidly diminishing in our wake of turbulence, the pilots barricaded behind their ISIS-proofed doors . . . I was really all alone. Just me and that silver moon and maybe a Jesus on the far side of this one unlucky solar system and so many millions more. Did I believe he was there? Did I trust in this faraway deity Dad blithely asserted was my best ever Friend?

The plane wings shuddered as a bank of disturbed molecules shot up and bumped against us. Nothing stopped them. If some meteor plunged through the outer skin of planet earth and sheared off this wing, I knew with certainty that any god watching would do just that and no more: *watch*. And be entirely silent during the 425 funerals.

Oh well. It is what it is. I had acted out roles before and I was wearily ready to do it again. I'd be Auntie Rachel's good little Christian deputy teacher; I'd read Bible passages to my charges and parrot all the right phrases in morning prayers. I wasn't so close to atheism that I couldn't do that.

But there was one thing I knew in my heart, and it wasn't because I had decided it to be so or had set up this BCS gig as some sort of millennial test case. But if

God didn't show himself to me during this coming school year, if he didn't reach down and actually heal my heart and banish my demons . . . well, I was done. I wasn't going to spend the next sixty years having things be like up till now.

I ADMIT, THOUGH, it was pretty amazing having Auntie Rachel come squealing up and embrace both of us together. "This is just so awesome!" she shouted, kissing me on the cheek, then Paloma. "Holy cats, you girls are both so pretty!"

She caught herself. "I'm totally sorry, Pranom. 'Girls'? You're my colleague now. 'Miss Daggett.' I'll never flub that again. I promise." Khemkaeng came up, his still professional self, and assured us all of BCS was just dying to welcome the two of us back. "Ratana sent out an email about you, Pranom. The *Matthayom* Six class is very excited that a student from their own ranks has returned to be a teacher."

Rachel Marie made an extravagant show out of introducing us to their children. "I can't remember if I was pregnant with Gage while you were still around, Pranom." Her son had an adorably impish smile that came straight off her face, and I felt myself warming up to this incredible missionary family. "And Katrina is three and we love her very much and she's been practicing all week to say 'Cousin Pranom.'"

Mom had already warned me about Rachel Marie's penchant for drafting all BCS newcomers right into the Chaisurivirat family tree. "First you're 'Auntie This or That.' Next thing you know, she'll have you teaching a Bible class at the church or singing the lead role in a Christian opera in the National Theater.'" I remembered her warning and grinned as I nuzzled the little girl.

Sue Carington was there too, and now stepped forward to drape the requisite orchid necklace around my neck. "Having you come back to us is a wonderful answer to prayer," she murmured, and I sensed genuine fondness in her voice. "Thanks." I found myself grinning despite my reservations. "It feels totally irreverent to call you 'Sue,' but I guess now it's okay."

"It's absolutely okay. And that's the amazing thing about Christian education," the older woman assured me. "You graduate; the Lord equips you for service. And now, my dear, we are peers all the way. 'Sue and Pranom.' And whatever in the world you need, you just come by my office and we'll make it happen." Her laugh was infectious. "And of course, your Uncle Khemkaeng is the go-to guy in all of Asia."

We wheeled our bags out to the curb, and I could tell the humidity was really hitting my sister right in the gut. "Yikes, it's hot," she sighed melodramatically as though the blanket of sticky steam was an unexpected travel hurdle.

"You knew it would be," I reminded her, forcing myself to maintain an optimistic façade. Uncle Khemkaeng motioned toward a white van. "Good! We don't have to wait long." He shot us a sympathetic look. "I'm sure you're both feeling the heat."

"A little bit," I lied. He grinned.

The ride into the city actually gave me a burst of curious energy. Of course, I'd finished a full seven grades of school here in Thailand, so retained most of my vocabulary and reading skills. There were massive billboards everywhere, boasting about the latest Samsung smart phones and glittering new condo developments. We were just getting off the elevated highway when Rachel Marie managed a clumsy bit of Thai directed at our van driver. He nodded and steered us toward a quieter *soi* off the main east-west artery.

"What's over here?" Even a decade later, I had a basic city map in my head and knew we were several kilometers east of Bangkok Christian School.

Sue leaned over and pointed. "We've discovered a nice tradition, and we're actually rather superstitious about it."

"What's that?" Paloma was gazing around, absorbing the frantic cacophony of *tuk-tuks* buzzing around our van like mosquitos.

"Well, we bring our newcomers to this nice Thai restaurant. We force-feed them a big plate of *kow neow ma-muang.*"

Both of us instantly recalled the kingdom's fabled dessert of sticky rice and chilled mangoes.

"And . . ." I grinned in anticipation.

"And whenever we do that, the teacher in question morphs into a superstar instructor and stays for a decade or so."

"Hmm." I pondered this, then retorted: "Well, this is just for one single year no matter how good the mangoes are." We all laughed, and even the driver, who spoke very little English, seemed to have comprehended the gag line.

It was a blast of comfort when the air-conditioned breezes enfolded us. A young Jamaican-looking man with a bright smile jumped up from a nearby bench and hustled over. "Miss Daggett! I've heard all about you. And little sister Paloma." He embraced both of us in turn. "My wife couldn't join us; sure sorry. But she's kind of got her hands full with nursing and diapers and now another already on the way and such."

The waitress came to our table with ornately embossed menus, and I found myself struggling with the Thai fonts. Rachel Marie noticed and grinned. "Looks like your bifocals need adjusting."

I sighed, sticking my nose even closer to the exotic culinary descriptions and trying to recall some of my favorites. "I know. I'm way overdue for a checkup and should have gotten it done before coming out here."

"Plus you've got to be way tired," she soothed. "Your eyeballs are still on West Coast time. You'll be okay when you get acclimated."

We were halfway through our dinner before I got the entire family tree sorted out. Pastor Gino was married to Khemkaeng's youngest sister. *Natty.* I repeated the name to myself several times, resolving to get up to speed and connected with my fellow teachers as soon as I could. Their little boy, Boonrat, was already sitting up and babbling, and Gino boasted endlessly about how smart he was, clicking us through an array of family photos.

"I can't remember if I ever met your wife," I told him, peering at the pictures. "I assume 'Natty' is short for something."

He nodded. "Correct. It's really Nattaporn, but we don't get around to that very often."

Sue draped a maternal arm around her adopted son. "I know I'm biased, but she's a brilliant teacher for us down in *Prathom* Three. And Pranom, I can just tell you're going to set our *Matthayom* folks on fire with all your calculus."

"I'll try," I promised her, meaning it.

The coveted silver tray of sticky rice finally arrived, and Gino held up his hand. "Before we absorb all this sweetness," he said, flashing his killer smile, "I got this feeling."

Paloma had been texting a note back to Mom and Dad, but set down her phone. "What?"

"Well, let's just hold hands around this table and pray for the Lord to really bless you, Pranom." His face sobered and I could see the kindness in his gaze. *Does he know?*

I felt the warmth of my sister's palm pressed against my own, and on the other side Khemkaeng's grasp was comforting and familial. The cool touch of my adopted uncle's wedding band was a golden reminder that joyous marriages could be forged out of broken pieces. "Lord God, this is such a blessed moment," Gino began. "We've got a new teacher for our school, and we already know she's going to energize our *Matthayom* program, Jesus, with her abilities and her enthusiasm. And also now we have Paloma. That's just so great, Jesus, for her to come back to BCS to finish up, and keep an eye on her sister."

There was almost a gentle wave of amusement, but it seems he really meant it, soldiering on without a pause. "Now, Jesus, please come so close to our two new team members. Bless Pranom in a remarkable way; help her to *feel* it. Show her your presence and your love and just give her the best year of her life here on our team. Bless all those high school students who come within the aura of her talents and all the love and ability she has to offer. Multiply it all like you did here on earth with those loaves and fishes."

His mention of the Lord's own lunch menu must

have reminded Gino that we did have that scrumptious plate of mangoes, juicy and still untouched. "So thanks for this great evening and now the dessert that blesses our taste buds," he concluded with a touch of levity. We all opened our eyes, and he was blushing. "Sorry; I kind of got carried away."

"No problem, sonny boy." Sue made a point of reaching across him and dishing out obscenely large pieces for Paloma and me.

"That's way too much," I protested, and the place busted up since it was clear I didn't mean it. Less than five minutes later my dessert plate was clean and I was oh so tempted to actually lick the surface for any last stray drops of that delicious tropical juice.

"It ain't bad, is it?" Rachel Marie reached around behind Khemkaeng and gave me an affectionate squeeze right above my elbow. "So glad you're here, sweetie." I felt myself flushing happily despite my earlier qualms in the plane.

It was late now, and even Gage was drooping in the back seat of the school van. But the Bangkok traffic was as snarled as I remembered from my childhood years; cars were stacked up at every red light, the *tuk tuks* and motorcycles in an endless sound war of gunned engines and testy horn honks. I vaguely remembered that we were close to the MBK Mall, and sure enough. One traffic signal later the massive high-rise came into view. There had always been a massive Pepsi sign near it, dancing with intricate neon playfulness, and the digital show was as impressive as ever. "I can't believe that thing's still up there," I murmured, feeling a bit anxious about how the edges of the soda display were fuzzing out on me. Right next to us was a jammed city bus, and as I looked out through our curtained windows, the Asian faces were blurry and indistinct.

You'll make an appointment. This can be fixed. I rubbed my right eye, trying to will some renewed acuity into my weary optic nerves.

As we pulled into the tiny courtyard of my new shared home, I strained to remember if I'd actually been here before. Way back when, this had been "Missie Stone's" startup home; in fact, I thought I'd heard laughing gossip about *Kuhn* Khemkaeng going up the flights of stairs, two at a time, with a bouquet in his hand for his new California girlfriend. They sat now in the bench seat in front of me, Rachel Marie's head resting against the shoulder of her husband of ten years.

I don't know if she was reading my mind, but just like that, she turned around and eyed me. "Don't forget that Apartment #305 is the luckiest love nest in all of Bangkok. I'm living proof of that. So you and Paloma be really, really careful. Even the paint on the walls just oozes romance and . . . and . . . really good-looking gentlemen. 'Cause this guy here is Exhibit A."

We laughed, but it was a jet-lagged bit of levity, and it took a few moments for us to clamber out and loosen our joints. Khemkaeng said a few words to the chauffeur, who obediently grabbed a suitcase and followed him up the stairs.

It was a cute little place, just a one-bedroom hide-away with an okay living room and cozy kitchen. The fridge was a three-quarter model tucked into the corner, and there was a two-burner stove and microwave. I glanced around the living room: it had a polished teakwood table and two chairs; the wall TV was an okay size, maybe fifty inches. On the way over, Rachel Marie had apologized ahead of time for the apartment's color scheme, which was a rather vivid shade of aqua. "It's actually okay," I assured her. "Kind of cheerful."

The bedroom light was already on, and I could hear the comforting hum of the wall AC. Khemkaeng set down his suitcase and took just a few minutes to show us around. "With two beds, it's a little tight," he conceded. "Sorry."

"We'll make it work," I shrugged, thankful as always for how nice this man was to people. "And it's only for the one term."

He gave me that teasing smile of his. "We shall see. Our campaign to extend your visit here has already begun." I returned his grin.

Rachel Marie made a little gesture toward a stunningly pretty painting of tropical Krabi; its frame was polished teak and I felt my pulse quicken. "That's our little housewarming gift," she murmured. "Uncle Khemkaeng and me."

"No way!" I gasped. "That's amazing." It was a beach scene from one of the resort islands along the southern peninsula of Thailand. There was a fishing boat in the far background, the long metal propeller blade jutting out into the blue-green water. White sand, a trio of coconut trees leaning in from the right. And a Thai couple, arm in arm, walking along in the shallow surf. The scene was one of idyllic contentment and endlessly fulfilled dreams, and I could hardly take my eyes off it.

"Well, it didn't cost all that much. And we just want you guys to feel loved and welcome-homed and all that good stuff."

"Thanks, Auntie Rachel."

She grinned. "That's the last time for 'Auntie' this

and that. From now on I'm 'Mrs. C' in front of the kids and just plain Rachel Marie the rest of the time."

I nodded, feeling the warmth of my aunt's grace.

Khemkaeng towed me toward the kitchen and showed me a generous stash of fruit already cooling in the refrigerator. "The 7-Eleven is right across the street. You saw it." I nodded. "But we got you enough water for a few days. And just a little food."

"This is great," I told him.

He handed me an envelope with some local currency. "Is this a pay advance?" I asked.

"No." He gave a nonchalant shrug. "We always give our new arrivals just a few baht. Until they can find their way around. But if you need an advance on the first paycheck, we can do that."

"No, we're good."

Paloma edged away from the group. "Well, the tour's great, but sorry to say, I've got to duck into the restroom."

"Sure."

As the door clicked behind her, I sensed a wordless moment pass between Rachel Marie and her husband. He cleared his throat. "Well, Pranom, we will see you at orientation Friday. Do you need us to come get you?"

"Oh, no. I remember how to go. It's just the Number Five bus, right?"

"That's amazing." Rachel Marie draped an arm around my shoulder. "That you still remember."

Khemkaeng stepped out onto the concrete walkway and shut the door behind him; the *click* seemed to have purpose and I braced myself.

Eyeing the still shut bathroom door, my mentor pulled me toward the flowered couch and we sat down together. "Listen, I hate to ask this, but I've got to."

I could tell I was back to chewing on my lower lip, which I always did in anxious moments. "Um . . . what?"

"Well, just . . . does your sister know what happened before? I mean, down at the beach?"

I shook my head. "Huh uh. We never told her."

The relief on Rachel Marie's face was a palpable thing and she let out a breath. "Whooh. I'm so glad. And just . . ."

I wasn't sure what was about to spill out, but all at once her eyes puddled. "I've thought about that a million times, how you were so hurt. And I swear, sweetie, I wouldn't have wanted you to come out here if I thought it would make you relive everything."

"I'll be all right," I managed, feeling unmoored by her emotional fragility.

"Well, look. Whatever you need, I'm here. Anytime. I want you to have my cell number, of course, and if you need to call me at four in the morning, I won't be mad one bit. 'Cause when you were here before, I just loved you like crazy, and that hasn't changed."

We could hear the muffled sound as Paloma flushed the toilet, and we exchanged watery grins. "Enough of that," Rachel Marie sighed theatrically. "And I promise you this. We're going to have the time of our lives. I can't wait for school to get started. Mrs. C and Miss Daggett are gonna explode BCS with our superstar teaching prowess."

SIX

I had to confess to myself that one new Thailand reality helped a whole bunch. It was quickly clear that I had a stalwart Christian army on my side. The church service at UCC was amazing. Pastor Gino preached a stirring sermon with his wife translating, and I honestly felt the familiar surge of Calvary joy, just like back home in Portland during those first months of recovery. We sat around the potluck tables until almost four in the afternoon, cracking jokes and exchanging gossip for the first day of instruction.

And then: Opening Day! It stunned me to stand there in the courtyard with my new faculty family and then look around at 1,500 students all in their burgundy-white uniforms. Paloma was being a good sport about the regimented wardrobe, and I have to concede she was awfully cute, her perky Caucasian features a white lily among a sea of such Bangkok beauty. She's got a knockout figure, and I could see the *Matthayom* Six guys eyeing her with unabashed interest.

Despite being a tad straitlaced, Khemkaeng managed a nice shtick of rehearsed humor as he welcomed back our hordes. "We have waited a long time for this day," he admitted. "I'm sure each of you has eagerly counted down the days as well. 'Only five more days until we have the joy of coming back to school. What a wonderful thing to do lessons again! To hear the lovely voices of our teachers! To take home stacks of books and papers and pencils and know you will experience no more boredom!'"

A groan went up from the high school kids, and he chuckled, his good humor washing over the assembly. I remembered how he was so hugely popular, especially way back when he first became a Christian. Now a decade later, there was still an aura of idol worship in the place, and I felt myself admiring Khemkaeng for his terms of faithful work here.

"Now, before anything else, we must meet our new teachers!" He gestured toward me, and also motioned for Sam Novarton to step forward. Sam was a plucky man from England, black as midnight and with a stiff accent that was part Big Ben and part Caribbean. He'd signed up to teach eighth grade world history and English, and I'd already enjoyed getting to know him. Now we stood side by side as Khemkaeng waxed eloquent about our arrival. "I do not believe we have ever had one of our own students come back to be a teacher," he boasted. "So this is a wonderful day. I remember Pranom as a sweet girl in *Prathom* Six; now she and I are partners in this wonderful work. Miss Daggett, beginning with this moment you are a professional woman, a respected teacher, and one of our leaders here in our *Matthayom* program. I know that you young people will not just learn calculus from Miss Daggett; she is also a light shining out to Bangkok about the goodness of God."

Uh oh. I knew this was the usual spiel; he had to say these things. And I guess I was okay with it. While here in this Christian school, I would be the dutiful ambassador. Frankly, as I felt the goodwill flowing toward me from my teaching peers, and also through the glances I got from students, I did feel bathed in heavenly blessings. It's quite something when fifteen hundred kids sing the Thai national anthem, and then follow up with four-part harmony on "Amazing Grace."

We'd all been on our feet for a good ten minutes, and I was itching to get to my classroom, but there was a bit more. Rachel Marie stepped forward, and there was a wave of affection from all the older kids. Several hundreds of them had passed through her *Prathom* Six classroom, and I knew she was virtually worshiped by the girls.

"Hi, you guys," she said, casting a glance over at her own row of twenty-six newcomers. "I can't wait for us to start this new year, and just want to read one Bible verse to you where God talks to us about that very thing. About the first day of something wonderful."

She had a small New Testament in her hand, and she juggled the mike for a moment, trying to find her spot. "Here it is," she murmured, her voice bleeding through. Then her words rang out clear. "This is our wonderful, amazing God speaking to the youth of Thailand. Listen to this." There was a sweet pause, the air-conditioned air wafting through the place and filling us all with a kind of anticipatory joy. "He who was seated on the throne said, 'I am making everything new!' That's God talking. He's getting a new world ready, and when we get there, it will be a place without pain or divorce or loneliness. No one will die. No one will ever hurt you. It will be just perfection and good things forever."

My adopted aunt closed her Bible and let her gaze sweep across the army of kids. "I know you all have stories to tell," she said. "Each person here. Little kids and all you wonderful *Matthayom* Six men and women, the highest jewels in our crown. We're so proud of you all. But if you came here this August with some sad things in your heart, you know, it's okay. Because God says to us: 'I'll make something new out of your life. I'll give you a new beginning. Together we can build a new adventure and even a whole new you.' Isn't that the best thing ever? I just want all of you to know that every day of this year, your teacher friends are praying for you and for your families and your homes. We love you guys and are so touched and happy and excited that you came back to be with us again."

Her words followed me up the stairs and I felt a rush of affection for "Aunt Rachel." As hundreds of us clattered up to the second floor together, I had to remind myself again that we were shedding the labels of Uncle and Aunt. This couple I adored were now peers; I was about to stand shoulder to shoulder with them for the next ten months. Despite my own fragile faith, I murmured an inward prayer for God to help me make good.

MAYBE THE BEST thing about Bangkok life is that we all dump our shoes just outside the door of a classroom. For that giddy sixty seconds, I was just one of the girls, and we eased into the comfort of being in stocking feet.

The place was deliciously air-conditioned, and I made my way to the front of the classroom fully aware that my pulse was really jumping.

The students were a dizzying array of maroon fabric; I was the only person out of uniform. I'd dressed carefully that morning, picking a pink blouse and cream-colored silk skirt. Looking in the mirror earlier, I winced; my trendy American dresses did tend to creep up my thigh, and I hoped Sue wouldn't call me in and give me a twenty-baht demerit my very first day.

I pushed such thoughts away. "Come on in and find places, everybody." I grinned. "I know that in America and here too, we always tend to sit in the same place all the time. So try and pick nice students to be near. Ladies, you have plenty of fine-looking gentlemen to choose from." There was nervous tittering at that, and in a few moments we were all settled in.

I took about ten minutes to get them oriented, explaining in rather sketchy terms how I'd spent three years here as a student myself and that, yes, I remembered when "Missie Stone" was a new and unattached lady in our Bangkok world. "Now she's my auntie," I cryptically added. "So it feels strange for me to jump up and now be her colleague as a teacher." A fresh impulse hit me and I added quickly: "So it shows the good ways where God can always lead us."

I offered to field some questions, and a boy in the back immediately raised his hand. "Yes? Do you mind if I ask you your name?"

He was a spunky lad with a bit of a trendy mustache, a rarity for Thai teens. "Yes. My name Udom."

"Very good." I caught myself. "Oops. Sorry, you

guys. But it's my job to nudge you to speak perfect English." I looked right at the boy. "Do you mind?"

"No. Is okay."

This guy must be new. I flashed him a smile. "We Thai people must always remember the word 'is.' So you should say to me: 'My name IS Udom.' Do you see?"

He nodded, unoffended.

"Okay. Try again."

He sat up straighter and affected a tone straight from Broadway. "My name IS . . . Mr. Udom." The place erupted in laughter and I joined in.

"Now you've forgotten your question."

"Oh. Sorry." He fumbled, now careful to not make mistakes. "Your sister, she is now here at BCS also?"

"Uh huh." I pointed vaguely toward the hallway. "But she's in the other section. I don't think you can miss her. She's the only white lady in *Matthayom* Six. In fact, I think in the whole school."

Udom grinned. "How do you have American sister, but we can see so much that you are Thai lady."

"'That you are A Thai lady,'" I offered.

"Yes. Okay."

"Well, that's an easy one." *Not really, but here goes.* "Back when I was here at BCS, there were some family problems. My mom died, which was really sad. But God kind of saved my life. He brought me to this wonderful, amazing American family and they adopted me." I paused and glanced around the room. "I don't know. Maybe a few of you have been here long enough to remember Mr. Daggett."

Hmmm. Nothing but blank faces, so I decided the enrollment rate had more turnover than I'd thought.

"Well, that's okay. He was the music teacher here and pretty awesome. But he and Mrs. Chaisurivirat's cousin, Miss Kidd, they fell in love while they were out here. And when they asked if they could adopt me, well, I felt like I'd gone right to heaven. Their little girl became my sister, and now she's all grownup too and here we are back in Bangkok."

Another girl blurted out without permission: "And you and her, is like you are really sisters all the time?"

"Totally," I said, meaning it. "I love her very much." I eyed the guys with feigned ferocity. "And if any of you gentlemen wish to know her better, you will have to make an application through me. And bring me five mangoes as a bribe." The place busted up, and I flushed, enjoying myself.

We launched right into the joys of calculus, and I proudly debuted Mom's PowerPoint file on the topic of limits. I knew my material cold, and it was a snap narrating the key points as they flashed up on the screen. Every little bit I would hit "B" on the computer keyboard and the images would blink into darkness so I could expound a theorem on our wall-to-wall whiteboard.

Toward the end of the lecture, I put a medium-level problem up on the screen. "Okay, ladies and gentlemen. Here's a problem I want you to try. This isn't a quiz; I just want to see if you're getting this idea of how a limit works. Do it in pairs if you want to, and let's see if we can get it finished in the next five minutes."

I patrolled the room, remote clicker in my hand, and tried to make eye contact and weave some start-up strands of camaraderie with as many as I could. I thought the girls were remarkably pretty; all had glistening black locks and the expected matching hair ribbons. Warm smiles, some of them still shy even though these ladies were just months away from filling out university applications.

Standing in the back of the room, though, I peered up at the screen again and felt myself sagging. From way back here, the graphs I was displaying were vague and blurry. I could hardly make out where the function values were undefined. Grumbling inwardly, I feigned nonchalance as I edged back toward the center of the room, peering over the kids' shoulders to monitor their progress.

Halfway through the lunch period I sidled over to Khemkaeng's table. He was chatting amiably with a couple of the older boys; I was pretty sure I'd just taught one of them, but my mind was still dizzy trying to catalogue faces and names.

He brightened. "Hello, Miss Daggett. How is your first day?"

"It's incredible," I admitted. "I had a wonderful time."

"Of course." He edged his chair toward our shared side of the dining table. "Anything you need?"

"Well, it's nothing, really. But I think I need to find an optometrist. I should have gotten a checkup before coming out, but I'm really feeling like my vision score is down to something like 20-6000."

He grinned amiably. "I think we have three different clinics we use. Want to come down after work and I can give you the information?"

"That'd be great."

There was a smallish food mart less than two blocks up from Orchid Garden Apartments; Paloma and I shared a cheerful half hour meandering the aisles together. I was going to be the breadwinner all this year, of course. But Mom and Dad had agreed to send over $200 a month for Paloma: half for some food, and the other half so she'd have spending money. So we teasingly bickered over various enticing morsels dangling in front of us. "It'll just be easiest if we split all the grocery bills fifty-fifty," Paloma suggested at last.

"Sure." I pretended to kick her ankle. "Then stop putting candy bars in the cart. If you want M & M's, you're on your own."

We ended up with two fairly stuffed grocery bags, and it was a rather humidity-drenched walk back to #305. Both of us had shiny foreheads by the time we lugged our loot up to Three. Paloma offered to whip up some supper, and I gratefully accepted the offer, plopping down on the couch with a dramatic sigh.

"You have papers to grade?"

"None tonight. Well, just that freebie quiz I gave both sections. But that's ten points across the board for everybody, so I already got the numbers put in."

We munched contentedly on our rice-and-chicken mix, occasionally spearing a bite of ripened pineapple. "This is amazing," I conceded. "You're a genius, Paloma dear."

She grinned. "*Kop kuhn kah.*"

"Oh yeah. So what are you up to when the rest of your class has its forty minutes of Thai linguistics?"

Paloma made a derisive raspberry sound. "Well, that's not going to work one bit," she informed me. "I know it's the rule and all, but I sat there like a moron for maybe ten minutes, and finally Mr. Thaugsuban came over, almost laughing, and said I might as well head to the library."

"Huh? You can't just skip the class."

"Why not? Next June we're heading back to Portland. I won't need Thai Vocab 415 to get into any universities back stateside. What's the point?"

I *hmmmed* for a second. "I bet you could duck back downstairs to something like *Prathom* Three and just sit in the back. Pick up some vocabulary at least."

Paloma grimaced. "You kidding? Me? A big old white lady wearing a bra and makeup, and all folded up into one of those mini-chairs like I was one of the Smurfs?"

"Well, I'm just saying. At least you'd learn some Thai."

She seemed unconvinced. "I'd do better all by myself in the library with a set of headphones and watching Thai vocab videos on Youtube."

"Maybe you're right."

We each had a couple scoops of vanilla ice cream out of the carton we'd just purchased, and then I remembered. "By the way, tomorrow can you just ride home on the Number Five by yourself? You mind?"

"How come?"

"Because I'm rapidly going blind and I really have to get an eye exam."

"Already? We've been here, like, four days."

"Hey," I told her. "When I stand in the back of the room, true story, I can't even read what I just wrote down on the board eight seconds earlier. We get to a traffic light and I'm not entirely positive if it's red or green."

Paloma sensed my exaggeration and I hastily backtracked. "Okay, it's not that bad. But really, I've got to get a better prescription."

We were just about to tumble into bed when she propped herself up on one elbow. "I got an idea. If you don't mind."

"Sure."

"Well, Mom kind of suggested that since we're forced to share a bedroom, we might finish things off each day just reading a few verses together." Paloma hesitated. "I mean, I don't know. Where your head is at with stuff like that. The last year or so I've kind of bogged down in terms of Bible reading."

Bogged down wasn't exactly the accurate description for my own religious barrenness, but I didn't say anything. It was more like *come to a dead stop*, but that was my business.

"Anyway, I figure most of the time we'll crash around the same time. So if you like, we could do it together. Plus," she added, "I think on every day except Monday the teachers at BCS kind of do read their kids a little something or other. One of the guys in my room was saying so, anyway."

I got the point immediately. "So maybe the same thing we read here, I could borrow again the next morning."

"Well, maybe. If it strikes a chord."

"Sure."

About a third of her stuff was still in the bottom of her suitcase and I teased her as she fished out her Bible. "You think by Thanksgiving you'll have everything put away?"

"Shut up, Miss Daggett." I grinned.

Nudging up closer to the light peering down from her headboard, she began to read in her trademark feathery voice. "*Paul, an apostle of Christ Jesus by the will of God, To the saints in Ephesus, the faithful in Christ Jesus: Grace and peace to you from God our Father and the Lord Jesus Christ.*"

As she read, a sweetly reminiscent memory floated back to me, where our roles were reversed out at Pattaya during the throes of my own recovery and I was reading to her from "The Cat and the Hat." I felt a bitter lump push its way up into my throat, and I forced the image away. A few lines later, I sat up straight. "Hang on. That's kind of nice."

"What I just read?" She scanned back and went over it a second time. "*For he chose us in him before the creation of the world to be holy and blameless in his sight. In love he predestined us to be adopted as his sons through Christ Jesus, in accordance with his pleasure and will.*"

At the mention of adoption Paloma set down her Bible and peered across the carpeted space separating us. "I guess that's us, huh?"

"Well, me for sure." But of course, even Paloma had gone through the overwhelming bath of paternal love when Tommy Daggett invited this blond waif into his heart and home. Both of us watched with childlike pleasure, wearing our matching red dresses and hair ribbons, as the name Daggett was legally bequeathed to us by the Portland law firm of Benfield & Salazar. Afterwards, it had been an evening of endless Ben & Jerry's with both sets of grandparents along for the celebration, presents stacked high on the restaurant table.

"I think I'm set for tomorrow morning then," I announced cheerfully.

My sister snapped off the night. "We sure lucked

out, didn't we?"

"Uh huh." I lay there in the darkness, covered just by the thin bedspread as the wall unit pushed comforting coolness into the space between us. On an impulse I blurted out: "*Rau bhen poo-ying choke dee.*"

Paloma gave her trademark snort. "Here we go then. So what's that mean?"

"Like you just said. 'We're a lucky pair of girls.'"

A pause. Then she said in a half-whisper: "Thank you, Tommy Daggett."

NEXT AFTERNOON I decided not to chance the Sky Train just yet. Clutching Khemkaeng's printout, I showed the top address to a cab driver loitering just outside the campus. "Can you take me here?" I asked in Thai.

He barely glanced at it, then nodded. Traffic was a clogged mess in what most citizens of Bangkok come to dread as a perpetual rush hour. Buses and industrial trucks nudged ahead one meter at a time as motorbikes threaded their weary way through clouds of diesel smoke. The air conditioning in my pink-and-blue chariot was puffing away gamely; my driver had some local talk show on the radio, and I strained to pick up the banter before giving up and staring ahead. It was almost a half hour before the glitter of the Siam Paragon Shopping Center came into view on the right.

"Is that it?" I asked. The guy nodded, stubbing out his drooping cigarette as he began coasting toward the curb.

Up on fourth floor I finally spotted the upscale ophthalmology center. The place was wreathed in artificial foliage and was all mirrors and mannequins and bilingual brochures touting the trendiest Hong Kong frames. A 60-inch Samsung TV was endlessly looping a video where skeletal European models donned one sexy Parisian pair of glasses after another as dapper gentlemen gathered around to flirt. I grinned at the shamelessness of it all.

A young man with a silky white shirt and blue tie motioned me over to his screen. "Do you have an appointment?" he asked me, in Thai, of course.

I nodded. "Four o'clock. Sorry I'm a few minutes late."

"*Mai bhen rai*." It's okay.

He tapped something into a couple of grids and then examined my medical card from Bangkok Christian School. "What do you do there?" he asked, pausing in his typing.

"Oh. I'm a new teacher."

"Really?" I imagined he wanted to comment on my glaring immaturity, but he thought better of it. "What do you teach?"

When I said I was the school's brand new calculus instructor, his eyes widened. "That is very hard!"

"Not if you prepare well."

He fell silent and finished logging in the rest of whatever.

"Let me show you where to go next," he offered. There was a maze of corridors behind us, with several examination rooms, and he motioned me into the second one. "Someone will be here to evaluate."

"Thanks."

I'd remembered to bring my Kindle with me, and had gotten through just a couple of pages in James Michener's *Alaska* when a pleasant-looking woman in a green pant suit came in. My chart was already up on the monitor, and after greeting me she peered at the data. "You have arrived here from America?" she asked, also in Thai.

"*Chai.*"

"And your last eye exam was this past December?"

Again I replied in the affirmative.

We went through an initial battery of tests and I felt a slowly creeping feeling of despair. All at once it felt like I couldn't make out a thing. If she asked me if Lens 3 was better or Lens 4, they were both a sickly blur. O's and Q's were indistinguishable ovals no matter how high-powered my glassy crutches were. "I feel like I'm blind," I grumbled, and the woman clucked sympathetically. "This is how we find out what your needs are, ma'am."

"But my eyes are worse, aren't they?"

"I think so. But wait until you are examined by Dr. Takuathung."

The assistant flipped the lights back on, and I peered angrily at the eye chart and its elusive codes. "So all along that was an L and not a T?" It surprised me that even here in Bangkok, the ophthalmology office used English lettering for the exam process, but apparently most patients had a working knowledge of the alphabet. She gave me a sympathetic look and then left, leaving the exam room door ajar.

I tried to get back to my novel, but my emotional reserves were down. Now even the words on the digital screen seemed a maze of hieroglyphics. Would I need to fall back on endless books-on-tape? Could Uncle Khemkaeng negotiate a seeing-eye dog to lead me through the hallways and up and down the stairways of

BCS? I realized I was just experiencing a psychosomatic funk, that my visual collapse was mostly mental.

"Excuse me. Miss Daggett?"

I looked up and tried to say hi at the same time I was attempting to nudge the Kindle to its off position. "Hello," I managed.

The ophthalmologist was a Thai man who looked like he was in his late twenties. Not much taller than I was, but even through his white coat I sensed that he was a wiry guy, perhaps an athlete. "I'm sorry you had to wait," he said, coming over toward me. He didn't offer the traditional *wai*; I suppose that in modern Bangkok, that's a fading ritual between peers. But he engaged in some cheerful small talk before looking at the sorry record left by his assistant. "Miss Sukhaphadhana tells me you are a teacher."

"That's right. And all at once I can hardly see the board and what I'm writing."

He grinned at the witticism. "When I was a boy, I always sat in the back row. And most everyone back there needs glasses. So I soon found it easy to choose this as a career."

All of this was in our native Thai, of course, and I felt myself relaxing. He had a disarming smile, which you don't often get from the head honcho in a medical office. And I kept on glancing at his necktie, which was a dazzling array of rainbow patterns. He caught me eyeing the fabric and shrugged. "Here in the mall, there are a million shopping temptations. But a lot of the merchants pass along discounts to one another. So it's not as pricy as you'd think."

"It's really pretty though." I hesitated, then added: "I'd love to get something like that for my dad. His birthday's coming up."

"Thanks. It's just one floor up. I can show you."

He directed me to place my chin into the plastic holder and hold my head perfectly still as he visually probed my eyeballs with his instruments. I fixed my gaze on the piercing red light as he instructed, breathing a subconscious prayer that perhaps the diagnosis wouldn't be as dire as I'd feared. It felt reassuring to be in the capable hands of this medical pro who oozed nonchalant optimism.

"Now let me just run through the last series of tests again," he told me.

"I hate doing them," I groaned. "Because it feels like I can't see anything at all. Whatever your assistant put on the screen, it was always a blur each time."

He actually chuckled. "That's very typical. So don't be distressed."

"Well, why can't you have me always pick between a 'really clear' and a 'really fuzzy' choice? Why is everything on the test so tiny like a mosquito leg?"

"You're right," he conceded. "But that's how we know what strength your new lenses need to be."

"I can already tell you I'll need the strongest thing you have here," I retorted, trying to mask my returning frustration.

To my relief, even though the litany of options he offered was still shrouded in mystery, his chairside manner disarmed me. "Look at both of these," he suggested mildly. "This one? Or this one?" When I asked for a repeat, he murmured an unoffended *dai, krahp*, "of course," and flipped right back. I felt mollified, even though my scores had to be sagging off the charts and definitely on the deficit side.

Sliding his rolling chair over to the wall switch, he eased the lights back on and then wheeled back in my direction.

"It's bad, isn't it?" I demanded. "What? Do I have cataracts already?"

Dr. Takuathung shook his head briskly. "No, of course not. That happens very rarely to a nice lady of your age. That's more a malady for people in their 60s and later."

I waited. He penciled something along the margins of the chart, and then turned back to face me. "Well, you've definitely had some visual deterioration since your last exam," he confirmed.

"But . . . what? Just really big and thick lenses?"

The doctor shook his head. "Well, if you're interested in hearing about it, I'd suggest that you're an almost perfect candidate for Lasik surgery."

I gulped. "I just know the barest details about it. They do some kinds of little cuts in your cornea or something." I didn't want to insult the guy by implying that of course, only the United States and perhaps Belgium would offer such high-tech procedures. The glitter and chrome of his medical practice practically shrieked that anything Beverly Hills had, he'd be able to boast as well.

"I've done them hundreds of times," he told me without a veneer of pride. "Of course. It's a simple procedure. Many Thai people are opting for this now."

He rattled off some statistics, and of course, the word "Lasik" was the only thing that wasn't Thai. Recovery time was rapid; many patients could be back to work within forty-eight hours. The one drawback was that it often wasn't covered under insurance plans.

"I don't know about where I work," I admitted. But when he offered a ballpark price, I was pleasantly surprised. "That's not so bad."

He launched into a story about an athlete he'd recently helped. "His vision was just about shot," he confided. "Nice young man, but he was trying to excel in badminton, where, you know, visual acuity is just so important. For precision play around the net."

"How'd it come out?"

I'd already noticed that Dr. Takuathung had an endearing habit, and he did it now again. He gave a little shrug of his right shoulder, and it was a blend of "oh, no big deal" and, I sensed, a cocksure bit of "well, of course; it went great. 'Cause, lady, I'm the best eye doc in the kingdom." But he simply added: "He's now *yee-sip, yee-sip.*" Even a kid in *Prathom* One can count to twenty. Or, in this case, 20-20. He ran a finger through his hair and grinned. "He was on TV just this past weekend. He came in third in a competition against Taiwan." Another smile, this one with a teasing twinkle to it. "I guess I should have bribed him to wear a jersey with our clinic's logo on it."

I giggled at that, enjoying myself, and just then his cell phone tinkled. "I'm sorry," he apologized, ignoring the call.

"Go ahead," I said. "It's all right."

"Are you sure?"

He pulled it loose and did a slight eye-roll as he glanced at the screen. And I swear I got the surprise of my life when he answered. "Hey," he said in absolutely flawless English. "I'm with a patient here. Can I call you back in about half an hour?'

There was a slight pause and then he said, again

sounding like a cute guy one row over at a Trailblazers game: "Sure. Talk to you then. . . . Uh huh. . . Okay, bye."

"Are you kidding me?" I began laughing and couldn't stop, and now it was his turn to be surprised. "What? You speak English too?"

"I just got here from Portland, Oregon," I informed him.

"No way."

"Yeah. My mom and dad are Americans; my sister's as blond as Jennifer Lawrence, and I'm the new calculus teacher at Bangkok Christian School, where anybody who speaks Thai has to fork over a twenty-baht fine."

He was immensely amused at our shared discovery. "That's totally amazing. Here we are both going on and on in Thai for forty-five minutes."

"So what's your story?" I demanded. "Because with a name like Takuathung, you're definitely a Thai man."

"I grew up in Baltimore," he said. "From eighth grade on. College and med school both. But my parents chose to return and after thinking about it and realizing how upscale practices are getting to be out here, I said, hey, why not."

To have this new friend flowing forth with flawless English after all the native formality had the effect of popping any remaining bubbles of tension. I sat there for the next twenty minutes as agog as a schoolgirl as he told me about his recent life on the East Coast and the sports awards he'd won in cycling. "I thought you looked kind of athletic," I said, hoping it didn't sound like I was trying to flirt.

That adorable shrug again. "It was a fun time."

All at once I noticed the wall clock over his shoulder. "You said you'd call your friend back," I reminded him.

"Oh yeah." He helped me out of the chair and we walked together to the clinic's entrance. "Okay, let me show you." *Holy cow, it freaked me out to hear this Thai man with diction like a linguistics professor.*

"Show me what?" I was puzzled for a moment till he took me by the arm and led me over to the escalator. "See right up there? That throbbing red neon sign?"

"Uh huh."

He hooked a thumb around his silk necktie. "That's where you'll find another one of these," he reminded. "For your dad."

SEVEN

So I rode back to Orchid Garden Apartments in a state of near-euphoria. First, it was a relief to know my gummed-up eyeballs were about to get repaired. From the sound of it, I'd be close to 20-20 again and be able to spot a sparrow up on a telephone pole from one end of Sukhumvit Road to the other.

But the more electric reality was that sexy doc in the white lab coat. Even thirty minutes later in the stale grit of this Bangkok taxi, I had Dr. Takuathung's face and chiseled facial features tattooed in my brain. I still had his business card in the palm of my hand, and I glanced down again at the small color photo in the corner. He wasn't rock-idol gorgeous in the matinee sense, but he sure had plenty in the handsome department to pique my interest. A great smile, with just enough of a crookedness to give him some allure. Nice hair, good masculine skin. He seemed broad-shouldered beneath his coat; I could visualize the taut crispness of his checked dress shirt, navy pinstripes on white, freshly ironed. And there'd been the one delicious moment when he'd reached over and nudged my gaze slightly to the left so he could get a better reading. I could still mentally retrieve the nice feel of his fingertips against my cheek. I was enjoying my reverie, and now remembered there was a bare hint of something nice, perhaps a cologne or aftershave he probably cadged at a discount price on the mall's seventh floor.

All of us with Thai blood in our veins have a similarity to our looks, of course: the jet-black hair and the dark eyes. And he had that too, but there was something about his eyes that seemed different than anyone else I might meet on the street. He carried around in that keen mind of his a boatload of vast knowledge and training, certainly. But there was a confident precision as he chatted with me about this and that, an appealing kind of in-control calm that came from being smart and well-read and just . . . *wise.*

I tried to assure myself I wasn't imagining this man's glorious resumé; he really had oozed warmth and engagement during my medical appointment. When he asked me questions about my work, he fixed his gaze on me and honestly seemed to want to know about teaching high school seniors things like derivatives and which infinity a function sails off to as it approaches an asymptote. When I wailed like a teenager about all the palm trees being blurry and why was his eye test so unfair, his gentle rejoinder seemed almost compassionate, that something in him honestly yearned for Miss Daggett, his soon-to-be-soulmate (of course), to enjoy perfect vision once again.

And holy cow, he'd sure made me jump when he so smoothly shifted over to English! Even before that *a-ha* moment, I'd already felt a girlish infatuation beginning to set in. But when the bilingual track gushed forth, it was as though Dr. Saman Takuathung was immediately twice as fascinating, twice as vibrant, twice the romantic prize.

And why might that be? I suppose part of it was the simple reality of his suave appeal. Even just in Thai, the guy was debonair. Add his Princeton-level English and his familiarity with American ways, and I felt giddy adolescent joy in thinking, foolishly, that he and I could have double the chemistry. I was a bilingual genius as well, a well-bred American lady wrapped up in exotic Bangkok DNA. Now likewise with my handsome matinee idol, the doctor of my dreams.

I lifted the thumbnail picture again, my pulse fluttering as I relived my really nice afternoon *in a doctor's office*. Did he like me? Was he already calling his other patients and regretfully cancelling appointments, clearing his schedule so he could rush over to Bangkok Christian School and commence courting me full-time? If we planned a Christmas wedding, well, I could certainly expect to get my Lasik surgery comped by my gorgeous and generous fiancé . . .

Hold the phones!! Pranom, dearie, you are one delusional nut-case. My romantic reverie splatted against the coffee-stained upholstery as the taximan skidded us to a rubber-burning stop on Ratchadamri Road just across the intersection from the Erawan Hotel's fabled Hindu shrine.

What was the matter with my gray matter? Was I so needy and unmoored that a kindly physician's chairside manner had me swooning about possible honeymoon sites? For all I knew, Dr. Takuathung was a married man with a pregnant wife and three children already. He might be gay. He might be an avowed hermit. Or an atheist. He might be a drunk or a gambling addict.

No, it couldn't be. I knew practically nothing about my hero's *curriculum vitae* except for his good vocabulary and those hunky eyebrows. For sure he was a gentleman, a gracious person. Beyond that, I had absolutely no clue. And it was an inescapable reality that the only future contact I might expect from my dreamboat M.D. would be to schedule a twenty-minute appointment with his microkeratome as he called out "Next," saw me standing there in his assembly line, and lasered my corneas into shape.

Sigh. Well, fantasies are sure fun while they last. The taxi guy wheeled into the tiny parking lot I now called home, and I grumpily fumbled in my purse for a trio of red bills. I murmured *kop kuhn* as I closed the door behind me and faced the stolid reality of those humidity-baked two flights of stairs. I was halfway to Apartment #305 when I remembered with a groan his folksy phone repartee with some invisible friend. Fragments came thudding back to me, dashing my spun-in-honey dreams. *Hey, I'm with a patient. Call you in half an hour.* Had he added a casual "babe" at the end? Was that a call to his girlfriend, likely a lingerie model whose image peered down on us from that Toyota billboard we'd just passed?

My lip curled as I considered that dratted lady, that vain, empty-headed hussy with her grasping schemes . . .

I pushed the door open and was greeted with the fragrance of a piping hot cheese pizza Paloma was just pulling free of the oven. "I'm really discouraged," I sang out, determined to make my afternoon love adventure a moment of light comedy. "And don't want to talk about it." Which of course we immediately did.

MY SISTER'S GAZE softened as I spilled my lovelorn tale over the shared treat. "Okay, so he's way cute," she acknowledged, surveying my meager bit of evidence on Dr. T's business card. "But look. You and I are at least trying to be Christians. This guy . . . I mean, he may have no clue about that. In fact, considering this is Bangkok, it's ninety-nine-to-one he's either a nominal rich ex-Buddhist or he's basically a guy out there to make money and enjoy secular life."

I sighed as I dabbed some tomato sauce off my chin. "Yeah, I got it. But, I don't know, I might be ready to just say 'that's enough for me too.'"

"What's enough?"

"You know. Just regular life. Marry a good guy, let him take me away from it all, and just live for daily happiness. I teach calc, he does eyes and designer frames, we make a ton of money, have babies . . ."

Paloma let her fork dangle in the air above her plate, a half-bite of salad perched there eavesdropping on us. "You really think the whole business of God and all that–you'd let it go?"

"Sometimes," I admitted.

"Yikes."

And that was that.

IN TERMS OF teaching math, though, I was in my seventh heaven. I honestly felt my pulse quickening as I got off the Number Five every weekday morning. Two weeks in, I had an okay handle on maybe two-thirds of my kids' names, and was beginning to catalog their personalities and fun quirks. It was hilarious having my Caucasiany baby sister right there in the classroom Tuesdays and Thursdays. She parked herself in the same spot, second row, by the window, next to a fawning lad named Klahan. Paloma typically demurred from asking questions in calculus class, but once in a while she did raise her hand. So of course, the entire class would begin tittering, the guys almost lifting their butts out of the seats in order to witness the sisterly ragging.

It was hard to mask my own amusement. "Yes, Miss Daggett?"

"I hate to ask, Miss Daggett, but I really don't get how to do number twenty-one."

"I know. You were talking about it in your sleep all last night."

"But it's not my fault. I think our teacher didn't explain it right last time."

"I'm sure that can't be it." Smirking, I turned to the others and feigned an apologetic pose. "I always say: 'It's so hard to teach calculus to a *farang*. They just don't have the right kind of brain for it.'" That brought down the house. Paloma slunk down into her chair, comically sulking. Then I'd heave a theatrical sigh. "Oh, go ahead. What is it, kid?"

Khemkaeng happened to be strolling by one Thursday morning just before our first scheduled chapter test, and caught a bit of the Daggett comedy act. He absorbed it with a wide grin, then, shaking his head in amusement, strolled on down the hallway. Later that afternoon, I got a cryptic Thai email from him. "Very good! Your act would work well in Las Vegas."

The next weekend Paloma rode home on the bus with me, all excited about the *Matthayom* Six party. "Where's it at again?"

She peered down at the colorfully printed invitation. "It's at *Kuhn* Somsak's house. I don't know where, but the school's sending the van."

"That's that kind of rich guy who keeps BCS afloat, huh?"

"That's what Uncle Khemkaeng says."

"What's the main thing? Just swimming?"

"Uh huh. And a whole lot of food."

"How much?"

"Three hundred baht."

I gave her hand a squeeze. "It sounds amazing. Especially in this heat." September had been a soggy sizzle here in southern Thailand, and a Saturday night pool party promised liquid relief. "Just watch out, 'cause I think that kind of shy guy sitting next to you has romantic intentions. Buried way down low, but when he sees you in that cute one-piece, he may get up his nerve." I grinned. "And just so you won't feel sorry for me, I got invited out to Rachel Marie's place the same night."

"For what?"

"Just, you know, supper and games. Play around with the kids. Maybe rent a movie, she said."

"Nice."

We spent a relaxing evening with watermelon slices and games of hide-and-seek, with Gage and Katrina shrieking as I tramped like a marauding giant from room to room trying to spot their hiding places. Katrina was an adorable bundle, already singing the ABC song with unflagging gusto and showing me all her baby pictures. I watched, amused, as Rachel Marie took both kids onto her lap and quietly read them a Bible story about when the princess of Egypt found a boy baby floating in a secret boat on the Nile River. "And a long time after that, when that little boy grew up to be a big man, God helped him to set all his people free. Which was really amazing and cool." She glanced in my direction. "Ready to show Auntie Pranom how we say prayers?"

"Is she really our auntie?"

"Well, not totally. But it's fun to call her that since she's such a nice friend."

Khemkaeng offered to take over the tucking-in chores and my friend tugged me down onto the couch next to her. "Want a soda or something?"

"You read my mind."

She had chilled cans of some Thai brand of cola, and we sipped the sweet liquid as I confessed about my girlish crush. She grinned amiably. "It's tough when a good-looking guy comes along and makes you weak in the knees. The next question always is, well, what else has this guy got? But it's nice to have things start with some sizzle." She eyed me over her drink, remembering her own earlier escapades. "If they ever do start, that is. When's your appointment? 'Cause I can tell you're squinting at church, trying to make out the song lyrics and Bible verses."

"It's next Friday afternoon."

"Ah. Good timing. Gives you the whole weekend to recover." Khemkaeng was coming back down the stairs, and he eased himself into the love seat across from us. "Will you need a ride home from the wherever-it-is?"

I shook my head. "Paloma can come with me. It just takes, like, half an hour. Then we'll catch a cab back to the apartment."

"Good."

I felt slightly intimidated with Khemkaeng listening in, but decided to spill my guts anyway. I tugged at the folded-up sheet of paper and showed it to Rachel Marie. "What's this?" she asked.

It was just a printout of the ophthalmologist appointment reminder, with the time and location and bilingual instructions about skipping all facial makeup and the necessity of adult accompaniment and a chaperoned ride home. "So you're good to go," Rachel Marie agreed, mystified.

"I know. But there's this too." I unzipped the side compartment of my purse and showed her the handwritten note that had arrived by snail mail just yesterday. Rachel Marie read it aloud. "'It will be good to see you again, Pranom. I wish you success with your new 20-20 vision and a good school year at Bangkok Christian School.' Signed: 'Saman Takuathung.'" She eyed me with warm curiosity. "It's nice."

"Yeah." I reached out for the note, reading the words again for myself. "You think that's a regular thing? A doctor sending out notes to all his patients?"

It took my friend a moment to assess the situation. "Ah. So you're wondering if these flickers of romantic interest run in both directions."

There was no point in hiding it. "Yeah. I guess so. 'Cause, hey, when I rode home in the cab after the first time, I really thought he could be something special."

"I have no clue." She turned toward her husband. "Honey, any idea about this guy? How'd the school get connected up with him?"

Khemkaeng shook his head. "The medical practice

belonged to someone else until two years ago. When this doctor came and purchased it, we continued the referral."

"But you don't know anything about him?"

"Mr. Bell said he got his checkup there. And that he was all right."

"Well, that doesn't help," I put in sarcastically. Khemkaeng grinned.

There was a muffled sound coming from one of the bedrooms, and Rachel Marie went to the foot of the stairs. "Go to sleep, Mr. Gage. No more noise."

"Did you try looking on Facebook?" Khemkaeng offered, enjoying the conversation.

"Of course." I sighed. "That's the first place anybody looks. But he wasn't even on it."

Rachel Marie left me and scooted in next to her husband, as if to model for me the sublime joys of wedded bliss. "I guess if you really want to know, you just ask him. What have you got to lose?"

EIGHT

S everal times that next Friday morning, as students were grinding through a pair of nasty chain-rule exercises, I tugged my glasses loose and peered at my soon-to-be-retired Coke-bottle lenses. In a few short hours, was I actually going to be healed like the needy Israelite folks in the Gospels? It seemed a blasphemous thought, but I was putting my suffering eyeballs in the hands of this miracle man from a high-rise Bangkok luxury mall. Despite Dr. Takuathung's serene assurances, though, I was experiencing a moderate case of trepidation. I mean, slicing open a flap on my eyeballs? Laser beams scorching my already damaged corneas? I was definitely going to accept the good doctor's offer of a Xanax tablet.

Several of the girls in my afternoon trig class came up to my desk after the closing bell. "Good luck, Miss Daggett."

"Oh. Thanks, you guys."

One giggled. "If you are not have to wear glasses, we think so soon you will have a nice *fan*."

You read my mind. I pretended to be offended. "There's more to life than finding a handsome *fan*."

They covered their mouths and tittered in unison. "See you Monday, okay?"

"All right, ladies. Thanks for your good work today. Don't forget that sine equals opposite-over-hypotenuse."

"We know it all okay. Except not to spell 'hypotenuse.'" I shooed them out the door and began stuffing textbooks into my rolling cart. I trundled down to the student locker area and grinned when I saw Klahan bashfully loitering next to my sister's locker. Did she want me to give this fragile moment some breathing room? Or perhaps she needed rescuing. I feigned a deep interest in my phone messages, and then about half a minute later did creep toward the awkward rendezvous. "Hi, you guys."

Paloma and I exchanged sisterly glances. "Hey, Miss Daggett."

"School's out," I reminded them both. "You, at least, can call me Pranom." Then to the stuttering lad: "But not you."

He managed a wan smile. "Okay, Miss Daggett."

"I assume you two are discussing inside functions and the chain rule."

"Right." Paloma gave her suitor an encouraging look and then slammed her locker shut. "Well, I have to take my sister to the eye doctor."

The boy took his cue. "Okay." He did summon up a shred of male bravado, wishing me good fortune in the forbidden tongue. "*Kaw hie choke dee.*"

"Thanks." I put a hand on his arm. "And since you're being nice to my little sister, I won't charge you twenty baht."

Paloma followed me toward Khemkaeng's office. "What'd you forget?"

"Nothing. It's just that the office is going to pay 25% of the fee. Even though Lasik's not covered by insurance."

"How come?"

"'Cause Uncle Khemkaeng's a good guy. And because the school figures it's a cheaper investment in the long run than buying all the teachers new glasses every other year."

She was scurrying to keep up with me. "So what's this gorgeous boy wonder charging?"

"It's not bad at all. About a grand per eye."

"How's that compare with Portland?"

"Only about half."

"Sweet. Dad's floating you the difference?"

"He said half him and half me. But that I could take till Christmas to pay my share."

She sighed melodramatically. "He's such an awesome guy."

We were about to push into the suite of admin offices when my cell phone dinged. "Hang on, kid." I examined the screen and felt my feminine antenna beginning to swivel toward the mall. An invisible chorus of angels sang in unison as I read: *Hi, Pranom. I wanted to let you know that you'll be my final patient of the day. If you like, I could serve as your driver/bodyguard going home. That would save your sister the wait.*

I knew I was flushing, but there was no question whatsoever about it: this was a small but significant victory in my subtle campaign. I let Paloma read it for herself. "Looks like you're off the hook."

"Wait a minute," she complained, grinning. "I need

to come along to keep an eye on things."

"'Eye on things.' That's hilarious."

"But look. You'll be spaced out on Xanax. He's a debonair authority figure, and you've already got the hots for him. I can't have you out there alone in such a vulnerable position."

"Oh, give it up." We went into Khemkaeng's office and Paloma immediately spilled the beans. "Pranom's new beau is going to chauffeur her home after the operation. Talk about a conflict of interest." She began to mimic a solicitious Dr. Takuathung. "'Feeling woozy, honey? Here. Take my hand. It's okay. There. Just lean your head against my shoulder. Isn't that cozy? Don't worry, we're just taking the scenic route to Orchid Garden. I'll have you there in about three hours.'"

Khemkaeng's face was wreathed in smiles. "So, Miss Daggett, you are really interested in this handsome and wealthy doctor?"

"He's probably married," I retorted. "But if not, yeah. I'm going to get my bid in."

"You think he's gorgeous now," Paloma cracked. "Wait till you can actually see him in sharp focus. You'll be weak in the knees."

I went closer to the senior administrator's door. "Mrs. Carington? Everybody's picking on me."

"She's not in," Khemkaeng observed blandly.

"All kidding aside, you guys wish me luck." A moment later I amended my request. "I mean in terms of the operation." We all shared a laugh at that, and Khemkaeng came over to offer me a half-embrace of support. "Here's the check; it's already made out."

"Thanks, Uncle Khemkaeng." He accepted the familial title and walked us out to the school's front gate.

IT WAS POSITIVELY ARCTIC in the surgical suite, and I was thankful for Dr. T's reminder to bring along a sweater. I was already feeling that coherent but vague spaciness as the relaxant bathed my nerve endings. Dr. Takuathung greeted me cheerfully and I hopefully imagined he was admiring my outfit and new hairdo.

"Are you feeling nervous at all?" He was getting his surgical tray ready, but came over close to me. "By the way, we can do this all in Thai if you'd rather."

"No, that's okay. And yeah, I'm a little jumpy. Even with the Xanax."

"It goes really quick. When it's done, you relax in postop for about an hour. I'll knock out some paper-work, and we'll get you home to your sister. What's her name again?"

"Paloma."

"Very good."

Despite my approaching torpor, I had an impulse to blurt out something along the lines of "I've got a crush! Have *you* got a crush! We're perfect for each other! And oh, by the way, who was that on the phone the other day? Huh? Huh?" But I forced myself into a series of obedient nods as he settled me in place, applied the numbing drops, and instructed me to relax and keep perfectly still. It was disconcerting to have my eyes bulging out, my reluctant gaze propped open by something he'd earlier described as a "lid speculum."

"It's so amazing that technology like this exists," I murmured as I heard the metallic *clink* of his instru-ments.

"It really is." His voice was soothing and melodic, and now he carefully shushed me. "We're about to start. Focus on that light right over there. Okay? Nice and easy now, Miss Pranom Daggett . . ."

I was surprised that in what felt like mere seconds it was done. He taped plastic eye shields in place and led me out to a warmer anteroom where some soft Thai pop music was coming through the speakers.

"Was it all okay?" My speech felt slow, but it was a wonderful sensation feeling my hand enfolded in his, professional though the gesture might be.

"Perfect." He gave my fingers a nice squeeze. "Why don't you just relax here for a while? I'll get some insurance things squared away and then we'll get you home." He paused. "And for sure, you want nothing but a really quiet weekend. Stay off the computer as much as possible." I heard his soft chuckle. "Give those calculus students a break."

"Okay." Even in my ethereal state, it was a constant temptation to inject some artifice into my replies, but I didn't know what. Breathiness? Shy vulnerability? Should I just be flat-out flirty?

You're spaced out, Pranom. Floating. Let it go.

"Is this music okay?" he asked. "I can put the TV on if you want. We've got CNN in here."

"No, the music's good." I swallowed, feeling the fragility of my punctured eyeballs. "I can work on my Thai."

"Good deal."

His carpeted footsteps led away, and I smiled inwardly. I mean, who knows? I was literally putty in this guy's hands, at least just now. My eyes were bandaged, my senses becalmed by legal opiates. And of course, my moral fences were already compromised by my infatuation for Dr. Takuathung. Did I dare to nudge things toward the more familiar? While still pondering my pleasant predicament, I slipped into a light doze.

It was the touch of his hand, not his voice, that tugged me back. "I think you took a small nap," he teased. "But we can go now if you're ready."

"Sure." My throat felt dry, though. "I could kind of use a drink of water."

"I thought so. Here." He pressed a paper cup into my hand. "Sorry it's not very cold."

"It's okay."

I had visions of this handsome medical pro leading me down four successive escalators to the ground level of Siam Paragon, throngs of shoppers gaping at my bandaged head. But apparently he had access to an employees-only elevator. "Careful," he murmured. "Pick up your feet a bit right . . . there." A moment later I heard the doors close and there was a slight shudder as we headed down. "I'm totally at your mercy, Dr. Takuathung," I managed, hoping to feign a desirable level of vulnerability. "If you trip, we'll both take a tumble."

"I'll be extra careful with such a nice patient in my care," he countered, and I flushed happily.

I'd already given him directions to Orchid Garden Apartments, and even the engine hum on his Mercedes seemed quiet and professional. "What color's your car?" I asked. "Don't forget I'm totally blind."

He chuckled. "It's really nice. I think they call it 'midnight blue.' I'm not sure what it said on the Thai sticker."

"You bought it right here in Bangkok?"

"Yeah. My dad has some connections."

I felt enveloped by the expensive upholstery and new-car fragrance. "You should take me home by way of Phuket," I managed lightly. "'Cause this is really plush and comfortable, Saman."

There. I said it. I'd crossed the red line and addressed this invisible hero by his familiar first name. Would he pull over to the curb and unceremoniously dump me out?

But he actually seemed charmed. "Well, then. I am Saman. You are Pranom. That's very nice."

I waited expectantly, barely hearing the grinding gears of the bus sliding past on our left, the soft strains of symphonic music I supposed Saman's iPod was feeding into his premium Mercedes sound system.

"I have an idea," he said all at once. I could make out the faint *tick tick tick* of the turn signal as he nosed our chariot to the left. In my mind's eye I could picture the thick traffic of Rama Road as we accelerated slightly.

"What's that?"

"Well," he said slowly, "you spend tonight with your eye shields on. All tomorrow you've got those hideous dark glasses to wear." He chuckled. "I get those in bulk for eighty baht, you know."

I waited.

"Anyway, after twenty-four hours, when you come back for the postop check, you'll be pretty much back to normal. And if I schedule things right, you could be the clinic's last patient of the day again."

"So what does that mean?" I felt myself flowing in a certain direction here, a dark but thrilling moment of expectation. My eyes were tightly closed, plus my vision was walled off by these cheap plastic eye shields. On top of which, I had no doubt, my wealthy friend's car windows were tinted to give Saman and any chosen lady friend a nice cove of privacy.

"Well, it could mean a detour for some dinner on the way home," he offered hopefully. "Someplace smoke-free, of course. I know a few really nice restaurants."

WELL, THERE WAS nothing to do but get Mommy on the phone. Paloma tends to take her showers the night before, which helps even out our generally cramped schedule. So once I heard the water flow through the bathroom door get up to speed, I dialed her up. "Hey, it's me."

"Hi, honey. How'd the surgery go?"

"Well, I guess okay. I'm going to keep the eye shields on till morning and then just lounge around the place in dark glasses. The postop visit's tomorrow afternoon."

"I'm proud of you for doing this. I think I'd be a trembling wreck, but if you end up at 20-20, I'll be one jealous mother."

I figured I had maybe eight minutes of confidentiality time here, so dumped the entire mess in my mother's lap. "Mom, he's just so amazing. He really is. He's smart and funny and I know it sounds like I have an idiot crush on him, but I can't help it." I told her about my flirtatious machinations and that I'd inveigled him into a dinner date.

"That sounds promising. I presume that at least implies he's single and unattached."

I hadn't even considered the idea that he might be a two-timing cad. "I hope so."

"Well, then, it's at least a possibility." I felt a tone of concern creep in. "Now, honey, hang on. Your dad and I really do not want you falling in love with somebody out there in Bangkok, no matter how wonderful he is. You're our girl forever, you know, and that means the big, beautiful state of Oregon. Or someplace really close by."

"I know," I sighed. "And it probably doesn't mean a thing."

"Dinner's not generally a nothing," Mom pointed out.

"I guess not."

Through the phone crackle, I heard the faint rumble of an engine cranking up. "You heading for work?"

"Yeah. I've still got a Friday to get through. But your dad's taking Tommy this morning so I've got the SUV to myself. We can talk a bit more."

It was awkward trying to verbalize to my own mom that I was experiencing my own crisis of faith. Mom and Dad were devout; they'd be devastated if they knew how far out in the wilderness of doubt I was at this moment. So I skirted around that, guardedly musing that Dr. Saman Takuathung might have zero connection with the things of Christianity.

"If he lived here in the States for very long, he'd at least have some knowledge of things like that," she pointed out.

"Oh sure. I mean, hey, he's very well-versed. Even if he's an atheist, I bet he could quote the Beatitudes just in order to win at *Jeopardy*."

Thankfully, Mom seemed unconcerned. "Listen, baby. That's why we go out with men. We find out if there's shared values and then make choices." There was some static on the line before she came back on. "Sorry; I had to change lanes 'cause the exit to the office is coming up." She settled in again, and I had a mental image of that long curvy drive, rhododendrons on both sides, elegant green-tinted windows against the copper-shade building with the white pillars.

"So you think it's okay?" I pressed.

Mom hesitated. "Look. I figure this. In nine months you're coming back home. Unless you want me to kill you. So in the meantime, there's that. If I had to bet, no, he's likely not a Christian and you're not that likely to marry him. But going to dinner, sure."

I felt my optimism beginning to leak out like air from a punctured tire. "But we've got just this amazing chemistry!"

"That's not something to take lightly," she admitted. "And if it's really a wonderful and unstoppable force, that might well mean the other two things I just said would solve themselves. If the perfect man falls in love with my born-again, amazing daughter, he'd be an idiot not to realize that it's the love of Jesus making you the prize you are."

Talk about mixed feelings. I heard the water in the shower slow to a crawl and then die away. "Paloma's almost out. Want to wait and say hi to her?"

"It's okay. Well, let me get up to my desk. If she wants to say a quick hi, that'd be wonderful. But I know it's bedtime for my girlies." She added the last with a light touch and I found myself with a wistful ache for the arms of my American mom.

NINE

I primped and dolled myself up with a severe case of confusion. I was eager to spend an evening with Saman. So I flipped through one outfit after another, Paloma offering her own giggly counsels, and we finally settled on a casual rose-colored blouse and a calf-length burgundy skirt. "These go together, don't they?"

"Sure."

I doffed my sunglasses for a brief session in front of the mirror, and sure enough, the bathroom lights did cause a kind of dim halo effect. "He said that would clear up," I reminded my sister hopefully.

"Better steer clear of any makeup around your eyes."

"I know."

It helps to fuss around with blush and things like that in front of a younger sister who's a calendar girl in her own right. But I peered at the pretty Thai features bouncing back at me off the mirror: even features with full lips, my hair pulled to the side in a twisted French braid Paloma had taught me just last year. I tried on a couple of smiles, imagining how one or the other would get to my dream guy's heart strings. I managed an impish grin, then a flirty dazzler that showed a lot of teeth. Then quiet, shy, *come and get me but it'll take you most of this school term.* Girls who know their way around can direct events just with a half-smile and a soulful look, and I breathed a prayer for God's wisdom as I accepted a hug from my baby sister.

"Good luck out there."

"I'll need it." I checked my purse to make sure I had sufficient cab fare. "What are you doing for supper?"

"Hiking up to the main road and getting a garden burger at Wendy's."

"That's original."

"Well, think of me while you're dining on filet mignon."

She waited with me for the few minutes it took for a stray cab to drift down our *thanon*. The guy nodded dourly when I told him I needed the Siam Paragon, but flipped the meter flag into position and I clambered in. Paloma leaned in for one last hug. "I'm glad the eye thing went okay. And hope this is all good too. Just don't do anything rash."

That last chance remark stuck with me as we pulled out into traffic and then painfully negotiated the clogged roundabout leading into the city's center. What sort of rash thing might Dr. Takuathung suggest? A tipsy row of martinis? A torrid night together in his bachelor pad? I pushed away the reality that for me to be on a romantic date here in Bangkok was uncomfortably close to the very thing I'd sworn to steer myself clear of these ten months. Dates led to feelings and feelings led to impulses and impulses are a direct conduit to a man's passions and I knew with agonizing clarity about how so many males in Bangkok settled that matter.

This is simply dinner. In a nice and well-lit restaurant. With a guy I find appealing. I was allowed to like a good man, a *gentleman*, I reminded myself as the front entrance of the towering high-rise mall came into view on Rama I Road. Just as I paid the taxi driver his expected fare I glanced up and happened to notice the BTS Sky Train station just half a block away. I made a mental note that should I need any follow-up care from my favorite ophthalmologist–a medical caution I fondly wished for–I could commute both ways on the elevated train and save a few hundred baht.

Miss Sukhaphadhana nodded officiously as I entered the well-appointed suite of offices. "Miss Daggett?"

"*Chai.*"

She explained that Dr. Takuathung was almost finished with a patient and asked if I minded waiting. "Did your procedure go well? How did your eyesight feel today?"

"I kept the glasses on all day. But it seems all right now. I didn't do any reading."

"Very wise. Well, I hope you are pleased with the results."

She returned to her monitor, clacking away on a Thai keyboard, her manicured nails noisy as she poked through long numerical addresses. There was a soft ding from the office intercom, and the receptionist glanced at me. "He's ready. Let me show you."

"*Kop kuhn.*"

I followed her to the main exam room; thankfully, it wasn't as icy cold as the surgical theater. Saman looked up from a chart and brightened. "Hi, Pranom!"

"Hey."

The Thai woman didn't seem surprised at our instinctive transition to English. "Since we are finished with the list of appointments, I will see you tomorrow, *Maw*," she added in polite Thai.

He gave her a casual half-wave and then motioned me to the patient chair. "How are your eyes feeling?"

"I guess okay. I kept things real quiet. We had the TV going, some news with that thing in Georgia. But I wasn't really watching."

"Well, starting tomorrow you can get back to a pretty regular schedule. Reading and all that. Just keep putting the drops in. And don't overdo in terms of eyestrain, reading, and such."

"Sure." I hesitated. "Starting Monday I'll be okay at school, won't I?"

"Absolutely."

He ran me through a preliminary set of eye exercises, and whistled appreciatively. "A bit of fuzziness is to be expected, but this is very good. I think you're about as close to 20-20 as we could hope for." He swiveled the massive device away to the left and cocked his head, seemingly pleased with his own work. "How's it all feel?"

"Feels great," I told him, meaning it. "For sure, if I end up chucking glasses, that'll be a dream come true."

"That's what we hope for."

Now that I was un-bandaged, he offered to take us down through the center part of the mall. "Actually, my favorite restaurant is down on the ground floor anyway.

But we can spend a few minutes window-shopping if you like."

"Sure."

We rode down successive levels, and Saman generously paused so I could take in all the glitz. Paragon is definitely a haven for the well-heeled of modern Bangkok, and some of the dress shops shrieked money and exorbitant prices. I examined a few price tags but immediately realized I could easily get similar items elsewhere for half the price. "You're really throwing away your baht here," I sighed. "But wow, these are pretty."

Way down at the far end of Floor One there was actually an indoor car dealership adjacent to an exclusive bank. I wondered idly if my two thousand dollars was about to flow through Saman's checking account and right into the vault behind the counter, but I pushed the thought away, then grinned inwardly. Just by going to dinner with him, I would at least recoup a bit of my Lasik adventure.

"Is this restaurant all right?" He gestured toward the trio of teakwood elephants guarding the entrance. "I already made a reservation, but we can go somewhere else."

"Are you kidding? It smells amazing even standing out here."

A waiter in a traditional long-sleeved Thai silk shirt with rounded fabric buttons bowed slightly and offered to show us to a table. I supposed he already knew my friend; it wouldn't surprise me if Saman regularly entertained influential clients here. Procedures like Lasik were sweeping across Asia, and I imagined well-heeled corporations would try to steer all their business to the same medical vendor if a group price was negotiated.

We nibbled on tasty seafood hors d'oeuvres while perusing the menu, and I tried not to notice the inflated prices. Saman seemed entirely unconcerned; he commented about some of the rare bargains one might find here in the mall, and how he sometimes scored good deals for friends. "Once in a while, a store will just have a fast sale: two or three hours. I got some shirts last month and they were down fifty percent."

"That one's nice," I commented, gesturing toward the one he was wearing. It was the sort of very pale blue often sported by TV anchors. He had a knotted necktie with tiny elephants, and the rich navy set off the elegance of the shirt. "Those colors really look good together."

"Well, *kop kuhn mahk.*"

I giggled, enjoying myself but not adding any commentary about how nicely the blue fabric highlighted my friend's perfect facial skin.

The waiter approached us with our main courses, the beef Wellington crisped to perfection and surrounded by a pile of steaming vegetables and small porcelain bowls of fluffy white rice. He warned us, unnecessarily, about how hot the plates were, then offered a modest bow and retreated.

I'd anticipated the next scene in my mind a hundred times, feeling as "in the dark" spiritually as physically these past twenty-four hours. Confused but vaguely determined, I held up a hand and then bowed my head for a silent prayer. I'm not sure why, but somehow as I took these possible first steps with Saman at my side, I had to at least know he'd be okay with my fragile faith.

He cocked his head to one side. "I didn't think

about that. I assume that was kind of like grace or something?"

I blushed and then managed a nonchalant shrug. "Well, hey. I'm the calculus teacher at Bangkok Christian School. So prayer before meals is kind of a thing."

He took a bite of his seasoned beef. "Is it a school 'thing' or are you religious yourself?"

Holy cow. This is not a good topic for you, Pranom. I picked at my vegetables while navigating carefully through an edited history of my journey of faith. "Well, see, I went to BCS way back when. Starting in *Prathom* Five. Then when Samantha and Tommy adopted me, they're totally born-again Christians. So that's my background."

"I get that. But what about *you*?" he pressed.

I decided to come clean. "I'm not sure."

Saman grinned amiably. "After so many years? And you're a teacher at a Christian school?"

"It's just . . . I'm trying to figure some stuff out. At some point I may make a decision that I'm all in or all out, but obviously that can't happen while I'm getting a paycheck from these guys."

Part of me wanted to lean across my plate of rice, seize those gifted hands of his, and squeeze hard and blurt it out: *What about YOU? What's in your head? You're so freakingly gorgeous, but if you're an atheist, it would break my heart to know this is our first and then also our last date!*

But I took a few bites, savoring the succulent flavors and Thai accents and the unlimited flow of chilled mango juice. To my surprise, we fell into an unhurried conversation where he let it slip that his own parents had dropped their nominal Buddhism during the family's sojourn to America. "I attended a Christian megachurch a few times with college friends," he admitted. "Just to be nice. And believe me, I'm not hostile toward God and all that. It just . . . I guess I never felt it was very urgent or anything. And as my practice here has grown, it kind of pushed stuff like that to the side."

He showed me some family pictures, and I found out his father was a successful OB/GYN doctor at the big city hospital out by the airport. "He's down to around three days a week now," Saman told me. "I figure he'll retire in the next few years, but it's easy work and he doesn't generally take many of the cases where he's got to go in at three in the morning."

His mom was a delicately beautiful lady, with long flowing hair and not a strand of gray. "What does she do?"

He grinned. "Spend Dad's money." A shrug. "My sister Pimpana's still back in Maryland. Corporate lawyer. Got an American husband, and so Mom jets back to the U.S. a couple times a year to see her grandkids. Here." He showed me cherubic photos of a little boy in a rental tux and an older girl, maybe four, wearing a red party dress.

"They're cute."

"Yeah. It's fun. I need to get on the phone with them more often. But I keep forgetting, and the time zones are a mess."

I tried to do a bit of mental geography. "America's Eastern time zone, that'd be straight around the globe, right? Twelve hours earlier than us?"

He nodded, still chewing on his rice. "Uh huh. Well, not now, during the summer. Just eleven until their daylight savings kicks off."

Our waiter came back over with the dessert menu, an ornate document all its own, and I was agog as my date flamboyantly ordered something called *pithivier*, the French pronunciation rolling easily off his tongue. "What are we in for?" I asked, feeling flushed and very much in over my head.

"Just wait, pretty thing."

When the pastry arrived, I dug into it and felt my taste buds going into ecstatic overload. "That's *aroy mahk*, isn't it? Tastes like almond."

"Yeah, it's not bad. I've had the staff down here a couple of times and they blackmail me into getting these."

Saman seemed content to linger over the exquisite dessert, and our conversation eased back over to the matter of Christianity. "So what exactly do you believe in?" I said, not wanting to press him but still curious. "You're educated; you've had occasion to think about these things."

"Well, I guess it's okay, God's probably out there in some form or other. I'm down with that. Somehow or other, he—or it or whatever—had a hand in the universe being shaped and all."

"What about Jesus and him being God's son?"

He grinned easily. "I had a couple med school friends who sure went on about it. And I didn't see it as a problem. If Jesus died on the cross and so forth, I guess I accept that it's likely a true story."

I felt an inward stab that someone so seemingly wise could casually pass over the cosmic significance of such a moral gift, then realized with an embarrassed flush that I was almost as negligent. "What about the resurrection?"

He finished his own dessert, then shrugged. "Who's to know? I mean, really? If it's just an urban legend or what." I'd not seen him be anything but affable, and he still was now, but a kind of brooding did settle over him. "I find it impossible to think that if there's a God, he has just this one salvation plan that leaves the whole kingdom of Thailand out in the cold. That seems monstrously unjust."

I remembered being at a Christian rock concert where Dad had given a quick devotional between music sets. Halfway through he'd talked about his one year in Bangkok, and how he was convinced a loving Father in heaven wouldn't hold Thai citizens responsible for the fact that they were born nine time zones away from the bastions of Christianity. "Hey, God has a way to figure that out," he blurted, peering owlishly into the TV cameras beaming his picture up on the two big screens. "The Bible says Jesus died for people's sins. It doesn't specifically say that everyone's got to hear about it and sign a pledge card in order to receive grace."

I tried to haltingly reconstruct the Tommy Daggett bullet points, and Saman listened with interest, trying to catalog my spiritual fragments. "So if that's true, what are you even doing here? Why should a place like Bangkok Christian School try to win kids over?"

"Well, we're not trying to win them *over*," I retorted, feeling a bit defensive. "As in raiding the opposition."

"Sure you are." He reached out and teasingly flicked my forearm. "Don't you guys have Bible classes every day?"

"Yeah."

"And do you make a big point of inviting students to attend whatever church is affiliated with the school?"

I hesitated, then felt a surge of born-again funk. "I don't go crazy with it, but yeah, that's in my job description." I took a final sip of my fruit drink, then leaned forward. "Speaking of which, how about you dropping in one of these weekends? I'd love to make all the pretty ladies at UCC jealous."

There was a candle chandelier just above our table, and the evening shadows danced pleasantly across my host's handsome face. "I'm not saying it'd be my first choice for weekend fun," he conceded. "But who knows? I might be able to tuck it into my schedule." He flashed a wicked grin. "When everyone kneels for prayer, does the preacher have everybody hold hands with the person next to them? That'd get me there for sure."

I tingled at the idea. "You show up at church," I promised extravagantly, "and I'll hold your hand during the prayer."

The waiter came back over, and Saman fished out a credit card and handed it over. "Everything was perfect," he said in Thai to the young man. "Thank very much."

We lingered a bit longer, enjoying the classical music. High-tech wireless speakers were embedded in the foliage ringing the large picture window opening out into the common area of the mall's ground floor. I glanced out there and saw the evening foot traffic beginning to ebb.

On our way out, we browsed at an international bookstore for a few minutes, and I teasingly offered to buy him a New Testament. "Would you promise to read it?"

He shook his head. "Better for me to get an audio download. Some days it takes me forty-five minutes to get here to the office."

Now that I was seeing decently, I *oohed* and *aahed* over his sleek Mercedes. "This is gorgeous, Saman." I leaned against him for a flirty moment. "And sure nice to know I helped pay for it."

"You're most kind." He gave my hand a squeeze as he helped me into the passenger side. "Are you paid okay at the school? It's got to be less than what you'd earn back in Portland."

I nodded. "Yeah. Which is why my being here is just a one-year gig."

Dragging my truncated calendar into our shared paradise brought our date back to earth in a hurry. Dr. Takuathung was a seriously gorgeous male specimen, and I had a case of the hots for him. But our shared spiritual thermometers were two notches above coma- tose, and I was already on borrowed time here in his kingdom.

Oh well.

I don't know if Saman sensed the doors slamming shut. If so, his response was marked by the affability I might have expected. "Well," he observed, as the traffic on Sukhumvit Road opened up and he moved out to pass a city bus, "I may need to schedule a follow-up Lasik consult, dear lady. One school term's just too short a time for us to get to know each other. Don't you think?"

TEN

For the next few days I floated from one class period to another, feeling repeated jolts of pleasure at my sparkling new vision. The halo effect of my surgery had already worn off, and as students clumped into my classroom with their backpacks and graphing calculators, I reveled in the bright pixilation of all I surveyed: a girl's dimples, the tiny scar on a senior boy's chin, the bright maroon fabric and silky hair ribbons sported by our ladies. BCS encourages its teachers to enforce a strict cell phone ban, and with my new eagle eyes, I could monitor things clear to the back row.

"You can text during break," I decreed. "Otherwise, no. All these fancy phones are just about the biggest time waster in the world."

"Is also true in U.S., Miss Daggett?" Prin, one of my struggling trig students, had sheepishly stuffed his sleek new iPhone in the corner pocket of his backpack.

"Are you kidding? Kids are totally addicted." I told

them about being at a Trailblazers game the previous Christmas. "This friend of mine got us really great tickets. Something like two thousand baht each. And all the people sitting around me just had their noses in their phones the entire game. They couldn't stop even though the action on the court was great."

During staff worship that morning, Sue had handed all the *Matthayom* faculty stacks of fliers, and I dutifully went up and down the aisles giving each math student an invitation. "This is for what?"

I shot Kraisri an admonishing look and she braced herself for a rebuke from the grammar sheriff.

"You mean, 'What is this for?' Try it again."

The pretty girl sighed delicately. "Don't feel bad," I urged. "This is your first year. So your English is actually very good, considering."

"Okay, Miss Daggett. 'What is this for?'"

"Much better. Well, we're having a really fun program tonight just for grades eleven and twelve. There's going to be tons of food, and Mr. Charoenkul and the band will play. And then I hear Pastor Ethan is going to talk a little bit."

"All Christian things?"

"Well, kind of. But the rock and roll will be pretty awesome, is what I hear. And most of you have heard Pastor Ethan before. 'Cause he was here for a while before moving to Phuket."

I wasn't contractually obligated to be there for a weekend program, but I knew Khemkaeng and Rachel Marie were attending and they'd be disappointed if I stayed home. Plus Paloma was bubbling with excitement over the social fest. I ribbed her as we rode the blue city bus the eight blocks back to our apartment. "Is that shy boy going to meet you there?"

She nodded airily. "Uh huh. And don't bother teasing me about him. I like him, he's sweet and he's cute, and I don't care what you think."

"I think it's awesome. If you like him, go for it. Goodness knows he could use the grammar help."

She clambered back to her feet, trying to tug her backpack off the sticky floorboards. "We're here already." As we exited into the Friday humidity, she eased closer to me. "We should have a little contest. See which of us collects the first kiss."

"That's no fair," I protested. "I don't know if I'll ever even see Saman again."

"Aren't you supposed to have a follow-up exam?"

"Not for a month. And even that's just if I'm having any problems. Otherwise, I can just go to the web site and click 'decline.'"

She giggled. "Oh, you'll make up some imaginary form of blindness."

"Watch what you say," I warned darkly. "We have a calc test Tuesday and if I'm in a bad mood when I grade yours, you're going to be galactically sorry."

"I'll just appeal to Uncle Khemkaeng." As usual, she had the last word.

THERE WASN'T ANY notable decoration in our school gym except for a hastily constructed paper banner draped across the platform. "Welcome back, Pastor Ethan!" it blared out. Rachel Marie went out of her way to introduce me to our Phuket visitor, and he embraced me warmly. "Everyone says they're excited that you're back in Thailand. Where you belong," he added impishly. I liked him right away.

He was clearly popular with the young people; even as the kids were going through the food line, one after another came up and wanted to get selfies with him. It didn't hurt that Ratana was there too; even clumping around with baby Sara in tow, she was a bonafide media star, and our *Matthayom* girls flocked around her, giggling and making goo-goo faces. Noah, the dutiful husband, kept shaking his head in mock horror. "Please! Only speak intelligently in front of this innocent child. I don't want her growing up sounding so foolish!"

Our BCS kitchen staff had toiled all afternoon on the menu, and there were massive vats of flavored fried rice, plenty enough to serve the twin lines snaking across the gym. All the band members from Eternal Love were back for the reunion show, but it was a struggle to get some of the *Matthayom* kids away from the dessert table and to their seats.

I was taking dainty bites of strawberry ice cream out of a paper bowl when there was an unladylike scream. "Pranom! You're here!"

The kids around me were craning to see, and then I spied her clear across the gym. She was wearing white slacks and an expensive silk blouse, and a long ten years had spun themselves out, but I would have known Vuthisit anywhere. She dashed up and gave me a big hug, laughing and almost crying at the same time. "I'm so glad you're here," she blurted out, forgetting and lapsing into Thai.

"Me too!" I backed off and looked her over. "You're still the prettiest girl in Missie Stone's class."

"No, don't be silly." But she did look absolutely stunning, a good four inches taller than me and with a spectacular figure.

"How come I haven't seen you over at the church?"

"Oh." She was still holding my hand, and finally did let go. "Jittisak and I were out of the city on holiday for a couple weeks, and just got back." She gave me the same impish look I remembered so well, and leaned close to my ear. "Shhh. Trying to get pregnant." Then added in a more conversational tone: "Sorry. I kept hoping and praying you were here already."

Giddy with joy, I towed her to a seat in the faculty section and proudly sat her down next to me; we paused to say a quick hi to Benjie and Chloe. Just then the music cranked up, though, and we leaned forward to absorb the praise songs. The band's set was crackling good fun; I'd heard in the faculty meeting that Gino and Noah had spent the previous weekend concocting some new comedy bits, and they tried them out on our BCS kids. There were cheerful jokes about Natty already being large with child again, and Ethan kidded her about taking up too much space on the stage. "We don't even have room for guitars up here anymore," he cracked, and the students giggled. Then Gino came out with a mini-ukulele in his hand, and the laughter grew. The guys kept tucking pillows underneath their shirts, and the humor was infectious.

Things got seriously thumpy as the band did an extended version of the school favorite: "Amazing Grace," sung to the tune of the old Tokens hit, "The Lion Sleeps Tonight." I hadn't heard this version before, even though Dad had once mentioned doing it at a Christian junior camp event up in Seattle. But most of our students seemed seriously enamored with it; even the staunchest Buddhists in the crowd were belting it out with abandon. *Oooh-um-um-e-weh!*

I felt mesmerized by Dr. Ratana's stage presence; the lady was absolutely dripping with star power. Her powerhouse vocals were filling up the gym, and even more than the lush notes was the *soul* that rushed into each phrase. It's rare to be present when a gifted performer so absolutely captivates an audience. These Buddhist kids kept pressing closer and closer to the stage, their eyes never leaving her. I thought to myself as applause swept through the building: *Wow, she could honestly do Broadway. One of these days BCS will have to send her on an American tour or something.*

I guess my aunt agreed with me, because toward the close, Rachel Marie sidled over to both of us, Katrina dozing lightly against her cheek. "Wait till you hear this one," she murmured, her voice already husky with anticipation. "This song is basically why your Uncle Khemkaeng and I found each other."

I had just a vague memory going back a decade, but it all came back to me with a rush as Ratana stood alone in the center spotlight and began to sing the haunting praise song: *Amazing love; how can it be? That you, my King, should die for me?* I'd never heard anything so stirring before, and as she stood there, hand in hand with her Noah and they harmonized together, I felt a sweet tightness in my own throat.

Pastor Ethan switched off his keyboard, and the PA board emitted an electronic *pop!* as all the sound machinery powered down. The rest of the Eternal Love band came down into the crowd and accepted seats among friends. I sat there, happy in the presence of my old friend, and we listened, entranced, as Pastor Ethan shared a brief devotional.

"The biggest question we ever hear in Bangkok is a

simple one," he admitted. "We have this great school. We have Christian churches. We invite you to come and share part of your life with us, as we talk about 'Jesus this' and 'Jesus that' and how a guy named Daniel spent the night sleeping with lions."

There was laughter at that, and he grinned. "But then I hear this question. And what a good question it is. Beautiful young people look me in the eye and ask: 'Pastor Ethan, really, what difference does it make? We can't know if God is real. We can't know if this story about Jesus is true. We can't know if there's actually a place called heaven. Even Thai TV shows talk about *sawan*, but nobody knows. We just want to be happy. We want to live a good life and make some money and be able to leave Bangkok traffic and go to Phuket or Hua Hin once in a while.'"

There was pleasant approval of that, and he paused.

"So I want to talk to you tonight about this question. Does it matter if you join the many others who are standing up and saying, 'Yes, okay. I do want to have a King named Jesus'? 'Does it make a difference if I accept God's offer? How can my choice count?'"

The high school audience grew reverently silent as he shared in his simple, unvarnished way about how much of an impact it makes when one Thai kid chooses to be an ambassador for the Lord. "Christianity isn't some new religion that's trying to 'beat' all the other religions," he told us. "I didn't come here to Bangkok to try and mentally wrestle with Thai people and say: 'My way is better!' That would be rude and crude . . . and wrong. It would be unkind."

My mind took me on a quick reverie journey to my old *Prathom* Six classroom where Missie Stone would read Vuthisit and me and the other kids stories about Jesus and then just fold her hands in her lap and tell us, like an older sister, what an amazing friend her Lord was. And now Pastor Ethan began to suggest the same theme.

"Think about living forever in a beautiful place. I mean, guys, consider it: *living forever.* And you're there because someone really generous wanted to give you that life as a gift. It's not a good life just because it runs for thousands of years. No, it's full up, brimming, exploding with joy and excitement and learning and adventure and seriously amazing music. We travel; we make friends. We eat the most delicious food, and it never runs out. We don't age; we don't tire; we don't get bored. And this wonderful Jesus keeps saying: 'I love having you here! This is such a reward for me! All the sacrifices were worth it now that you and I are together for always and such happy friends.'"

Ethan allowed this to settle in, and I admit I did feel a sweet wistfulness begin to envelop me. "So listen, ladies and gentlemen. Does it make a difference when even one awesome Thai young person steps forward and says: 'Yes, I want to be an ambassador for this wonderful King who has died for us'? Yes! One by one, you young people can change the world. You graduate from here, and you go to a university or a trade school, and the whole time you're there, people always think: 'This person is different! They are happy. They are calm. They are unselfish. They seem to have more time to give, more love to share, more friendship to spread among more people. How do they do it?'"

Gino and Noah began strumming their guitars as the band members drifted back up to the stage. The slow, poignant anthem began, and I wrestled with my emotions as Vuthisit seized my left hand and Benjie my right. "I have decided to follow Jesus. No turning back, no turning back." All the kids were singing, even the non-believers, with all the teachers around us adding their harmony. Across the room, I spied my sister Paloma; she was holding hands with Klahan, a contented look on her face, and they were both singing and aglow.

Okay, Jesus, this is pretty much wonderful. I admit it. If things could always be like this, and if you could just keep that damned Pattaya girlie bar out of my brain and those red envelopes with fifteen hundred baht . . .

I forced the intruding poison out of my soul and focused on the lyrics as Pastor Ethan kept leading us forward: "The world behind me, the cross before me. No turning back, no turning back."

After the program, my new friend and I sought out Pastor Ethan again and thanked him for the good message. He brightened, and when he heard how Vuthisit and I were enjoying such a reunion, he fished out his phone and demanded a quick picture of the two of us with Missie Stone. Our former teacher joined the shot, beaming with pride, and it took all my composure to keep the tears back.

I sought out Paloma, taking note of the fact that she and her Thai boyfriend were still hand in hand. *I'm probably going to lose that kissing wager,* I grumbled inwardly. But I told her Vuthisit and I were going to hang around for a while and that she should take the Number Five back to the house by herself.

"I have our family driver here," Klahan said quickly. "We can give ride to Paloma. It is no problem."

I nodded, not wanting to seem like a chaperone. But

I gave Paloma a sisterly glance: *Okay, help this guy with his grammar. And this is a first date!*

The BCS crowd thinned out, and I led Vuthisit over to the bench right next to the outdoor flagpole. We sank down onto it, contented with our renewed friendship. And we sat there until almost midnight as Bangkok settled into a Friday night calm of sorts, the huff of buses and motorcycles a distant rumble blended into the concert of crickets and nearby river frogs. We talked about our old memories, the school play we'd done together as sixth graders, how we both had a crush on Siroj until we figured out he was kind of a pill, how much fun it had been learning under the generous care of a rookie teacher from the land of Disneyland and the Los Angeles Dodgers.

Before I realized what was happening, I spilled the entire story. Pattaya, life as a thirteen-year-old hooker, Tommy coming to rescue me, the HIV test at a beach clinic, the whole ugly, scab-covered saga, German guys demanding oral sex and slapping me when I tried to resist, my uncle the pimp. Her eyes misted over and her lip quivered, and when I'd said all there was to say, my old friend burst into tears and I ended up having to comfort her.

We shared a taxi ride back to Orchid Garden Apartments, holding hands in that grimy back seat, saying nothing as the digits on the meter clicked by.

ELEVEN

A week went by and my seniors were whizzing nicely through calculus's quotient rule before I heard again from Prince Charming. He caught me during my lunch break, and I'm sure Rachel Marie and Audrey could see me blushing as I took his cell call. "Greetings, Dr. Takuathung," I said, hoping my voice didn't betray me. Across the table, my peers nudged each other and leaned forward in comic eavesdropping fashion.

"Hi, Pranom. How are you doing, vision-wise?"

"Well, so far it's perfect. No glasses. I feel like I'm 20-20."

"Sweet. I'm sure glad it went well."

"Thanks to you," I told him. "I've been bragging all over school about this really awesome eye doctor."

"Well, we can always use the business," he teased. "If you send anybody over, I'll make sure a nice referral fee comes your way." He paused for effect. "Hopefully, you'll let me pay you off in nice seafood dinner dates."

"That might work out," I allowed.

"How's this weekend?"

I glanced over at my fellow teachers, who were now both giggling into their paper napkins. "Can you hold the line for about sixty seconds? I'm being spied on here."

"You bet, sweet thing."

I held my phone away from my face as I strode toward the exit of our buzzing BCS food court. I was sure all the juniors and seniors were focused on this romantic soap opera, and tried to look like I was taking a soiled napkin to the nearest trash can. Out in the hallway, I managed to continue the conversation. "Okay, now I can talk."

"How about dinner this weekend? I've got both Saturday and Sunday off."

I thought fast. "Here's my counter-offer. You come to church with me. And please don't say no because it's pretty much an amazing place. You'll like it; you really will. Then after that, we always have this super-good potluck lunch, and Paloma and I are bringing a mango custard."

"But I wanted to take you out to eat," he protested.

"Well, this is better 'cause we'll save a bunch of money. And I want you to meet all my friends. Plus," I added as a quick afterthought, "when lunch is done, hey, we could take a drive out in the country or something."

"Ah. Yeah, I could see that working out."

"See?"

That evening I shared the good news with Paloma over plates of steaming hot spaghetti. "He's really coming to church?"

I shrugged, hoping to mask my feminine tingles. "He said he'd be there."

"Very good." As we were finishing our carrot salad, she coughed and then told me she had something to confess.

"Um, I think I can guess."

"Yeah. You owe me a whatever-the-prize-is."

"Have you no shame? That shy Thai boy gave you a kiss? Already?"

"He sure did."

"When?"

"When his chauffeur gave me a ride home. After that concert."

"That was more than a week ago! How come I'm just hearing about it now? What kind of sister are you?"

She blushed. "Well, you know. I felt kind of funny."

"How come?"

"'Cause I didn't know if your friend was ever going to call. Now that he did, then . . . you know."

"You nut. I'm happy for you. So tell me about it."

"Just like I said. The guy drove me over here, we were holding hands in the backseat, Klahan hiked up here to the third floor with the chauffeur down below and the motor running. I got out my key, Klahan was kind of clumsy, but he leaned right in and kissed me. Then said in English: 'I like you very much, Paloma. Very much.'"

"'And you like me too?'" I tried to mimic a Thai boy's stiff English, and we both giggled.

"Well, I said something like, 'Sure.'" She blushed. "I mean, he's really sweet. It's just for this one year and what can come of it? But I really like him."

"Very nice." I made a grand show of seizing my purse and waving it around in extravagant fashion.

"Follow me, please, sister dear."

"Follow you where?"

"To the land of rewards. You got the first kiss; I'm a lady of my word."

We tripped down the stairs and across the street to the neighborhood donut shop. I sprung for a pair of jelly-filled, both oozing with sweet red stuff, and as we ate, the sticky frosting clinging to our fingernails till we licked them clean, we reminisced about Missie Stone's first night in Bangkok and how she'd come right down to this same shop and bought herself a donut to scare away her jet lag. Maybe that's how all great love stories begin: a 28-baht pastry.

THE BIBLE STUDY hour had just begun when I saw him standing at the door. He was casually dressed in tan slacks and a navy-blue polo shirt; I caught his eye and motioned him over. I was sure thirty pairs of eyes were following him, but he sat down next to me with an easy grin. "Sorry I'm late."

"It's all right. We just got started."

Khemkaeng was leading a discussion on the Beatitudes, and a Thai college girl I didn't know had just begun to read through the first part of Matthew 5. I leaned over to whisper. "We can go over to a Thai lesson if you'd rather."

"No, this is all right."

The discussion went on all around us, and I worried that our BCS teachers were monopolizing the discussion. But Khemkaeng, ever the astute host, soon noticed that and jokingly announced that for the rest of the period, he was putting a temporary freeze on all comments made by faculty members. "They talk too much even during the week." We all chuckled at that.

A moment later, as the lesson flow moved over to the point of "peacemakers," I was pleasantly surprised when Saman raised his hand. Khemkaeng beamed. "Pranom, I think you should introduce your friend to all of us. It's wonderful to have a visitor."

"Sure." I flushed. "This is Dr. Saman Takuathung. He's very good at things like eye surgery, and all of a sudden I can see to read my Bible a whole lot better." The place erupted in laughter, and I was relieved when Saman good-naturedly joined in.

"So what is your comment, Saman?" Khemkaeng asked.

"Well, this is all way new to me," he admitted. "But I know that no matter what the Bible says, even people who are Christians get into arguments. The Internet is full of people squabbling about religion. Not that I read much of that, but it's definitely there."

"So true," Khemkaeng conceded. "And even at BCS, we often have to work to put away a dispute."

"So how do you do that? Where I work, over at my offices at Paragon, there are legal disputes. People who sue their employers. What does someone do to really get past that and find peace?"

"A very good question," the leader nodded. "Class? What ideas do we have to share with each other?"

The flow continued, and my new friend followed along with interest. After church was over, I was pleased when Vuthisit introduced both of us to her husband. He was tall for a Thai man, with a pair of thick black glasses. I teasingly suggested that my friend Saman could help put his eyewear in a welfare bag, and Jittisak seemed mildly interested. Over a lunch of watermelon slices and bowls of rice, he described his position as a claims adjustor for Thai Airways.

"Can you get my sister and me a bargain fare to Phuket?" I asked, and then immediately regretted the question. Phuket Island wasn't Pattaya, and the two resorts had a markedly different ambience. Still, beaches and brothels were prominent features at both places, and I felt my stomach lurch. But he nodded affably and said, sure, he could pull a few strings. Sitting next to me, I wondered if Saman was filing away the idea of a romantic getaway.

We helped put away the clean dishes and tablecloths, and I sought out my sister. "Saman and I are going for a drive. You'll be okay?"

"Oh sure." She shrugged. "I'm kind of zonked. Maybe I'll take a nap for a bit, and then give Mom a call."

"Better wait till I get back," I said. "'Cause I think we both have things to confess to her." She grinned and made a show of giving Saman a comradely hug.

I was grateful for his thoroughly western mindset; he accepted the familiar gesture with aplomb. "It's funny to think of you girls as sisters."

"Well, we've been fighting and making up for the whole last ten years," Paloma informed him. "And if you're mean to Pranom, even the tiniest bit, I'll track you down and kill you."

"I believe you." And all at once he seemed entirely serious.

I followed him downstairs to street level, pausing to give hugs to Gage and Katrina. "See you back at school," Rachel Marie said, her eyes full of meaning as she inspected my new boyfriend.

I sank into the expensive butter-like leather of that luscious Mercedes, enjoying the ambience as it shielded us from the grit of downtown Bangkok. "Where shall we drive to?" I asked him.

He glanced over at me. "It's about an hour and a half down to Bangsaen."

I remembered that was a pleasantly quiet beach resort, not nearly as cacophonous as its bawdy sister to the south. "That'd be nice."

"Yeah. We can just walk along the beach and watch the sunset and all."

I leaned over, the seat belt tugging at my torso, and planted a teasing kiss on his shirt sleeve. "Dr. Takua-thung, you're filled with good ideas."

"I have many of those."

We were just a few blocks away from the elevated toll highway, and he casually flipped a fifty-baht bill out of his pocket and handed it to the clerk. He thanked her in precise Thai, and I felt a new rush of pleasure that Saman and I were seemingly such compatible friends. "How far is it to the southern highway?"

"Oh, it's not far." Traffic flowed easily on the divided highway, and he pointed out various landmarks, reminding me of major hotels and tourist sites.

"I don't remember ever seeing that one," I sighed as a huge Buddhist complex of temples came into view on the right.

"We can go together and see it sometime," he offered. "I haven't been for a really long time."

"Sure."

We flowed pleasantly along the Bang Na-Chon Buri highway, and a scant hour later Saman pushed a button and our windows opened a crack. He sniffed eagerly. "Smell the beach?"

"A bit. Are we almost there?"

He nodded. We spent a nice hour browsing at the fabled aquarium maintained by Burapha, the local university. Then, just as the sun was beginning to settle close to the western horizon, he drove me over to the beach. Parking the car, we rolled up our pant legs and he led me close to water's edge. "What do you think?"

"Pretty good." I eyed the cool green flow as the small waves rippled around my ankles. "Is there much pollution here?" I saw just a few bathers still out in the water.

"Not much. This place doesn't get a lot of inter-national traffic."

We walked south along the expansive stretch of sandy beach, and about halfway through he reached for my hand. We conversed easily: about school and math tests and the work ethic of Bangkok high school kids. "Do they prepare well?"

"For the most part. I have a few who don't take it seriously. They show up on test day and clearly haven't cracked a book."

"Probably out at the cinema," he agreed. "Or too much texting."

"Tell me about it. That's the curse of all high schools now."

The weather was absolutely perfect, with a fragrant breeze wafting the essence of coconuts and orchids across the gently splashing waves. I noticed just a sliver of moonlight as the faraway orb struggled to climb up into the cloudless sky. The lights of nearby hotels began to twinkle, and I felt happy as my new friend squeezed my hand and described the intricacies of his medical work.

"What if a patient sues you?" I wondered.

"Well, there's not much risk in Lasik. But the practice has an insurance policy. There are always trial lawyers trying to scare up a group malpractice suit."

"Got it."

We got to the tip end of the promontory, and I gazed back over the distance we'd come. "I need a tiny breather before we head back."

"Sure." He fished in his pocket for some coins, and we paid a local attendant a few baht so we could bask in rented beach chairs. We chatted some more as the moon rose into the night sky, and then lapsed into a comfortable silence that filled the space between us.

Jesus, I really like this guy! But . . .

But what? I honestly didn't know. I was happy by this nice man's side. But my mind was ablaze with a million competing variables. I had this new home in Bangkok, this abbreviated rookie career at BCS. I was tentatively happy at United Christian Church, feeling enormously encouraged by Pastor Gino's weekly sermon messages and the extravagant friendships I savored during our potluck feasts.

We got up from our unspoken reveries and headed in the northward direction along the curve of the beach; the moonlight was spilling out now across the nearly white sand as families headed for cars and hotel rooms and hamburgers and *pad thai* at a host of restaurants and beachfront bars.

It felt delicious having my hand enfolded in Saman's, and yet the questions kept poking at me. He wasn't saying anything, content to let the beach ambience and the silent splash of the waves be the entire soundtrack to our evening. But as we walked along, I spotted a board floating out in the dark green of the incoming flow. It bobbed up and down, hidden by waves and then poking through again. An incoming wave with a slight foaming break pushed the board toward the shoreline, but then some hidden barrier must have grabbed at it, because this brown object's floating trek toward dry land was again halted.

And I peered at it as Saman's footsteps matched my own: *left right left right,* our tracks spelling out a burgeoning love story behind us. I had no doubt that a myriad of forces was working on that two-foot bit of lumber: the incoming flow and tug of the currents, then the receding riptide as gallons of H_2O went back out into the deep. Above us the moon was beaming down, not just spilling silver paint on the water's surface, but gently exerting its own tug in the form of a faraway tide power. Beneath the water, were small fishlike creatures poking and prodding and murmuring, *hey, over here!* in their own aquatic language?

And the board, having no mind or will or noticeable inherent powers of physics or determination, was obliged to succumb to whichever vectors or combination of commands won the evening.

I, on the other hand, was a modern Thai/American woman: cleverly bilingual in two languages and with a prestigious master's degree. I could choose my fate and decide on Door A, B, or C. I had enough in the looks and sex-appeal department to probably snag this studly gent or any of ten thousand others. I could embrace the Christian faith of my BCS friends or make a cool and calculated decision to turn toward secularism and a life of money and *Matthayom* perks.

"Getting hungry?" Saman's gentle voice abruptly cut through my internal dialogue, and I shook my head, determined not to be irritable. *He doesn't know I'm standing here in the vast Valley of Decision, my heart up in my throat.*

"Not really," I responded, squeezing his hand. "Well, maybe some French fries or something. Or a bit of *kanom*. But not a whole meal."

"Sure." He pointed to where the lights of commerce were now ablaze. "We'll find a snack or something."

We passed by that bit of waterlogged lumber, still thrashing about in the mild tumble and ripple of currents, and I saw that it hadn't moved more than a meter away from where it and I had begun this lab experiment. *Not to decide is to decide . . .*

I glanced to my right, taking in Saman's profile. Good chin, his sideburns neatly trimmed, his haircut expensive. I could feel the cool metal of his wristwatch against my forearm and we continued holding hands and walking together.

My mind flitted back to Khemkaeng's Bible study class earlier today. His thoughtful questions. The verses people found in their Thai New Testaments. Saman's raised hand and his cautious query about blessed are the peacemakers. I supposed I could allow my own choice to follow his. If he embraced Christianity, well, that would be my pick also. But if he took me out to an Italian restaurant this next week and said with a shrug that, um, all that God stuff wasn't really for him and he hoped I understood, are we still a possible item, okay, I could say, yeah, me too. In that case, I'd quietly finish out my term at BCS, keep my head down, keep my morning prayers innocuous and politically correct with all the

Sue-approved phrases, and then jump ship, marry my
Mr. Wonderful, and settle into a life of money and
basking in my guy's handsomeness and generous indul-
gence.

But as I remembered that floating, unprotestingly
obedient board, I had an abrupt moment of gestalt
awareness. It was foolish, spiritually juvenile, for me to
choose my own spiritual destiny on the basis of what this
cute ophthalmologist decided. Because for sure, Saman
was like that board floating in the salty water out there.
He didn't know from straight up about the beauty of
Jesus' love and character, the awe and power of
"Amazing Grace" and the enormous cost borne by my
Savior on the cross. He didn't have a clue. Why would I
follow his shake-the-eight-ball decision?

I remembered now how my teaching partner, Natty
Carington, had spent restless nights thinking about two
really great guys. One a Christian, the other not. And for
a while, she fretted inwardly: *the faith I choose determines the guy I get.* Which seemed a bizarre bit of
matrimonial lotto. Still, though, it made much more
sense for a Christian woman to choose her life's destiny
that way than the other way around. To have the guy
choose the faith was disastrously shortsighted.

We got to the initial row of restaurants and bars, the
evening mood beginning to brighten with the bass of
disco songs and live bands tuning up. Saman pointed to
the first one, where a waitress was bringing a tray of
drinks to a knot of Thai vacationers. "We could probably
get a sandwich and some fries right here," he offered.

"Great."

We found a spare table against an open window,
and he gallantly offered me the seat with the view of the

moon-spangled beach. "Nice breeze coming through, huh?"

"Yeah, this is great."

The waitress found us, and again, I was amazed as always at how smoothly Dr. Takuathung could transition to our local dialect. He ordered me a grilled cheese sandwich and a diet Coke. "And please bring us some French fries," he added. "Lots of fries! And I'll have a beer."

Oops. I didn't mind some guy I was dating having a beer. But just his simple request was a reminder that Saman was by no means BCS-approved except in the wielding of optical instruments. This nice man was definitely not a deacon of our church.

The food arrived just moments later, and Saman retreated, amused, as I again murmured an inner prayer, adding a plea for heavenly wisdom to my thanks for the salty snack. I munched on fries and sipped on the ice-cold soda, and made small talk as we scanned the football action on the wall-mounted flat-screen TV.

"Isn't that the team from where you live?" he asked suddenly, peering up at the satellite images.

I shook my head. "Huh uh. Portland doesn't have NFL football."

"Oh." He half-rose out of his chair for a closer look. "But that's the Seahawks. Seattle, right?"

"I guess." I was half-done with a bite of my sandwich, and hastily swallowed. "Except for baseball and the Angels, my dad's not much into sports, but I had a boyfriend who liked the Seahawks. I never got the rules of the game, though."

He smiled at that, and we continued eating in wordless camaraderie. From across the street, the enthusiastic beat of an American classic rock hit traveled across the sand and actually rattled the glass louvers of our shared window. "Sounds like fun music," Saman mused.

But the insistent beat had the opposite effect on me. *Why can't you be . . . good to me? Why can't you be . . . good to me?* A whole decade later, the misery-drenched wail of Tina Turner's and that godawful Pussycat club in Pattaya was still with me, bringing back the memory of that night where a chunky music teacher from BCS walked in, sat down at the bar, and saw his choir-girl student up on the hardwood, shuffling along with the beat.

Tourists were pushing past us, some calling out to friends, others craning to see if Dallas had made that long field goal. But I shrank back in my seat, thinking hard now. I was feeling the call of my Lord, the gravitational tug of Calvary . . . and on the other side, the disco beat and the memory of that shameful white bikini with the top that always got peeled off at 11:00 p.m.

No, I should not choose or deny Jesus Christ because of anything said or selected by a good-looking eye doctor. But was it equally insane for me to turn my back on God and his Son Jesus because I'd been badly scarred in a brothel? Why should a girl so badly beaten up run away . . . FROM THE HEALER?

Hold on, Pranom. Just hold on a blasted moment. Don't make a rash decision. These people really cut you up. What happened was galactically unfair. You have a good legal case, kid!

My gentle friend, so blissfully unaware that I was being wooed toward my end-game destiny, paid our tab, left a hundred-baht bill on the table, and motioned me toward the parking lot. "This was sure nice, babe," he said, sounding very western and hip as he held the door open for me.

"I know. Thanks."

It was a quiet ride back into Bangkok, and instead of conversing, I deferred to Saman's luxury sound system. I was relieved that my friend seemed okay with brief quiet stretches; he hummed along with the instrumental tracks, looking over at me just once in a while. "You all right?"

"Yeah. Just enjoying the ride."

I wasn't sure, but it felt like our shared walk on the beach had moved me toward an unexpected decision. No matter how this friendship played itself out, or how the rest of my rookie teaching year unfolded, I wanted to hang onto my fledgling faith in Jesus. There were times when, in the throes of despair, I'd considered chucking it all. But now, with the memory of those ocean waves, the surging *infinity* that was the wellspring of Christ's love, I began to feel more sure of myself. The cross had to come first; my identity as a redeemed Christian woman trumped even the adoption papers Tommy and Samantha Daggett had so generously signed in a Portland suite of legal offices.

Okay, kid. So that matter's settled. Kind of, at least. Now talk to the poor guy.

I pasted on a cheery smile, made a small joke about my reborn eyeballs, and we gossiped about TV soap operas until we arrived at Orchid Garden Apartments.

I'd halfway figured this would be the night Saman would kiss me, but apparently the surf at Bangsaen had distracted him too. He walked me up to #305, squeezed my hand and then offered nothing but a clumsy hug. Not a word about what's next or hey, I'll call you real soon. Paloma was waiting inside wearing a tank top and a scolding smirk, but I shushed her and didn't offer a word of explanation until the taillights of that sleek Mercedes disappeared around the corner.

TWELVE

Over the next couple of school days, I didn't have a clue about where Saman's head was at. Had the morning at church freaked him out? Were we done? The relationship was still in such a virginal state, I didn't know if the word *done* even counted. Was there anything here to even fret over?

But all my angst was for nothing. Tuesday I was inputting some quiz scores into the grading system when my cell phone dinged hopefully. Thankful that my classroom was empty, I shoved the stack of papers to the edge of my desk. "Hey, doc."

"Working hard?" he teased.

"Not particularly. In calculus we learn all about maximums and minimums, and I try hard to make sure grading is always a 'min.'"

"Good for you." He laughed. "Luckily, I've got two very nice ladies who handle most of the paperwork for the clinic."

"I'd love to pay one of our seniors a few baht an

hour just to stick the grade numbers into the LMS for me," I admitted. "But the boss says I better keep that under my own control."

We talked for a few minutes before he came to the point. "There's a pretty big badminton tournament over at Chula. Tomorrow night. I can get free passes if you're interested."

I'd always enjoyed the game, even going clear back to sixth grade where I managed to whop Rachel Marie right on her skull a few times. Most Thai kids have some enforced encounters with a birdie and a net. And tournament action was sometimes blazing quick, with lithe athletes scurrying up for intricate net play, and then back to retrieve a deep drop shot. "It sounds fun," I agreed, feeling my pulse rate spike.

"It starts at six, so maybe we could just get fast food or something before."

"Okay."

We agreed to meet at a KFC two blocks away from the university entrance, and he told me I should hop off the Sky Train at the National Station exit. "You'll see the Kentucky Fried place as soon as you get to the bottom of the stairs." A pause. "Of course, I'll be glad to drive you home afterward."

"Okay." I didn't have to feign my pleasure. "I was hoping you'd call."

So for the next month we fell into a nice rhythm of weekly dates. I borrowed a recommendation from Chloe about D'Sens, an upscale restaurant she and Benjie claimed had a super-romantic aura high up in the Dusit Thani Hotel. Saman saw a web site boasting about a blues concert at the basement nightclub of the Novotel; we spent a smoky Saturday night sipping Cokes and watching the bass player run up and down the frets. A new Spiderman film spun its web, ha ha, throughout all of Asia, and my new boyfriend gallantly paid for paired reclining seats that sported a shared mini-table for sushi and various Thai menu delicacies.

And all the while he was pulling thousand-baht notes from his wallet, this intriguing guy who radiated such masculinity . . . he didn't make a move to kiss me.

Paloma just kept shaking her head in wonderment as I came back to #305 and changed into my night-clothes. "I can see you holding hands coming and going," she accused. "But you're telling the truth? Not a single kiss yet."

"It's no big deal," I remonstrated, not at all meaning it. "When it's time, I'm sure it'll be great."

"Man." That's all she could manage in response.

I was cautious about dragging Saman back to United Christian Church. Three weeks after our beach outing, I hinted at it, telling him I'd heard that Noah and Company were about to spring an awesome new praise song on us. But he grumbled about a Lasik procedure that had been postponed into the weekend, and that he needed to hang around for the guy's post-op. "I'm not putting you off," he insisted. "I swear. It's just a bad week is all."

The next Friday I was doing some unofficial parking lot duty with my fellow high school teachers, waving to parents and generally spreading around the goodwill. Tuition is a major investment for many Thai families, and our faculty mingling with them pays nice dividends. I made a point of greeting Klahan's mom and gossiping with her about her son's romantic overtures toward my American sister. Just then I spotted Sue heading back toward the inner sanctum of admin offices. She caught my eye and motioned me to follow her.

"*Kaw todt.*" I excused myself, apologizing to my new friend. "But our headmistress seems to want something."

"Of course." She gave me a demure *wai* and thanked me for teaching mathematics to her children. "Klahan says he is learning a great deal."

"I'm glad."

I checked to make sure my phone was switched off and followed Mrs. C into her office, pausing to say hi to the office help. "What can I do for you?"

She motioned toward the nearest chair and then sank down into her own. "Well, after a month of teaching, how are you enjoying it?"

"I love it," I said immediately. "I really didn't have any idea it could be such a blast. I really get into it with the kids. And they're doing terrific at calculus."

Her face lit up in a smile. "I just had a feeling. Somehow, with your mom and dad being so very good at it, I knew you'd come along and be a superstar too." Sue's face took on a comically forceful edge, and I grinned, my radar humming and detecting an assault. "Are you sure we can't bribe you to sign up with us for a decade or so?"

"I'd love to," I countered. "But Paloma finishes up in June. And I think Tommy would kill me. And you too."

"I suppose." She heaved a sigh and gave me an *oh well, I had to try* look. "Anyway, that's really not why I called you over."

Uh oh. I wondered if maybe she was concerned about my rather well-publicized friendship with a sexy ophthalmologist.

"You know that Khemkaeng is pretty decently connected over at the government ed offices," she began.

"Sure." After some fifteen years of service, he was a well-known figure with all the locals over at city hall. That made sense.

"Anyway, we're in the pipeline for a lot of symposiums and such," she went on. "And I probably wouldn't have had this catch my eye if it was just a little thing here locally, but there's a group putting together a major four-day shindig happening up in Chiang Mai."

"What about?"

My boss hesitated, and I felt a twinge of anxiety. *What?*

"Well, I really almost hate to get into it, but hey, you're a grownup now. And the main focus of the thing is the same as always: the sex trade. What to do, why don't things get better, how do we keep young village girls out of such a mess." She eyed me with her kind gaze, and then blurted it right out. "They'd love to hear from someone who was right in the clutches of it all, and then managed to get free." What she said next came in a verbal torrent. "Look, I know it was a heartbreaking thing. And I honestly have no idea just how much you might still be bleeding and fragile. But Pranom, you're a beautiful Christian woman. Your survival from that horrible thing at Pattaya still moves me to tears sometimes when I stop and think about it. I watch you teach, and then I walk past Rachel Marie's room with all those sweet little girls, and I sometimes just want to come back in here, close the door, and pound my fists on my desk. I swear to God I do."

I gulped, feeling a tornado of memories and

emotions. It was true I was a grateful survivor; what Tommy and my BCS friends had done to get me free was a precious, heroic tale. It would make a dramatic presentation, and I didn't doubt I could offer my testimony effectively. Still . . .

"I know ten years is a long time. And yet it's not a long time," Sue said carefully. "But of course, if you thought you could go up there and represent Bangkok Christian School, and also UCC, well, it'd be amazing. Naturally, we'd send someone like Rachel Marie along. Or Paloma, if you liked. And besides the speaking appointment, it could be a nice getaway trip. Complimentary hotel, flight there and back, and all that. We'd find a sub for your classes, of course."

I was about to blurt out that, hey, nice of you to ask, but there's no way. However, just then there was a timid knock at the door and Paloma eased herself into the office. "Hey," she blurted. "I'm ready to go if you are."

And I froze. My brain and my emotional defense mechanisms just seized up on me, the gears locking. I suppose I could have glibly managed, "Sure, we'll be two more minutes," or something equally innocuous. And my kid sister would likely have taken her cue. But somehow seeing my adopted sibling framed there in the doorway while Sue and I talked about me baring my soul in a hotel ballroom with educators and maybe newspaper reporters sitting there with a whole row of their iPhone voice recorders activated–well, like I said, I just plain froze up. There was no way in this whole world I wanted Paloma to get wind of what Mrs. Carington had just put on our Friday afternoon agenda.

My mind sputtering helplessly, I seized on the first thing I could come up with. "So you're telling me that all the test scores I put in for Calc One and Calc Two got processed the wrong way? I have to redo the entire list? Sue, that'll take me hours!"

It was a bit of macabre nonsense, a hasty lie, and I was sure I was flushing seventy shades of bright maroon, matching my sister's uniform skirt. My boss, her facial muscles quivering as she attempted to process my sudden attack of inanity, took a moment to recover. "Um, well, yeah, I'm really sorry. But *Kuhn* Srirook says it's a pretty common flub for some of our new-comer teachers. Says he apologizes for not getting you off on the right foot. But it does have to get redone."

Somehow we both paddled to the raft of my hastily concocted cover story. "It's just test scores? What about all my homework data?"

"He says they're fine." She bobbed her head energetically now, helping me solidify our deception.

Paloma, thoroughly baffled, slowly retreated. "Um, I guess I'll wait out by the gate. If you think it's much longer, I'll just catch the bus."

"No, it was just this," Sue told her. "Let me just schedule a time when she and Srirook can get together and recover the numbers. I'll scoot your sister right out to you."

Paloma padded up the hallway and out of earshot, and Sue visibly sagged. "Oh, sweetie, I had no idea! Your sister doesn't know, does she?"

I shook my head miserably. "It's just . . . well, it was so ugly, and for a long time I couldn't talk about it one bit. But I think it was the first Christmas back in Portland, Mom and Dad and I got together one night after Paloma was asleep. And we just decided we'd try to bury it forever. Back when I joined the family she was barely eight, so of course, that was way too soon anyway."

"Oh, I totally get it." My mentor was visibly overcome, and had to dab at her eyes with a corner of her sleeve. "Oh, sweetie, I should have thought it all through before asking you," she moaned. "Please, just put it out of your mind. We'll tell them it's not possible."

My armpits were swimming in dampness, and all I could manage was a feeble nod. "I know it's dumb and maybe infantile. Sure sorry."

"No, no." Sue got up from her seat and offered me a matronly hug. Somehow being enfolded in this kind older woman's embrace did feel soothing, and we lingered together for a nice few moments. "You're a brick, you know," she said, consoling me. "I can't believe how brave you were back then, and still are now."

IT HELPED A whole lot when Saman strolled into UCC the very next weekend, scanning the place until he spotted me. Khemkaeng was up front translating as Pastor Gino made some opening announcements, and I sensed both of them masking smiles as people dutifully scooted down one seat to make room for the newcomer. Right next to me, of course.

Gino was partway through a sermon series on sharing our faith, and as he and Khemkaeng dissected the New Testament story of a demon-possessed man healed by Jesus, I found myself fretting. Would Saman think all this was immensely corny? More to the point, would he think I was intent on "converting" him? Would all our romantic discussions come under close scrutiny?

But he was an affable guest during our afternoon potluck feast, bantering with Charles and Audrey and giving her pronunciation tips on her Thai. "You do very well for someone who hasn't lived here that long," he complimented. The four of us lingered over helpings of lemon cake, and he seemed genuinely interested in all the classes Charles was teaching out at Redeemer College. The guys compared notes on sports, and I was at least able to talk intelligently about the Chulalongkorn badminton tourney Saman and I had attended.

UCC had recently hired two of our *Matthayom* Five girls to serve as hostesses at the church, and they waved at us, giggling, as we trooped downstairs with Gino and Natty. "I'll probably hear about it all next week at school," I grumbled good-naturedly. "'Miss Daggett has a *fan*.'"

Natty grinned, relieved to have a few hours away from mommy duties. "A single teacher at BCS isn't going to hear very much else." She and Gino hopped into the back of my friend's gleaming car, and I could tell they were impressed. "This isn't bad," he sang out as we pulled into traffic. "You get a good deal on it?"

"No," Saman retorted immediately, and we all laughed.

Even though it's just a few kilometers over to Lumphini Park, it must have taken us half an hour, and more than once Saman sighed theatrically as our progress was held up by traffic signals. "Lucky we're not in any hurry," he said, eyeing both side mirror and looking for an escape valve.

There was some pleasant overcast, though, as we got to the park and strolled together along the concrete pathways, watching the action as kids scampered here and there through the humid late afternoon. A knot of college boys was kicking a *takraw* ball around, gyrating themselves into knots with trick shots and comic routines. We paused to take in the action, and I was pleased when Saman reached for my hand.

"You should join those guys," I teased. "Are you good at stuff like that?"

He shook his head. "I'm not very coordinated. Just biking, really. If we played badminton, you'd probably beat me."

"I doubt that." I felt a surge of funk, and added: "I got all my DNA from my adopted dad, and he's a pasty white man who plays the piano for a living."

Gino cracked up. "I've met Tommy, and you're right about that."

Natty tugged at my sleeve. "Come over here and I'll take a picture of you guys together."

Lumphini's central park area sports a whole maze of ornate shrubs all sculpted into open-shaped hearts. She nudged Saman and me into position together in one of them, and made a big show of trying to get just the right lighting. "This is going on the BCS web site," she warned. "So I want to get it right." We Thais have an expression: *naa-raak*. Loosely translated: "Oh, what a lovable face. Kissee kissee." She trotted it out several times, hamming it up, and I was thoroughly enjoying myself.

We traded positions then, and Gino kept kidding around about how his bride's swollen abdomen could hardly fit in the heart-shaped vacant spot. "Let's hurry and have this kid," he announced. "I can't wait to get at double piles of extra-poopy diapers."

The park was already quieting down, but we spotted a street performer clad in a red-and-white striped shirt. He was juggling tennis balls, and a small crowd had coalesced around his clever tricks. His eye-hand coordination was dizzying, yet he didn't miss a beat as he entertained us with humorous banter, all in Thai, of course. When it was done, Gino approached him and asked for a business card. "We might have a gig for you at our church some weekend," he suggested, and Natty stepped up and translated for the performer's benefit.

It was getting fairly close to sundown now, but the four of us opted for a half-hour rental of Lumphini paddle boats. These were sturdy plastic two-seaters, and we teasingly scooted across the pond in a race mostly powered by the guys. A bit later Natty spotted a row of ducks, and she cajoled Gino into chasing after them.

"We're staying put," I called after them. "Hurry back."

I rested my head against Saman's shoulder and sighed happily. "It's nice out here."

"I know."

I twisted around and looked up at him adoringly. "Thanks for coming to church today. I really liked having you along."

"Sure."

"And . . . well, you weren't obliged to spend the whole afternoon with me."

"I enjoy us being together."

I felt a rush of joy at hearing him say that. "Me too."

Our little craft was getting a bit too close to the shoreline, and he gave the pedals a halfhearted kick in reverse until we nudged away. "Next weekend I'm out of town though."

"Really? Work stuff."

He hesitated. "Yeah. And just some family thing

I've been meaning to get to."

Well, I don't own you. "I guess I'll write some new tests for calculus," I teased. "That should be fun."

He grinned. "Just please don't ask me to take one. I doubt if I'd get forty percent."

Sometimes, just on a lark, we would spin over to Thai instead of English, and we did that now, chatting idly about the weather and the lunch menu at BCS. It seemed odd, I mused, even as we bantered, how in our moments as a couple, we seemed to function mostly in English. Despite our both being Thai, and enjoying natural fluency in our native languages, most of our shared moments were rather American in flavor.

On the ride back home, I asked him why. He seemed startled by the idea. "I hadn't really noticed." Then a grin. "You started it."

"I don't think so."

In the back seat, Gino shifted to give his bride's expanding torso more room. "You're two very professional people; both of you work in a world where English is a prominent thing. I think that just subconsciously colors your relationship."

I peered back at him through the bucket seats. "How much Thai do you know by now, Pastor Gino?"

"*Nit noi.* A pretty pathetically small bit."

Just to be ornery, Natty shifted into Thai herself and launched into a windy critique of the day's sermon. Saman and I chimed in merrily, and we shared a laugh at Gino's discomfiture. He pretended to sulk, peering out the window and whistling in admiration whenever pretty girls went by in the opposite direction.

THIRTEEN

So I was feeling rather glum as my old-maid weekend approached. Bangkok Christian School has the wonderful tradition of dismissing at 12:30 on Fridays, and I hatched the perfect scheme to comfort myself. "Pack your bathing suit," I ordered Paloma that morning as we dressed and vied for mirror time in the bathroom. "It's a girls' afternoon out."

My sister wheedled for details, but I shook my head. "Huh uh. It's a surprise."

It cost us a whopping four hundred baht for the taxi ride, but when we emerged at Fantasia Lagoon, her eyes about popped out of her head. "This is totally awesome! I didn't know it was here."

"That's what the Internet can do for a modern girl," I told her.

The huge water park was perched atop one of Bangkok's better malls, and we got in for the paltry sum of a hundred baht each. "Are you kidding me?" Paloma gaped. "Wow, I'm here once a week from now on."

We scooted down the tubular slides a few times, but then launched ourselves on a languid float journey around and around the lazy river. The sun was mostly hiding behind October cloud cover, but we still did some occasional dog-paddling to stay in the shade, and to also avoid the cold gushes of water spilling down from a pirate's open maw. I managed to crook my left leg through part of my sister's inner tube. "There, now we won't drift apart," I announced as the current carried us cheerfully along, bathed and refreshed by the cool liquid bath.

There wasn't much of a crowd there for a Friday afternoon, so we had plenty of time to talk and just bond with each other. I described my date with Saman at Bangsaen Beach, and my odd "Jesus reverie" about that mossy board floating in the surf. Paloma listened intently, and I could see her brighten as I mentioned my renewed determination to hang onto my Christian faith.

"That's totally cool, Pranom. So you really feel like this is it? You're all in?"

"Well, like I'm saying. It's just dumb to ever go: well, hey, if things go great I'll stay with God. If this great guy pops the question, I'll say thanks to God by being a Christian. If this or that gets fixed in my life"– again, I had to swallow my scarlet resumé from Pattaya Beach–"then I'll join the church."

We clambered out and I fished in the tiny baggie I'd pinned to the inside of my bathing suit. There were enough coins there for two sodas, and we sat in the shade underneath a massive green umbrella and watched the Thai kids cavorting in the pool and lining up to ride down the baby slide.

"It's like Aunt Rachel said once," I mused, peering at the last two inches of my icy treat.

"Sorry, I forget."

"Oh, you know. 'Jesus paid it all; all to him I owe.' We've both had some bad stuff happen. But nothing's as big as him dying on the cross for us."

She peered down at her pruny fingertips, saying nothing. "What?" I pressed.

"Just thinking."

"But that's right. Don't you think?"

She nodded. "In terms of cosmic scales, sure. If Calvary's true, and you and I get offered an eternity in heaven, nothing down here would be enough to cancel that out."

Of course the two of us share a keen appreciation for the idea of infinity, and how a calculus function shoots toward the distant constellations whenever a denominator edges toward zero. We sat there in the shade of that Bangkok fun park, the giggles of children receding into the background along with the distant rumble of *tuk tuks*, and just tried to imagine a life that goes on and on and on along the number line of Eden without ever ending.

"I don't get it," Paloma finally said with a dainty sigh. "But it's nice, huh?"

"If it's true, it's amazing," I admitted, unwittingly hedging my bets.

We spent another forty-five minutes back in the circular eight of blissful flow, and I tried to imagine God's kingdom in those terms: pleasures forevermore, endless joy, unlimited contentment . . .

Ahhh.

WE BOLDLY SUMMONED a *tuk-tuk* for the ride back to the apartment. Paloma held back as I dickered with the driver; we settled on two hundred fifty baht, which of course means three hundred for any Christian generous enough to tip these underappreciated road warriors. Traffic was a snarling mess, but the motorbike operator did throttle back at some of the roundabout intersections, and we continued our sisterly chat. I asked how things were with Klahan, and she did one of those hand-wobble gestures to indicate so-so.

"What? He seems totally stuck on you."

"I guess. And I really like him too. But it's just weird with him being Thai and me American."

"Weird how?"

"It's mostly language. I don't speak any Thai beyond 'hello' and counting to ten. So we're in English whenever we're together."

"And he's lousy with it?"

Paloma grinned. "He really is. Which is cute up to a point. But then . . ."

The din of competitive driving rose up again like a Jericho shout, and we paused the confession until two blocks down. I was thinking in my mind what it must be like to be in a relationship where every word shared was labored: mentally translated and catalogued.

"Well, it's not just that he struggles to come out with anything," she added. "He knows enough to get by. But it kind of makes our friendship, I don't know, upside-down."

The reference left me mystified. "Like how?"

"Well, you know. There's always a little bit of: guy takes charge, girl says okay, sounds good. But with us . . ."

I waited, wondering just how far down the track Paloma's romance with this shy lad had progressed.

"See, I'm the fluent one. So the whole thing kind of

inverts, and he's down below trying to qualify to get me to like him. Which isn't how it is, but I think he feels that way."

"Yikes."

Left unstated was the old mission axiom about the wonderful, benevolent, *white* savior sailing into port from the great America. And how the locals would spread out a red carpet and offer a hundred *wais* of obeisance to the grand newcomer. My sister fidgeted around that idea, and I waved it off. "Come on. Things aren't like that here in the 21st century. Are they?"

"Well, it doesn't feel that way to me. Maybe 'cause you and I grew up in the same house and were always just, you know, sisters."

We giggled at that. Within a week of arriving together in Portland, I was definitely the bossy big sister, and the Daggett pecking order had always reflected that. Still, I could see now, looking back, how old colonialist views might linger on.

As we paid the cabby and dragged ourselves up to Apartment #305, it struck me that the entire culture of trafficking here in Asia largely rested on that exact twisted notion: guys from any western country can fly here with a passport and a wallet stuffed with currency . . . and buy Thai girls for their selfish pleasure. Slap them around. Stiff them. Hurt them. Then go home and boast to their friends.

I went in after Paloma, flipped on the light, and slammed the door shut harder than I intended. She glanced back at me but said nothing.

THERE'S A FIRST time for everything, and I felt a surge of happiness when Paloma's special guy poked his head in the door of United Christian Church. Blushing cheerfully, she hopped up and seized his hand. I offered him a teasing *wai* of welcome, and beamed proudly as the three of us sat there enjoying Pastor Gino's sermon. This was our first time to hear his bride translate, and I breathed a prayer that Klahan's heart would be touched by the thoughtful devotional. Natty was brilliant up front, funny and adding just the right touch of Bangkok folksiness to her husband's manuscript.

Rachel Marie came over during our mango fest to commiserate with me. "You were saying Prince Charming's out of town?"

"Yeah. Some work stuff, I guess."

She snapped her fingers to keep Katrina in line, then gave me a hopeful look. "Do you think he's honestly interested in Christianity?"

"Well, he's been twice. And whenever we talk about it, for sure he's not hostile. Or . . . you know. Just going along with it to keep our friendship going."

"And how's that part?"

I hesitated. "Slow and steady. I don't know really how to answer. Dates once a week. Nice discussions." We were both avoiding the same snuffling elephant-in-the-room, and I rolled my eyes. "No kisses yet, since I know that's what you're thinking. Holding hands, yes. But not that."

She laughed amiably. "Khemkaeng was the same way. I was ready and sending out signals a whole long time before he got around to it."

I felt somewhat mollified by her admission and promised to keep her fully briefed.

We were just dishing up bowls of spumoni ice cream when a hulking foreigner came ambling over to our table, a white medical coat covering his green hospital scrubs. It took me a moment to recall that this was Gino's dad. *Um . . . um . . . Dr. Carington. Duh!* I'd had the briefest bits of connection with him right after my long-ago mess down the coast. He and Sue were just beginning to court during my final safe-harbor semester at BCS, *Matthayom* Two, with Tommy and me waiting out the required adoption probation period before heading off to America. I had a dim recollection of singing in Handel's "Messiah" with a whole bunch of Christians the week before leaving Thailand, and seeing the balding physician looking mushy-eyed at Sue from over in the baritone section.

He strode right into the conversation like we'd never even said goodbye. "Miss Pranom, what a wondrous treat to see you. My dear girl, you're all grown up and beautiful!" I got halfway out of my chair and accepted a warm embrace. He made a fuss over Paloma too, said a stiff *sawatdee* to Klahan, and then proceeded to dish himself an obscenely large helping of ice cream.

"My my." Sue flicked him on the forearm, a gesture I remembered from way before. "That's all you're having?"

Natty went back to the kitchen and fetched him a small plate of rice topped with curry. "Here, Grandpa." That brought raucous applause from the entire table, and he bowed affably. "Many thanks, dear friends. Yes, Grandpappy is anxiously awaiting the arrival of more Carington beauty into his noble family tree."

The BCS family was in a contented frame of mind, so a few minutes later I actually fished out my cellphone and passed around the recent Lumphini pictures for everyone to see. Rachel Marie set down her daughter and gave Saman the once-over. "He's good-looking enough. You can check off that box for sure."

"And an okay car," Gino called out from his end of the table. "Show everybody that delicious Mercedes."

"I think I'd best take a look also," Dr. Carington declared, motioning for Klahan to pass the phone over for his inspection. "It's my task to vet these young men with all their romantic wiles."

He slid his finger across the screen and cocked his head, looking. For a moment he seemed puzzled, then carefully set the iPhone down and nudged it back toward me without comment.

Uh oh. I wondered for a moment if the Caringtons inwardly disapproved that I was dating an ophthalmologist who wasn't a believer. I was a paid employee at Bangkok Christian School; it was certainly expected that my friendships would reflect the high ideals of both BCS and this affiliate church. And even from my years with Mom and Dad in Oregon, I was brutally aware of the scriptural dictum about *do not be yoked together with unbelievers.*

But the banter continued and before the ice cream carton was emptied, I'd been conned into doing the translating for Pastor Gino the following weekend.

FOURTEEN

I was drilling myself on a Youtube trig video Monday afternoon when Paloma popped her head in the door, breathlessly happy. "Aunt Rachel just invited Klahan and me over for some pizza."

"Very nice." I sensed a momentary twinge of jealousy, but actually felt relieved. I was happy for my sister, but didn't exactly relish hanging around as a third wheel. As far as I knew, Saman was still out of town; plus, he and I were about forty laps behind them on the racetrack of love.

We commiserated for just a few minutes, then I pulled out a marker and scoldingly nudged her through one of the math brain-twisters at the end of the section. "Next time you mess up subtracting those negative exponents, I'm going to hit you over the head with my shoe," I warned darkly.

"Oops. Sorry." She giggled and erased the offending numbers.

Paloma had just scooted down to the parking lot

when Sue ambled through the open door. "Hey, Miss Daggett."

Her visits are always a pleasant intrusion. "Hi. How's everything?"

"Good."

I shut my computer off and peered at her over the screen. "Sure was nice seeing Dr. C again. I don't think he's changed one bit in the last ten years."

"Oh, I think perhaps he's gone up one shirt size," she acknowledged. "The man has a thing for *kanom*." I'd seen him endlessly nibbling on local sweets during the recent church dinner.

"Yeah, me too."

"Listen," she said, coming closer. "Are you maybe free for some supper? Over at my place?"

The invitation startled me, but I recovered quickly. "Wow. That'd be wonderful. My sister just ran off on me and I didn't really feel like going home to an empty apartment." I shrugged, then added casually: "My gentleman friend is still gone too, so I shouldn't be expecting any out-of-the-blue dinner invites from him."

"Well, we'd love to have you over," Sue said. "I'm heading out around five if that works."

"Sure."

I knew she and Dr. Carington leased a fairly pricy condo just a few blocks up from the fabled Chao Phraya River. And sure enough. The elevator whisked us up twenty-seven floors, and the breezes that high up were refreshing and cool. I could see evening lights along the river already blinking on; I sipped on a diet 7-Up and made small talk with Sue as she diced potatoes and efficiently assembled a salad.

"You like any particular dressing?"

"Whatever you've got," I told her. "Paloma and I aren't fussy."

"Us either." Sue is a pleasantly padded woman, and she reached around behind her to untie the apron strings. "Miles ought to be home any second."

He came in a couple minutes later, calling out a greeting. "I'm home, lovie dear." He spied me and grinned, a beaming smile that sent upturned wrinkles right up to the middle of his scalp. "So good to have you come over, Pranom. Susie said she had talked you into it.

"Hi, Dr. C." He came over again for a platonic hug and I felt a renewed kinship with this affable gentleman.

All during supper he regaled us with stories from the surgical suite at Mission Hospital. "We get these little student nurses in there," he said. "And most of them do just great. But a few turn all shades of pasty white when there's blood oozing out through the cut. And every now and then when an accident victim comes rolling in, ye gods, there's red stuff all over the gowns and the floor and then all at once, one of these dear children is leaning over the nearest waste basket heaving her lunch away."

I shuddered. "I don't think I could ever do that kind of work."

"Pish tosh," he said with a casual wave. "You'd be fine." He glanced over at his wife. "Course the word on the street is that you're a superstar in our little education project."

"She sure is," Sue affirmed, reaching over and putting a hand over my own.

With appropriate fanfare, she went back into the kitchen and soon emerged with a lemon meringue pie.

"Where'd you get that?" I almost gasped. "Thai folks don't go much for pie."

"Oh, there's a bakery near the hospital that does them," Dr. C told me. "It's a few extra baht for something so nice, but when Susie here said you were coming over, I traded in most of my vast holdings and brought home this plate of sweetness."

"Wow." It really was delicious, and I ate slowly, savoring the tart flavor of the rich yellow filling.

We had just finished, plates shoved to the side, when I could tell some *thing* was coming in for a landing on the runway of unspoken thoughts. Dr. Carington cleared his throat, took another sip of his bottled water, glanced at his wife, and then back to me. "Well, look, Pranom. This is lovely and everything, and it's awfully nice getting to be friends again. We're so glad you're back in town, dear."

"That's right," Sue chimed in, her eyes soft and caring. "And we just don't want for you to get hurt."

I felt confused, but still relaxed and contented in the company of such nice people. "I think I'm doing okay. What are you talking about, Dr. C?"

He drew a breath, and then leaned forward slightly. "It's just this. About your friend the eye doctor."

"Saman?"

"Yeh. I wasn't positive of his last name, but I looked it up on the roster today. 'Takuathung.'"

I nodded, still unaware. "Yeah." Then my gaze widened. "Wait a minute. Do you know him?"

"Well, just a bit," he hastened. "I think it's maybe one day a month, he comes over to our place. Contracts himself out, see? Just does routine eye exams and so forth. Then if something's serious, the case is shipped over to his clinic. But when traffic's a bit slow, that's kind of a standard thing."

"Oh. Okay." I still didn't get why there was suddenly this air of caution, of a warning to be shared.

"Look, Pranom," Dr. Carington said, weighing each word. "There's no good way to tell you this, so I'll just be a Christian ally and come out with it."

Oh no . . .

"The fact is, Dr. Takuathung, he's in a rather serious relationship. With a young lady. She lives in Hawaii, and maybe three times a year he flies there and they spend a week together. It's been that way for, oh, the last year and a half."

"What!"

"I'm so sorry," he said, and then repeated himself clumsily. "So sorry. And the only reason I know is because, like I say, he's out our way every now and then. We had a lunch together, just a sandwich, see, maybe in August. Of course, I had no idea he had any connection with one of our BCS professors."

"Oh my God."

Sue slid her chair closer to mine and seized my trembling hand in both of hers. "Honey, honey. I'm really sorry. We just don't want you to get hurt. That's all."

My mind was blazing with indignation. "But, I mean, he's been taking me out for the last month. We've been out to the beach; he took me to dinner. Movies . . ." I was babbling, trying to keep from crying.

"It's a total mess," Sue acknowledged. "And see, it was all a case of the left hand not knowing what the right hand was up to. I knew you were seeing him. But I had no idea he had any connection to the Adventist hospital and was putting in a shift there. Or that Miles was acquainted with him."

"See, love, it's like this." Miles wagged his head, emanating sympathy as he bit his lip. "I saw your picture the other day during our nice get-together. And right away, I went: 'Oh no.' But just didn't want to say anything publicly and cause distress."

All at once, a light bulb went on in my fevered brain. "Hang on. So you guys inviting me over here was just to tell me all this?"

Sue nodded miserably. "Well, of course we care about you. And it's wonderful spending time with friends. But yes. We wanted to find the kindest possible way to let you know to please be careful."

I felt like I was about to be sick. "What about Paloma? She gets invited out to dinner, and that frees me up." I looked at my mentor with a pleading expression. "What, did you set that up? Try to get my sister out of the way so you could tell me?"

To my amazement, Sue Carington actually teared up and had to snatch up one of the freshly laundered white napkins we'd used for our impromptu feast. "I'm so sorry. Yes, I just didn't know how else to let you down easy."

I sat there in the shadows of this nice couple's hideaway, feeling foolish and bereft and emotionally naked. "I've been such an idiot." My mouth was dry, my heart quivering within me, but at least I wasn't bawling right in front of my boss. "He never said a word to me about Hawaii or anything. And I guess I was dumb enough to think he cared about me."

No one said anything for a long, miserable minute. Just then a memory fragment came back to me from my first eye exam at Saman's lavish office. He'd gotten that phone call and switched so smoothly into English, giving me such a delicious shock. What had he said? *I'll call you later.* I was almost too fragile now to calculate the time zones, but it took just a glum minute or two to figure that with the International Date Line in place Hawaii was seventeen time zones earlier than we were. It was likely around eleven p.m. the evening before when Little Miss Girlfriend had called him to say good night.

I followed the Caringtons out onto their balcony, and tried to push away the hurt with a second slice of her pie. But I was keenly feeling the sense of betrayal. How could Saman so glibly go out on weekly dates with a gullible Thai chick, a fragile Bangkok newcomer, while already in a state of near-engagement with someone else? It seemed so out of character for him, I thought, and then immediately rebuked myself. I, Pranom Niratpattanasai, was obviously a failure at judging characters. Getting myself adopted by Tommy and Samantha was about the only sane relational thing I'd ever done.

It was lovely beyond words up there in that secluded eyrie, far above the grind and grit of Petchburi and all the riverfront traffic. But I set down the pie plate and sighed heavily. "Guess I'd better go," I mumbled, not bothering to hide my resentment. "And not do my pouting in front of you guys."

"Oh, sweetie." Sue enfolded me in a generous embrace. "You're a princess; you deserve so much better. You just wait and see. God has someone absolutely amazing waiting in the wings."

It took all my fortitude to force a smile. "Yeah." I gave her husband a wan smile. "Thanks so much, Dr. C.

It had to be hard telling me something that yucky, but you figured out the least awful way of doing it."

"I'm sorry as can be," he assured me. "Thanks for being dear about it all."

He gallantly offered me a drive back to Orchid Garden, making careful small talk and pointing to interesting store displays. "You could give me a calculus quiz," he quipped, trying to cheer me up, and when I tepidly offered him a pair of easy function derivatives, he rattled them off with aplomb.

"Pretty good," I managed, determined to be gracious. He dropped me off with a sympathetic wave, and I watched from the landing as his taillights disappeared into the snarl of departing traffic. Through the locked door of #305, I could hear the faint murmur of the TV set, and braced myself for an evening of sisterly commiseration and revenge plotting.

FIFTEEN

Y ou should just call him up right now," Paloma spat out over our cornflakes the following morning. "Just get him on the phone and say, 'You are so busted, sonny boy.'"

"What good would that do?" I was too emotionally beaten down to calculate those seventeen hours again; with my unlucky timing, the wretched Dr. Takuathung was likely lolling on the beach in his lady friend's arms at this exact moment. "Anyway, he didn't owe me anything. We went out; that's it. It's not like I . . . gave away . . . um . . ." I couldn't think how to complete that sentence without swerving over into an anatomical confession I wasn't about to offer up.

"I don't care. The guy is tacky, tacky, tacky."

I'm not aware of a decent Thai word with that exact meaning, but there were plenty of other leaden epithets occupying my mind the next few days at BCS. I led my calc students in morning prayer; I proctored quizzes and parked myself in the back during our weekly staff meeting. Every afternoon I dutifully went out to the parking lot and waved to moms and dads and older brothers detouring over to our campus from Chula and Thammasat University. Rachel Marie sidled over to me once and draped an affectionate arm around my shoulders. "You doin' okay?"

"Sure." I shrugged. "He was just a guy."

"I know. But it's a mess when men don't treat us right." There were a million unstated postscripts to her observation, and I sensed she was regretting the remark. A moment later she brightened. "That's a decently cute guy there. What do you think?" She pointed to the older sibling of one of my trig students.

"Too young."

"I suppose."

Foot traffic was thinning out already, and my adopted aunt towed me toward the playground swings. We sat together in the October shade, two grown ladies idly pushing ourselves in tiny back-and-forth arcs, and she commiserated over the hardships of dating and finding the right man. "Once in a while you just plain get lucky," she admitted at last. "Not everybody gets the miracle, I know. But me and Khemkaeng . . ."

We talked for a bit more, and she sagely reminded me of one thing. A woman who puts her trust in the Lord and makes the permanent choice to fully obey him definitely improves her odds in the game of love. "I mean, I don't know squat about this guy. What was his name?"

"Saman."

"Yeah. And I'm sure he had a lot of good about him. Money, good career, educated. You'd have had a lot of nice stuff."

I felt a disconsolate stab of resentment; her whole narrative was decidedly in the past tense. Which I realized was the fact of it all, even though a tiny, pathetic part of my heart clung to the illusion that perhaps it was all a massive misunderstanding, that Saman was caring for an aged spinster aunt in Oahu and just giving some old biddy Epsom Salts and back rubs. *Sigh*.

I finally blurted out the stark fact: I'd come out here to my childhood haunt with gnawing doubts about God's care for me. But that I'd recently glued together a tentative commitment to him, wanting to put that choice beyond my daily vacillations.

"Good for you." Rachel Marie didn't say anything else for several long moments. We sat there in unspoken union, our swings gliding back and forth as if guided by a Will or mind beyond the two of us. "Nothing bad down here can ever obliterate the wonder of what God has masterminded for us." She paused, then pushed her swing closer to mine and strained across the chains until she actually kissed me on the cheek. "Especially for a treasure like you are." Her eyes dampened. "Dear God, I still remember how your mama, meaning Samantha, just was so in love with you. 'It makes me ache,' she said once. 'I want to just hold that kid and take care of her and beat back any enemies.'" She smiled with the remembering of it, then gave my hand a squeeze. "Better give her a call tonight."

The three of us had already had a long debrief about it; Paloma and I tended to seek out quick doses of Portland affection every couple of days. But that night I did retreat to the bedroom while my sister was cramming for a physics test. We talked till past midnight, and I drifted off to sleep with her assurance: "Your dad and I pray so hard every single day for the two of you. You guys are our angels; please don't ever let go of that."

THE FOLLOWING WEEKEND Paloma and I joined Noah, Pastor Gino, and a knot of *Prathom* boys in a quick service adventure to the Alzheimer's ward at Saint Catherine Hospital. The third-floor retreat was painted an optimistic teal, and nurses glided up the aisles ministering to their charges. Gino drafted one of the eighth-grade boys to translate, and cheerfully beckoned the senior citizens into a semicircle around the parlor television set. "These are all Christian songs," he admitted. "And maybe you don't know all of them. But we are all fashioned by the same God who loves us, and it makes me so happy that *Pra Jow* is interested in our lives and knows where we are each day."

We all joined in on the spirited Thai song fest; I made sure to keep a smile on my face and try to make eye contact with as many of the blank-eyed patrons as I could. Noah was a wonder; he knew just how to temper his guitar-playing so our fragile friends wouldn't find the music jarring. When we were done singing, Gino shared a brief devotional message, telling the old Bible story of Joseph who was dragged far, far away from his home and his loved ones.

"But the entire time he was away from his family . . ." Gino waited while Wannasilpa translated, offering up just a precise line at a time. "The entire time, God was right there with Joseph and looking after him. Joseph was never once alone. And the end of the story turned out in a wonderful, royal way!"

"You were terrific," I murmured to the Thai boy as we went down to the lobby. "Translating can be really hard, but you did a good job."

He beamed. "*Kop kuhn mahk.*"

I gave him a teasing smile. "I guess we should always be speaking English, but we're not at BCS, are we? I won't tell if you don't."

"I feel way out of it," Paloma announced loudly, and we all shared a laugh.

The Sky Train station was two blocks away from Saint Catherine, but as we approached, Pastor Gino pointed us down a dilapidated *soi*. "Let's take a quick look down here," he urged.

"How come?" Paloma peered into the gloom.

"Just . . . once in a while it's good to be reminded of how hard some folks have it."

We hadn't gone more than fifty or so meters before the side street came to an end. There was a narrow walkway threading a path between makeshift shelters mostly built up of layers of discarded tin roofing and a forlorn stack of deconstructed cardboard shipping containers. We were immediately assaulted by the stiff fragrance of unwashed bodies, urine, and unattended piles of feces. A little girl, clad in a torn T-shirt but bare from the waist down, bolted across the path, looking at us with what even I could see were badly crossed eyes.

"What's your name?" Noah sang out, trying to be friendly. The girl blubbered something and then whirled at the harsh barking of a female behind a graffiti-marked tin wall. "Come back here!" the invisible mom spat out, and the waif ducked out of our vision.

"This is way grungy," Paloma said, trying to absorb the human suffering. "And yikes, you can't even walk here. There's . . . *goo* all over the place, you guys."

It was hard to take a measure of the neighborhood;

the squalor spread out for what looked like two hundred meters. "How many people you think live here?" I whispered to Noah.

"Beats me. Several hundred, I guess." I sensed he was clutching his guitar with extra protective zeal.

"The sad thing is, there's just not a whole lot we could do," Pastor Gino sighed as we gazed around at the bleak heartbreak, acutely aware of our own tailored clothes, our overstocked fridges back home, the pure air flowing through our wall AC units. I had an education and a job. A scant eight months from now I'd be back on a plane and soaring away to the creature comforts of the most prosperous nation on the globe.

"Yeah." Noah drew the Thai boys closer, and they dialogued about what sorts of life circumstances led families to this hell. "Sometimes the daddy, he is go to jail," Wannasilpa offered. "And then if Mom has no money, and kids and many expense things, then they must come to be here like this people."

Yeah. You tell 'em, kid.

We trudged back toward the train station, all of us in a collective emotional pause. Oddly, I thought about my biological dad, still pacing aimlessly in some anonymous Thai prison yard. But what was to be done here? Could United Christian Church at least come back to this blighted spot once a month and . . . what? Set up a soup kitchen? A rice bank? Find jobs for a few of these able-bodied people? Bring clean sheets and pillows? The yawning chasm of need mocked us as we fished in our wallets for the necessary coins to buy tokens that would allow us to escape these foul images.

We were waiting for the northbound train to pull in when my cellphone dinged. I glanced down and my heart did a tumble. *A text message from Saman.*

"Oh crap," I blurted out, and Gino caught my gaffe. He made as if to shield me from the innocent students tagging along behind us. "Everything all right?"

"Yeah. It's just . . . him."

"Oh boy." He shook his head sagely. "Say a good long prayer before you send off an answer."

All of us sat crowded together on the Sky Train commute back toward the city center, my mind in an angry muddle. I forced myself to be grateful for my surrounding friends, and Paloma was right there, her arm draped affectionately around my shoulders. The *Prathom* guys were unaware; they engaged in a raucous Thai game called *O Soam*, just an endless tournament of paper-rock-scissors. But I had my iPhone burning a hole in my skirt pocket. What new deceptions did it hold?

We elected to just walk the eight blocks home from Bangkok Christian School, but I waited until we were two traffic lights away before I paused in the shadow of a 7-Eleven and thumbed down to the incoming message.

"What's that idiot have to say?"

I peered at the innocuous message. *Hey, Pranom. I've been missing you. Back to work and all. How about dinner or something Monday night? Pick anyplace you like.*

"Holy cow, he's a nervy bastard," she breathed, reading over my shoulder. "Figures he can pick up right where he left off."

I was honestly feeling more *blank* than angry, but we trudged up the two flights of stairs and I tossed the toxic phone onto my bedspread. "You going to answer in any way?" Paloma asked.

"Yeah," I bit off. "Just . . . I got to think what to do

about this."

"You're not going to go out with him?" she almost shrieked.

"No. Course not. But I want to . . . you know. I've got to go out with some class."

"Oh, forget that. He's your typical jerk. Tell him to go to hell and hit send. If you can't spell hell, it's got two L's in it."

"Just hang on." I eased myself down onto my favorite side of the living room couch and peered over at my younger sister. "I have to think, and I for sure know I've got to pray about this first."

The last remark seemed to blow an unexpected spirit of calm into the turmoil of Apartment #305. "Oh wow," Paloma managed. "Pranom, you're right." She scooted over toward me and offered a gingerly hug. "You're so awesome; you really are."

"No, I've been pretty much a fool. But I've made my decision about Jesus and all that. So from now on I've got to live with that being the number one factor."

"Boy," she mused. "Boy." Then: "You know what? You and me both."

I SPENT ALL of Monday like a wound-up Bangkok robot, fielding math questions about one-sided limits and related rates and going through the faculty line at the school's buzzing food court. But all the time I patrolled my *Matthayom* Six fiefdom, my guts and brain were screaming at me. *It's over! This isn't savable! You can't take this relationship to Dr. Carington's Emergency Room and have someone call a Code Blue on it.*

Still, a desperate part of me clung to the wan hope that somehow it had all been a misunderstanding. Maybe the Hawaii love nest wasn't real; perhaps Dr. Takua-thung had just gone to an ophthalmological convention in Hong Kong. But I knew deep down that Dr. C's intel was reliable. My boyfriend was already sharing a life and a bed with some lady in Honolulu. And honestly thought he could indefinitely two-time her and me both. *Wow.*

I'd already sent off a bland acceptance of his offer, and at the stroke of 5:30 I was seated and fully armed at one of the outdoor tables at Peperoni, the Narai's pizza palace. My stomach did a flip-flip when I saw Saman approaching; he gave me a casual wave through the throng of students, and then looked confused when he saw Paloma next to me, still in her maroon *Matthayom* uniform.

"Oh, hi," he said, flustered as he tried to decipher the scene. "I didn't know you were coming along too, Paloma, but that's totally fine."

"Well, we can't stay and eat," I said coolly. "I just wanted to have her present when I said a proper goodbye to you, Dr. Takuathung."

A strained moment lodged itself between us as he digested that. "And I guess I'll have to ask you to email my Lasik records over to BCS," I added. "It's probably best if we just don't see each other again."

"Hang on. Hang on. What the hell?" He had begun to sit down, but now jumped back up. "Pranom, honey, you're not making any sense. What did I do?"

"You've got a girlfriend." I was breathing a prayer that God would just see me through this nightmarish moment. *Jesus, oh my Savior Lord, please don't let me burst out bawling like one of those girls who gets dumped on a Thai soap novella.* "You just got back from

Hawaii; you spent five days and nights"–I paused to let that last sink in–"with some lady you're pretty much engaged to over in Oahu." All at once something spurred me to switch over into Thai, and my diatribe left my sister staring blankly back and forth between the two of us like at a ferocious tennis match. "Why'd you decide to treat me like that? What am I, some kind of idiot? My God, I really thought you were special or something. I guess I can really pick them."

He managed a terse curse word, back in English, and spun himself away from the two of us, his fists clenching and unclenching. *Busted!* I wondered for a moment if he might simply take off and stride back toward wherever he'd parked that obscenely gorgeous Mercedes-Benz of his. But he came back toward us and adopted a pleading expression. "Okay, okay," he managed. "Yeah. It's all true. I don't know how you got . . . I mean, how you know and all. But yeah. I was with Melanie over the long weekend."

Paloma's face was uncharacteristically beet-red. She snatched up some departed patron's unused paper napkin, wadded it up, and flung it in his general direction. "That's beautiful," she snapped. "Man, you're a piece of work. You treat my sister like garbage and then show up here like things are fine."

"I swear to God it's not like that . . .'"

I actually leaned over and pushed Saman down into the one vacant seat. "I'll give you sixty seconds," I managed. "Right now, frankly, you're a zero to me. But let's hear it."

Saman glanced over at my sister, hesitating. "She stays," I decreed.

"All right." He drew a deep breath. "This is all I can

say. You came to my clinic, and the first moment I saw you, I just thought you were awesome. You got to me. But there was Melanie. We had issues that were going nowhere, but I didn't know what to do about it. So I didn't say anything, and that's unfair. I absolutely admit it. But when I began going to church with you a couple of times and that stuff, I honestly began to say: 'Wow. I kind of like this. It's what I want.'"

"Oh hell." Paloma folded her arms across her chest.

"Just wait," I ordered her. "I want to hear this."

"Okay. Like I said, I felt kind of stuck. I was hugely interested in you, but it seemed tacky to just call Melanie up and say: 'That's it. I'm out with someone else.' But see, remember? When we were going out and all, I just . . . I never once tried to kiss you or anything. Because I knew it'd be wrong to get to that level with someone else."

He had a point there, and my mind whirred anxiously, trying to process his babbling. Then my face tightened again. "No way. Over in Hawaii, you spent just about a whole week with your girlfriend," I charged. "What, did you rent a separate hotel room and stay up reading the Gideon Bible every night?"

He had enough dignity to blush. "No. It was . . . okay, it was a mess. We did spend some time together like you just said. But two days before my return ticket, I did tell her she and I were finished. And I left her and booked a room across town."

That last bit caught me by surprise. "Yeah," he managed. "I actually thought about just cashing in my ticket and coming back and telling you. But then figured, hey, I'll probably never be here in Hawaii again. So I just kind of hung around the beach and walked around, trying to get my head back on straight."

Now I had him cold. "So what happened to flying back to Bangkok and telling me the whole story? Instead of Dr. Carington having to tell on you?"

He looked down sheepishly. "Look, Pranom. I honestly like you. I mean, a lot. I care about you. And I was ashamed. I guess a weak part of me was hoping I could, you know, just put that failed story behind me, take it nice and slow with you, start going to church and stuff, and see if we might have something." His gaze now was pleading, not at all the suave Thai medical pro who had so bewitched me before. "I totally get that you're a Christian lady. You'd have no future with me unless it was along those lines. So I'm here. I'm ready to date you nice and slow, church together fifty-two weeks a year, the whole thing."

I felt dizzy and bereft, but all at once this gorgeous, pleading man began to actually make some sense. I looked over at my sister, whose face was a dismayed blank. "What do you think?" I hissed.

Paloma shook her head, her blond curls jiggling, and I could tell she was still steaming. To her credit, though, her answer made sense. "I don't know. But if you're honestly going the whole Christian route, then hey. Forgiveness and all that is definitely part of the deal."

It felt only right to let Dr. Takuathung at least salvage a supper with me. I sent my sister to the indoor counter with a stack of my date's Thai currency, and we sat there together in awkward silence as the nightlife of downtown Bangkok hummed its way around us. "I feel very ashamed," he admitted, and his crooked half-smile didn't have any of the old charm. "Is there any way you could forgive me?"

"I don't know," I admitted. "Before, yeah, I really liked you a whole lot. In here"–I gestured toward my badly bruised heart–"what we were heading toward felt very special. But look, Saman. To a woman, betrayal and deception are just killers. When I sat at that dinner table and had Dr. Carington tell me, 'This guy you're dating flew clear off to Hawaii and has, like, a fiancée,' I felt like a mountain had fallen right on me. And right in front of my boss. Just: 'I'm an idiot.'"

"Man." He did reach over and squeeze my hand quickly, and then let go. "But look. I'm here. And I'd love to start from square one if you'd let me. I'll earn your trust one weekend at a time, sitting next to you at church."

I was sorely tempted to say: *And just hand over your cell phone, you sneaky cad. 'Cause I'll be monitoring all your incoming and outgoing from here on.* But I didn't. A few minutes later, a waiter brought our tray with a piping-hot pizza on it. We chewed on it in wordless contemplation, an awkward Bangkok trio. When it was done, Saman fished in his pocket for his keys. "Please. Let me drive you ladies home."

I shook my head forcefully, and hid a smile as I saw that Paloma and I were shaking in tandem. "Not this time," I told him. "Us ladies will take a cab."

We talked until way past our bedtimes, Paloma and I did. Before drifting off amid my blurted prayers, I thought that maybe, just maybe, I'd give Dr. Saman Takuathung a second chance.

The following morning I got to my classroom and found a massive bouquet there, at least thirty orchids, spilling all over my desk.

SIXTEEN

Thinking later about our laborious journey back toward normalcy, I have to concede that Saman was a model penitent. He didn't press; he didn't overcompensate. He accepted that as a couple, we were clear back to the starting gate. But the following week he dutifully showed up at United Christian Church, knelt next to me for prayer, sang the praise tunes as best he could, and kept his hands to himself. During lunch, he was a devoted gentleman, fetching extra bowls of pineapple chunks for all my BCS mates and plying Noah with questions about the *Matthayom* choir's upcoming two-day tour to Chiang Mai. After dessert he got down on his hands and knees and willingly gave Gage, Katrina, and Jaidee horsey rides.

A few days later he sent me a text message, and I was surprised to find he was as big a fan as I was of that mall-top water park. He treated me to a sunset-drenched evening of floating endless loops around the lazy river, the evening lights of high-rise luxury hotels blinking pleasantly down on us. Afterward, we walked hand in hand through the jewelry section of the city, giggling at some of the pricy displays. At the far end of the district was a McDonald's, and Saman fished out enough baht to sate my ravenous appetite. He watched, grinning, as I gobbled up a second McFlurry, draining the last sweet drops of the frozen treat out of the upended paper cup. "You seem to like those."

"Well, with all that paddling around we did, I think I'll break even in the calorie department."

"You're the prettiest girl in Asia, you know."

I accepted the compliment with wary pleasure, and sent myself a reluctant internal memo that any first kiss for Dr. Takuathung was way off nestled among the clouds of a distant horizon.

The following weekend he came through the back door of UCC a few minutes late, but hunted me down and proudly introduced an older Thai woman. "Pranom, this is my mom."

Oops. I felt my face going pink, but offered her a polite *wai*. "It's nice to meet you," I said, staying in our shared native Thai.

"And you also." She was an attractive woman, and I could easily see her son's features imprinted on her face. "Saman says he has enjoyed several nice evenings with you."

I nodded, setting aside the unstated baggage accompanying Mommy's greeting. "It's been good getting acquainted. And I was thankful when my eye operation was a success. Dr. Takuathung did an excellent job." I instinctively reverted to his medical title, hoping she would understand the tentative nature of our relationship. Then to Saman: "You know I'm translating the sermon today."

"Oh, sure." He grinned, and the same deadly charm seemed to be there once again. "That's why we're here." He paused. "Plus Dad is off at some medical seminar he wanted to record over at the Asoka Hotel."

This was my second try at translating, but Pastor Gino was skilled at pacing his English remarks, and it was easy for me to read the Thai Bible verses off the computer monitor perched on a pair of front-row seats. His message was on the temptation of discouragement, and how Satan utilizes such a tool to separate new Christians from the Lord. It pleased both of us to see a quartet of my *Matthayom* girls on the back row absorbing the gospel message, and I could tell they were more tuned in to my side of the presentation than the pastor's.

Gino shrugged amiably when we discussed it during the luncheon. "Oh, sure, I get that. I mean, okay, they listen a bit to the English side, since they're learning that at school. But their main emotional connection will be with you, Pranom." Even though Saman and his mother were seated at the same table, he didn't hold back. "I think your Christian life is a very effective witness to some of these high school young people. Especially the girls."

He soon slipped over to another table to make a connection with our first-time visitors, and I managed some small talk with Mrs. Takuathung. Her first name was Palanee, which reminded me that Vuthisit and I had so long ago enjoyed playing after school with a classmate who shared that unusual name. "How is it," she carefully asked, "to return to Bangkok after such a long time in the U.S.A.? And now be a professor at your old school?"

"Oh. Well, I like both parts of that," I said. "Thailand is always my native home, certainly. And as a girl, I thought BCS was just amazing. So to now be able to come and help in my own small way, and to be a teacher instead of a pupil, is a lot of fun."

Paloma, sitting hand in hand with Klahan on the other side of the long table, piped in. "She's really good too!" Saman's mom smiled at that, but deferred to her son for the rest of the afternoon banter.

"Can I call you later this evening?" he asked, as I walked them over to his car. "Maybe we could just meet for some coffee."

"I'd like that."

We were getting well into November before Sue came by and tapped again on my classroom door. "Knock knock."

"Hi, Sue. You should have been by here earlier. We gave back some tests, and fourteen kids got A's. I gave them some reward candy, and that cost me a lot of baht."

She beamed as she came over and took the one spare seat next to my desk. "I knew you'd do a bang-up job for us, Pranom. And the parents are just delighted as can be. Khemkaeng forwards some of the emails to me."

"I'm really glad. And it's tons of fun."

"Very good." She peered cheerfully at me across the top of her glasses. "And you seem to be proceeding very cautiously with this gentleman. Now that he's for sure focusing one hundred percent of his attentions on Miss Daggett."

"Well, we're taking it really easy. But I'm beginning to feel like, yes, he is earning my trust. Slow but steady."

"That's great." She nodded. "And of course, it's

true that people do deserve a second chance. God's grace and all that."

I knew that only the Lord could read men's hearts, but it was undeniably true that Saman had faithfully sat at my side for a month of church services. He'd absorbed an entire sermon series by Pastor Gino. And when he drove me to dinner dates, I sometimes heard the same praise songs Noah and his band taught us coming through the car speakers. "I know you and Dr. C always pray for us," I managed faintly. "And that means a ton to me; that's for sure."

"Oh, of course." She smiled. "If you fall in love with a good man over here in Asia, we might just be able to hang onto our favorite calculus professor for more than one school term."

"Um . . . I can't make any promises."

Sue laughed. "By the way," she said, tacking in a different direction, "I realize you and I squashed the idea of, you know, you doing a workshop on that issue of trafficking."

Uh oh. I said nothing.

"There's a three-hour thing Thursday afternoon," she said carefully, pulling a brochure out of her purse. "And I mean, it'd just be something to attend. And sit in the back. If you thought it might be helpful."

I didn't want to, but I did reach over and accept the government publication. There were three workshops being offered, and I scanned the titles. "I don't know," I said slowly. "It's just . . . what would I learn that I didn't already know the hard way?"

My mentor nodded. "I get that. But I was seeing that third plenary dealing with the aftermath and how these young girls need so much help to come out safely on the other side." Her face softened, and Sue reached over and seized my hand. "It's just . . . honey, if you ever thought it would help to hear the experiences of others, maybe it'd be worth attending." Her eyes searched out my own. "If you want, we can get a sub for that last school period. And no one in the office would know where you'd gone. This is all between just you and me."

So I took Sue up on her offer. I concocted a lie for Paloma and said I was dickering with the Thai government's education folks about our graduation rates. She shrugged and said okay, she'd probably have pizza with Klahan and a couple of his nerd friends.

It was a quick Sky Train ride over to the stately government complex where the workshops were being offered. I had a yellow notepad just in case, and scooped up a set of bilingual fliers at the back table. And then sat alone toward the rear of the hall, penned in by my memories as a panel of so-called sociological experts shared case studies on what happens to young hookers trying to escape from Patpong Road's raucous lifestyle.

Fortunately, the workshop didn't delve into the detailed horrors of Thailand's sex trade. The talk was clinical, with crammed-together PowerPoint files, all in Thai, cataloguing the miserable statistics. The whole sordid saga boiled down mostly to a sad list of options; young girls get traded into prostitution when there don't seem to be viable choices. Some, like I had been, are coerced into the trade by a greedy relative/pimp. Others have no way to care for their dependent children, and will actually turn tricks in a cheap hotel bedroom while their own toddlers try to sleep in the bathroom.

Once when the anecdotes began hitting too close to

home, I simply set down my pen, closed my eyes, and let my soul escape back to Mom and Dad and our Sunday night burger-and-fries dinners in Portland. I'd secreted a small gold crucifix underneath my blouse, and I fingered it, tracing along the perpendicular lines of the Calvary crossbeam. *You saw me through it, Jesus. I'm okay. I'm here. You're present right now . . .*

On my way back to the metro station, I popped into a KFC and just ordered a small dish of ice cream. Pushing small, frozen bites into my mouth I sent off a cryptic text to my boss. *I got through it but didn't really learn much. Too many potholes in the road, to be honest. Sorry, Sue. But your concern for me is a super gift. P.*

BANGKOK CHRISTIAN SCHOOL was just creeping up on its in-house celebrating of the Christmas season. Bangkok is decidedly secular during the month of December, but Gino and the pastoral team had gone all out to give our church a festive holiday look. We boasted a full-size Christmas tree downstairs close to the lobby staircase and there were even icicle lights strung along the perimeter of the warehouse sanctuary. Rumor had it that Natty was too large with child to squeeze herself through the door of a Bethlehem stable; at least, that's how Gino joked during one of his worships with my *Matthayom* Six students. Still, she found time to ride a taxi over to the MBK Shopping Center and find a trio of Christmas-themed paintings at the Christian book-store.

"But there's no snow," I sighed as Saman hiked up the stairs and grabbed a pair of seats next to Chloe and Benjie. I waved at Vuthisit and made a mental note to connect with my old classmate during lunch.

But I got a sweet December surprise during the worship period. Halfway through the carols, Gino nodded in our direction and Saman hopped up to his feet. He tugged loose a thin paperback New Testament, leafed over to the gospel of Matthew, and began to read in his precise English, pausing as Khemkaeng translated the saga of how a virgin named Mary was told she would bring hope to our world by having a Son.

"And this is the finest part," my non-believing boyfriend concluded. "Listen to this. *And they will call him Immanuel, which means 'God with us.'*" He stood next to his translator as the Thai words rolled out, and I felt warmed by his nice smile and his seeming acceptance of the grandeur of our church's communal hope.

"I didn't know you were reading today," I whispered, leaning over and giving his hand a loyal squeeze.

He grinned. "Your boss sent me a text message a few days ago and I said okay."

"Wow." Pastor Gino was standing up for his sermon and we fell silent, but then I felt compelled to add: "I bet you'd be an amazing translator for our church."

Saman hesitated, then nodded. "Yeah, maybe."

MY BOYFRIEND HAD ducked out to the men's room for a break during our holiday feast, so Vuthisit seized her moment. "Things are going well?"

A shrug. "Well, we're not rushing things. But he seems interested in Christianity."

Her eyes danced knowingly. "My calendar says you're not here that much longer."

"That's kind of a problem. But all I can do is to take one step at a time. And let God steer things this way or that."

"Sure."

The Christmas banter went on so long it was almost dusk as we got the last bits of trash put away and the plates and silverware washed and stored. Saman went over to my sister and Klahan and murmured something, teasingly dangling the keys to his luxury car in front of them. The Thai student brightened, and the three of them bounded over. "Can we all go?" Paloma pleaded. "Pretty please?"

"What are you talking about?"

Klahan grinned. "Saman say, we can all go for boat ride. Nice dinner and also music."

"What? We just ate. You're not hungry again, are you?"

Saman draped an arm around me. "We don't have to stuff ourselves. But they've got some nice Italian pasta and stuff like that. Soda and drinks." He caught himself. "We won't do that, of course. But Dad likes to take my mom out there maybe twice a year, and it's real festive."

"Is it expensive?"

"Not much." He gave Klahan a man-to-man glance. "It's my treat," he added in Thai.

Klahan whipped out his cell and clicked in a rapid text message to his parents. There was an affirming *ding* in reply, and he put it away with satisfaction. "Is okay for me to go."

Paloma pinched his forearm. "Come on, boyfriend. 'It is okay for me to go with my beautiful American girlfriend.'"

He obediently parroted the line, and Rachel Marie guffawed as she swept past us, Katrina in tow. "That's the way to teach English," she observed. "Mingle in adolescent hormones and Thai boys will pick it up at seven times the normal rate."

It took some threading through traffic to get down to the Chao Phraya; once Saman turned the wrong way and we found ourselves stuck on a tight one-way alley. But an amenable taxi driver on his cigarette break cheerfully pointed us toward an escape *soi*, and Klahan called out from the back seat that he'd spotted a pair of vacant parking stalls. "Is it safe to park here?" Paloma wondered, easing down the power window and peering out.

"Yes, is okay here." Klahan immediately sensed that yet another grammar lesson was about to pop loose, and recoiled visibly as we shared a laugh.

We made the dinner hour cruise with perhaps three minutes to spare, and Paloma's eyes bugged out as my boyfriend casually tossed out a stack of tan thousand-baht bills. "This lad's loaded," she murmured to me as the guys handled the paperwork.

"I know. But really, he's been nothing but sweet since . . . you know."

There was a cozy bank of December clouds pushing their way up and past the skyline, now beginning to glimmer with incandescent nightlife, as discos and movie theaters fired up for a good Bangkok dose of *sanuk* (fun). The four of us snagged a circular table on the upper deck, with the tropical breezes rippling our hair. Saman doffed his suit coat and draped it over the back of his chair, and we made small talk as Klahan went below to fetch us a quartet of diet Cokes.

It was one of those really magical nights where a girl can instinctively tell her special friend is smitten. I'd been to Rachel Marie's favorite dressmaker around Thanksgiving, and came home with a pretty outfit especially for UCC. It was cherry red with ribbon trimmings, and sparkling sequins along the collar. I'd gone back twice to get the perfect tailored fit, and Paloma kept smirking behind her glass of cola as Saman eyed my clingy outfit. We dissected the morning sermon, bantered about whether the new *Spiderman* film was worth 120 baht, and made up fantasy lists of Christmas presents. "Just in case Santa Claus rides all the way out to Bangkok," Saman jested, teasing me.

"Of course he's coming," Paloma countered. "I've been way, way good."

"You did get a B- on your last calculus test," I said, scolding her.

"And Paloma beat me by four percent," Klahan sighed. "I study so hard, and then forget always to put 'plus C' on integral."

"Well, I warned you about that. In both English and Thai," I reminded him, and he grinned, enjoying an evening where the usual boundary lines between professor and student were melting away in the cheerful river ambience.

The dinner bell rang, and we went through the buffet line, carefully choosing from the array of pasta dishes. The ravioli had a butternut squash filling, and I moaned at the thought of limiting my intake. "Those are my favorite in the universe."

"Well, then don't have so much pineapple."

I shot Saman a poisonous look to let him know exactly what I thought of his ridiculous suggestion.

The pastas actually had a light flavor, and the Alfredo sauce was brimming with just the right amount of spice. Drinks were included, and I wondered if Saman was missing his usual libations. But he seemed perfectly content, sharing half a slice of carrot cake with me and going back through line to get me a refill on my soda.

It was nearly dark now, and waiters in short white coats moved through the maze of top-deck tables, clearing away dishes and inviting us to scoot our tables close to the perimeter and clear some deck space. Our pleasure craft chugged along pleasantly, and we waved to partygoers in nearby vessels, the general ambience glowing with what I was sure must be a champagne-fueled haze. Smaller canoes bobbed along in our wake, with local merchants hoping we might stop and dicker for carved elephants and other Thai art treasures.

There was a small three-piece combo setting up their gear in the back of the boat, and I spotted speakers dangling from the overhead mast. "You didn't tell me there'd be live music," I said to Saman, pleased.

"I didn't know either. But let's see how good they are."

The tunes were actually just all right; the guitarist had his amp turned up too high and some of the chords were fuzzing out. But the singer was a spritely Thai lady in a white top and navy blue miniskirt; she had a good range and the pace was cheerful. The third member was a keyboard player, and I finally figured out that the bass and percussion parts were coming our way courtesy of a MacBook Pro.

Some of the guests had shed their coats and entrusted purses and packages to friends, and were beginning to sway to the beat. But the four of us kept on chatting, enjoying the elegance and carefree pleasure of being out on the water, and the band swung into a long medley of Abba hits.

"Is it illegal to dance?" Paloma asked, glancing over at me like I was a deputized BCS chaperone and daring me to say no.

"I won't tell Mrs. Carington."

She seized Klahan by the hand and led him toward an open spot. I grinned and turned my attention back to Saman. "This is just great," I told him. "You really . . . well, thanks a whole bunch. And bringing my kid sister along and all that."

He eyed me, still basking in the vibes coming off my red sequins. "I should give Klahan a hundred baht to go over to the other side of the boat."

Um . . . I actually like the sound of that, sweetie. I didn't say any such thing, of course, but sitting there in his pinstripe blue trousers and his neatly starched dress shirt, Saman was scary-good-looking. The wind was ruffling his hair, and his eyes had a wonderful softness to them, so filled with protective happiness.

Jesus, can it just be like this for a long, long time?

The combo's lead singer said something in clumsy English about only two more songs, and "we hope you have so fine time in Bangkok; please come again, okay." The main musician switched over to his nylon-stringed guitar, and began a slow arpeggio that made goose bumps form on my arm. I pushed my chair back and reached out for my boyfriend's hand. "We have to dance to this one."

Saman looked surprised, perhaps not expecting this from his Christian girlfriend. "How come?"

"I love this song. Just be quiet and hold me."

He brightened. "Well, that I can do."

Two years before, Mom and Dad had splurged at

Christmastime and gotten us tickets to a live performance of *Mamma Mia*. Now the lead singer began to do the poignant anthem about a girl whose heart has been crushed by past betrayals.

Chiquitita, tell me what's wrong. You're enchained by your own sorrow. In your eyes there is no hope for tomorrow.

I suppose the tune was a bit biographical, and on any other night it would have made me think of Pattaya Beach and my sad juvenile confession. But now, with Saman holding me close and his cheek pressed up against mine, the vocalist's words had a hopeful sweetness to them. We weren't really dancing, just kind of *there*, the gentle beat from the computer track nudging us into a rhythm that matched the ripples on the wake behind our boat.

Chiquitita, tell me the truth. I'm a shoulder you can cry on. Your best friend, I'm the one you must rely on.

There on the wooden deck of a Thai party boat, with cocktail glasses all around, and now with the guitar player leaning into the mike to add his harmonies to the Abba chorus, I didn't honestly know if Saman Takuathung could step forward and be my soulmate. Yeah, he'd deceived me once; he had let me down in the most hurtful way possible. But now he was coming to church with me; he'd put in five weeks of solid, earnest effort, trying to regain my trust and then win my heart. Was he getting there? I didn't know that for sure, but I surely was happy now in his arms, floating along with the slight essence of his cologne, mingled with the lingering fragrance of our shared dinner.

Chiquitita, you and I know how the heartaches come and they go and the scars they're leaving. You'll be dancing once again and the pain will end; you will have no time for grieving.

In the Broadway play, the performers sing "Chiquitita" while Sophie Sheridan ponders the reality that a biological dad had failed to be present and faithful in her life. I didn't pause now to think about the parallels with me and my own locked-away father; instead, I pressed my heart, literally and spiritually, against my friend's chest, trying to swallow the lump in my throat.

"You okay, babe?" He murmured it in my ear, but with the music still going I wasn't sure I had heard him right. He lifted my chin until our eyes met. "Sweetie, are you all right?"

"Yeah," I nodded. "This is nice. And I'm very happy."

There were just a few bars left in the music, but my mind skipped across the river current and back to our worship service. It was my new boyfriend who had read the biblical promise of a God who would come to our world and then remain for many Christmases. *Immanuel: God with us.* Was Christ my Lord with me here on this pleasure boat, with the bartender down below handing out martinis in exchange for hundred-baht bills? Could I find something healing and good and wondrous with this gracious eye doctor, this man with a look of resolve?

I gave his hand a squeeze filled with meaning, and gazed up again into his handsome face. It was an expectant look, and he was certainly man enough to read it and respond. "Merry Christmas, my sweetheart," he murmured in Thai. And then as the last notes from the acoustical guitar floated from the back of the ship and into our embrace, Saman drew my face closer to his and kissed me. We held our lips together for a nice long moment, and I tried not to let my eyes swim with tears.

Sing a new song, Chiquitita. Try once more like you did before, Sing a new song, Chiquitita.

SEVENTEEN

Three nights before Christmas Paloma and I were watching a holiday movie on the international HBO channel when Rachel Marie called. "Natty just went into labor," she exulted. "Khemkaeng's okay with watching the kids, so I'm going over to the hospital to wait things out. You want to come along? It'll be fun."

We immediately switched off the TV; it was a show we'd watched the previous December with Mom and Dad anyway. "Which hospital?" I asked.

"Mission Hospital. It's kind of our family tradition. Anything good, anything bad, the taxi man takes us there."

"Does the Sky Train go by there?"

"Huh uh. Just grab a taxi. Tell him *roang payaban mitchun.*"

Even after a decade here in Thailand, my aunt's pronunciation was woefully stiff. I stifled a giggle. "Sure. We can play Crazy Eights in the waiting room."

It took us a crawling forty-five minutes to traverse the clogged length of *Thanon* Phitsanulok, so by the time we got there Natty was already dilated up to seven centimeters and panting hard. We popped in, said hi, kissed her on the forehead, said good luck to Gino, and retreated to a cramped anteroom across from the nursing station. We deferred to Rachel Marie, who claimed special privileges as a sister-in-law; she kept ducking in and out of the delivery room, snapping pictures with her iPhone and popping off text messages to her in-laws in Chiang Mai. "They're getting the last shuttle flight down," she told me, waving the screen in our direction. "Aroon says he's about to bust."

"How many grandkids is this for him?"

"This makes five. Two, two, and one, so we can go nuts with the hand-me-downs."

Paloma brightened. "That reminds me of a joke Dad told me."

"Oh no," I groaned. "They're so bad."

"This is from Bob Hope." My sister began cackling even before she launched into it. "He said when he was a kid with a million brothers, by the time a pair of pants got down to him, the fabric was so worn he could sit on a dime and tell if it was heads or tails."

Rachel Marie shook her head, laughing. "My dad loved Bob Hope, but I never heard that one."

"How about this one. With so many kids in the house, his dad bought the family a dachshund."

"Why's that funny?" my aunt wanted to know.

"Oh. 'Cause it's so long all the boys could pet it at the same time."

I leaned over and threatened to throttle Paloma. "Those are totally lame."

"And I'll bet you'll borrow both of them for class next week."

I did tend to try out corny bits of humor on the seniors, and generally got little more than polite titters. Rachel Marie, hoping to fend off any more cheesy humor from the Daggett archives, headed for the ice machine, and then popped her head into the delivery ward where Dr. Pradchaphet was holding court.

"Very soon now," he sang out, and she rushed back to tell us. "Looks like we might beat midnight by five or ten minutes."

Paloma glanced up the hallway. "We should say a little prayer, you guys."

My aunt's face softened. "Oh, honey, you're a genius. What a good idea."

We held hands as my sister prayed. "Lord, it's so great to be here. Thank you that Pranom and I have gotten to be in Bangkok for such a precious event. Please bless Aunt Natty right now, and be with the doctors. Help the baby to be born safely and then help us to love her and be a good Christian community for her. Amen."

Her words were so simple and pitch-perfect, I hardly knew what to say. It amazed me, really, how these few months in Bangkok, living as a kind of quasi-missionary, had filled my kid sister with such solid discipleship bone marrow.

One of the Adventist nurses appeared in the doorway. "Doctor say you can come and see baby is born. If you stand in the back only. Is exciting to see."

"Natty doesn't mind?" I asked the nurse in Thai, and she shot me a grateful look. "No, it's all right."

By now things were in a state of anatomical

undress, but Natty seemed in good humor. "Don't try to talk me into some other baby name," she called out between gasps. "Gino and I have our minds made up."

He peered up at us, grinning, then gave his wife's hand another squeeze. "It's crowning, babe. Even the back of her head looks awesome. Like Queen Esther, maybe."

"Oh brother." She almost got to laughing, but the doctor shushed the joviality. "One more contraction and we must push very hard," he admonished.

Less than a minute later, a lusty cry rattled the window louvers and we all applauded eagerly. "Oh, honey, she's just absolutely perfect. What an adorable face!" Rachel Marie breathed. "I think she looks a little bit like Katrina, actually." She began fishing for her cell phone again. "Soon as we can, I want to send a picture over to the house. Khemkaeng might wake up the kids and show them."

The nurse carefully weighed our little newcomer and made the grand announcement. "Little girl is weigh 2.9 kilo." Then, peering at the digits again, pushed a button. "Is six pound and four ounces."

"She is a fine daughter," the Thai doctor said proudly. "*Kuhn* Gino, God has blessed you and your wife. All our medical team here wishes you many blessings from heaven and for your girl to always love God and serve him in a good way."

"Thank you, Dr. P," Gino murmured, suddenly overcome with emotion.

Paloma and I lingered at the hospital just long enough to greet the incoming grandparents, who had snagged a cab from Suvarnabhumi Airport. Aroon was wreathed in smiles as he held the squawling infant.

"What a noisy baby!" He edged closer to Gino. "I believe this part of her must come from you, Gino. Because Nattaporn has always been a quiet girl."

He said this tongue in cheek, of course; all of BCS knew Khemkaeng's kid sister had a reputation for spitting out colorful jokes and insults.

Rachel Marie walked us out to the elevator and actually led us down to the circular drive where there was a queue of cabs even at two in the morning. "Sure was good of you guys to come over," she murmured, giving me an affectionate squeeze. "We're proud to be related to you." She eyed me gently. "You're still on for your little adventure tomorrow?"

I nodded, too pleasantly confused to elaborate.

On the taxi ride back to our flat, though, I leaned back against the oily upholstery, thinking about my own biological dad and tomorrow's agenda. Would I be able to track him down through Bangkok's notoriously spotty penal system? He'd been locked away for more than a decade now; might he actually make parole while I was still here in Thailand? Would he accept visits? Would seeing him again set back my lurching spiritual journey?

Paloma asked me that very question as we were lying there in the early-morning darkness, still too keyed up to get to sleep. "Will that freak you out? Seeing your real dad?"

"Hey. Tommy's my real dad now."

"I know. But . . . just saying."

"I don't know." In my heart, I realized that the issue wasn't Dad. Sure, he'd gotten busted for running drugs through tourist networks. But he wasn't the Satan in my still wounded soul.

It's Uncle Viroj I can't ever see or think about

again. Kuhn Viroj Niratpattanasai. The man who abducted me under the guise of charity, being an angel of mercy. And then sold me into prostitution at the age of thirteen.

It took me more than an hour to get to sleep, and prayer was labored that night. Because I knew full well that if my Christian faith had to stack up against an encounter with my captor, that snake, I was still likely to trade in Calvary for one screaming, vengeful rant against the one man I truly, truly loathed.

PALOMA HAD SNAGGED an invite to enjoy a pool-side breakfast with one of her *Matthayom* girlfriends, and I assured her I wanted her to go have a great time. "If I strike out, hey, I'll just come back here. I'm two quizzes behind in grading."

"Okay."

The central clearing authority for all Bangkok was in a fairly nondescript, older trio of buildings a block away from Rama Road. I had a vague memory of Natty's recent brush with the law, and wondered as I hiked over from the Sky Train whether she'd been forced to testify somewhere in this same complex. There was a massive directory in the lobby, and I scanned the endless array of numbers until I realized I'd come in the wrong way. The information desk for incarcerations was down a long corridor and with its own straggling line. I joined the tail end of the queue and shuffled along, reading a bit of Colossians on my Kindle as the overhead PA cut in with various announcements about visiting hours and on which floor such-and-such hearing had been scheduled.

I was already dragging by the time I finally got to

the window. "Name please?" An older man with nicotine-stained fingers jabbed at a computer keyboard, and his gaze didn't depart from an ancient monochrome screen going back to at least my own childhood days.

"Pranom Niratpattanasai."

"Address?"

I told him, and he clicked it in.

"What do you wish, miss?"

"I have a relative who is incarcerated. But I don't know where."

"How long ago was he sentenced?"

"Eleven years ago."

The official glanced up at me. "That is a long time. You have not paid this person any visits before?"

"I just returned to Bangkok."

He paused, drumming his fingers. "Do you have a more precise date?"

I was able to offer him the month and year, and he frowned. "Our records for that time are not so good. But I will try." He spaced down a bit in the computer field; I could see the green cursor blinking furiously. "What is this inmate's name, and what is your relationship?"

"He's my father. I mean, my biological parent," I amended. "Since then, it became necessary for other friends to adopt me. So I lived for a long time in America."

"His name?" The man prompted me again.

"Oh. It's Anuman Niratpattanasai."

Both names are common enough in Thailand that he pecked it in using his Thai keyboard, and didn't need to ask me about the spelling. He looked at the screen, watching as the Internet slowly hummed through its internal processes. After a long pause, he shook his head.

"I am sorry. But some of our records are not well processed. I do not see your father's name here."

"Well, there has to be a record somewhere," I protested, keeping my voice even. Truthfully, I was half hoping for a failed search; still, I felt it incumbent upon me to at least make an effort. "He's not old; only forty-six."

That gave him an idea. "I should have asked you for his birthdate."

I rattled off the digits, not sure if he wanted the Buddhist accounting or an A.D. edition. When I began with a 10-5, meaning October 5, he asked me to clarify. "Here in Thailand," he reminded, "it is customary to say the day first, the month second. Is your father born on May 10 . . . or October 5?"

"Oh," I apologized. "In October. In America it's done the other way."

He rolled his eyes. Typing in the amended digits, he hit enter again and peered listlessly at the screen. "I'm sorry," he said, almost instinctively, as if he knew the antiquated system would fail him. "There is nothing."

"But in the entire computer system," I countered, "how can he not be there?"

He shrugged, then suddenly seemed to brighten. "It's possible he has already been released," he mused. "The original sentence was for fifteen years?"

"I think so."

"And that was eleven years ago?"

I nodded.

"There is a good chance he is released," the official informed me. "It is very expensive to house prisoners for long periods of time. Often, if they show penitence and are rehabilitated, the sentence is shortened." He picked up a laminated sheet of pink paper, looking down a long row of office numbers. "It is the same everywhere, I am sure. Even in America."

I had no idea what he was examining, so simply waited, trying to form a mental picture of my dad shuffling out of some jail cell, having a bored official hand him a small paper bag filled with personal effects and maybe a thousand baht or so of rehab currency.

"You could try the parole division," the man suggested. "I should have already told you. If your father has been freed, he would be cooperating with them. A parole official would be advising him on how to be a successful free person once again."

I had absolutely no clue how advanced or primitive such a network might be. But he told me I would need to walk two blocks to the other sector. "That building is smaller. Blue, only two stories. A parking lot is on this side here." He took out a small pad of paper, and sketched a crude map for me. "Here is *Thanon* Seppita. See? Here is the building. There is a Caltex petrol station on the other side. If you see that, you are right where you wish."

"Who do I ask for?"

"Oh. All queries must be at the main desk. Give them the name of your father and also these same dates." He shrugged as if to confirm that I was still likely chasing a phantom. "I hope you are successful, Miss Niratpattanasai."

I don't know why, but I said with some force: "My name is now Daggett."

This official was just doing his job; I realized that. I was about to murmur an apology, but he nodded as if to say he understood there was a long and scarred story hiding behind my pursed lips and flaring emotions.

I WAS SURPRISED to find an Indian clerk at the information desk, but the woman spoke flawless Thai and nodded when I explained how the other officer had sent me over to her. "Yes, if he was paroled, we should have a record here," she agreed. "What is your father's name?"

I spelled it out, and was tempted to ask about her fluency in a foreign language. But of course, all sorts of interesting people are born and raised in Bangkok despite a foreign heritage. She clicked the name in, listening intently as I spelled it out. At least over here the computer monitors were sleek and up to date, I mused, as the color screen flickered in digesting the information. My new friend cocked her head to one side, sidestepped one information box, and then brightened. "Very interesting."

"What?"

"It appears your father was released four years ago."

"What!"

"Yes." She read off the date. "That is unusually early for such a serious offense." Then she smiled. "It appears that perhaps your father was diligent in seeking rehabilitation."

Oh. I hardly knew what to say to that. Yes, Dad–meaning my biological father–wasn't a bad sort, actually. In a way, it was unfair for me to lay the entire curse of my childhood on his one rash and desperate error. He had always loved me; he was mostly a generous parent. Still, to take such risks when I had no other familial protection . . . for the longest time in

Oregon, I had harbored an inexpressible rage toward the man and fantasized about the venom I would spew at him if I ever got the opportunity.

"So what happened to him?" I asked faintly.

"He would have been on parole. For two years."

"But that's over already."

"Oh yes." Her responses were cautious now; she likely sensed uncertainty about my reactions. I hadn't let out a whoop of joy; that's for sure.

"So if I wanted to get in touch with him, would that be possible?"

The woman pondered this. "Such information wouldn't be in our system. But the parole officer might have records."

I waited while she researched this. A moment later I had a phone number, along with her apology for the reality that many such personnel operated in a rather freelance way. "Such officials do not always have offices within the system."

I went out behind the building; next to the parking lot was a bus stop where a few commuters were taking refuge from the mid-morning sun. Despite this being December, Bangkok was unseasonably warm, and I claimed a small corner of the protected bench. I dialed the number and waited for someone to pick up.

"Hello?"

It was a male voice, and I stuttered my request. "I'm back here from America, but thought I would seek to find my biological parent. You handled his case."

It took him a moment, but I gave him the bare details of Dad's arrest for accepting drug shipments from the infamous opium territory in the remote hills of northern Thailand. "Yes, I remember him now," he agreed. "*Kuhn* Anuman."

"Are you still working with him?"

"Oh no," he said quickly. "Two years; that is all."

"But he was doing okay."

"Yes, very well. He is a good man." The parole officer's voice became gentle. "I am sure, miss, that the loss of him was difficult for you. But he served his time without incident. I worked with him to get back into the travel industry: arranging guides and so forth. He swore to me–I remember this well–that he would never commit such an error again."

I listened to all this with mixed emotions. For more than a decade, I'd pushed away all happy memories. Dad was a jailhouse convict. His blunders had been costly, leaving me in the hands of a callous monster. I'd not thought about him in anything beyond those wildly aggrieved terms.

"Would you still have any point of contact with him?" I asked, trying to sound hopeful but not succeeding.

"I know he was with an agency dealing with NGOs," he said, a tidbit which surprised me. "You know, wealthy American groups that wish to provide aid in Asia to children with HIV infections and so forth."

"Really?"

"Yes. But the employers he had went out of business. I recall hearing this."

"So where would my father have gone?"

"I cannot imagine. But he seemed very steady. I suppose he is still in Bangkok, doing similar work for another group. That is the most likely expectation."

"Do you have any suggestions?"

He actually chuckled. "My son always says: 'Try

Facebook.' If you type in a person's name, more than
half of all attempts lead to a hit."

I said nothing. Truth be told, I'd actually done that
before leaving Portland. But nothing came up. The other
possibility would have been to type in my uncle's name
and see if somehow he had eluded justice and was still
operating in some shadowy enterprise. Of course, any
such temptation was fleeting indeed.

"Thanks very much," I said to my benefactor, trying
to sound appreciative. "It's good to know that he came
out well and is hopefully all right."

There was a pause. "It seems you are prospering,
miss. It must have been hard to lose your father for so
many years."

You have no idea, my friend. "God has offered me
many blessings," I told him, meaning it. "A Christian
family in America adopted me and gave me a wonderful
life. I have a beautiful sister, and we are together
spending one year back in Thailand serving at Bangkok
Christian School."

"Excellent." The line crackled and then he
admitted: "I have heard of your school, actually. My
sister's boy is in *Prathom* Five."

"What's his name?"

"Chawat."

"I see." I explained that the school had well over a
thousand pupils, and I was assigned to the calculus
classes in *Matthayom* Six. "But my aunt teaches one
grade above where Chawat is. I'll ask her if she's
noticed him."

He said goodbye, and I sat there at the bus stop for
several minutes, reflecting on the fact that in this
teeming corner of Asia, I still had a Thai father who got

up each day, washed his face, ate some breakfast, and then went to work and functioned and earned a living just as before. Dad had always been clever; of course, being too clever had been his downfall. But it was a reasonable bet he was doing moderately okay, and wasn't sleeping behind a shed somewhere down by the Chao Phraya River.

EIGHTEEN

The guy did have an address to offer me, warning me as he read it out over the phone that parolees tended to move around quite a bit, especially once their mandated time of supervision is over. "I do not know, *Kuhn* Pranom, if your father is still even in Bangkok. But you can try."

I didn't want to go alone, so Khemkaeng graciously volunteered to drive me. We gossiped about his house bulging over with guests and the excitement over the new baby. "Are you excited to be an uncle again?" I asked him. "I mean, an uncle for real?" Going back to Paloma's first sojourn here in Bangkok, she'd always called him "Uncle Khemkaeng" and shamelessly exploited the moniker to wheedle ice cream treats out of him.

"Well, with Tiang's little girl, Esther, I am an uncle three times now."

"Right. I forgot."

The address I showed him was difficult to find, and

I felt chagrin when the drive stretched out to forty-five minutes. But he had cheerful Christmas music flowing through the car stereo, and we finally found a sagging apartment complex. Khemkaeng followed me up to the second floor, and I could feel my pulse skipping around. But when we knocked, a tired-looking woman came to answer. She had a cigarette going and was on a cell phone tucked up against her cheek, and shook her head when I asked about my dad. "No one like that lives around here," she said, juggling the two conversations at once. "I have been here for more than a year. And the person before me was an old man. I think he went to a Buddhist rest home."

I thanked her and actually felt a stab of relief. It was just easier this way; I'd put all thoughts and memories of my former life away, be always grateful to the Lord for Mr. Tommy Daggett, and now pour myself into romancing Saman.

Khemkaeng nodded as I shared my ebbing anxieties. "Of course," he soothed. "This man has been out of your experience for more than a decade. And Tommy is a wonderful father, I know."

"That's for sure."

He confided that Rachel Marie was trying to bribe Paloma to do some Christmas Eve babysitting. "My parents have a favorite restaurant here in Bangkok. Quite expensive, but they enjoy taking us. Natty, of course, will be home with the baby."

I shrugged, feeling relaxed in the passenger seat of my uncle's fairly new Honda. "Saman and I haven't set up a date or anything, but maybe we'll go out that night too. I know we're going to do some shopping Christmas day and maybe catch that new car-chase movie all the kids are talking about."

Saman responded eagerly when I sent him a text message. *Perfect! I'd love spending Christmas Eve with you, babe. My folks are at a concert so don't have any expectations.* I thumbed in a quick offer. *I could make you dinner. Or would you rather have some Christmas Eve flavor at a restaurant.*

Moments later my phone dinged. "Where could we go that would even have a Christmas tree?"

"Probably one of the better hotel buffets."

"True." I heard him say something to his assistant, then he came back on. "You know what? I haven't had the chance of trying out your cooking. Are you any good?"

"Just okay," I admitted. "But that would give me a chance to see where you live."

There was a comedic pause, and he went *ummmm.* Then laughed. "You'll be surprised at how Spartan it is."

"Really?" Extrapolating from his office suite and that sexy car he drove, I'd always figured he had a sumptuous bachelor pad overlooking the river, with a uniformed guard letting only the most well-heeled visitors in and out.

Bangkok has its share of gourmet supermarkets; there are a few you honestly could mistake for a Trader Joe's. Saman followed me around, wheeling the cart for me, and we enjoyed teasing banter over one pricy goodie after another. "This is going to melt your credit card," I warned, wincing as I eyed the sticker price on some of the prepackaged desserts.

"Yes, but Christmas only comes once a year."

"It's your dime."

He nudged me toward a decadent array of imported

pastas, all boasting cheese trimmings directly from the hillsides of Italian farms. "Make that 'it's your three hundred baht.' Holy cow, Saman."

The beverage section had a French drink bottled almost like a Martinelli's back home, one of Dad's indulgences. "This stuff is pretty good."

He plopped a pair of them into the cart. "I actually have the real thing at the apartment," he admitted.

I shrugged. "I don't drink, though. So these will be nice to have."

I hadn't seen a single slice of cheesecake since arriving in Asia, but hey, this place had four kinds. I drooled over each of them, bouncing up and down and moaning in the throes of indecision. He teasingly took my hands, led me to the caramel one, and together we lifted the heavenly gift to the top of the growing pile of Yuletide pleasantries.

"That had better be all," I warned. "Even if you can afford it, there's enough in here to make me add five pounds."

Mid-afternoon traffic was light and I gave my sister a quick phone call as we loitered at the Victory Monument. "Are you there yet?"

"Yeah. Aroon and all them just headed out. I'm playing a game with Gage."

"Are the folks nice?"

"They seem great. The mom brought presents for you and me."

"You're kidding."

"Says we're all family."

"Tell them thanks when they get back."

"Sure. You guys have fun."

I suspected Paloma still harbored reservations about

Saman, but was gracious enough to not say so. I hung up and sighed contentedly. "She's so awesome."

He grinned. "The two of you are really the prettiest ladies in all Thailand; that's for sure."

"She's cute, isn't she?"

"You've got her beat, but it's close." I reached over and slapped his hand.

In a way, though, he was right. About Spartan, that is. When we got to the apartment complex, it was a rather ordinary four-story structure across the street from a smallish strip mall. Older-model cars filled up the parking lot and there was a convenience store/gas station adjacent to the property. I could see a swimming pool shielded by an iron-bar fence, but no one was anywhere near the brackish water, and the sign out front was dimly lit.

I tried to mask my dismay but he must have noticed because he gave his characteristic shrug. "I know what you're thinking. Pretty lame, isn't it?"

"Well, I mean . . ." I was kind of sputtering, but then nodded. "Yeah. It's not as shiny as that gorgeous office of yours."

He picked up the two largest grocery bags and nudged me toward the smallest one. "Can you grab that?"

At least there was an elevator, and we rode in silence up to the third floor. As we went down the concrete walkway, arms beginning to grow heavy, he explained. "See, my practice is still kind of new. And when I got out of med school, man, it was a mountain of debt. All U.S. prices, see? I've got ugly school loans still going. Dad said he'd be okay with helping me with a down payment if I wanted to buy a place, but for at least the next two years, I really wouldn't be able to swing the mortgage that would come with it."

"It's okay," I assured him. "You should see our tiny apartment. I mean, really. Paloma and I can hardly fit in the kitchen at the same time together."

He had to fumble, trying to manage the grocery bag along with his apartment keys, but when he pushed the door open, I felt a cheering glow of relief. At least the interior was pleasant and all kept up properly. The hallway opened into a decent-size living room, with facing couches and an ornate coffee table down the middle. He had an impressive bookcase along the interior wall, although most of his books appeared to be medical texts. There was some nature art arranged in an intriguing spiral motif; most of the framed photos seemed rather European: mountainous Alps, castles, scenic lakes. "Did you do all these?"

He shrugged. "Mom's good with that kind of stuff. A few of these my sister paid for as a going-away gift."

"Pretty nice." I wondered idly if his former *fan* had her fingerprints on any of the furnishings, but pushed the alien thought to the side.

Most Bangkok apartments have abbreviated kitchens, and his was no exception. But I began organizing our private banquet-for-two: stirring up the sauce for our pasta, shredding a pair of carrots for our salad. "I haven't had ranch dressing in a long time," I told him, my appetite already beginning to bubble over.

Saman watched, fascinated, as I whizzed the mashed potatoes into submission and set the microwave timer. "This is really nice."

"I know."

I'd almost forgotten about the Asian Martinelli's,

but then spotted the pair of bottles still leaning against the supporting pillar separating the kitchen from the common area. "Could you hand me those? I should get them chilling in the fridge."

He slid them across the counter and I found a spot for them next to a loaf of bread. Toward the back I did spot a bottle of what looked like inexpensive wine. Mom and Dad didn't drink, thankfully, and I'd actually never once experimented with alcohol in any form. "What kind of wine can people buy out here in Thailand?" I wanted to know.

"Oh, I guess all kinds." He made a deprecating gesture. "I'm really not into it, so please don't fret. I think that bottle's been holding down that spot since July." I grinned, enjoying the pleasant banter and the homey feeling of sharing a kitchen with this gracious gentleman.

The aromas of our coalescing dinner began to awaken our appetites, and I scolded Saman when he began nibbling out of a small bag of roasted peanuts we grabbed at the checkout counter. "Spoil your dinner."

"No, I swear it."

"You could set the table," I suggested. "And use the good china."

"Uh, about the expensive china . . ."

At least it wasn't paper plates. He did have an okay collection of six: plates, salad bowls, side plates for dessert. He got up on tiptoes and pulled out a pair of elegant wine glasses. I watched as he poured out a generous offering of the apple cider for me, and then, after a moment of hesitation, fished out the wine and filled his own glass to the halfway point.

Just before eating, Saman came around to the other

side of the kitchen island, and took my hand in his. "What?"

"Just this." He put his hand on my shoulder, and pulled me close for a kiss. It was intoxicating sharing this nice moment with him, and I flushed happily. "Merry Christmas, my beautiful friend," he murmured, kissing me again.

I returned the gesture, then added a spunky peck on the cheek. "Enough of that," I decreed. Then added a coy: "For now." He brightened noticeably.

Saman pulled out my chair and gestured grandly. "Please, my lady. Grace my table with your delectable presence."

That sounded very un-Thai, and I giggled, giving him yet another kiss on the cheek. "*Kop kuhn kah.*"

He agreeably held my hand as I said grace. "Lord God, we're remembering that this is your Son's birthday, and today we honor him and thank you for sending him to die for our sins. Thank you for this amazing meal, and the blessing that we have the means to enjoy it. Thanks for our friendship and please always guide and protect us. Amen."

"That's very nice," he said quickly, and I could tell he meant it. Then, looking at the array of menu options, asked me, "What can I pass you?"

"It's only the two of us," I responded. "Let's just dig in and eat."

The string beans were absolutely divine, if I say so myself. Maybe a bit on the buttery side, but it was a decadent Christmas privilege, along with the pasta and berry Jell-o. Saman sipped carefully at his wine, and made sure my own glass was filled.

"You actually ought to try this Thai wine," he said

at last. "Not to corrupt you in any way, but it's sur-
prisingly nice. And boy, does it go with your mashed
potatoes."

I peered at the dancing red liquid, so sparkling and
intriguing in his glass. "Never have had a sip."

"Sure, but take just a taste to see if you like it." He
nudged his own glass in my direction.

The liquid was cool on my tongue, and I held it
there for a long moment. "You like it?"

"I don't know," I admitted. "I mean, it hardly tastes
different from other things I've had. There's really
alcohol in that?"

"Not very much. But some wines leave a funny
taste in your mouth all evening, and this is really better
than I remembered."

I had just one more sip, and then passed his glass
back to him. "I better not have any more."

We'd picked up a small jar of really crunchy
American peanut butter, and I scooped an obscene glob
of it to put on my hot buttered roll. "Oh yeah," I sighed
in dramatic contentment. "That is just way amazing."

He grinned, then went over to the stereo to change
CDs. "I've got some great old stuff my American
brother-in-law gave me," he called out. "Frank Sinatra
holiday songs. Want to hear them?"

"Sure." While he was fishing through his collection,
I did take just one more cautious sip of his wine,
admitting to myself there was a cheering glow that came
with the samples. I felt bright and relaxed and happy and
wonderfully pleased that our evening together was
unfolding in such elegant fashion.

The cheesecake was all that my imagination had
promised and more. "Wow, that's yummy," I gushed. "I

don't want to beg, but you'd better send me home with a second slice for later. Plus one for Paloma. She'd die for some of this."

"Glad you like it."

I motioned toward his wine bottle. "Just pour, like, an inch into my glass. It's actually not bad."

"Yes, my lady."

We had seconds on the cheesecake, for sure, and every few moments he reached over and kissed my hand again. The ambience there in his dining room was intimate, warm, very much a Christmas-Eve-for-two. Saman cracked jokes, mimicking Thai friends who mangled their attempts at English, and I found his humor endearing. I certainly wasn't tipsy, but the repeated dribs and drabs of his offered Thai wine had warmed my blood, and I found myself slipping into the magnetic circle of my boyfriend's charms.

"Just leave the dishes for later," he instructed, as we polished off our last shared piece of caramel cheesecake. "I'll get to it tomorrow."

He led me by the hand over to the sofa, and we nestled there together as Sinatra brought out his good friend Bing Crosby to sing about a white Christmas and all the American GIs serving the cause of liberty around the globe. "Must have been World War II," I mused, remembering my high school history classes from Portland. A moment later, I took a chance and rested my head against his shoulder, and a whisper of his cologne filled my senses. *Nice.*

We kept chatting, about school and UCC and that divine water park and when could we go again, and whenever I had to answer a question or tease him with a girlish quip, that made me lift my head, give him a flirty look, and then ease right back into that so-comforting position. A couple of times, he did kiss the top of my head and call me "Sugar Pie," which sounded corny coming from a Thai guy, but I was definitely in no mood to quibble.

After the oldies Christmas CD wound itself down, though, I extricated myself and got to my feet. "I need a quick trip down the hall."

"Oh. Right there." He pointed. "I'll miss you."

"You're sweet."

When I reemerged, he wasn't there, but I heard him scuffling around for something down in the bedroom. "Where'd you go?" I called out.

"Just over here."

I followed the sound, and saw Saman coming out of his miniature walk-in closet. "What have you got there?"

It was an elegantly wrapped gift, and the paper actually had reindeer and snowflakes. "It's nothing."

"But I didn't get you anything," I half-wailed.

"Don't worry about it. I just . . . you know, I'm working at Paragon day after day. There's stuff on sale all the time."

I plopped myself down on the edge of his queen-sized bed and tore gaily at the wrapping paper. "You wrap this yourself?"

"Are you kidding? The salesgirl at the store did it for just twenty baht."

"Pretty nice."

I slid my thumbnail along the edge to undo the Scotch tape, and then gasped. It was an embroidered blouse, obviously handstitched, with the most exquisite silk fabric I'd ever touched. It felt slippery and deliciously decadent, and I sprang up and held it in front of myself, peering at the image in the mirror. "Oh, sweetie, it's gorgeous! I love it!"

He was nothing but gallant. "It'll look even better on you, I'll bet."

I hesitated. "Only one way to find out."

"I could close my eyes," he offered.

I responded by sticking my tongue out. "Just step aside and prepare yourself." He grinned as I brushed past him and into the bathroom. I eased out of my own top, and carefully buttoned his Yuletide gift. It clung to me and gave me a delicious feeling of being, I don't know, *curvaceous*.

"Ready?" I called out.

"Both eyeballs prepared."

I made my debut, and his grin was enthusiastically male. "Wow! I'd say I got my money's worth."

"Well, I'm going to make sure of that." I eased myself into his arms, and offered up a kiss that could only be described as generous. "Merry Christmas, Dr. Takuathung. Your girlfriend adores her present."

"Mmm." There was another kiss, this one initiated by him, and it didn't surprise me when it grew both moist and lingering. The lighting was soft in his room, and I felt both desirable and cheerfully helpless in Saman's embrace. Being in his arms, clad in his generous, perfect-fitting gift, it was a giddy, spontaneous moment. Looking back later, I guess my guard was down . . . not that my friend had anything sinister in mind. We'd simply wandered into a trap, and I didn't realize it.

"You really do look amazing, baby," he murmured, his voice husky now. He pulled back for a moment and eyed my form with appraising hunger. "That's the best money I've spent in months."

He kissed me again, and now his affections began to have purpose and a direction to them. Saman pulled me closer, one hand around the back of my neck, and instead of several kisses it was now just one that went on . . . and on . . .

"I think the BCS employee handbook has something to say about moments like these," I managed, my pulse rate hammering wildly now.

"It's Christmas Eve." He grinned for just a second, the same cocksure smile that made me weak in the knees, and then kissed me once more. There was some noticeable body heat between us now, and even as the bedroom AC hummed and tried to intervene, I was starting to sense all of his *body*, his form, his insistent maleness beginning to press against me.

And I was enjoying the sensations, the pleasure of knowing a guy like this thought I was desirable. Saman traced his hand along my cheek as we continued to kiss with increasing abandon. "Baby, you're just so very beautiful."

"Mmm." I was getting near to some kind of tipping point, but pulled away long enough to manage something like: "I'm sort of into the way you look too, you know." But the last of it was swallowed up by his return for more kissing, and now these were definitely not the kinds of staid kisses a kid might get from their aunt.

"You being so gorgeous in that blouse made me think of an old line," he blurted out all at once.

I had an idea where he might be going with this, but cast aside my cautions. "What's that?"

"Just . . . it would look even better dropped down on the floor of this bedroom, Miss Pranom Daggett."

There. It was out. Saman and I were necking, passionately exploring each other while standing in the Christmasy seclusion of his bedroom. We had the night to ourselves. Mom and Dad were nine time zones away. Paloma was babysitting the Chaisurivirat kids and fully accounted for these next few delicious hours. No one else was around; there were no prying eyes.

I don't know if he was waiting for some kind of feminine response to his blouse-on-the-floor quip–any kind of green light. But almost without either of us realizing it, we were sitting together on the edge of his bed, our hands still stroking, touching, exploring, while our tongues and lips were blazing away in a joint adventure.

It was delicious and wanton and I suppose now that I think about it, there is such a thing as wine having an impact on a woman's safeguards and inhibitions. But I felt his fingers at the top button of my luscious silk blouse, his hundred-dollar present on Christmas Eve, the one with my name on the package, and I didn't protest. I could feel the movement of his fingers running down along the fabric, one button after the other coming undone, and the fabric slowly, gently separating. Saman pulled away just long enough to gaze down and verbally drink in what was there to see. I didn't recall anything at all about what bra I'd fished out of the drawer that morning as Paloma and I gossiped about Klahan's new haircut. But at this unguarded moment, my boyfriend and hoping-to-be lover was basking in whatever visual joy men get when a woman's top begins to head for the carpeting.

I sank down onto the coverlet of his bed, still not protesting. The kisses continued as his hands began to roam exactly where I hoped they would. But as our foreplay continued, all at once it began to be this *thing* in my brain. I didn't intend it; all my female impulses guarded and hastily regrouped. Yet the ideas were there and I had to begin to both kiss and morally formulate at the same time.

Because I wanted to do this thing. I really did. I wanted to have this go right on down the road and to the sweet, glorious finish line. Already I could tell that my necessary body parts were responding, getting ready for Saman to finish disrobing me and then himself. The delicate mechanism my creative Lord had designed for a man and woman's shared coupling were intact and ready to function even before we exchanged "I do's."

And yet as my brassiere came off and he carefully dropped it off the side of the bed, I knew I would have to fend off a host of Pattaya memories. There were so many other men before Saman; scores of them had seen me wearing less than this. Men young and old, some clumsy and others brutish, had run their fingers over my nipples for just that brief detour before getting down to business and getting what their fifteen hundred baht had purchased for them.

So when Saman's gentle fingers traced along that same coveted prize, I had to squint and push away the recollections. That one Chinese businessman, obscenely overweight, who had spent too long there, muttering to himself in a foreign dialect. A high school boy losing his virginity on a dare, gaping at me with foolish fascination. Always it was the same, though: no one knew I was Pranom, a schoolgirl with dreams and feelings of my own. No, it was always the same: gawk at the boobs, feel them for twenty seconds, then move south and get this thing done.

Even as my thoughts thudded back and forth between that damned nightclub by the beach and this still-sweet Christmas Eve with a good-hearted doctor, now with his shirt tossed over to that chair by the TV, I was responding to Saman's kisses. His hands were gentle, still, not abusive or possessive. But they were occupying those same places on the map of old, and as his right hand slowly slid down and began to push at the fabric of my silk panties, I felt a rancid lump come into my throat. It got there and wouldn't leave.

Because there was this also. *I wanted to please Jesus! Jesus Christ was my newly chosen Lord!* I wanted to make love with Saman, yes; I was fully and agonizingly aware of my feminine impulses and built-in wanton nature. But now I was facing an impossible maze, like a long, black corridor in a House of Horrors, narrowing as one lurched along the damp floorboards and hoping for some exit in the murky future. There was Pattaya and those ghouls; on the other side, I had to keep my brain away from any visions of Calvary and Tommy Daggett's praise songs about beautiful Savior and my cherished Christian hopes about a honeymoon night.

Down the middle was the safe place to be. Here. Now. Saman and me. I had no idea how fulfilling it would finally be when we were joined together and fully in the throes of lovemaking. But I could never truly experience it unless I could keep my quivering thoughts down the center of that hallway. Not this way . . . not that way either . . . careful, girl, broken glass everywhere, you're overcorrecting now, *bump, crash!*

Saman just about had me all the way unclothed when all at once it hit me. What was happening was impossible tonight, and maybe impossible forever. Even if he were to become my husband and we could head to a honeymoon night blessed by the vows written and delivered by Pastor Gino Carington and witnessed by Paloma-Maid-of-Honor, there was still Pattaya. How could I ever experience and share a genuine sexual climax with this generous friend, even as a husband, as long as my mind and collective nerve endings were all occupied and forever fried by the sordid memories of that Greek male flight attendant who slapped me around a dimly lit hotel room, called me an ugly bitch, and then raped me from behind?

I was trying to hold my quivering soul in that center crevice of safety, when an equally toxic third guardrail slammed into the frame. *We don't have a condom! I'm not protected; Saman didn't plan for this either . . . is this an okay time of the month?* A hundred lurid folktales from the dingy "short-time" motel rooms of Pattaya Beach sprang to my mind, and in less time than it takes to turn off the purring engine of my boyfriend's Mercedes-Benz, I felt my body absolutely seizing up. The motor was conked and about to sputter over to the shoulder of the highway.

Overwhelmed and confused, I didn't know what to do except push him away. Not intending to, I burst into tears and snatched up my underclothes. "Sorry," I sobbed, my voice clotted and ashamed. "I'm so sorry. It's like I led you on, Saman. But I can't do any of this."

He sprang up from the bed and tried to step toward me, but I pushed up a hand, not threatening but simply to protect what space I had left. "I can't tell you," I wailed. "Swear to God, I can't tell you. Believe me, it's not you. But I'm totally messed up and we're not going to be able to do this."

"What do you mean?"

"Just . . . I'm sorry." I picked up the now forlorn blue blouse and carefully set it on his dresser. "I probably shouldn't even take this." I went over to the bathroom, found my own top, and tugged it on over my head. "I don't even know what to say except sorry that I ruined your Christmas."

"Honey, honey, honey." He was babbling help-lessly, now hastily buttoning his own shirt, and I could tell his own reaction was more confusion than indig-nation. *He probably thinks it's some idiotic Christian impulse,* I thought, my scorched memories still madly crashing into each other. "Look, I'll just get a cab."

"Don't be . . ." I don't know what word he had in mind to finish that sentence, but he wisely bit it off. "You're my friend and I'll take you home, honey."

NINETEEN

It was a hellish ride back to the apartment. Saman, his hair mussed, was genuinely confused and, I suppose, resentful over my whimpering. His expensive Dolby stereo had gone dark, and I felt assaulted by the grim silence between us. At every traffic light, I could tell questions were trembling at his lips, but I held up my hand, pushing him away, and I guess he managed to choke them back. A block from home, he did manage to say: "Look, Pranom. I guess you've got something really big to work out. But I care about you; I really do. Even if we can't be, you know, together, I hope someday you can tell me. And get things worked out. I'll always be your friend."

That, at least, was generous. I refused to let him walk me up the flights of stairs, and he numbly accepted the hollow goodbye.

Some Christmas Eve. My eyes puddled with tears again and it took me almost half a minute to find my apartment key. In the reflection off the glass window, I could barely make out the red taillights of his luxury car as Dr. Saman Takuathung backed out of my life.

I pushed the door open, and to my amazement, Rachel Marie was there with my sister. They were nibbling on a shared bit of Thai *kanom*, giggling through the sugary treat, and both gazed at me in surprise. "Sweetie, oh no! What's wrong? What happened?"

In that exact moment, my quivering soul was transported back to the beach and the night Dad came to the club and rescued me. I recalled with absolute clarity the white bikini, me stumbling out of the go-go club with Tommy Daggett's arm around me. "Just say nothing," he had murmured. "Just look like this is any other night. I'm a regular guy with a bucket of money. Thirty more seconds, Pranom, and you'll be free, sweetheart. I promise."

We'd collapsed into the back seat of Uncle Khemkaeng's chauffeured car, me sitting next to the Bangkok Christian School choir director, relieved and yet so embarrassed that a faculty member had just seen me topless. But he was already gently enfolding me in a man's long-sleeve shirt, murmuring that I was safe now, that my friends would take care of me.

And then the priceless moment of redemption when he opened up the door to that Christian doctor's beach house and I saw John and Marilyn Garvey leaping up from their seats, arms outstretched. And Samantha Kidd, who wasn't my mom yet, but just this gangly math teacher from the *Matthayom* level. I'd seen her in the food court a few times and offered up a shy earliteen smile.

But the moment I saw Rachel Marie, my teacher from the previous year, all the agonies and abuses had melted away into my dash to a savior's embrace. I remembered with icy precision my heartrending scream. "Oh, Missie Stone!" And then bursting into tears, into gut-heaving sobs that felt endless.

Now, more than a decade later, it was still her. My teacher, whose own face was melting as she saw my tears. "Oh, kid! Oh, honey! What happened? Did your friend . . . oh, dear God, what?"

And I couldn't even make it to the couch. I fell to my knees, sobbing there on the floor next to the lampstand, and then onto the rug, pounding my fist into the carpeting over and over. "Goddammit! Oh, God! Dammit! Dammit! Dammit! Jesus, get me out of this place!"

Above me I could hear my sister screaming an obscenity. "Pranom, what?" The two of them hovered over me, watching helplessly as I sobbed out my rage.

It took a couple minutes for them to get me to my feet and then to my bedroom, where I collapsed into my aunt's arms. "Okay, baby," she murmured, stroking my hair. "Something terrible. But we're here and we love you, and I won't leave until I at least hear it all."

I wanted to tell them, but for the moment my chest was heaving and I couldn't stop sniffling. Twice I tried to get some words out, but they wouldn't come, and I pushed away the impulse to run to the bathroom and heave my guts up.

Paloma brought me a drink of water, and I took careful sips, so thankful to have Rachel Marie's arm around my shoulders. Maybe she guessed what had happened; I mean, it was actually a rather predictable story plot. But nothing in the world, nothing any of the three of us could have imagined, matched the torrent of memories I spilled out into that third-story apartment on

Christmas Eve of one year ago.

My little sister, who knew absolutely squat, zero, nothing, about my former life as a kid hooker, sat on the edge of the bed, white-faced and in total shock, as I dumped the river of sewage right in her lap. I told the entire tale, beginning with tonight's exploded tryst with Saman. And then back in time to the horrors of a decade earlier: how my uncle had tricked me into going to the club overlooking the beach. His smooth stories about maybe getting to be in TV films. Making a lot of money. Why, the minute I was eighteen, he was sure I would already have my own car. I'd be signing autographs at fairs, maybe singing at wedding karaoke parties. Wouldn't my dad be surprised when he finished his prison term and came out to find out that his own daughter had earned him a four-bedroom house in the suburbs north of Bangkok?

Instead, there had been this endless and immediate lineup of men. Men with leers and men with perverse appetites. Men who could come at me three times for one low price. Men who got off on violence. Men who went limp in the motel room and vented their rage by breaking a window or slapping my cheek until welts formed and I had to take two nights off. There were nights when I entertained seven or eight men in succession and nights when one hateful foreigner would roam my weary body until the sun came up over the ocean water, titillating their selfish own selves and saying not a word to me, never noticing that I had lips that might form words and a mind that could think and a heart that was most certainly breaking into small, unfixable pieces.

"My first week there, the lady at the club took me

into the restroom and gave me this tube of stuff," I said now, in a voice almost corpse-like. "And I was so stupid, I stared at her. Like: 'What's this for?' And she said if I needed it, 'cause of course, I was probably too young to ever get slippery down there, the way men liked, well, I could wait till they weren't looking, and then put in a dab."

"Dammit!" Paloma spat out. "Auntie Rachel, my God, weren't you guys there? How did something like this happen to my sister?"

"We just didn't know," Rachel Marie admitted, then looked at me. "One week you were at school; the next you stopped coming. And I guess with such a big school, we didn't follow it up like we should have."

I was about to spill out some more when my aunt held up a hand. "Shhh," she managed, her own eyes red-rimmed with tears. "Sweetheart, I'm so sorry you had to tell us all this."

The tears began to hit me again, and even as she held my head against her shoulder, Rachel Marie fished out her cell phone and pushed the first number on her list. I could barely hear Uncle Khemkaeng's voice on the other end. Rachel Marie said in a careful voice: "Honey, the folks are there, aren't they?"

I couldn't hear his response, but she went on quickly. "We need you over here. Right now."

"No, it's okay," I managed, feeling ashamed, but she put up her hand with authority. "Shush, sweetheart. We love you and this is important."

Paloma brought me a slice of bread with jam on it; I was oddly thankful it wasn't peanut butter, because that would have brought back a tangled host of Saman memories. I ate slowly, wordlessly, thankful for the presence of these dear family members, and marveling that even though I was Thai and Rachel Marie was an American lady with zero shared DNA, my love for her was deeper than *family*. She held my hand now, her fingers laced with my own, and it was like heaven holding me fast. Like angels embracing me.

There was a tap on the door, and Paloma went over to open it. Khemkaeng came into the room, and somehow just knew. He saw my face and there must have been a wordless flow of my broken biography going between his wife and his own perceptive soul. He embraced me in a hug, my shoulders shaking against his upper chest, and he said how sorry he was.

I couldn't speak, so Rachel Marie told him briefly how I'd been on a date with Saman. "Things went a little farther than she meant, and sure, that happens to a lot of us. So we won't think about that. But then it brought back all these memories and she just, you know, needs for her family to love her and be with her."

I honestly don't know if Aunt Rachel had ever seen her husband cry. And it was only for a few seconds; his demeanor crumpled and he put a fist up to his face, clenching it hard. But then he regained his composure. "Listen to me, Pranom," he said, choosing his words carefully. "I cannot say that I understand. No man could fully grasp how deep your hurt cut into you. But the one thing I can say, at least I know is true. Jesus is so mighty. For a long time I didn't know it. But your aunt came to BCS and helped me to learn it. Jesus is mighty beyond the worst things than can stab at us. Tonight, right now, he is nowhere more than here. In this apartment." He glanced around for a moment as if to remind us all that Apartment #305 was the place of other healings and other reborn dreams.

"Someday," he told me, peace radiating from him to me with every word he chose, "someday, Pranom, you will live in the fullest experience of God's gift of marriage. Sometimes we break God's gifts, but they are never given to us broken or damaged. This I can promise. You will be married one day; God is telling me this. You will love a man, and he will love you. And when that time comes, you will see that the healing in your heart, the erasing of Pattaya Beach, will be finished. You will be all well, and your sister and your auntie and I, we will be so happy to share in your happiness."

AFTER EVERYONE DRIED their tears, Uncle Khemkaeng agreed his wife should stay the rest of the night with us. Paloma dug out a T-shirt she could borrow as pajamas, and Khemkaeng embraced all three of us in turn, awkwardly patting my cheek before letting me go. "You are a very special part of my family," he assured me. "And tomorrow will still be a wonderful day."

I'd completely forgotten that, now at one in the morning, we had staggered into Christmas Day. But in a way, the thought of Christ being born into the epicenter of our world's hurts and griefs, intent on rescuing lost girls just like me . . . I felt a quiet slice of peace nudging into my heart.

Paloma tugged me over toward her own bed, and we huddled together in the darkness, her soft breathing right next to my shoulder. "Sure love you, sis," she murmured. "I mean, I for sure do. You're so amazing. And this'll all be good someday."

"I know."

Rachel Marie was already asleep in the other twin bed, and I could barely make out her form outlined in the silent moonlight creeping in through the overhead window. My aunt had her own scars measuring the cruelty of Bangkok, and it helped for me to ponder the fullness of how God had healed her and then rearmed her as one of his foremost ambassadors in this faraway kingdom.

I was just getting drowsy, trying to let my grief seep out into the mattress, when I picked up this faint message. *He accepts you at your worst, when he is hoping for the best. Jesus loves you–Jesus loves you. He will never ever leave, and he will never ever forsake. Jesus loves you–Jesus loves you.*

It was my kid sister, murmuring and half-singing the Daggett theme song we'd all picked up and embraced from our adopted dad. It was on Samantha's debut weekend in Bangkok, her confusion and self-loathing awash in a pity party of jet lag, when a bearded keyboard player peered out over the Asian congregation and began to sing about healing.

All Paloma's DNA came from the tone-deaf side of the family tree, but nothing had ever sounded so sweet, so guaranteed, as her spotty rendition of Mom's favorite praise song. *He is proud of who you are and he has faith in who you'll become. He's not like us. He loves you just because.*

I felt a lump come into my throat, and I reached my right hand around behind me, until I found my sister's and squeezed it hard. "I love you, kid," I managed, trying to not awaken Rachel Marie. "Thanks for saving me, okay?"

"Yeah." There was a pause to her soulful offering; I

236 DAVID B. SMITH

could feel her lips pressing against my shoulder, and a moment later I knew she was overcome and crying again, her own frame shaking. The chorus went to a higher note, and she couldn't quite get there, the words wobbly but oh so perfect for this awful, sweet moment. *Brokenhearted, do you want your healing?* Paloma hugged me close to her, kissing my shoulder again, and added in a choked alto rich with promise: *Trust again, there is love in his right hand.*

OUR CHRISTMAS DINNER was back over at Khemkaeng's place, and it felt nice to be surrounded by a hubbub of holiday energy. I still had this empty, unwashed feeling, kind of like when you pull an all-nighter with a close friend at Urgent Care, and are behind on sleep. And yeah, my nerves were shot and my eyes red from crying. Still, though, it was Christmas afternoon and I was surrounded by some of this planet's most heroic friends. My adopted relatives even had a decorated three-foot fake tree there in the living room, and I felt cheered playing scootball with Katrina and accepting her gummy kisses.

"What's my name?" I prompted, forcing myself to smile.

"Aunt Pranom," she lisped, proud of herself.

"Well, not exactly your auntie," I confessed, still enjoying the sound of it. "But I love you just as much as if I was."

"Daddy give me presents."

"They didn't come from Santa Claus?"

She looked confused, her eyes glancing up to the ceiling as if to look for reindeer tracks along the stucco. "Huh uh. Daddy got it."

"Pretty nice." She had a stuffed animal that looked like a knockoff item from *Lion King*. I showed her how to squeeze it around the abdomen, and a mild roar came from the toy's digital bowels. "It's not going to bite you, is it?"

Already she knew how to feign horror. Then cackled merrily: "He's a nice lion. He doesn't eat girls."

"Well, very good. Especially on Christmas."

We sat down around a crowded table supplemented with two flimsy card tables erected on each side. Aroon, the family patriarch, thanked each of us for coming and declared himself the most fortunate man in all Thailand. "I believe God has blessed me in a fine way," he admitted. "Look at how many grandchildren I have! Five! And maybe some more soon." He eyed Tiang, his older daughter, with a teasing expression, and her husband guffawed. "No more babies for a long time!"

The older man's kindly gaze fell on Paloma and me, and I wondered how much he knew of our scarlet confessional the evening before. "And this is so nice to have cousins here with us," he added brightly. "Pranom and Paloma, we love you also. Pakpao and I are very happy to be like uncle and auntie to you. Thank you for coming and to celebrate the birth of Jesus with so many Chaisurivirat people."

His wife had spent most of the morning in the kitchen, and the huge bowls of fried rice were delicious; I felt my better nature slowly reviving as we scooped second helpings onto our plates and teased each other for the biggest mango slices. Halfway through the meal, Paloma's cell phone dinged, and she blushed, easing into the kitchen to exchange girlish endearments with her Thai boyfriend.

"Is he coming over here to try and find you under the mistletoe?" I teased.

My sister grinned, and I saw a spot of pink come into her cheeks. "He might come over later and take me out to the movies." She caught herself. "If you don't mind."

"No, I'm good."

There was a rugby game on satellite TV, and I nibbled out of a box of Aroon's fabled candies, enjoying the feeling of baby Kanda nestled in my arms. "She's pretty amazing," I told Natty, reluctant to give him up. "You ready to nurse her again?"

She must have sensed my fragility because she shrugged. "Keep her a bit longer if you like. I could use a break."

I found myself subconsciously counting and timing her shallow, slumbering breaths. *One . . . two . . . three . . .* She gave a tiny hiccup, and peered up at me as if to shift blame, her drooping left eye taking in the Yuletide glow. "Are you a good girl?" I murmured, wondering as I cooed and made a fuss if the Lord would ever heal me to where I could spend a night in my own delivery room, cheerfully huffing and puffing and obeying the OB doc's directive to *push!*

The entire clan, all fifteen of us, did a cheerful loop around the neighborhood, still snacking on goodies from the Chiang Mai candy empire. Natty graciously let Paloma and me take turns with the stroller, little Kanda snuggled up in a pink blanket with tiny elephants chasing each other through the banana plants. Rachel Marie seemed to have made friends with some of her neighbors, and waved affably as we passed them, calling out greetings in her awkward Thai.

Khemkaeng gave us a quick shuttle back to the apartment, our arms filled with comp boxes of his dad's pricy candy. "We won't need to cook for a month," Paloma declared, eyeing the decadent color artwork on the box lids. "Uncle Khemkaeng, this stuff is sinful beyond words." He grinned, then gave me a quiet look.

"No classes till Monday. I hope you both enjoy the rest of our holiday."

"We will." I gave him a grateful peck on the cheek, and he nodded, accepting the gesture. "We will pray each day for you, Pranom."

Halfway up the stairs, my sister's phone did a soft *brrr*, and she paused on the landing, grumbling at the incoming news. "Klahan's family party is running way over, so I guess we're not going to the show. Oh well." She pushed ahead of me. "Maybe there's a Christmas movie on HBO." Our apartment complex did pull in a trio of international networks that mostly ran films with Thai subtitles flickering along the bottom.

I collapsed on my own bed, still with my shoes on, and tugged my pillow around so I could double it over and peer through the bedroom door and see the TV screen. Paloma ran through the English-language channels and brightened when an oldie episode of *Friends* came on. "Let's see this, and then maybe just have a sandwich."

"Not hungry," I sighed, but closed my eyes and let the giggly banter from the television wash past me. I wondered idly about Saman and his Christmas Day spent with his own parents. Had he already regrouped and selected another name from a long file of possible romantic interests? Would he circle back and give his Hawaiian lady friend a second look? What was her name again? I ran through my ABCs until getting to the M's. Melanie. That was it. Assistant manager of a pricy Japanese restaurant in Honolulu. *Why her and not me? Oh well . . .*

I didn't dare allow myself to replay the physicality of my busted Christmas Eve, to recall the touches, that growing delicious *ache*, and then the clogging of my machinery. Would I ever love a man? Ever once in this whole world? I supposed that, yes, I'd make do. Someone would come along. I'd drag myself through enough therapy to push Pattaya to the back of the closet; our married moments of coupling would either satisfy or they wouldn't, but I'd survive and grit my way through. But—*watch out now, Pranom, the flickering pink neon of the beach club is coming into the frame, put on your turn signal and get out of this intersection right quick now*—it was inconceivable that I could ever have any kind of virgin experience, anything climactic and sweet and deliciously unstoppable with a husband, a kindred spirit. After so many men already, no man could ever be a soulmate to Miss Pranom Niratpattanasai.

Being holed up in the bedroom, I didn't hear the gentle knock on the door, but Paloma set down the loaf of bread. "Looks like we got company."

"Tell them to go away," I groaned.

My sister pulled the door open, and there, framed in the doorway, were Pastor Gino and Saman. It wasn't quite dark yet, the December twilight sweet and encouraging as the breezes blew through the leaves of the nearby trees ringing Orchid Garden Apartments. Gino was still wearing the same short-sleeve green T-shirt from our Christmas dinner. Saman had a charcoal suit from our dinner date at the fabled Sheraton buffet:

white shirt, tieless, hair a bit rumpled in the breeze.

Confused, I managed to get myself to a sitting position, still in the bedroom, and Paloma stood her ground. "What . . . what do you guys need?"

When he spoke, Gino was subdued, almost timid. "We both know it's an intrusion," he said apologetically. "That last night was pretty much a bust. But Saman was hoping we could just, you know, do some talking. With your sister."

It was almost the hardest thing I've ever done, but I was able to push myself up onto my feet. The moment felt wobbly; I was confused and disoriented, seeing this maddeningly beautiful man standing there just beyond the borders of Apartment #305. What in the world could he be doing here? What could Dr. Takuathung possibly want with a wreck like me?

"What's . . . what's up?" I managed, hating the feeble waver in my voice. Paloma looked from me to them, and I could sense her blond American temper beginning to gather up and flex its muscles.

Saman held up a hand as if to ward off my sibling's hostility. "Look, Pranom. I feel so bad and ashamed about last night. Things went kind of crazy there, and it's all my fault. But I called up Pastor Gino and asked him if there was any chance he'd come over here with me."

"But how come? I mean, for what? What's the point?" I was babbling my way through my own bleak frustration, and I gave him a wan *what's the use* gesture.

"Can I tell you one thing?" he asked. "Just one thing. I swear it. And then if you and Paloma want us to leave, yeah. We'll go and you won't need to see me again."

What the hell. An aching part deep inside of me was

still infatuated with this beautiful man, and he was being respectfully cautious, still parked on the doorstep and not invading our space.

"Okay," he said, looking down at the carpeting and then back at me. "Look. Pranom Daggett, I'm completely in love with you. I love you just . . . totally. You're all that I want. But I know now that I've got to make a decision about Christianity. That's why I'm here with the pastor. And if you'll let me, I want to hear your story about, you know, last night. What in the world happened. I know it's my fault, and from right now till forever, I'll be just this straightforward guy. I'll guard your purity like it's the king's jewels."

SO MY BABY SISTER and I followed the guys down the steps and into the fragrant twilight of December 25. There was a bare-bones Thai diner, indoor seating but just folding chairs nudged up to unbalanced square tables sticky with the residue from a thousand spilled 7-Up drinks. Saman took charge in his nicely understated way, ordering a pot of white rice and some beef curry. Cokes and a plate of mango slices. There was a clumsy stiffness to the conversation as we waited for the food to arrive; Pastor Gino asked Paloma about her plans after graduation and how were things with Klahan. "He's always invited to church, you know," he assured her. "Keep him coming."

The main course arrived and I allowed Saman to spoon a modest helping onto my plastic pink plate and add a bit of the spicy topping. We exchanged nervous glances back and forth, and Gino eased the tension with his trademark grin. "Oh, all right; I'm the preacher. I'll pray." His grace was simple and heartfelt, thanking Jesus for his Christmas gift of coming to our messed-up world and surrendering his life for our salvation. "And thanks for this food," he prayed. "As we're blessed by your Word, we're also willing for you to sustain our bodies with this delicious rice and curry."

Saman allowed me time to have a few bites, and the topping's savory nutrients did seem to flow right into my digestive system. Then he set down his spoon. "Listen, sweetheart," he began. "I meant what I said up there." He made a head bob toward the street in the general direction of our apartment. "I'm totally in love with you. I really am. And I'd love to earn a place by your side for a really long time. Meaning, you know. Marriage and all that wonderful stuff."

I waited, still dazed and wondering how this could all happen. "Anyway, I lived in the States for a long time. I know a decent amount about Christianity and such. And I told the pastor this afternoon over the phone: 'I see what it's done to the community at UCC. And I want it.'" He reached for my hand and gave it a squeeze. "Sweetheart, I want to be with you. I want to be a man who has confidence and influence like your Uncle Khemkaeng. And if you're willing, we can start right here. Let Pastor begin teaching us. I'll study the whole thing; I'll take as long as you think it needs to take. And in the end, if you think you might be able to fall in love with me, that'd be amazing. If not, well, I want to be a Christian anyway, so it's all good." He did give me his crooked smile, and I felt that same exquisite weakness in my knees that had already floored me so many times before.

"My sister's only here in Thailand five more months," Paloma tried to interject, but the objection died away, and she went back to her plate of rice.

Saman slid his chair closer to mine, and then carefully put his arm around my shoulders. When I didn't object, he said in a voice low and protective: "Listen, honey, I'm so very sorry about last night. It was wrong to make a move like that, and I swear, I didn't invite you over with that idea in mind. But would you still take a chance on me? Tell me what went so wrong? I know it's something huge, but . . ." He glanced at our pastor, and a masculine look passed between them. "Look, if the power of Jesus is all that Pastor preaches about, and that the Bible talks about, then whatever's wrong, I think God can fix it."

It amazed me to hear this suave ophthalmologist talking so openly about the divine invincibility of Christ, and as he made his unpolished pitch for a second chance, I began to sense something truly wondrous. My past memories from Pattaya Beach were just that: *memories*. They had happened; they were real. But those men were gone now, erased from my life. I was a redeemed woman; Jesus loved me and valued me enough to script himself into a story entitled Calvary. He had bled and died to erase those horrid, hateful chapters. Was I really going to spend the remainder of my life in resentful isolation, a bitter spinster endlessly rehearsing her scars and grievances from decades earlier?

It made me think of that floating, aimless piece of wood down at Bangsaen Beach, and also how the moonlight that magical evening had spilled out across the waves, creating a frolicking silver freeway toward a reborn life. Could Pastor Gino minister to us in this unwashed diner with the dilapidated Singha Beer sign up on the wall next to the cash register? Would the spilled blood of my chosen Redeemer be able to drip down and wash away my years of sexual slavery? Then could the Creator of the entire universe step up to his easel, pull me over to stand by his side, and then back up his offer of: "Watch, my child, as I paint a honeymoon celebration you will remember and treasure for ten thousand years"?

With Gino's encouragement, I began to retell my Pattaya story. Paloma had already endured the ride down this sordid road less than twenty-four hours earlier, but I told it again. Although this time I felt something different, something new and strong begin to settle within me. I didn't embellish or sugarcoat the ugly details about anatomy and bruises and missed menstrual periods, about the commiseration of my sisters in the trade. I simply outlined how, for four months, I earned money for a pimp by selling my body night after night in a go-go club. It was terrible; I had endured it; I was now free. I had the most amazing dad in the world: Mr. Tommy Daggett. I also had a heavenly dad who was by my side, embracing me and filling my heart with his eternal, unshakable promises.

"So that's it," I said at last, staring down at the last uneaten bits of rice and curry. "I got myself messed up. And last night it all came back." On an impulse, I reached out and seized my boyfriend's hand. "I don't know if we'd be good with each other. But yes, I love you too. I do." I cast a sisterly look at my kid sister, and her eyes were glowing. "If you want to be a Christian, I'll celebrate like crazy whether or not you decide to stay in love with me. But it'd be awesome to grow together, in church and all that. And then see what God wants to do in both our lives."

"Our lives together," Saman amended, and I flushed happily as he squeezed my hand.

Pastor Gino pumped his fist, and then, with a grand flourish, speared the final slice of mango with his fork and jammed nearly all of it into his mouth, a tropical blast that made all four of us burst into laughter. And it felt so amazing to be bonded together in that moment of shared hilarity. "Here's the deal then," he offered. "Every Thursday night, my friend." He clapped the doctor on the shoulder. "We'll study the Bible together, the three of us." Then he glanced at my kid sister. "Paloma, if you and your boyfriend would like to join us, that'd be a sweet miracle for sure, eh?" Then to Saman: "And I hear you're a man of considerable means, so in whatever restaurant these studies take place, you, my friend, will pick up the check."

Saman nodded eagerly. "Absolutely."

Gino took an extravagant moment to type the new appointment into his phone. Then he tugged off his glasses and rested his kindly gaze directly upon me and my bruised soul. "May I tell you something, Pranom? My sister?"

I nodded, suddenly not trusting myself to speak.

"See, we sing: 'I once was lost but now am found.' And that's me. I was near death and you guys know the story."

Paloma set down her fork, her reddened eyes sober again. All three of us nodded.

"But the Lord Jesus redeeming me from the grave, that's honestly not the big thing. It's not the miracle. Bone marrow and Sue Baines and a six-for-six marker match. I mean, yeah, it's cool and it's stupendous odds.

But that's just Vegas. In Los Angeles, the City of Hope computers put together patients and donors all the time."

I waited, fascinated.

"But the real Calvary miracle is that Christ released me from bondage to hate. See, I was in prison, you guys. To my bitterness and my grudges and my rage against my own dad. That was the poison that was killing me, not the renegade white cells. And when Mom—I mean, 'Mrs. Carington'—baptized me in that hotel swimming pool, I came up out to the water and I just felt this eternal surge of Calvary power. New body, new soul, new heart."

Pastor Gino respectfully set his Bible down, took my hand in his own and held it to his lips in a gesture that was entirely sacred. "The cross of Jesus did that for me, and I promise you, Pranom, it will do the same for you."

TWENTY

So January and February were paradise to me; they honestly were. Saman was like a high school kid; he courted me with unabashed joy, his face lighting up whenever I came into view. If he had a cancellation at the clinic, he would speed over to BCS, crash the front gate and hunt me down in the *Matthayom* crowd, grandly holding my hand and distributing business cards to parents and chauffeurs as they came by.

I loved getting text messages from him; they were pure and eloquent. *Can't stop thinking about you, my beautiful queen*, he declared in flawless Thai one morning. I blushed all the way down to assembly, and Khemkaeng caught my eye and grinned, wagging his head in mock severity.

Now that I knew my boyfriend was on a budget, I sometimes fretted about the weekly bouquet he delivered to our apartment. "Don't worry about it," he assured me. "I was able to squeeze in a tiny fee increase, and Lasik bookings are solid through May."

Paloma's friendship with Klahan was getting rather serious as well, and every time we got on the phone to Portland, Mom heaved theatrical sighs and went on about *what's the point*. But the three of us sometimes stayed up past midnight for Zoom sessions–my sister and I huddled together around her laptop screen, squeezing both of us into the frame.

And the Thursday dinner dates were such treasures. Saman did scour Bangkok web sites in order to hunt down discounts. But we dined on Italian recipes; we gorged ourselves on the Sheraton buffet; we gave Sizzler's a workout one rainy evening where the stormy weather battered the window right next to our booth and the busboys could barely make themselves heard.

But through the wondrous two months, Pastor Gino was such a blessing. Without histrionics or embellishing, he laid out the simple and inescapably joyous truth: *Jesus is everything.* Saman would sometimes sit there, dessert untouched, eyes wide with awe and childish fascination, as our mentor described the intensity of God's love for our crumbling world. "He doesn't give up; he just never does," he declared over and over, and I could see Klahan nodding. "Look at me. I was at death's door. I told Christ to leave me be, that I hated religion and the fantasy of heaven. But he just kept coming at me, just kept pulling me toward my own miracle."

It got to be a sweet loop through the suburbs of Bangkok after our double dates. Klahan's family lived fairly close to the BCS campus, so we dropped him off first, Saman and I exchanging grins as some chaste kissing went on just beyond the humid film on the Mercedes' side windows. Then the sweet goodbye when

my boyfriend would climb free, let me out, give my kid
sister a half-hug and a quip, and then offer me a trio of
just perfect, tender, not-ambitious kisses. "Love you
more each day," he'd whisper, either in English or Thai
and sometimes a bit of both if that gave him a second set
of triplets. "Enough already," Paloma would sing out
from the upstairs landing, and we would reluctantly tear
ourselves apart. "See you at church, babe" was his
reliable refrain, and I felt my soul singing as Paloma and
I stood next to our apartment door and watched him
wheel out into the gummed-up machinery of our new
and beautiful Thailand home.

With my heart steadily being repaired by our
weekly gospel doses, all at once I realized I was
absolutely loving my new life as a high school teacher.
Bangkok Christian School's seniors were charging
through Calc II with a vengeance, almost half the kids
getting A's and cracking jokes about L'Hôpital's Rule
and does such-and-such series converge or diverge. Two
of my *Matthayom* Six ladies had gone in for Lasik
procedures as well, and we compared notes during the
mid-morning break.

"I see really good now," boasted Nisachong, one of
my favorites in the B section. "And Miss Daggett, you
know what I also see?"

"I have no idea."

"Dr. Takuathung, he has such a big picture of you!
In his office! I see it and I say to him, 'Oh my! This is
my teacher.' And he laugh and say, 'Sure. I know.'" She
fixed me with a saucy grin. "Miss Daggett, I can say one
hundred percent, he is much in love. Don't worry. In
very soon time, you can always marry him." Then
caught herself. "But no matter if you are wife of rich

doctor. You must still teach at BCS for many years."

I choked back my grammar fixes and rolled my high-priced eyeballs. The girls burst into peals of laughter, and I was still smiling inwardly as we slogged through the PowerPoint file for the new lesson.

The closing bell had just rung when I got an incoming text from my favorite Asian correspondent. *Pastor G says tonight finishes up his usual series of Bible studies. I'm totally ready to say yes! Pls help me think of a perfect baptism venue. P.S. How does Japanese food sound? P.S.S. I'm soooo in love with Miss Daggett.*

I showed it to Paloma as we milled around in the courtyard waving to departing friends. "Japanese is good for me."

"I know, but . . ." I felt a twinge of regret that our weekly Bible studies were concluding. "This has been so awesome."

"We can still just double date," my sister pointed out. "But look. Pastor Gino, he's busy. He took us through the series, and he's got other folks to study with."

"I know." I made eye contact with one of the moms who had solicited my help with her son's ailing trigonometry grade. "By the way, when we order tonight, just kind of ease up."

"How come?" Paloma gave me a knowing nudge. "Your boyfriend's rich. It's kind of nice grabbing everything we like off the menu."

"Well, 'cause he's not that rich." I'd already confided to her how my boyfriend's apartment was anything but lavish, and that he was sending a huge cut of his monthly net to the college-loan hounds at some

New Jersey clearinghouse.

She sighed theatrically. "Fine. I'll just go to the kitchen help here and ask them to make me an egg sandwich."

"Don't be like that. I'm just saying."

Paloma snorted that any guy who had flowers delivered weekly to his lady friend's apartment couldn't be too hard up, and I conceded she had me there.

Bangkok traffic was nastier than usual that night, and Saman grumbled as a parking lot attendant waved him off. "I guess we'll have to try on the other side," he told us. "But that's a hard four blocks walking back to the restaurant."

"It is okay," Klahan said from the back seat. "But then we must pass Patpong Road."

Oops. I'd forgotten that this part of downtown Bangkok was right where the infamous row of nightclubs and strip joints operated with impunity. It's a colorful oddity: the capital's thriving (and legit) night bazaar, a hive of bartering and endless sales booths, juts up adjacent to a long, narrow den of decadence. Touts out front hand out mimeographed sheets hinting at dark pleasures and prurient anatomical displays, definitely not for the morally faint of heart. It's a twin image of what I'd endured at Pattaya Beach, and I could tell Saman was embarrassed that we had to even thread our way through the perimeter of the pink-tinged lab of licentious pleasure.

"That's so ugly," he murmured anxiously, trying to inject himself as a buffer between me and the market of female flesh.

"It's all right," I managed, my face tightening as I averted my eyes.

Thankfully, the massive Japanese letters soon blinked their welcome along with tempting aromas, and the maître d' bowed stiffly in welcoming us to the elegant eatery. Gino waved to us from a corner booth, and I heaved a sigh of relief. *Okay. This is better.*

I actually felt a small surge of strength. I did it. I'd heard the disco beat and even spotted those obscene brass poles where the girls had to shuffle through their ritualized dance moves, and I hadn't freaked out. I supposed by now there was a numbness of sorts, a calcifying of my heart. In addition, I had Saman's caring defenses around me, and also the fortifying Calvary hope which these Thursday dinners always offered.

My optimism grew as we held hands around the table and each said a prayer. Saman hesitated before adding: "Lord God, we saw something ugly tonight out there on the street, but thank you so much that we're now here in this sanctuary of friendship. Especially please bless Pranom and shield her with your love and the good news that she has such a great new life at BCS."

In a few sentences, Saman explained to Pastor Gino about our unfortunate detour. He nodded gravely. "Yeah. I knew this restaurant was close to that stuff, but didn't think you'd have to walk past it that way." He reached over for my hand and gave it a squeeze. "I'm so sorry."

"I'm okay."

I tossed Paloma an approving wink as she theatrically scanned the menu, then settled for a modestly-priced order of *omurice*. I was tempted by the Japanese-style omelet, but conferred with Saman, who'd been here before, and we agreed to split a huge plate of *udon*. "As long as we share that too." I pointed to the back page of the menu and the tempting color photo of *korokke*, which I remembered was deep-fried patties. "My dad always gets that back home."

As we ate and bantered, Pastor Gino let the jovialities mingle in with our study, but we did dig seriously into the First Corinthians passage where Paul describes spiritual gifts and how any new member needs to find a place to contribute. "Here's the thing," he told us, his dark eyes growing sober. "Every single person in God's family has a gift. A thing to contribute. A specialty. Look, Saman. You're a doctor. This isn't saying you have to do Lasik on everybody for free, hint hint; that's not the point. But God might call on you to help run a mission clinic for a week. Or donate your medical expertise in lecturing at BCS once a month. Or just, I don't know. Maybe you're a really great singer and we haven't figured it out yet."

"I'm quite sure that's not it," he cracked, and we all chuckled.

"Sure. But the point is this. And hey, especially here in Thailand where the Christian community is still so fledgling. We need every soldier armed for combat. We all dig in; we all have to be in service mode all the time."

I reflected on that as we enjoyed the restaurant's recommended *kakigori*, the tart watermelon flavor of the shaved ice dessert lingering on our tongues. Was calculus my gift? Did my lectures at BCS count? Or, with that being a secular occupation and the natural flowering of my master's degree, did I need to find something more unique and *Pranom-only*? What could I and only I offer to this novice movement trembling and about to spring forth with power here in *Krung Thep*?

After we dropped Klahan off at his place, Saman asked if he could borrow another half hour from me. "Just something I want to talk about."

I tingled pleasantly. "Sure. That'd be great."

"I'll just sit down in the lobby staring at the paint on the walls," Paloma grumped, not meaning it.

"No. I want you to hear this too."

He followed us up to the apartment, and I fished a soda out of the refrigerator for him. "I shouldn't," he said, but took it anyway. "I'll be up half the night."

I followed him over to the loveseat, and didn't mind when Paloma brought a chair over from the dining room table. "So what's up?" I asked him.

"Well, it's just about my baptism."

Impulsively, I leaned over and kissed him enthusiastically on the cheek as my sister groaned. "I'm so happy, babe."

"I know. Me too."

"So what have you got in mind?" I already knew most of Pastor Gino's baptisms happened over at Somsak's house and were typically tied to nocturnal pool parties.

"Well, maybe this is weird. I don't know. But walking past that red-light place tonight made me think of it."

I pursed my lips, but the reality was that it hadn't really bugged me that severely. "It was . . . well, not that bad," I said at last. "Maybe I'm getting my head on straight."

"Well, that's what I'm praying for," he told us both. "I realize we had that big painful mess on Christmas Eve. Which is all my fault."

I shook my head quickly. "Not really. It was just

one of those perfect storms."

"Well, whatever. But look. Here's what I think."

We waited.

"Maybe a couple weeks from now. We have church; we have potluck. All that stuff. And then, when it's all done, maybe just, I don't know, one van of us."

It was an incomplete thought, and after an odd pause I pushed him on it. "One van of us what?"

"Well, let's say just your best friends. Khemkaeng and Rachel Marie. Natty and Pastor and his folks, of course. And we all head right out to the beach and I get baptized there."

Okay. Which beach?

He knew that's what I was thinking, and his voice softened. "If you can't do it, I totally get it. But what if we just walked right past that place where you got hurt? Together. God's little invincible army. And then keep right on going, because, you know, together in Christ we're just plain unbeatable. And then we walk right into the surf, and I'm baptized, so it's my new beginning. And maybe if you're standing right there in the water with me getting fortified, and all that sorrow just stays on the beach and God sends along a nice breeze, who knows?"

I could tell Saman was fighting a lump in his throat, and he even had to rub his hand against his eyes. "Sorry," he muttered.

"No, sweetie. And I think it's good."

"You do?"

"Well, let me pray about it, sure. But the symbolism of it is amazing. We walk right past the devil's old place, and into the surf and then we just don't look back."

"Hang on." Paloma rose up from her chair and

pulled it closer to the sofa, and there was vehement body English to the movement. "You're not serious."

"I think it'd be okay."

"But what if it's not?" Her eyes had that familiar fire from when we used to fight as kids back in Portland. "Let's say we get there and the place is going full blast. All that R-rated rock music. And those sleazy guys out front passing around their 'you see sexy show' sheets of paper." She pointed a finger right at Saman, as if to imply that every male in Thailand bore some responsibility for the scourge. "Do you know what kind of crap they're offering?"

He colored a bit, and did bow his head. "I'm sure it's awful."

"And what about this?" My sister wasn't about to be deterred. "Holy cow, Pranom, what if your uncle's down there someplace? He might still be lurking around there a decade later, still making money off . . . you know."

I honestly hadn't thought about that. What had my notorious Uncle Viroj done since the Daggetts had spirited away his one and only juvenile source of income? Had he expanded his empire of kid hookers? Built up a lucrative network of prepubescent sex slaves? I knew full well that unscrupulous guys just like Dad's brother scoured distant villages for fresh-faced innocents free from HIV infections. A bribe as low as $50 often added an unsuspecting victim to the flesh feasts of Pattaya.

"That would be bad," I conceded, half-turning toward Saman. "Maybe we'd better think of something else."

"Sure." Thankfully, he wasn't wedded to the idea,

and we chatted about the upcoming Buddhist holiday and a possible return to that high-level water park. "Me and Klahan are in for sure," Paloma said, relief evident on her face that we'd dropped the other matter.

BUT MONDAY NOON at lunch, I impulsively blurted out the scheme to Rachel Marie, and she sat there next to me just chewing on her fist. "I think it sounds amazing. I mean, if you could handle it." She seized my hand and looked into my eyes. "Oh, sweetie. I just don't want you to get hurt ever again. But that would be such a witness."

Even now, neither of us wanted to really dial up those old memories, but she told me she was pretty sure a club like that wouldn't be operating in mid-afternoon. "It's all evenings and midnight specials and evil stuff like that," she said quickly. "If we got down to the ocean by mid-afternoon"–she seemed to carefully steer away even from the loaded word *beach*, and I felt a rush of affection for my adopted aunt–"we could just walk by this shuttered-up place, signs aren't on yet, no music, nothing but their, you know, creepy silence." She stared off into space, like she was trying to penetrate right through the smoke and the stars surrounding our beat-up planet and connect us up with God's throne room. "But it'd be so cool to have Saman baptized there in the ocean, you next to him, virgin beginnings all around."

I timidly brought up the idea of accidentally encountering a specter like my criminally evil uncle, Viroj Niratpattanasai. Even the idea that I still legally shared a name with such a person made my guts tighten up, and I had to acknowledge that some of my own forgiveness projects still had a long ways to go. But Rachel Marie tried to allay my concern. "I just don't imagine he's still around there, honey. That was more than ten years ago. If he was living such a fast life, there's a good chance he's pushing up daisies somewhere. We can always hope, anyway."

It was such a wonderful, earthy thing to say I leaned over and hugged her right in front of five hundred students. "Auntie Rachel, you're just too much. Every single day, you're this awesome blessing."

"Aw. Now I'm going to cry," she teased.

"I'm not kidding."

Her face softened. "I know. But it's sure easy to love you, kid."

PALOMA HAD A SUPPER date with Klahan next evening, and I wished her well, grumbling about a whole stack of calc quizzes I'd let pile up in the bottom of my backpack. "Both sections," I sighed. "I bet it'll take me till nine."

"Sorry," she offered, but I could tell she was eager to be off.

"You guys just meeting at the mall?"

"Uh huh."

"Be good."

I resolved to get into the paper flow without delay, so I got some Handel flowing through my ear buds and tore into the stack with a vengeance. To my surprise, half the kids had really nailed the idea of integration by parts, and I was writing a whole series of cheery *10*s on the tops of a lot of papers. "Miss Daggett, you are just so awesome as a teacher," I murmured half-aloud, mocking myself. "You superstar thing." It was just a lucky week; I realized that. Next week these same kids would feign complete ignorance of anything I'd ever told them.

But I polished off the entire pile in less than ninety minutes, and simply sat there in the quiet hum of #305's air-conditioning unit. What next? I hadn't had supper yet, and my recent conversation with Aunt Rachel was poking at me. Did I really want to ride down to Pattaya Beach and confront my demons? Even with Saman at my side, was I ready to see that garish citadel of sexual conquest? No one but me had memories from *inside* the dance club; I realized that now. Even an indignant friend like John Garvey—who had heroically teamed up with Khemkaeng and Dad to rescue me—really had no clue. Nobody but me knew the feeling of standing on that long plywood runway, the seductive *thump* of American disco hits vibrating the boards, and seeing sweaty, eager men looking up at my bikini panties and then higher. Top, panties, top, panties, *come on, now, girlie, unhook that bra, let's have a look-see* . . . never my face or my tired, thirteen-year-old *Matthayom* One pasted-on smile.

"Jesus, what do I do?" I forced my mind away from the images, fully aware that if Saman and I and our UCC family did undertake The Quest, there would be hurt involved. I'd bleed down at Pattaya, at least a little bit. But I'd have my sister along. And Auntie Rachel. And my boyfriend.

And Jesus. Would even my mighty Savior be enough for that long six-block walk to the beach?

I made an abrupt decision and picked up my purse and cell phone. I was a bit low on cash, but a foray to McDonald's wouldn't be more than 150 baht. Plus the Sky Train fare, I reminded myself.

The car was only half-filled, and I idly scanned the wall ads: deodorant, Honda motorcycles, a soccer tournament at Chulalongkorn University with five visiting countries sending teams. My days in this foreign kingdom were waning fast, and I absorbed the glistening Thai-ness of the posters, the cheerful fonts hyping Bangkok pleasures. What was about to happen to me? To my relationship with Saman? To my satisfying identity as a high school calculus instructor who made a daily difference in the lives of fresh-faced kids? I realized with a start that I was woefully unprepared to make a lasting choice about my own destiny.

Oh well. For now, I was determined just to focus on counting the stops and getting something hot and delicious into my grumbling stomach.

I arrived at the Sala Daeng Station, and clumped down the stairs along with maybe fifty other riders. Already I could see the golden arches up ahead, but something nudged me past them. There was a mid-level mall right across the street from McDonald's, and I rode the escalator up to the fourth floor and perused the food court. Right in the corner next to a KFC was a modestly decorated Thai diner with two employees out front offering photocopied menus to passers-by. I accepted one of the blue sheets and scanned the options.

I still had an American craving for a McFlurry, but reminded myself I could always top off with that later. For tonight, it suddenly seemed important to linger in my Thai world, to consider my future while surrounded by Asian aromas and appetizers that were vibratingly spicy, *pet* being the operative Thai word. I accepted the girl's directions and entered the Thai restaurant, looking over the available tables and choosing one by the window. From my vantage point, I could look down on the thick crowds still pushing their way along the sidewalk, many pausing to pick through bootleg DVDs or hand-stitched native blouses.

I ordered a plate of *gai paat prik*, chicken fried with chilies, and made sure the appetizer included a small bowl of fried rice, my favorite. The food arrived almost immediately, and I had to remind myself to murmur an inward prayer of thanks.

An older couple was dining just a few feet away from me, the aroma of seafood wafting over to my table, but their conversation was muted and I fell into a kind of thoughtful reverie as I ate, the muted cacophony of street traffic below us floating up to where I sat but not quite penetrating the glass windows. An occasional loud snort of diesel fumes from a *tuk tuk* would pop into my brain, and I smiled as I ate, watching as the blue motor-trikes charged across the intersection and into the red morass of taillights on the other side.

I was halfway through my meal before I realized something. At the very boundary of where I could see through the glass, the commerce of Patpong Road was humming along. There was a stretch of night-market booths hawking men's shirts and faux leather purses. Americans and Australian tourists were gawking at the polo-shirt displays and dickering for wooden souvenir elephants. But just on the other side of a blue tarp, there it was. The pink-tinged alleyway where bikinis and beer and rattling disco speakers mingled together to titillate those who dared the naughty stroll through Gomorrah.

I didn't want to look, but part of me felt drawn to the faraway image, the pink and the flashing neon somehow anesthetized by the tint on the window pane. From this distance, I couldn't even make out the glowing marquee signs. But just like in Pattaya, I didn't doubt all of them referred in some glib way to *Available Females*.

Girls and the attached anatomy were available for lease just like a half-hour taxi ride to the Victory Monument.

There was barely a dab left of my *kao paat*, and I slowed down, taking in just a few grains of the delicious rice with each nibbled bite. My gaze stayed on that distant quadrant, the seductive images of Patpong, and I wondered anew about the idea of circling back to invade Pattaya for my boyfriend's baptism. Was my soul sufficiently redeemed and healed that I could walk past the old go-go club and not collapse? Could Christ be my safeguard and my surety here? I thought so; I chose to believe so. But I still wasn't sure.

Again I was struck by the oddity of having Patpong Road and the Bangkok night bazaar in such proximity. The market was a freewheeling, cheerful, and usually kindly place of commerce where shopkeepers bargained in good faith with clients, acknowledging the cheesiness of the offers and so-called specials. *Hello! Pretty lady! For you only, special price!* But folks dug in wallets and purses for stacks of baht, and they got okay deals on luggage and pajamas and gaudy T-shirts and knockoff Houston Astros baseball jerseys. Every wheeler-dealer had a big-screen calculator so visitors from all over could crunch the numbers and know how many baht to surrender. It was all math, all buy-two-get-one-free, all decimals and percents and what's-today's-exchange-rate.

And I had my own math to consider. Not calculus and not second derivatives. Just a tally of stats and assets.

Because on my plus side, I had the love of a good and reformed man. Saman was my treasure; I loved him desperately. He was solicitous and kind and thoughtful, determined to make up for his earlier betrayal and win my heart. Despite the earlier setbacks, my account with him was solidly in the black by now.

I also had my own growing Christian family. Mom and Dad and my oh-so-amazing little sister. Paloma had almost literally saved my life back on Christmas Eve; I knew it down to my socks, and I loved her with an inexpressible ache. On top of that, there was Auntie Rachel and Uncle Khemkaeng and all the others. Pastor Gino and Natty. Ratana and Noah. All the kids coming along now, with their sticky hugs and missing-tooth smiles at church.

I had my life at BCS, the joy of not just teaching math but embracing a student and saying a first prayer with a teary-eyed convert. That was amazing stuff, and I adored my new role as a Christian mentor, as an admired and adult presence in the lives of these beautiful Thai kids.

And then there was one more thing.

I had Jesus. This crucified carpenter King from so long ago had come into my heart and I was determined he would abide and rule there always. I was just *so happy* being his child, worshiping and representing him. I was finally happy as a Christian, happy to be the girlfriend and almost-fiancée of a giddy-in-the-Lord convert like Saman. Happy to worship my risen Savior along with my church family at UCC, my brothers and sisters in the faith.

All of that went into the plus ledger that, even now in this darkened corner of Bangkok, teetered in my brain's recesses. So much good. So many pluses and sweet advantages.

All there was on the other side was Lucifer's attacks and those four months at the Pussycat Club. That was the eternal debit, the crippling foe, the hidden cancer marked on X-ray films I kept locked in a closet and didn't want to acknowledge.

I'm Pranom. I used to be a child hooker. I'm forever damaged. Soiled beyond repair.

Really? Wasn't my glowing list of pluses enough to beat back that sordid February-May of infamy? Wasn't the embrace of Tommy and Samantha and Paloma Daggett and Tommy Junior–and their priceless gift of adoption–enough? Wasn't the story recorded in Matthew, Mark, Luke, and John sufficient to beat back Pattaya Beach?

Of course I knew the answer. I had chosen an alliance with Jesus Christ, and he was my everything. His gift to me at Calvary was the pure essence of mathematical *infinity*. In my heart, the cross was a sideways eight and it evoked in me an undistilled ardor.

Even then I couldn't be sure it was all enough. All the math in the heavens above couldn't obliterate the cold fact that I was a damaged woman. I might never again be right, gospel or no gospel. Even as I sat here with my bowl of rice and with the music coming through the restaurant PA and these thick glass windows shielding me from the raucous cries of the sex-show touts two hundred meters up the street, I knew my spiritual resumé was as suspect as a counterfeit Rolex. I might ride to Pattaya with Saman and experience a spectacular collapse requiring long-term psychiatric care. I might marry this gorgeous man only to have my worst fears confirmed: that my destiny was to be a failed honeymoon bride, a broken lady with frigidity chained around her by the ghosts of her former life.

I shuffled up to the counter and paid my bill, trying

to understand the anxiety in my own heart. Was I hopeful? Doubtful? Optimistic? Foolish and awash in self-denial? I didn't know. I didn't understand my own heart. All I could do was go down to the street, avert my gaze, buy my BTS token, and go home.

And pray. Oh my God, I surely did pray.

TWENTY-ONE

Three days before our scheduled D-Day assault on Pattaya, Sue Carington came into the back of my Calculus B classroom with a breezy smile. "Hello, young people," she boomed out. "I'd like to learn a bit of calculus with you. Is that all right?" There was one desk free and she plopped herself down, making a big show of getting ready to scrutinize my performance and record every verbal bobble on a yellow pad of paper. "Does Miss Daggett smile as she teaches?" she mused aloud. "Has she prepared her lessons well? Does she know her times tables?"

There was good-natured chuckling all around, and then she slid the notebook free. "I really just wanted to enjoy twenty or so minutes with BCS's elite students. You young people don't mind, do you?"

"You can telling Miss Daggett to give all students extra credit?" Udom was never shy about grabbing some bonus points.

"Well, let's try that again, my friend," she

prompted. "That did not sound like perfect *Matthayom* Six English."

The nearby girls cracked up and he put his head down on the desk, pretending to moan. "To speak English well is so impossible! All day teachers say to me: 'No good! Speak so bad!'" The laughter grew and I waved off his protest. "That's too many flubs to fix in one go, Mr. Udom."

After the brief session, she stood by the door and offered nice *wais* to one and all, exchanging hugs with a few of the soon-graduating girls. "So glad you're doing well," she repeated over and over. "You ladies are pure amazing."

I had enjoyed her presence and told her so. "I guess having you come by should make me feel nervous, but I really don't. And the kids love it when you interrupt us."

"Well, you're just so good at this," she gushed, filling me with a cheering glow. "Khemkaeng says your mom was just the same. Got here on a Friday. By Monday, her first day here, she got the hang of it. Kids loved her. Within a week Mr. Garvey was downtown trying to get a Teacher of the Year plaque engraved already."

Her humor was a wee bit over the top and I laughed, enjoying our visit. "Was there anything else?" I caught myself. "You and Dr. C are for sure coming to Pattaya after church, aren't you?"

"Oh, honey, of course. I've hardly thought of anything else all week." She came over and hugged me. "You're so amazing and brave." A smile. "I keep forgetting the Thai word for 'brave.'"

"*Gla-haan*," I prompted.

"Oh yes. I think Natty was telling her kids the old

David and Goliath story, and one of them popped up with that. So all the children whipped right around and looked at me to see if I was going to slap him with a twenty-baht fine."

"Which I'm sure you didn't."

Sue sighed. "I don't think we've scored a language fine in the last two years. It's just too hard to enforce that rule consistently."

She broke toward the door and made a point of easing it closed. I felt something tighten in my tummy. *Uh oh.*

"I got a massive favor to ask," she said quietly, coming back and looking right into my eyes. "Actually, it's not a favor, but more of a ministry challenge."

"I'll try."

She looked down at her shoes for a moment, and then seized my hand. "This thing with Saman and you pushing back against what happened before . . . honey, I think it's just hugely courageous. I mean it."

"Well, I hope I make it through," I said, pushing away the jagged impulses already gathering strength and moving toward my inner core. "I've got all my friends and everything."

"I know, sweetheart. Anyway, here's what I'm thinking." Sue gestured through the windows to our high school campus. "We have all these girls here. Even with what we offer–the solid core instruction, the STEM classes, the Christian element–look. The fact is a whole lot of them are still vulnerable to the same thing that happened to you. These ladies don't all end up at university getting a master's degree and then getting married in a white bridal gown. And the offramp heading to some real pain is just way too traveled here in

Bangkok."

I fell silent, knowing that everything she said was true. Many bright young girls, brimming with potential, still fall into the swamp of Patpong Road and *Soi* Cowboy. A family member gets sick and a girl quits school, just temporarily, of course. Two months later they're turning tricks in a sordid alleyway or renting a bargain hotel room hour by hour. Others can't manage the tuition payments for a full college education, so they fall back and manage trade school for a semester, and then quit when problems mount. Before long they're making a living the only way they know how.

The most painful reality of all was one our teachers anguished over in faculty meetings. Some of Bangkok's clever girls get suckered by the reality that tourist males are just so easy to con. An incoming visitor meets a bar girl; they spend a promiscuous night together. In her mangled English–and enterprising ladies quickly learn how to stumble linguistically in a way that arouses a gentleman's sympathy–she assures him there's nothing she craves more than a long-term relationship. "I never meet nice man like you until now. I think soon we can be always together. Okay?" Even after his plane soars out of Thailand airspace, why, in this fragile fantasy she thinks of nothing but him. If she can just save up enough money, say, a thousand dollars or so, she can leave this horrid lifestyle behind and marry a nice foreigner. Of course, she does still have to take care of her mom and her younger brother who needs surgery for an infected ear.

Sue recounted some of these breezy scams with me and then concluded by gravely shaking her head. "It sounds awful to say. But we've got high school ladies who see the action on the street and then wonder to themselves: 'Why should I get a job in a department store making ninety cents an hour. I'm pretty. I'm bright. I'm way bilingual now, thanks to BCS. If I market my *self* the right way, I'll soon have that condo by the river and a chauffeured car.'"

I found the notion appalling, and Sue could tell I was beginning to seethe. "Just think about this," she urged. "Maybe one of these days we have a chapel. Just the *Matthayom* girls. And you open up to them. Not the ugly details. But just enough for them to know: *hey, the life I got pushed into is nothing but heartbreak.*" She had to swallow hard and I was getting emotional as well. "But then add for sure that Jesus Christ is always our protection and our healing." She took my hand in both of her own and cradled it, letting her nurturing love flow through her fingertips and into mine. "If this isn't something you could ever do, of course I'd understand. But the way the Lord rescued you is one of the most thrilling things I've ever gotten to witness. I praise him every time I consider it."

I promised her I would definitely think about it. "That's all I can ask," she responded, getting up from her seat and offering another quick hug.

Not really meaning to, I blurted out what I'd been thinking all through our conversation. "I guess it really depends on our ride to the beach. And how that goes. If I feel okay during all that, I think I could definitely handle this too."

"That'd be just so sweet," she nodded, leaning over and kissing my cheek. "Love you, my dear friend."

"You too."

RIGHT BEFORE HIS SERMON, Pastor Gino called Saman forward and then, as an afterthought, gestured for me to join them. "I wish all of you could come along," he announced, "but some of us are driving to the beach this evening for a baptism. We've all gotten to know and love Dr. T; he's a good guy and a nice blessing to United Christian Church. And this evening it's official! He'll be a bonafide part of the body of Christ and a pillar here in our spiritual community."

Saman shot me a grateful look as I slipped my hand into his. "It has been amazing," he admitted, "to fall in love with Jesus this way." I blushed when he hastened to add: "And my heart has tumbled down more than one hill, I guess." A quartet of my *Matthayom* girls were sitting close to the front and I saw them beaming and exchanging giggling comments under their breath. I flounced away from them, pretended to be mad, and the church noticed, a ripple of amusement sweeping through our ranks.

"Anyway," he went on, "thank you for being good friends to me. And for sure, thanks to Pastor Gino for the Bible studies. Every week when we got together, I'd drive home just thinking: 'This all sounds true and wonderful.'"

I felt cautiously optimistic as we climbed into the BCS van later that afternoon. Aunt Rachel had procured the babysitting services of Kraisri so it was just an intrepid knot of adult friends accompanying Saman and me on our spiritual quest. Khemkaeng had on some Christian music, and I felt cheered when a pair of Dad's songs were in his playlist.

"There's one wrong note," Paloma announced, and we all fell silent, listening hard. "There," she said, pointing at the in-dash stereo. "The bass was off and they didn't notice until the master had been duplicated, and Dad finally said oh well."

"He's the only guy who would ever even pick it out," Rachel Marie said.

Sue and Natty had put together a killer picnic supper, and the aroma of potato salad was already starting to get to me, but I knew we weren't going to eat until afterward. I tried to keep my nerves calm, but I began feeling twitchy as billboards soon dotted the divided highway, all announcing hotel bargains and zip-line adventures.

The first exits for the resort areas of Pattaya came into view, and Khemkaeng slowed down at the first one. "Saman, where do you and Pastor Gino intend to do your baptism?"

My boyfriend paused and I felt his fingers tighten around my own. "Well, just . . . you know, the beach."

I could tell my friends were tiptoeing around the subject at hand, and Saman glanced at me before laying it all out there. "Pranom and I just want to have all you guys gather around. And say a prayer for her and for me. Then we walk right past that old, you know. That dance place. We walk past it, we just hang onto each other and remind ourselves that Christ is our mighty friend. And then we walk straight to the beach and we never look back. Ever again."

I was about to tear up, and got absolutely puddly with what he said next. "I'm just telling everybody this. I love Pranom with everything I've got. And I want her to be safe. All that other stuff out of our lives. Wedding day, honeymoon, and for the next fifty years."

Are you kidding me? Had my boyfriend actually

blurted out the words "wedding day" right in front of the entire brain trust of BCS? But the van didn't swerve off into a banana plant. Khemkaeng offered me a quiet smile and a few blocks later he pulled into the parking lot of a tourist-type convenience store. "The beach is right down there," he pointed. "And the club . . ." His voice tightened, and we waited until he could manage. "I think it is quite close."

We got out of the van, and Gino handed bundles of food to the guys in our entourage, then remembered. Setting his down on the pavement, he drew close to Saman and me. "Let's pray, folks."

My heart was beginning to beat a tattoo in my chest and I felt both exhilarated and scared witless. But his prayer was short and calming, thanking Jesus for being nothing but victorious, our perfect Savior and rescuer. "We need you right now, Lord," he pleaded. "Especially for Saman and Pranom, this is the moment when we know you will be their ally and battle warrior. Jesus, nothing can stop you; nothing can defeat those who have you standing in their corner."

There was a sweet, muscular pause, and then, without even saying amen, Pastor Gino announced cheerfully: "And here we go!"

I smiled despite my jumpy nerves, and gratefully tugged Saman's arm into place around my shoulders. "Don't you dare let go of me," I murmured.

"Never."

One block later, on the right side of the street, there it was. The letters were unlit, the neon flow shut off until twilight. But it was still the Pussycat Club, with the same brass-ringed letters out front, the exact same wooden two-side easel listing inflated cocktail prices. Someone had swept the parking lot clean, but I spotted a wadded-up tangle of pink photocopied half-sheets, and had no doubt they described the X-rated displays a visitor could ogle up on the second floor.

The nine of us paused, and I realized everyone was trying to both insulate me and allow me whatever processing time I needed. But I stared at the structure, at the pink paint, the unlit signs, the industrial-grade stereo wiring that ran through rain-proof tubes in order to feed outdoor speakers and draw tourists to come take a look at the dancing ladies in their halter tops and thongs. Right here is where Uncle Viroj had dragged me night after night. He sometimes loitered in the parking lot, greedily evaluating the scene as a man would lead me toward a nearby flophouse.

"Don't think about . . . just . . . don't think about what happened," Pastor Gino whispered, putting a hand on my shoulder. "You survived all this. You beat this awful racket, Pranom. You really did. In the name of Jesus, you're victorious."

I nodded, relieved that a sort of gospel anesthetic seemed to have dulled my former agonies. "I'm good, you guys. Let's get to the beach."

"Pranom Daggett, you are such a brick," Sue declared. "Praise God for how he's given you this courage."

It was close to sundown now, and the beach was beginning to empty out. About a kilometer to the south of us I spied a tiny dot against the blackening sky, a man dangling beneath a red-and-white parasail, but the towing speedboat was heading toward the shoreline and he was coming in for an expensive landing. Saman, plainly relieved that our shared encounter with the brothel had gone well, gaped at the scene. "I'd love to try that one of these days."

"I'll bring you," I told him, feeling in a celebratory mood.

We stood at water's edge for a sweet moment, and I was thankful for Rachel Marie's arm circling my waist. "You were amazing back there, sweetie," she told me, awe in her voice.

"Thanks. But it's not me."

"I know."

I hadn't realized it, but all my friends had planned ahead and brought extra clothes. Pastor Gino and Khemkaeng dumped the picnic bags in the sand and all nine of us tramped grandly into the surf, giddy with pleasure at the beautiful night our triumphant Lord painted in the night skies above. The water was pleasantly cool and I savored the ripples splashing against my thighs. A larger wave surged toward us and almost lifted me off my feet, and I giggled with the sheer relief of being with friends I loved and a prince like Saman Takuathung.

"This deep enough?" Gino asked as the surf reached his waist.

"I think we're good."

The ceremony itself was short and sweet. We'd already said our prayers, so Pastor Gino just pointed toward the sky and reminded us that loyalty to the Trinity—God the Father, God the Son, God the Spirit—was any man or woman's highest calling. "Saman, my brother, we've already scored a great victory just walking to this beach," he said carefully, glancing over at me. "And now heaven wins again because you've joined the Lord's unbeatable team. I love you, we all love you, Pranom loves you, and most of all, Jesus is looking down and crying through the heavens: 'I love this man! I died for him!'"

"Amen." Saman's eyes were uncharacteristically damp as Pastor gently lowered him beneath the surface. He emerged sputtering but cheerful, and quickly embraced me. "I love you so much, honey."

"I know. I love you too."

"Enough!" Paloma hollered out, and we all laughed, savoring the sweet moment.

We began splashing toward the shore, an army giddy in triumph, and eager now to get into dry clothes and dive into Sue's gourmet supper. The water was still at mid-thigh when I saw that the go-go bar's neon lights had flickered on. We could barely hear it, but the speakers were now live with music, and I supposed that the first customers would begin to buzz toward the action like bugs drawn to a light bulb.

But it's all right. Saman and I are a Christian couple. Jesus is mighty; he really and truly is. It's okay.

And I thought that. I felt it. I believed it. So what if the neon lights were switched on? The music CDs playing? The brothel madam at her place in the corner of the bar, tracking the comings and goings of pimps and johns? Christ was our defender, our shield and buckler. I still wasn't sure what a buckler was, but it sounded sturdy as I splashed toward the sandy shore.

I felt like I was safe now. That my faith in the Lord was settled. That I was likely to marry this amazing, thoughtful man and be very happy.

And yet, as I accepted a big pile of potato salad and popped the top on a diet soda and saw a nearly full moon rise up gloriously out of the faraway deep blue, a strangely unsettled mood crept up next to me on the beach.

This is all good. It's blessed and it's good. But somehow, Jesus, oh, Jesus, it's not . . . DONE.

TWENTY-TWO

Wanting to please Sue, I spent the next two weeks prayerfully outlining a chapel talk describing my rescue from Pattaya. Some of the girls in my audience would be mere seventh-graders, so my testimony needed to be carefully expurgated. But even prepubescent females in Bangkok know what Patpong Road is all about, and have some concept of "short-time" and fifteen hundred baht and "hello, handsome American man." More than once as I wrote down memories and then backtracked and edited an overly graphic moment, I felt my stomach lurch.

But the core message did seem to pierce through the polluted fog of Thailand's original sin. Jesus is a healer and a rescuer, heaven's own Tommy Daggett. A girl can begin again, especially if friends surround her with their love.

The second reality is that Bangkok's beautiful girls, virgins and princesses all, need to stand up straight and tall, arms linked in a display of sister power. No man has a right to our bodies; our heavenly Father has a claim on our purity. Even a trusted family member who points toward Pattaya as a lucrative adventure needs to be reported and scorned.

Paloma and I, along with our guys, spent a nice Sunday afternoon back at the waterpark, and as we floated around the lazy river in slow circle-eights, I tried out the gist of my presentation on the men. Several times Paloma bristled, but in the end they all nodded approval. "Sweetheart, are you sure you can make this presentation?" Saman reached over and squeezed my hand. "And not get too emotional?"

No, I wasn't sure about that. But there was only one way to find out. By now, I honestly felt I owed my Savior this moment of witness.

Paloma and I lingered in the women's changing room, talking in sober tones about it as she toweled her blond locks and fumbled in her travel bag for fresh underwear. "It still just steams me that you went through something so vicious," she admitted, gravel in her voice. "And sure, Dad was amazing. But still, I don't see how BCS didn't figure this out."

"It was just . . . you know, kids leave. You got a thousand-plus students enrolled, and somebody drops out." I laced up my shoes and looked up at her. "It's not like in the States where the computer goes *ding* and somebody calls a contact number by ten in the morning if a kid doesn't show up."

"Yeah." She still had one shoe left to put on, and she stared at it, her eyes hard. Then she slammed it against the concrete floor, a sharp *whack!* bouncing off the hard surface. "There," she said with satisfaction, looking to make sure I concurred with her indignant body English.

All the next Thursday I felt on edge as the wall clock crept toward 2:00. I showed my trig students how to convert degrees to radians and clicked through my PowerPoint file, my voice on autopilot as I narrated. But I kept thinking of my chapel talk and my opening paragraph. Would I be able to tell my story? How would the young ladies of Bangkok Christian School respond?

By the time the chapel bell rang, I was definitely a bundle of jumping nerves. But as I went out into the hallway and looked for my shoes, Auntie Rachel came up the stairs. Catching my eye, she wove her way through the bustle of students and came right up to me. "Oh, sweetie, I've done nothing but pray all day," she said, embracing me. "Are you okay?"

"Not really," I told her. "But I'm doing it."

"You're so awesomely awesome," she said, borrowing a favorite expression. "But hey. Come back inside here and let me say a prayer for you."

That meant the world to me, and I felt my eyes welling up with tears. "Thanks."

We shooed a couple of straggling guys out. I knew our biology teacher and some of the office staff were going to be supervising mass male mayhem on the basketball courts while we had our Ladies Chapel hour, and Rachel Marie made a point of forcefully shutting the door, giving us a few moments of privacy. She draped both arms around my neck and just blurted out a prayer. "Jesus, oh mighty, wonderful Jesus, how much we need you this afternoon. Pranom has a story to tell; Jesus, you lived it with her. You were by her side then and now and forever. Please, Lord, fill her up this afternoon. Give her peace and give her all your healing might and love.

Make every word count. Please bless each young girl who sits in those chairs and absorbs this story of victory."

When she was done, we just stood there in the shadows of early afternoon; I honestly thought I could feel my auntie's heart beating through her black polo top.

"Come along, you brave soldier," she smiled through her tears. "I mean, you brave soldierette."

That made me smile and as we made our way downstairs, I felt myself being bathed with a sense of eagerness. Perhaps telling my story would be its own kind of catharsis.

The assembly hall was already almost full as I walked in with my aunt, the place a cauldron of feminine energy: all blouses and hair ribbons and regulation maroon skirts. Tuitt was a junior who usually ran the PA for our chapel programs; he came over and led me to the sound booth. "I cannot stay for program," he told me with a grin. "Mr. Chaisurivirat say is for ladies only. But is okay if I help do microphone. And then leave." I don't think he had a clue about our subject matter, but his fingers were gentle as he affixed the wireless mike apparatus around my ear and twisted the small wire until the speaker head was just grazing my cheek. "It feel okay?"

I nodded. "Yeah. Thanks."

Another smile. "Okay." Then he lowered his voice conspiratorially. "*Kaw hie choke dee*," he murmured. Good luck!

Noah got up, guitar strap dangling loosely from around his neck. "Okay, beautiful ladies," he called out through the main mike. "Let's sing a praise song to our

Lord."

I don't know if he had consulted with Sue, but his choice was pitch perfect. "Mighty to Save" had been one of BCS's favorites all term, and the girls sang with gusto. *Savior, He can move the mountains. Our God is mighty to save. Forever, author of salvation.*

There was a lump in my throat as I glanced toward the back and saw my beautiful Saman edge in through the back door. His gaze swept the arena until his eyes found me, and I saw him mouth: *I love you.*

I guess Noah must have realized what was about to come next, because the second verse of the Hillsong hit was perfect. *So take me as You find me; All my fears and failures. Fill my life again. I give my life to follow everything I believe in.*

Those of us in the teaching ranks did always try to sing along, to be an example to our *Matthayom* students, but my mind was blazing with emotions and trying to keep my memorized paragraphs in the right order. I could hear slender seventh-graders on the front row, their unison voices blended together on Noah's final chorus. *Our God is mighty to save, mighty to save.* I sensed a wordless prayer rising up within my breast. *Jesus, please do save and protect these pretty young girls, these virginal treasures.*

I was waiting for an introduction, and got a sweet surprise when my old childhood friend came through the door and went right up on the stage. "Hello, young ladies," she sang out as she looked around at the garden of blooming womanhood. "What a beautiful army of princesses God has brought together! Thank you for choosing the best school in all Asia. My name is Vuthisit, and I think it was ten years ago when I was right here at BCS too! We called our teacher Missie Stone and I loved her so much. I'm happy that she is still here, and as sweet and wonderful as when I was in *Prathom* Six.

That last did give me a start. Aunt Rachel's class wasn't supposed to be in here; for obvious reasons, this was strictly an upper-grades chapel program. It took me an emotional moment to realize she must have arranged for a substitute so she could come down here to the chapel and lend me her emotional support.

"One of my best friends, when I was right here and at the age when I was becoming a young lady, was Pranom Niratpattanasai. We had many good times and even went on a vacation together. But then, the next year, when we were both in *Matthayom* One, there was a sad day when Pranom was no longer in the classroom. No one knew where, and I was sad to lose my friend. But the story I learned, so long after, is a story my friend Pranom is going to tell you today."

The room was still, even though these three hundred young ladies had no idea what was about to unfold before them. Vuthisit motioned for me to join her, and I did so, my knees feeling wobbly and the three sheets of notes in my left hand almost fluttering with my stage fright. Vuthisit slipped her arm about my waist before continuing. "Today our school is very blessed. Now my friend Pranom is 'Miss Daggett.' She teaches trigonometry and calculus and I know you ladies love and admire her. But today please pray for my friend as she tells you a story about how Jesus saved her."

The girls looked up at us, confused, and there was a smattering of polite applause. I understood the awkward silence; after all, I had been an authority figure all year.

These girls had seen me teach, lead out in daily worships, offer closing prayers, tease some of them about their *fans* and romantic escapades. What secret was I about to unveil?

I'd made sure to have at least my first three paragraphs memorized, so I swallowed hard and then launched right in. I was a seventh grader. Doing well in math. Singing Christian songs in Mr. Daggett's choir. Trying hard to speak English without any accent.

And then my mom lost her struggle with cancer. My dad tried to do a good job, but he was often away. Sometimes his job kept him away half the night and I would have to lock the doors on the house and go to bed in the awful stillness of being all by myself in the darkness.

And then there was jail. And my Uncle Viroj. And that short, unsuspecting drive down to Pattaya Beach. The rented condo was really nice: fourth floor in an almost new subdivision. From the kitchen window we could just barely see the beach and all the parasailing visitors floating up so high next to the clouds. I thought I would be going to a new school, and even though it wasn't BCS, and I was already missing my friends, I thought it would be a good adventure to live right in a fun tourist place like Pattaya.

"Maybe you can guess what happened next," I said, pausing to allow the dark possibilities to fill the assembly hall. "My uncle never once had an idea of caring for me. I was not going to go to school. I was not going to graduate. I was never going to get to attend university or make plans to teach or be a doctor or a successful businesswoman. No. I was going to wear a white bikini and dance in a go-go bar. Men would look at me. And most of the men, as they looked, with a beer in their hand, would move their fingers like this." I made a sort of crude waving gesture. "They all said the same thing. 'Take off what you are wearing. Let us see the rest of you, little girl.'"

The silence in that chapel was electric; I could tell the younger girls, the seventh and eighth graders, were floored by the abrupt shift in the saga.

I went on, telling about the first night where I was expected to follow a man to his hotel room. That I had an envelope with me; it was my duty to get at least a thousand baht from each gentleman I "entertained."

I hadn't planned this part, but several times as I spoke, I came up to English words I wasn't sure the girls would fully grasp. Hesitating, I impulsively switched over to Thai, unburdening my testimony the best I could, and going back to English as soon as I could regain some emotional equilibrium.

I painted the sordid experience in broad strokes, leaving out most of the anatomical horrors, but wanting to impress this army of young woman with how deadly a life it can be. And how thankful I was that generous Christians had put their own reputations on the line, risking physical danger in order to pull me free and give me a brand new start in Jesus.

"So here I am," I said as the last few minutes of the hour ticked away. The place was awash in a holy hush; I almost wondered if my students were even *breathing*. "That was then. This is now. Today. All those men, they attacked me. They tried to leave their mark. For the Pussycat Club, I was just a name. One more girl standing on the bar in a white bikini. To my uncle, I was just his little money machine.

"But today," I went on, raising my fist above my head, "I am Miss Daggett. I am a Christian woman, and I am a BCS teacher, and I am a new creation in Jesus, totally liberated and free, and I have a man who loves me and wants to be with me forever, and I want to tell you that God is just so wonderful and powerful and caring. He loves me just as I am! When I was finally free of Pattaya and my uncle, my new auntie and my new mom said something to me I will never forget. They said to me: 'Pranom, those men did not leave a mark. Not any mark that counts. No! You are clean! You are free! You are wonderful and you are a special prize!'"

The room exploded in thunderous applause, the girls hopping up to their feet, surging forward, and I felt my tear ducts surrendering. I had to pause and dab at my eyes, and in the back of the room I saw that Saman and my own Aunt Rachel were arm in arm, and his shoulders were shaking. Rachel Marie said something to him and I could tell he was nodding in agreement.

Noah came back to the stage, and for a long, precious moment he just stood next to me. Then he reached out and took my hand. "Ladies," he said, addressing the wave of womanhood seated there before the two of us, "I have never heard a miracle like this one. Isn't Jesus amazing? Wow!"

He didn't have his guitar, but he went right back to the chorus and within two words, all three hundred girls were with him, singing in unison. *So take me as you find me. All my fears and failures, Fill my life again.* Halfway through the chorus, Saman got to the stage, his eyes red-rimmed, and nothing felt so good as his strong arm around me. I rested my head against his shoulder, thankful beyond words that I was in the care of a generous Redeemer and a prince like Saman.

WE HAD STAFF MEETING after school, but there really wasn't much on the agenda except for about forty people all coming up and hugging me. Benjie Cey was still blowing his nose, sweetly emotional, and I got teary all over again with the kind things he murmured.

Sue waited until we adjourned, and then called me to the front. "That was truly, truly magnificent," she affirmed. "Pranom, our dear champion, I'm so proud I could bust. I saw those girls; believe me, you touched their hearts. You got to them."

"I'm glad," I responded, meaning it. "I worked a long time on what to say."

"I know you did. And the Lord just blessed you wonderfully. I could see his power flowing through you. That one time where you were getting kind of emotional and sort of lost it . . . and then you seemed to take a breath and the light came back into your face, and you had it together again."

I knew the exact moment she was recalling. "Yeah. That was kind of biblical."

"Pretty nice. Anyway, Pranom, us finding you for BCS was a stroke of divine providence. Praise the Lord."

That last remark stayed with me as Paloma and I rode the bus back to #305. Was that why my baptism felt wonderful and yet oddly incomplete? Was I still destined to leave Thailand and return to Portland in seven weeks? What about Saman? I was madly in love with him, and quietly confident that he returned my affections. He seemed to want to commit to a lifetime together: marriage, honeymoon, kids, shared vacations and joy and sorrows and bills and birthday parties for the next five or so decades. How was that going to happen?

I thought about this while the wheels on the bus went round and round. It was impossible to consider ever leaving this rich new experience. Saman. BCS. Auntie Rachel and my teaching pals. Pastor Gino and United Christian Church. I adored being a teacher; I was good at it without having to agonize. Calculus and bits of life wisdom just flowed out of me; sweet chunks of Christian witness fell from my lips like candy out of a piñata. My army of *Matthayom* students admired me and were adeptly carving out careers and fledgling faith experiences under my tutelage.

BUT . . . back home in the United States were two people whose souls were inseparable from my own. Dad and Mom. Now more than ever, I loved them with a desperation that bordered on ache. I couldn't wait to be with them again, to feel my mother's arms around me, and Daddy's bass guffaw, his beard against my cheek as he called me sweetheart.

My sister and I hadn't exchanged two words the whole bus ride home, and I don't think I said anything out loud, but her head suddenly jerked up. A woman across from us, arms loaded with packages from a nearby department store, seemed jolted out of her reverie as well. "Did you say something?" Paloma murmured.

"Huh uh."

"Oh. Thought you did."

"Maybe just thinking brilliant thoughts to myself and one slipped out," I managed, blushing.

As we were climbing free and looking both ways to see if the *thanon* was clear, she stepped closer to me. "I was so proud of you, you know."

There was a really nice glow between us, and I feared I might start blubbering right there on the curb. "Thanks. It was great having you sitting there, giving me all your prayers and support."

"For sure."

I was about to ask her how she was processing the idea of breaking up with Klahan and showing her passport to an airline officer at Suvarnabhumi Airport in less than two months. But the words died in my throat. Because resting against our nondescript and battered apartment door was a cheerful bouquet of orchids. It clearly came from an upscale florist, one of the boutique places now sprouting, no pun intended, all over the nicer neighborhoods in Bangkok.

"Wow. Someone else liked your little tell-all too," Paloma teased. "I thought lover boy was on a budget these days."

"Shush." I plucked the tiny card loose from its plastic holder and eased a thumbnail underneath the flap.

"What's he say?"

"Oh." It took me a moment to process what I was reading. "Um, it's not from Saman."

"No way. The good doctor's got competition?"

"Huh uh." I was halfway through the message, but paused. "My friend Vuthisit sent these, I guess."

"Wow. They're gorgeous."

"Sure are." I handed her the card and she read it aloud as we stood there on the stoop, backpacks sprawled on the rough concrete. *Dear Pranom: You were amazing! I prayed many times for God to give you a good message, and he answered my prayer. Thank you for sharing the story of your rescue. Vuthisit.*

Penned along the bottom in her neat penmanship

was a concluding line, this one in Thai, and my sister thrust it back in my hand. "No fair," she protested. "I can't decipher the secret code."

"Oh." I'd already absorbed the message, but read it again for her benefit. "*Chahn samart taam tuk sing die doy Pra Kris poo songe hie gaam laang chahn.*"

"Thank you," she yodeled sarcastically. "Not helpful. Gibberish. Twenty baht."

I sighed happily, still basking in my relief over having been so blessed by my Savior. "It's just Philippians 4:13."

"Ah." We recited it together as I fished for the apartment key. "*I can do all things through Christ who strengthens me.*"

We were halfway through our supper of soup and fried-egg sandwiches before I noticed my friend's text message. *I hope you got the bouquet, Pranom. Please call me when you can.*

292   DAVID B. SMITH

TWENTY-THREE

I was pleasantly disoriented by the attention my chapel talk had created, but Vuthisit was a lady on a mission. The very next afternoon she took off from her high-powered banking job and marched me down to Sue's office. The boss lady grinned as if she'd been expecting the interruption, although I found out later the two of them had put their heads together the previous day.

"That was very excellent yesterday," my friend gushed, reaching out and seizing my hand again. "Don't you think, Mrs. C?

"It surely was."

"So this is what I believe." Vuthisit didn't have quite the linguistic advantage I'd gained from a decade in Oregon, and chose her English words with care. "God can prepare a plan; I am sure of it. And then Pranom can share this story with many young people."

She'd only given me the barest glimpse of what she had in mind, and now she unfolded her dream. A two-week tour of schools, both Christian and secular. Redeemer College, where Audrey's husband taught religion. The big Christian academy in Chiang Mai. Our sister school in the Ekamai district. Perhaps even Bangkok College or Chula. "It is a certainty that if Doctor Ratana joins Pranom and does some good music, even these big universities would be very pleased to hear this program."

I felt myself blushing. It was one thing to stand up front and tell how God and a colorful keyboard guy named Tommy had plucked me from the swamp of sin. But Chulalongkorn University with its teeming and urbane student population? Did my childhood friend really think we could put together a lecture tour and hit Phuket Island?

"That's something Pastor Ethan could help us with," Sue pointed out. "His wife is influential at Prince of Songkhla U."

Vuthisit squeezed my hand again, and I almost laughed out loud at her bubbly enthusiasm. "Don't pinch too hard."

"But I am very excited! Your message is so important, Pranom."

"What about classes here?" I remonstrated, eager to join the adventure but also knowing that my calculus students were down to a scant seven weeks left. "And I really wouldn't want to be going here and there alone. At least somebody should come along and, you know, just help with details. PA and all that." An absurd mental picture popped into my brain: me being followed around by an entourage of helpers and flunkies, dusting off my airplane seat before I boarded the first-class section of a Thai Airways flight. Chartered, no less. It was a ridiculous image, and I pushed the idea away.

Sue sat there, glancing from one of us to the other. "Ladies, ladies," she smiled. "This is a big opportunity; I'm with you on that."

"Yeah, but . . ." I tried to envision the upcoming April/May calendar with its many academic and social events, especially for soon-to-graduate *Matthayom* students.

"I've got a brainstorm," my boss put in suddenly, energetically tapping a pencil on her desktop. "See what you ladies think."

"Yes, Mrs. C?" Vuthisit leaned forward, her dark eyes snapping with eager energy.

"Well, let's take the next couple of weeks to see about the schedule. Khemkaeng would be brilliant at that, of course; he seems to know everybody in all Thailand."

We both grinned.

"Then we line up as many places as we can: back-to-back-to-back. Maybe some days you could do two events, Pranom, one in the morning and another after lunch if it's not too far away. If we send you to Chiang Mai, of course we'd try to do three or four places while up north." A sudden inspiration hit. "I'll bet if Pastor Gino and Noah just went back to the entire list of schools where the band played these past two terms, most of them would want to have us back."

"But what about my classes here?" I said again, not wanting to squelch the dream, but still wanting to be practical.

"Well. That," Sue responded, "all hinges on one important thing. Can we get somebody really bright to step in for a two-week stint of substitute teaching? Who do we know who could pop right over here and teach high-end calculus?" She got a mischievous smile on her face, and I thought my pulse would go right off the charts with what came next. "And maybe the person we get to sub could save us a few baht by sharing a one-bedroom apartment with her two daughters."

I WAS LITERALLY BABBLING as Vuthisit and I floated out of the ad building and hunted down Paloma in the parking lot. She and Klahan were holding hands and scrolling through photos from the senior class's recent banquet at the Sheraton, and I emitted a most un-faculty-level shriek as I pushed his iPhone away. "Forget that! Mrs. C's going to bring Mom out here to teach for a couple weeks!"

"What!"

Of course, nobody had bothered to place an international call to the other side of the world. But Vuthisit assured my sister that, sure, this was all a done deal. "My husband and I will make this our missionary project for this term," she announced happily. "Please tell your mom that we will purchase her plane ticket if she can come."

Overcome with excitement, I hugged her hard, feeling a tear of happiness slide down my cheek. All at once I caught myself. "But wait. If my mom comes and teaches my classes, and I'm going here and there doing these programs, I'll hardly see her."

Paloma purposely stepped on my toe. "Sure you will. Just . . . you know, here and there. You do an afternoon program at Chula, but you'll be home for dinner and all that. We'll figure it all out."

There was something else in the humid Bangkok

air, which so suddenly seemed sweetly perfumed and fragrant with promise. Vuthisit glanced around to make sure we were alone. "There is also this, Pranom," she said. "We can all see that Dr. Saman plans to marry you. So your mom needs to come. She must meet him and help to make wedding plans."

Oops. So there it was. It was actually possible I might be planting my flag of residence right here in Bangkok. And having to deal with a topsy-turvy summer of sorting out my life journey. But my anxiety over that was subsumed by the joy of having my mom come floating into Suvarnabhumi Airport and mentor me through some of the decisions that lay ahead.

MRS. C IS RIGHT. My Uncle Khemkaeng is pretty much a miracle man. In less than two weeks, he and Noah had burned up the phone lines and gotten me booked on a speaking tour loop. It began in Bangkok, jetted me up to four whirlwind events in Chiang Mai, shuttled east to both Chiang Rai and Ubon, and then back down to the capital for a newsworthy double bill: my concluding presentation along with a brief Christian pop concert by *Maw* Ratana at prestigious Chulalongkorn University. Pastor Gino worked with me to establish a web page and a blog, and already some of the BCS girls were filling it up with nice comments about how my story had inspired them.

Our entire teaching staff wanted to make the airport run with me, but in the end we decided on just Aunt Rachel. I was breathless with anticipation as we all climbed into Saman's Mercedes for the pickup. I know global separations aren't like they were fifty years ago, when missionaries to the Far East said goodbye to

American loved ones and then disappeared from their lives for interminable five-year stints. This whole school term, Mom and I had spoken at least weekly by phone, instinctively calculating the fifteen hours of time difference between our two work worlds. And Zoom chats were a soul-saving blessing, such a quick jolt of familial comfort. Still, there's nothing like a mom's physical hug and her voice in your ear when you just feel like leaning against a parent's shoulder to wail out your anguishes, genuine or frivolous.

FAA regulations are the same the world over, so we weren't permitted to hang out at Mom's arrival gate. The three of us paced back and forth on the other side of the huge Customs queue, antsy with anticipation and scanning our cell phones. Finally my screen lit up. *Touchdown! Can't wait, sweetie!! Don't leave the airport without me, lol. I'll be out in a quick flash. Mom.*

Paloma and I went ape, hugging each other and bouncing up and down like twins sharing a single pogo stick. *Boing! Boing! Boing!* I'm sure Saman was feeling his own version of Bangkok butterflies, but he absorbed our histrionics with an indulgent smile.

Maybe twenty excruciating minutes later, we spotted our mother's gangly, beautiful form as she wheeled a silver airport cart directly toward us. "Yay!!!!" Paloma shrieked, sprinting into Mom's arms. I was right behind her, and the three of us clung to each other for a happy couple of minutes. "Don't squeeze all the oxygen out of me," Mom gasped, comically trying to regain her breath. "It takes a lot of air to explain hyperbolic graphs and asymptotes."

I finally tugged myself loose and brought my boyfriend into the picture. "Mom, this is Saman, my um

. . . special friend. Sweetie, this is my mom, who is way more amazing than I am. And if you don't get along with her, I'll never speak to you again."

He laughed, and I was jealous of his urbane sense of ease. "Hi, Mrs. Daggett. I'm really glad to meet you." With a burst of funk, he added smoothly: "*Yindee dhon raap.*" Welcome!

"Let me look you over, young man. My daughter hints about wanting to overstay her scheduled airplane return ticket, and I suspect you're the main culprit." We all laughed, and Mom did indeed look over this new possible Asian addition to her family.

He led us out to the parking garage, and indulgently allowed the three of us to babble in girlish delight all the way into the city. "Are you hungry, Mrs. Daggett? How about some dinner?"

Mom shook her head. "Look, it's going to waste my whole trip if you keep 'Mrs. Daggetting' me the entire time I'm here. 'Samantha' will be just fine and dandy. And no, they fed me and fed me and endlessly fed me on the plane."

Despite her jet lag, Mom managed to stay up past midnight with us girls, as we gossiped about weddings and my pending speaking tour. "I'd love to hear every one of them, sugar," she sighed as we finally doused the bedroom light. "But for sure I'll be there to hear your grand finale at the university. Since BCS doesn't have classes on Friday afternoons."

"She did amazing, Mom," Paloma chimed in loyally, and I gave her a squeeze before we drifted off to sleep in a contented state of mind.

The tour itself was a thrilling marathon. My talks were pretty close to verbatim at each school or church venue, but before stepping to the podium, I always prayed for God to give me a fresh passion for the unique girls in my audience. For most of the Bangkok events, Ratana was able to slip away from Mission Hospital and perform an opening and closing number, either with Noah on his guitar or using a digital track through the house PA. And as I shared my testimony, and made eye contact with one young female and then another, I felt the Lord swelling my confidence and empowering me to share unguarded memories.

"This is just so good," Sue affirmed with a giant hug as we wrapped up my Thursday engagement at the big megachurch on Wattana Road. "There must have been over 250 here. And with the video, I guess they can post it for everyone else to hear as well."

Early the next morning it was Uncle Khemkaeng who boarded the northbound air shuttle with me for the quick ride to Chiang Mai. His wealthy parents still lived up there, so he was the natural choice. He chatted briefly with me as the plane sped north, but was also a model of executive efficiency, thumbing in a flurry of text messages and directives for BCS staffers to follow back home.

I had never been to our huge sister academy on the outskirts of Chiang Mai, and Khemkaeng regaled me with the story of how he and Rachel Marie had visited the place very early in their own courtship. "It was during the Christmas holiday," he recalled. "She rode up with me on the train to visit my parents." A grin. "I was already very much in love, and she came along with her brother and sister-in-law."

"Time to meet the parents already?" I teased, and he almost seemed to blush. He steered our rental car carefully through some smallish, barely paved roads, and finally pointed to a sign. "We're almost there."

The campus had a lovely Christian church at the far end, and I was pleased to see that even just the *Matthayom* ladies streaming in almost filled up the sanctuary. Uncle Khemkaeng and the school's American administrator jointly greeted everyone, including neighborhood guests, and explained the purpose of our tour. I got up, my heart overflowing with thankfulness for the power of Christian education, and testified how my mighty Savior Jesus had brought me out of such a risky life. This was my first time to share the entire saga in my native Thai language, and I felt a sense of comfort as I related how God's people had schemed and sacrificed in order to bring me to freedom.

"See, this is all that Christianity is," I asserted toward the close. "Liberty. God came into my life and he shattered the chains that had me in that evil club, that bar where girls were bought and sold. I can never forget that moment when my Uncle Khemkaeng . . ." I caught myself. "Well, he is my uncle today! Back then, he was just this kind Christian man who wanted to be a part of God's liberation plan." I glanced behind me, and Khemkaeng's face was wreathed in smiles.

Back at the hotel, he dutifully uploaded a five-minute video of part of my talk to our BCS web page, and I sat out by the pool, my feet and ankles dangling in the water, gossiping with Mom and Paloma till past midnight. As an afterthought, I began reminiscing about Saman's Pattaya Beach baptism and my odd sense of unease, that in my triumphant conversion party, some element, some *thing* had gotten left out. "I'm still a teeny bit weirded out about it," I told her. "I guess it's just because I don't know for sure how things will end up with Saman. Meaning, you know, do I end up living here or back home. But . . . I don't know . . ." My voice trailed off, and I could hear both of them mentally processing on the other end, no one speaking.

At last Mom came back on. Just a long maternal sigh at first, and I waited along with Paloma for her to reveal some parental wisdom. But she shook me off. "I know what it is," she said guardedly. "And it's not that."

"Huh?" *How could she know if I didn't?*

"Look, baby," she said quickly. "Obviously it's a big, scary idea if you end up staying in Bangkok. But really, you need to make whatever life plans fulfill you. If you marry this man, and live here in Asia, we're happy with that. We can come see you; you'll make trips to the States to show us our grandkids. We've got the Internet. And now Zoom parties. So that's not as big as I ever made it."

I didn't know if she had seen the determined gleam in my boyfriend's eyes and was now simply bowing to the inevitable. But she seemed eerily calm.

So I almost began to splutter. "Well, if that's not it, then what's bugging me? 'Cause for sure, even though I feel really good about God and stuff, it's like I'm not quite there yet."

"That's because you're not."

Her blunt assessment hit me right in the face. "What then?"

Silence. Then she said in her crisp mom tone: "Get some sleep, honey. You guys have two more events in Chiang Mai, then Ubon, then back here for the big one at the college."

She was about to sign off without further elaboration, and I could almost feel my little sister's teasing smile through the phone line. *They're probably talking behind my back the whole time I'm up here.* I retreated to my hotel room and stared out the window at the meandering Ping River, thinking and praying. *God, I give you my all. I WANT to give you my all. But it feels like I haven't yet, and I don't even know what it is I've held back. If you show me, I'll at least try to cut it loose.*

It was nearly midnight before I climbed into bed, thinking as I donned my pajamas: *if God wants me to surrender my relationship with Saman, that'd be impossible. It can't be that. Can it?*

I resolved not to keep fretting about a seemingly unanswerable question. I rode with Uncle Khemkaeng to the airport, we flew to Ubon, I accepted the greetings of the hostesses who met us at the next stop, I offered *wais*, we went out to dinner, I gave my talks. It was actually a delight signing autographs after the school assembly, hugging teenage girls and assuring them that, yes, they were awesome and special.

By Friday afternoon I was almost beginning to feel wobbly as I deplaned back in Bangkok. We had a tight schedule; my headline event at Chula was scheduled for six and traffic was ferocious as we approached the city. Mom and Paloma had ridden out to meet us in the BCS van, and I had Saman's text-message guarantee that he'd be there as well. I spotted him coming through the crowd just before Ratana stepped up to the stage to begin performing. He gave me a lingering hug and even scored a chaste kiss before Noah warmed up the crowd with a series of cute jokes about life with a pop-music celebrity.

Her first two songs were actually secular favorites that had swept through the Bangkok club scene since

Christmas, and I had to admit my friend Ratana exuded raw star power. Her vocals were amazing; I could feel the energy sweeping through the auditorium as she shimmied across the stage. Noah had told me to brace myself for her performance of "Precious Lord," and when she went back and forth between English and Thai, drawing the college kids in with her spiritual presence, I felt almost overcome with emotion. "Your wife is unbelievable," I murmured to Noah, and he nodded, seeming surprised himself.

In such a cosmopolitan setting, I had been asked to share in English, and I expanded my testimony to add little bits about how this gawky American woman had poured herself into the redemption of a scarred Thai kid barely into her teens. "And then my rescuer adopted me," I told the hushed crowd. "She gave me her heart and her fortune and even her name. I will always be a Thai woman through and through, and yet on all the visa papers it says 'Daggett.'"

Girls were craning to spot my adopted mother, and Samantha blushed and then half-stood to give them a wave. "Here is my last thing to say," I told the gathering of mostly young females. "I do not come to Chula to talk about Jesus Christ. Even though both *Maw* Ratana and I have found our new faith to be a thing of power and beauty in our lives. But I will say that *Pra Jow* is real to us. We worship him; we pray to him; we are his ambassadors. To live a life sustained by a Father in heaven is precious to both of us, and I hope as you meditate on the ways where you have felt a strange, quiet blessing, you will soon know that it is God who tugs on our heart. It is God who makes all things new. Not us. It is God."

It was deathly still there in the university auditorium, and then began a slow, respectful applause. I
bowed my head, acknowledging the kindness of my new
friends, and then made my way to stand next to Ratana,
who was signing autographs and handing out blog
brochures to her fans. Two university officials came up
and gave us both *wais*, thanking us for sharing with the
Chula community. Noah was right behind them, and he
had a youngish TV executive in tow. "Pranom, my
friend Sopon wants to get just a couple clips on tape. Is
that okay?"

I said sure, and he led me to a back room where a
cameraman was already waiting, audio gear strung out
and hooked into the equipment. He asked me, still in
Thai, what I hoped would be gained by my sharing such
a personal story. I barely had time to mentally compose
a halfway non-sectarian reply, but felt a flash of
inspiration as the technician counted down with his
fingers. *Three . . . two . . . one . . . you're on!*

"This is what I think," I said into the camera.
"Every girl in our nation should be able to grow up
knowing she is respected, that she is a person, a being
with value and thoughts. We are women. We are not
meat! We are not toys. I hope every father and every
brother . . ." I had to force myself to say what came next.
"I hope every uncle and every man who is a boss or a
person of influence or power will begin to realize that
we, the women of Thailand, are beautiful people with
minds to value and hearts filled with love and souls that
need to be nurtured and fed with education and beauty
and culture. The selfishness of Patpong Road and the
Pussycat Club–Thailand's dignity will always be scarred
while such things are tolerated. I was very blessed to

escape. But no girl should have to endure such scorn and disrespect."

Sopon thanked me profusely, and after I signed the release papers allowing his TV station to use the footage, I rejoined Saman and my family.

He drove us away from the college, and just three kilometers away from the sprawling campus, pulled over to the curb. "Are we eating here?" I asked.

He shook his head. "Look. We can have meals anytime. Your mother leaves for home in two days. The three of you ought to have a good dinner together." I loved him for this thoughtfulness and reached over to squeeze his hand. "But I'll try to come to the apartment later so I can hear all about Chiang Mai."

"That'd be wonderful."

I didn't know the various restaurants in this part of Bangkok, but was surprised when Mom took Paloma and me in tow and marched us directly toward the golden arches. "Are you kidding, Mom?" Paloma cackled. "You come all the way to Bangkok and we're going to order Big Macs?"

"There's a method to my madness," she informed Paloma, and the two of us exchanged bemused shrugs.

We went up to the counter and Mom fished in her purse, pulling out an assortment of Thai bills. "Get anything you want, girlies. Your dad insisted we do this, and it's all on me."

"Well, then, let's go crazy," I giggled, relieved and in a somewhat celebratory mood now that my grand tour was successfully concluded. "I'm going to get both flavors of their McFlurrys."

"I thought I raised you better than that," Samantha sighed, then tossed me the wicked grin I loved so much from way back when.

While we were waiting for our food, my mom pointed up at the menu sign. "Not you, Pranom," she said. "Stay out of this. But Paloma, can you read what it says right there?"

She squinted. "Well, duh. I know it's 'Coca-Cola' 'cause it says so in English right next to it. But I can kind of figure it out from the Thai. That big squiggle there makes an 'o,' and I guess that other thing's the 'k' consonant. So hey. 'Co-ca-co-la.'"

All at once a ghostly bit of remembering crossed her face. "Holy cow, Mom. We did this way back in third grade too. I just remembered."

"That's right," Mom nodded. "When you were eight years old. We came here, just you and me, for a last mother-daughter dinner."

Oh yeah. Now I remembered last year's quick junk-food trip in Portland where Mom told me about the decade-old appointment.

"This exact McDonald's? Silom Square?"

Mom nodded. "Uh huh. I was finishing up my term at BCS, about to head back to the States. Pranom, honey, this is before you and I . . . you know, before you and I got together. And fell in love," she added awkwardly. "But honey, I was about to tell you that it was possible I'd marry Tommy. We came here, you and I talked about it, you said it'd be okay with you, and that next weekend, down at Pattaya, he asked me."

"Wow," she managed. "Now I for sure remember. And I spelled out 'Coca-Cola just like today.'"

"Yep." Samantha smiled, remembering. "You had on that little yellow top Auntie Rachel got for you at the Chiang Mai night bazaar. I could hardly get you to take that silly thing off at bedtime. But I knew we had to have a mother-daughter talk, that a pair of milkshakes might make it go down better, and we came right there." Mom actually pivoted and pointed to a corner stall. "Ten years ago, girlies, I think we sat right there for our summit meeting. So let's go there again."

"Uh oh." I felt a rush of love for my American mom, but still wondered if she might be about to let loose with her grand revelation. We held hands and said a prayer together, not minding the likely stares of nearby diners. I dipped a pair of my fries in the ketchup and then waited. "I guess it's my turn then."

Mom smiled knowingly. "Sure. If that's okay."

I figured she was going to spill some drippy mom emotions on me about how, okay, she and Dad would buck up and figure out how to survive my permanent move to Dr. Takuathung's world. And how we'd make do with frequent flier miles and a choreographed rendezvous in Maui or something. But instead, she dropped a bombshell on me that neither of us girls had anticipated.

"I've prayed about this a thousand times since watching you both get on the plane to come over here."

"What, Mom?" It was Paloma who asked.

"Well, honey, this is for your sister."

I swallowed hard and then braced myself with a hit of diet Coke. "Sure."

Mom did a little bite thing with her lower lip, a gesture I remembered from way earlier. Then reached across the table and took my hands in her own. "Honey, I think it's wonderful that you and your sister came to Bangkok and, you know, found your true soul again. And your dad and I are just so thankful that your walk with Jesus is more solid than ever."

I nodded, grateful beyond words. "But I can tell you what the one more thing is," she said softly. "It's not got to do with plans or where you live. That part's fine; it's okay. There are ways to make that work, and maybe even miracles we don't know about. That's not it at all." Now her eyes began to grow moist, and I felt a strange scary feeling enter the fast-food restaurant. "Sweetheart, baby, you're safe now. You have Daddy and me and Paloma and your BCS family. And Jesus. But sweetie, there's one more thing."

What? Oh my God, Mom . . .

"Honey, it's your other dad. And your uncle. You can't really get all the way well until you forgive them."

And I simply stared at her. No way. There was an untouched hamburger on my tray, one torn ketchup wrapper, an order of fries, my soda. My sister Paloma, her blond curls tangled around her blue eyes. Four or five meters away was a Ronald McDonald clown figure, and beyond that a trio of Thai kids were tussling in the kid playground. Digital screens were flickering with scrumptious footage of milkshakes and crispy McNuggets. Stacks of baht were flowing into the cash registers and the calories piled up. But above and impossibly beyond it all was this moral Golgotha: *forgive thine enemy*.

I didn't really think that in my heart, forgiveness for my biological dad was any big thing. I wasn't horrendously angry at him. But to forgive Uncle Viroj? Are you kidding me? My entire testimony on this grand tour was built around the glory that Christ had rescued me from that man's betrayal. Uncle Viroj was the judas in the story. He was the villain who made Tommy's bold foray into the Pussycat Club such a dramatic, stirring crowd-pleaser.

"Mom, that's ridiculous." It was Paloma who found her voice first. "That man's a bum. He's total scum. He's probably locked up, but if he's not he ought to be."

"Yeah." I didn't know whether to feel indignant or simply helplessly overwhelmed. "And anyway, Mom, he's gone. Nobody knows where he is. I already looked around, and both of them are just . . . they're not around. So they're out of the picture."

"None of that matters," she said softly. Then to me: "Honey, are you angry with your uncle?"

"Of course I am," I said, not bitterly but with some ferocity. "Mom, you know what he did."

"Yes. It was evil and he's evil too."

"Then why should I forgive him? And . . . I mean, how? How would I tell him?"

She shook her head. "Honey, you don't tell him. You tell yourself and you tell the Lord."

That was a new thought, and I took less than four seconds to digest it and then spit it out. "Mom, that's just totally dumb. If I can't tell him, then I can't . . . there's no process. I can't forgive him."

"Yeah. And Mom . . ." Paloma was steaming, and she actually reached over and clutched my forearm, her fingers digging into my own sinew until it almost hurt. "Mom, we're not idiots, see? We're not going to just overlook something as evil as this is. Didn't you hear Pranom's talk? What happened to her was a nightmare. And this Viroj jerk, he did all that. I don't hear him coming around and saying, 'Please forgive me.'" She caught herself and it was an awkward interlude. "Um, I guess if he did manage to find us and all, heaven forbid, then Pranom would have to process that when it happened. But she doesn't owe this creep one thing." She swallowed hard. "And if you're saying she can't be an okay Christian without forgiving something like this, well, then I guess neither of us would be very good Christians. 'Cause that's how things are."

I didn't want my entire testimony to be nothing but a *me too*, but I nodded abjectly, my appetite gone. I did force another couple of fries into my mouth, but there was no taste to them and I could hardly chew.

Mom absorbed the twin outbursts without apparent emotion, and then smiled, a sort of inward thing not even aimed at us. Then she told us both, her voice serene: "Eat some food, girls. And I'll tell you a story."

We did begin to nibble on our Big Macs, and as we did so, Mom spilled her own testimony. How she came out here to Bangkok as a writhing, bitter, almost swallowed-up-in-venom mess. "I hated your dad with a passion," she told us, nodding in Paloma's direction to indicate that she was referencing Brian, that loser guy down by the Portland wharf. "He betrayed me over and over. He was a lousy dad, sorry to say. And I got here to Thailand with a heart filled with pus. It was all I could think about. But while I was down at Pattaya, right during the time, sweetie, when the Lord was getting you out of that hell you were in, your Auntie Rachel helped me to understand what forgiveness really is."

It took Mom maybe another five minutes to lead us, two trembling souls, her daughters, down to what she and Auntie Rachel called The Ocean. So close to the Pussycat Club is our mighty Lord's ocean of grace. Trillions of gallons of surging hope and forgiveness. All the iniquities of the world can be washed away, buried, swallowed up in the deep Calvary currents that remove the stain of rebellion.

"So you are in that ocean, my sweet child," Mom said, taking my hand and not letting it go. "But to really feel it and have it, you must allow your first daddy to walk into it too. And even this uncle that you hate and that Paloma hates and that I hate. I do. I hate that man. But I forgive him."

"What's that mean!" I burst out. "Mom, those are just words! 'I forgive him'? Huh?" I slapped on an expletive without even meaning to.

She accepted my profane outburst with utter calm. "You forgiving this uncle means only one thing. And not any other thing. You're not saying it didn't happen. You're not saying it wasn't terrible. You're not saying it wasn't wrong. You're not saying you weren't hurt or scarred or that he doesn't owe you to the moon and back. It just says: 'Uncle Viroj, I am in this ocean. I am at peace in the ocean of God's forgiveness and grace. And I *release you*. Your life, your fate, is between you and my mighty God. He can save you if he wants. He can send you to hell if he wants. If you respond and he takes you to heaven someday, that is okay with me because the love of God's mighty ocean bathing and comforting me is so good that even your sin, Uncle, is swallowed up.'" Mom reached over and borrowed a napkin from the dispenser, dabbing futilely at her eyes. "Forgiveness is nothing but giving up that other person to God's infinite wisdom, trusting him to do the best thing there is to do."

TWENTY-FOUR

Those two hours at the Silom Square McDonald's were my Armageddon; that's for sure. I sat there in glum agony, my gaze fixated on a ketchup-stained napkin next to the discarded paper burger wrapping. That soiled tissue was a metaphor for my current state, I realized. My anger against this criminal man, this phantom sinner, Uncle Viroj, was locked away in a closet. But it wasn't gone. It was an invisible infection, a cancer that might metastasize until it consumed both me and the man I loved.

My appetite was shot, so I didn't treat myself to that second McFlurry, but Paloma and I traded forced bites of the one dessert. "You're probably right," I told Mom. "But it sounds impossible. I'm sorry."

My sister didn't say anything but her expression was both eloquent and X-rated. She finished off the ice cream treat and set the empty cup down next to the pile of gooey trash with some force. "The best thing would just be if he's dead," she said, daring Mom to contradict her.

"And maybe he is," she agreed, apparently deciding she'd done enough witnessing for one afternoon.

We rode together in an air-conditioned taxi back to the apartment: Paloma up front and me sharing the back seat with my mother. She craned to see as many sights as possible, occasionally asking me about Bangkok landmarks, but my mind was a muddle over this new, waterlogged burden. Really, what did people want me to do? Sing out into the humid night air of Thailand: *If you're out there, Uncle, I forgive you*? My sister was right. What would be the point of such an empty gesture? *If a tree falls in the forest, does it make a sound? If you "forgive" a monster who's a thousand kilometers away, does some cosmic burden shift in the heavenly scales?*

Mom paid the cabbie and we climbed out, but we were a morose trio ascending the two flights of stairs. We plodded toward #305, and I took a deep breath, determined to get off this moral carousel and simply enjoy my mother's company for the rest of our stay together. "Okay, you guys," I announced, pushing the front door open, "Let's just be happy. I have a dad; his name is Tommy Daggett. If that's not good enough for everybody, then I guess that's tough. But Mom, it's awesome having you here, and I want for us to have fun the rest of while you're with us."

"You got it, sweetie," she sang out, and I felt cheered by her resolute enthusiasm. Mom had brought me a stack of calculus tests to grade, but I actually giggled now as I shoved them under the bed. "I'm officially procrastinating that stuff," I announced. "I'll do them on the trip back from the airport after we drop you off."

"Don't even say 'airport,'" Paloma moaned, flopping down on the couch. "Come on, you guys. We've got three episodes of 'The Big Bang Theory' recorded."

I perched myself on the carpeting and rested my head on Mom's lap as the sitcom spun itself out. I was the only one who could zip through the Thai subtitles, and I managed a wan smile as the jokes rolled along, with Raj and Leonard picking on Sheldon. But my brain was still in fret mode, and I pondered the Christian ideal of *simply deciding*. You, Sir, Are Forgiven. I *will* that it be done. *Wow.* It seemed impossible and completely otherworldly. Even on the ride home, I'd spotted an emaciated pair of Thai hookers on a street corner, one of them tapping a reply into her cell phone. I had no doubt she was wearily agreeing to some pimp's ambitious schedule for the night.

The ding of our doorbell interrupted the cheap laugh track, and Paloma pushed the pause button on the remote. "Did we forget to pay the rent?" She grunted as she pushed up to a standing position. "I'm the youngest; I'll get it," she grumped, but tossed us a high-school smile to show she was teasing.

To our surprise, it was her boyfriend. "Hey," Paloma blurted out, surprised to see Klahan all gussied up in a black suit. "Yikes. Did we have a date? I musta forgot."

"No, no." Despite being a senior, he was a rather shy guy and still woefully clumsy in English. "We have surprise for Miss Daggett. Can she come out?"

"Looks like it's for you," Paloma said. "Some big surprise."

"Oh, man." I hid a sigh, but Klahan's tux was anything but trivial. I'd changed into a pair of shorts and a tank top, and felt scruffy as I went to the door. "Hey, Klahan. Did you come to say 'sorry' for flubbing my mom's calc quiz?"

"I got 'A' on test," he said, but brushed aside my quip. "Please, Miss Daggett. Hurry."

"What is it?"

I stepped out onto the narrow concrete wall and leaned over the railing. To my surprise, Noah was down there with a knot of at least fifteen BCS choir members. The guys were in their performing tuxedos and all the *Matthayom* ladies had their elegant mid-thigh black banquet dresses. "Oh, you guys . . ."

Noah managed a teasing wave from the street below, then turned to the students and hit a note on his pitch pipe. "All right, ladies and gents," I heard him murmur. "This is way important. If we want Miss Daggett to stay at BCS, please don't sing off-key."

What?

His guitar was leaning against the school van, and he picked it up, caressing the neck and strumming a bit. I remembered he had a battery-operated portable amp that didn't need a plug, and he did a bluesy riff to match the disheveled state of my soul on this gray Friday evening. It took a few bars for me to get the gist of it, but the tenors and basses kicked in with a subdued sort of pop thing: *shoo-bap-a-dap, shoo-bap-a-dap.* Suddenly I remembered all this from an oldies FM station in Portland, and felt my flesh tingle when a man's solo wafted up to me from two floors below.

Are the stars out tonight? I don't know if it's cloudy or bright. I only have eyes for you, dear . . .

I couldn't hear who was singing, but all at once my beloved Saman stepped out from underneath the balcony where he'd hidden himself away. He wasn't much of a vocalist, but nothing had ever sounded so poignantly sweet as his voice as he strained to send a message up to me.

Yikes! This is the moment. He's going to propose marriage!!

The choir girls, all my Thai sisters, were masking smiles as they did the background vocals on the chorus. Saman paused now as the gents, along with Noah, did four more reps of the male doo-wop vocals: *shoo-bap-a-dap, shoo-bap-a-dap.*

Mom pressed up behind me. "Sweetie, this is going to be it," she murmured, and I could tell she was almost crying. Paloma was sniffling, and I felt her hand slide into mine. "Love you," she murmured. "This is so awesome, Pranom."

Saman came to the song's concluding lines and I was sure my heart was going to bust itself wide open. I wanted so badly to marry him; I did. *I love you so much!* I wanted to scream it out so everyone in Bangkok could hear me. I wanted to be his wife and live here in Bangkok and raise a family and be the mother to his cute little sons and daughters. I wanted to sit together in UCC week by week and listen as my husband helped teach the Bible lesson and translate for Pastor Gino.

And yes, all at once I knew something deep and wonderful and demanding in my soul. I wanted to be absolutely free of the Pussycat Club. And my bitterness toward Uncle Viroj. I recalled now with icy clarity a vignette Mom had tugged loose over that tasteless bit of a Big Mac earlier this Friday afternoon. Some story about how a Jewish rabbi had survived the Nazi holocaust during World War II. The concentration camps, the gas chambers, the torturing and the monstrous war crimes committed by the high command in Berlin. But before the liberated priest stepped off the boat in New York Harbor, he had quietly prayed and then actually granted absolution to the worst Nazi of them all. "I had to forgive him before I got here," he confessed later. "I did not want to bring Adolf Hitler inside of me to my new world."

So I actually blurted it out loud as I stood there in the sweet twilight, Saman's lyrics still floating up . . . up . . . up to my waiting ears. *Jesus, help me, oh Jesus, please Jesus, I do. I do! I forgive Uncle Viroj. You have him; you take him. I'm done with my past. I forgive Dad and Uncle Viroj.*

"Sweetie, oh my God." Mom must have heard me, because she was absorbing both my suitor's entreaty from below and now my babble, my murmured submission. "Are you sure?"

"I've got to," I said under my breath, not wanting to miss my lover's pledge. It came to me now, and nothing had ever sounded so fine as Saman's song. *You are here; so am I. Baby, millions of people go by . . .*

I leaned over the rail, my shoulders shaking with unbridled joy. I was absolutely liberated and free; I knew it. I could say yes; I could love and marry this wonderful man and know that it was just Saman and me and my Redeemer, Jesus Christ. The men who had betrayed me were gone, forgiven, erased, forgotten . . . even perhaps *accepted?*

Saman seemed almost unable to get through the concluding line himself, but he managed it. I don't know if Noah supplemented a bit, but I heard it just fine: *But they all disappear from view. And I only have eyes for you.*

Those sweetest of words wafted into my heart and then up to the rooftop of Orchid Garden Apartments. The swelling heavens accepted the rising anthem, and then I watched, my eyes flooded and cheeks drenched, as the *Matthayom* students took their cue and each lifted up a cell phone. The screens were perfectly choreographed–I've got no clue how Saman pulled it off–but I could read the message, one huge letter per smart phone. W-I-L-L-Y-O-U-M-A-R-R-Y-M-E-?

"Yes!" I shrieked. "Yes! Saman Takuathung, I love you! I'm coming down! Oh, sweetie, this is unbelievable!"

I almost tripped in my mad dash down the steps; Paloma was right behind me, laughing maniacally. "If you were in on this, I swear I will kill you," I managed breathlessly as we rounded the last corner together. I flung myself into my lover's arms, passionately kissing him, and the girls in the choir whooped their approval.

IT TURNED OUT SAMAN and Noah had a massive engagement-party sheet cake secreted away in the back of the school van. But none of us got a taste of it until the *Matthayom* boys had picked up both him and me and gleefully dumped us in the Orchid swimming pool. "You'll all flunk!" I hollered, wagging my finger in their faces. "I've got all your names! You'll be taking calculus over and over until you're old and gray." The hilarity was infectious, and before the celebrating was done half the guys were in the deep end with us, splashing us both with unbridled gaiety.

Halfway through the hoopla, Saman motioned for quiet. "A real man does his own talking," he announced. "Pranom, my sweet lady, my request cannot come through fifteen cell phones. So are you listening to me?"

"I am," I managed, my throat suddenly tight.

"All right then." He glanced around at the dripping-wet musical troupe. "No songs, no background vocals. Just me saying this: I love you very, very much. I am so much in love I want to pick you up and fly through the clouds. Pranom Daggett, will you please marry me?"

I began to puddle up, and Paloma sidled over to squeeze me hard. It took a breath for me to get it out, but I nodded vigorously. "Yes, my love. I will marry you and live with you and worship with you for as long as we are both alive in this world." In a burst of inspiration, I added: "And Bangkok will always be my home and BCS will always be my ministry." I pointed at Klahan. "I will teach there for as many years as it takes for him to finish math with a passing grade."

There was more laughter at this, but it died quickly as Saman fumbled in his drenched tuxedo trousers. He pulled loose a small jewelry box and the young ladies in Noah's chorale gasped. It was a lovely diamond ring, pure and exactly the right size and color for this happiest of nights. He slipped it onto my finger and then held my hand to his lips for an achingly perfect moment. I'd long ago shed the Asian impulse to cover my mouth during a moment of overwhelming emotion, but I did so now out of habit. Mom, standing by the side of the pool, motioned me to the nearby steps, and I collapsed into her arms, sublimely happy and oh so relieved to be spiritually liberated.

The merriment went on for another half hour, but

soon the cake was consumed and our paper plates tossed in the trash bin next to the manager's office. The business lady came out, effusive in her congratulations, and accepted a small orphan slice of the frosting-laden treat. "Congratulations, Miss Pranom," she offered in Thai, and I nodded, beaming through my damp clothes.

Noah shooed the students back into the van, tossing me a smile and guaranteeing that the upcoming church service was going to be hot with gossip. "I'm so happy for you, Pranom," he said, giving me a brotherly hug. "Many happy years are coming up for you, kid."

"I know."

Saman splashed up to the third floor with us, and I loaned him a baggy pair of sweat pants and one of Paloma's BCS sports T-shirts. We spent a familial three hours on the couch, arms wrapped around each other, Paloma and Mom bursting in with irreverent wedding ideas. "Your daddy's going to pop," Mom declared, glancing at her watch. "But let's wait another hour. I don't think he's awake yet."

I kept preening with my ring, holding it up to the light and swooning until Paloma hit me on the side of the head with a sofa cushion. "Enough already. I'm burning up with jealousy."

"Isn't it pretty?"

Saman took the opportunity to apologize. "It's not as pricy as I'd love to give you," he lamented. "But like I said, with things being the way they are, I really should have gotten on a budget sooner." He caught himself. "I mean, we'll be fine, honey. And I promise you, for the wedding we'll go all out. But these next few years we're for sure going to be stuck in that little apartment of mine."

"It's fine," I said loyally, pushing away the memory of my one busted evening at his postage-stamp place. "I'll be happy as long as we're together."

Mom straightened up. "You know it's the bride's family that pays for the wedding."

He grinned appreciatively. "I was counting on that! And listen, Mrs. D, I swear to you, I'll work my tail off to make sure Pranom shares a good life with me. But just lately, the way they changed the U.S. tax laws, my student loans are going to take twice as long to pay off. Stuff like that."

"Your apartment's fine," I assured him. "I mean, okay, the outside of it's kind of blah." I giggled. "Not that this place has anything going for it."

Saman leaned over and gave me a robust kiss on the cheek. "Right now it's the most beautiful place in the world. It's a paradise."

It was almost midnight before we Daggett ladies ushered Saman to the front door, each of us embracing him in turn. "Welcome to our family, honey," Mom offered, patting his cheek. "I'm ecstatic for both of you."

"Thanks, Mom." I flushed with pleasure at how natural that sounded coming from Saman. He noticed my smile and gave my hand a squeeze.

Paloma handed him the still dripping tuxedo trousers. "Gonna cost you another two hundred baht for dry cleaning," she scolded. "So your budget lifestyle will have to wait until tomorrow."

He shook his head. "Nope. I didn't even rent that. Borrowed it from one of the choir guys who couldn't make it. So see, I'm already tightening my belt."

"Ha ha." She accepted his hug, and as he headed for the stairs, he called back up to her. "You're next, you know. Klahan's crazy in love with you."

"I'm just a high school girl," she retorted. "And out of here in two months. Right after the wedding reception, you have to drive me to the airport."

We were safely back inside before I nudged her in the ribs. "I'll betcha don't."

TWENTY-FIVE

We piled into a taxi for the commute over to United Christian Church, and the entire ride there, I was consumed with one glorious reality: *this was now my permanent world.* Rama Road and these Bangkok malls and the roundabouts and the Victory Monument were going to be the physical landmarks of my adult life. With my renewed confidence, I even felt I could brave a romantic weekend getaway to Pattaya. As I watched the red digits head toward the 200-baht mark, Dad's long-distance words rang in my ears. "I'm on my way, baby. And you tell Sue Carington and the folks at BCS that I'm bringing my keyboard out with me. We're going to rock all of Bangkok during the reception."

I was thankful my parents were taking the news so cheerfully. Even though I was a college graduate and my own adult life and portfolio might have skidded me way across the American map, Bangkok Christian School really still was on the other side of the globe, Google and

Skype notwithstanding.

"We won't be wealthy for a while, sounds like," I admitted, sheepishly allowing my mom to fish in her purse for the cab fare. "But once we get things figured out and the family budget going better, I promise you guys, I'll make a trip to Portland once a year."

"Forget that. Let's just meet in Hawaii," Paloma interjected.

"You just say that so you can keep things going with Klahan," I teased.

She reddened. "I really like him. So yeah, that's a mess."

"Where's he off to next year?"

"Thammasat U. Some degree in international finance."

"Wow."

Understandably, Sue and Khemkaeng hustled right over and gave us all big squeezes. Aunt Rachel held onto me for a long time. "This is all just so amazing. Plus now you get to stay!"

"I know."

I'd already sent her a midnight text about Saman's proposal, and also about heaven's gift of forgiveness. "See?" she murmured in my ear now, her hair tickling my cheek. "'The Ocean.' Isn't that amazing?"

And all I could do was nod.

Pastor Gino was in an expansive mood, and right after the morning offering he took his spot behind the podium, but left his Bible and sermon notes on the chair next to Natty. "Before we open up God's Word today," he teased, eyeing me, "I think most of you have already heard. But UCC and Bangkok Christian School are exploding with headlines. Mrs. Carington, why don't you please come up here and tell us what everybody already seems to know."

There was some applause at this, and I noticed there were more of our high school students here than usual. But Sue adjusted the microphone and then motioned for me to join her. "Well, I said a year ago, I would do almost anything to make sure Miss Daggett becomes part of our permanent team of superstar teachers. But I swear to all of you, I *did not* write this amazing movie plot. I did not bribe Dr. Takuathung to fall in love. He and our Lord Jesus Christ pulled that off without my nosy intervention." Even before Chloe's translation, laughter swept through the place.

"Anyway, you've all heard the news. Miss Daggett is getting married to a certain eye doctor, and is planning to stay right here in the City of Angels. So we lay claim to her right now. For the next twenty years!"

There was general clapping and merriment at this, and Saman stood up and bowed grandly. Some of the high school kids began moving through the congregation, handing out something I couldn't quite see. When Puengpet got to the front and handed me a pink souvenir, I realized it was a balloon. Already folks were blowing them up, and a large heart appeared. Both our names were inscribed in it: "Saman and Pranom: United in Jesus!"

"You stinker," I murmured, edging closer to him. "I thought we were going on a budget."

He gave a dismissive wave. "It was, like, two hundred baht is all. There's a guy at the mall."

"Okay. But from now on we vote on everything financial."

He grinned.

Pastor Gino tried to restore order. "Mrs. C, there's a bit more, I understand."

"There really is." Taking my cue, I followed Saman back to our seats. I watched, fascinated, as our video screen flickered to life. It was network video from my talk at Chulalongkorn University, but this footage was of Ratana's standout performance. Even on our 50" television monitor, the sound was pure adrenalin, and I could feel the energy rolling through our own church aisles. Gino let it go for just about a minute, then motioned to the sound guy. "This is going to blow you all away," he told us. "But Noah got a contract Fed Exed to him Thursday afternoon. Our own Dr. Ratana is touring America the next seven months with two of the top Christian bands out there. Five nights a week, a U.S. recording contract of her own, three TV specials, and a book deal."

What? It was something we'd all gossiped about at the school, and every time I heard my friend sing, she seemed destined for higher orbits. But for real?

"So today's a worship day of good news, and then bad, and then good again," our principal informed us. "We just got Pranom for full-time. But now, what I hear is that Noah is going to follow his wife to America. Partly because I think the man's in love and is a new daddy, but also because he's going to be a part of the U.S. audio team for the entire tour."

It made sense, of course. They were a family. If Ratana was launching an American tour, her family was tagging along. But that was for sure a yawning chasm in the BCS lineup. Noah was a powerhouse presence on our campus, with his ever-flowing talent as a choir director and producer of class-act school programs.

But I could hardly absorb what our principal said next. Her gaze carefully avoiding our side of the auditorium, Sue went on without missing a beat. "God is good, saints. He most surely is. Because time zones do not stop the work of the Lord. I was on the phone half the night, and I think our great *Matthayom* choirs are going to carry right on like always. A certain music man says he's ready to come right back out to Bangkok. I have a text message to read all of you."

No way. Are you kidding me? NO . . . WAY! But somehow I just KNEW. Next to me Paloma's mouth was hanging open as Sue thumbed through her incoming messages. "Here it is," she teased, pretending to squint. "Dear BCS: I'm ready to return. On one condition. Here it is. 'I want a grandson! Or a granddaughter! I don't care which. I love weddings; I love baby showers! As long as there is plenty of *kanom cake*. Please do not interview anyone else. I, Tommy Daggett, am your candidate.'"

"MOM! ARE YOU SERIOUS? You already knew?"

I honestly feared Paloma might just split in two and explode right over the potluck lunch table. Both of us girls were absolutely floored by the morning headline. *Our parents were heading back here to Bangkok.*

"Sue called Tommy a couple days ago," she told us. "After hearing about Noah."

"I know, but . . ." My mind was whirring. "I mean, it's amazing and all that. So after the wedding, you just stay?"

Mom calmly explained that after a prosperous decade at Evergreen Academy, Dad was ready for something new. "We'll just keep the house; we already own it free and clear. So it'll be a good rental."

"What about your job?"

She grinned. "I got up way early this morning and went down by the pool. Sat there for an hour and talked with my boss."

I remembered him from recent corporate Christmas parties: a big, kind-of-bloated sweetheart. Very, very born-again, prone to hugs and pricy presents for families and friends.

"What's his name again?" I prompted.

"Barney. Gibson."

"Oh yeah."

"He gave us those matching sweaters we really like," Paloma reminded me.

"Anyway, it's not perfect, but I can do half-time work for them long-distance if I want to," Mom said. "Most of the day, back in Portland, I was just staring at a screen and running stats through our adapted formulas. If I don't mind an occasional get-up-at-three phone call to a client, he really thinks I can make it work. And if not, hey, I'll just follow your dad around from one Bangkok concert hall to the next one." She cast a glance over to where Sue was bantering with some of our juniors. "Who knows? I know my daughter's got trig and calc locked up, but maybe I could teach baby algebra."

"This blows my mind," Paloma said for about the fifteenth time.

I concocted some cheesy excuse about not knowing where the pineapple juice was, and she followed me into the kitchen. "This is amazing," I hissed under my breath, "but what about you?"

"What do you mean?"

"Everybody's going to be out here! So are you

going to stay? Go back to Portland all alone? That's weird. But, I mean, are you up for going to Chula and taking college classes in their international division?"

She colored again, and I could tell she'd already been plotting. "Well, probably Thammasat. 'Cause that's where Klahan is."

"Holy cow. Are you really that in love with him?"

Paloma gave me a searching look. "Hey. It happened to you. Why's it so weird if I'm getting kind of head-over-heels too?"

I hugged her right there in the kitchen, the hum of the refrigerator providing its own cheerful soundtrack to our sisterly love, which right now transcended my bilingual vocabulary. "You know I love you more than I can even think to put into words," I managed, hoping I wouldn't cry. "To have you around for next year just saves my life, kid."

We returned to the potluck table and all our friends. I eyed Paloma to make sure it was okay, then cleared my throat. "Attention, everybody. My baby sister just whispered in my ear that if Klahan gets up his courage and gives her a kiss right this very second, then hey, she'll stay here in Bangkok and go to Thammasat with him in the fall."

Klahan, ever the shy prince, buried his face in his hands, then managed a bashful grin and did indeed plant a rather generous kiss on my baby sister. Sue rapped her knuckles on the table. "Page fourteen of the BCS handbook," she warned. "That one kiss is okay because you're seniors, but no more, kiddies."

Klahan straightened up manfully. "Yes, Mrs. C. No more." He caught Khemkaeng's eye and the two exchanged masculine smiles.

THAT EVENING SUE hosted our entire family on the cramped balcony of her cheerful hideaway way up on the twenty-seventh floor. We had to shuttle back into the kitchen for more hors d'oeuvres, but it was a sumptuous feast and we basked in the elegant atmosphere as the twinkling glories below us glided slowly toward the meandering edge of the river picking up passengers.

"By the way," she told me as we dished out bowls of strawberry ice cream, "I'm in serious negotiations with Pastor Ethan. Down in Phuket."

"He's still working on that thing?"

She nodded briskly, eyeing the last dab of dessert in the bottom of the carton. "Do me a favor and finish this off."

I grinned. "Oh, fine."

Sue went on. "The man's got ambitions; I'll give him that. He wants all of our senior girls down there. Plus the twelfth-graders from Ekamai and Chiang Mai. I guess there's a little school in Haad Yai, not so big, but maybe thirty girls from there. And he's already in touch with two of these halfway houses where they help shelter a few of the kids who got drafted into the sex industry right out of little villages in the hills."

I accepted the last without any particular flutter of emotion. "But Sue, that's a huge undertaking!"

"Yeah. It sounds like it. And beyond that, he's going to fly Ratana in and really get the town revved up with a concert the first Saturday night you're there."

"How long a thing?"

"Three days."

"Wow. That's hugely expensive, isn't it?"

She nodded. "I'm worried about that. I mean, look. A lot of our parents have money. And Somsak has generally said to us, 'If you need funds for something worthwhile, just tell me.' But this sounds like a whopping price tag."

We finished our dessert and I stacked up the bowls. Over in the corner, Saman and Miles were in serious conversation about something medical, and Sue motioned me back inside. "Tell you what. Let's try and get Ethan on the phone right now. He ought to be free. 'Cause you're right. It sounds just way ambitious."

He answered on the second ring, and Sue switched it over to speaker mode. "I've got Pranom with me," Sue sang out. "You remember her?"

"I sure do. Hi, Pranom. And the good news has already gotten to Phuket. Congratulations and all that. I'm thrilled for you guys."

"Thanks, Pastor Ethan." I remembered how quickly I had come to admire this gentle giant, basking in his own healed relationship with a special new lover, now his wife.

"Well, we're halfway firm with some dates," he told us, marking out a long weekend in late May. "I don't know if every single one of your *Matthayom* Six ladies can get down here, but it'd be a headline three days. Good hotel food, Pranom speaking, two other amazing women I've got lined up, Ratana doing music. Et cetera. A whole lot of et ceteras."

"Well, we're very, very interested," Sue agreed. "But Pastor Ethan, we're just fretting about the logistics. And financing. It sounds like this is close to two hundred young people. Most of them flying in. I know Phuket's a bargain trip, and it's not that break-the-bank. But are you sure it can all get handled?"

When he came back on, his voice was ringing with

optimism. "That part's okay, ladies. It really is. If you just say yes, and open up your schedules, and bring us your godly passion, and Pranom, your amazing, amazing story, the idea of who stays in what room and getting folks shuttled back and forth, no problem. I've got a few super-talented people here who, that's all they do. I didn't think Christians could be such wizards, but just yesterday, they gave me a spread sheet and I about hit the roof when I saw the bargains they stitched together. I kid you not."

We exchanged glances, and then Sue grinned. "Pastor Ethan, it sounds like a big 'wow' on our side. Pranom is nodding her head yes."

He cackled with merriment on his end of the line. "Sounds like saying 'yes' is all she's been doing of late. Hey, Pranom! Can you please donate fifty thousand baht to our church's 'new hymnal' fund?"

"No," I immediately sang out, and we shared a laugh. I followed her back out to the balcony and eased into my fiancé's embrace. "Hey, good-looking. How does a free long weekend in Phuket sound?"

TWENTY-SIX

Yothin brought a glittering packet up to my classroom a couple weeks later. I had a coveted window seat down to Phuket, 42A, and the computerized hotel voucher had "Paloma Daggett" listed as my assigned roommate. A Tropical Fun Book was enclosed, four-color artwork, and a thick stack of 2-for-1 coupons for things like putt-putt golf and *muay Thai* boxing exhibitions. I didn't imagine our busy convention schedule would grant me much getaway time, but hey, if I was in the mood for a zip-line adventure, Pastor Ethan's connections had arranged sixty-percent discounts for all clients from Bangkok Christian School.

Paloma buzzed into the room brandishing her own packet. "This is totally amazing," she cooed. "And the whole thing's, like, ninety bucks. I just texted Dad and he said sure."

Of course, my own trip to the tropical paradise was being comped by the school, and Paloma sagged a bit as I trumped her good deal. "But it sure looks like this Pastor Ethan knows how to stage an event." We already knew the conference was going to be Ratana's farewell performance before heading off to America, so our own high school ladies had been signing up at a brisk pace. The hotel brochure artwork was high on pristine swimming pools, and it was hard to keep order in my calculus classes the next week. "I thought kids were going to be going nuts over graduation," I told Khem-kaeng during our next-to-last staff meeting. "But this junket to Phuket has the students really excited."

He grinned. "I'm glad. And the board is pleased with what a bargain Pastor Ethan arranged. Our friend *Kuhn* Somsak didn't even have to make his usual contribution."

Saman drove both of us to the airport, and it was a reluctant farewell at the curb just outside the domestic departure lounge. "I hate missing this first day," he grumbled good-naturedly. "And flying with you, sweetie. But I've got four procedures this afternoon and evening. For sure I'll jet down there in time to hear your presentation."

"Did you get the same awesome deal as we did?" Paloma peered at her watch and tugged on my sleeve.

He nodded. "It's all the same group rate since Pastor Ethan and his church friends in Phuket contracted with the airline. Nineteen hundred baht, I think. Which is dirt cheap." He gave my sister an affectionate half-hug and then enfolded me for a more generous interval. "I'm sure proud of you, babe. You'll be great, I know."

It felt like a third of the plane was our Bangkok Christian School female army. They weren't in their usual maroon-and-white uniforms, of course, and I tripped up and down both aisles of the wide-body aircraft, exchanging smiles and greetings and making note of cute outfits. "Everybody has a swimming suit?" I called out, waving at Sue over the tops of the seat backs. "Because every time there's a break in the schedule, I'm going to be the judge for a contest. 'Who can make the biggest splash and get Pastor Gino all wet.'" He overheard me and grinned affably.

The Thai Airways plane thundered down the runway and into an azure sky crowded with clouds. Paloma and I giggled like school kids, trading snacks with her fellow seniors, and just as we reached cruising altitude I looked out the window and smiled. It was indeed The Ocean down far below, endless kilometers of surging blue forgiveness. We were so high above the vastness of it all, I could barely make out the white fleck on some of the waves as they tossed and cavorted beneath the heavens. It took me another few moments to realize that, yes indeed, my bitterness toward Uncle Viroj had honestly been absorbed into the miracle my Christian friends called Calvary.

Paloma noticed my reverie. "Wow, you're deep in thought," she teased.

"Why do you say that?"

"Um, well, when your lips are moving, I figure either you're praying, or you're talking to yourself a little bit, or maybe you're kind of, you know, mentally unbalanced."

"Thanks a lot."

She rested her head against my shoulder and we shared the view for a bit longer. "It's so amazing."

"I know." I shifted just slightly, not enough to disrupt our nice physical connection. "I'm glad we get to stay in Thailand."

"You and me both."

I reached over to her tray table for my last bit of soda. "Is Klahan mad about not getting to come to this?"

Paloma shook her head. "He knows it's Ladies Only."

We touched down on Phuket Island less than an hour later and there was a nice female whoop as we rolled to a stop. Even before the jetway was wheeled into position, a cheering tropical feeling of *aaah . . . sabai* permeated the main cabin. Despite the somber reason for this trip, our ladies were excited about being in this grand paradise.

Down at baggage claim, I could already see Pastor Ethan waving at our faculty members. Two young Thai women were standing nearby, iPads in hand, and as we gave them our names, they quickly punched in ID numbers and nodded. "Yes, okay," they said over and over, having obviously been briefed that BCS expected them to conduct business in English as much as possible.

Pastor Ethan enfolded us both in cheerful hugs, and promised to introduce his new bride Vasana that evening. "She can't wait to meet you," he told me. "And of course, our whole church wants front-row seats when Ratana sings."

Apparently his connections had arranged for two massive tour buses to shuttle us to the hotel complex, and there was plenty of giggling and jockeying for seats perched up on the upper deck. The operators had assigned a guide to each bus, and they did lapse into Thai during the fifteen-minute commute. Dinner this evening was a buffet in the main ballroom. Each hotel room had complimentary bottles of water, but the minibars were expensive, the guide warned with a smile. The pool had extended its hours "only for beautiful BCS ladies," she intoned, and joked about please not staying out past midnight. If we wanted to go scuba diving Sunday afternoon following the last convention event, that was an available option added since the brochure had gone to the printer. Only thirteen hundred baht, and I saw some of the girls nodding and whispering to each other.

We were both agog as we stepped into the air-conditioned lobby of the Bali Lagoon. The carpeting was all done in a tropical motif, with coral reefs and waterfalls and undulating rare forms of sea life. The tour ladies had already handed out our digital key cards during the bus ride, so we headed right up to the sixteenth floor. The bellboy beamed when I handed him a gratuity, and he made a big show of opening up the drapes to let in a floor-to-ceiling view of the beach, fishing boats lazily floating out in the deep. "This is way amazing," I breathed to Paloma, tempted to add another twenty-baht to the tip.

"Because you are feature speaker, madam," the kid managed in his careful English. "So hotel is give you junior suite. Very nice! I hope it is so comfortable for you."

I responded in Thai, and he looked relieved, offering us a *wai* as he backed away and out into the hallway.

Ratana's concert that evening was in the Bali's premier ballroom, and the place was wall-to-wall humanity. The convention attendees all gained entrance with their laminated passes, but the local churches had sold individual tickets as well, and there was close to a thousand people jammed into every available seat. Pastor Ethan asked for a show of hands to find out how many college students had come over from the nearby university, and at least fifty waved and cheered.

The concert was a blend of live-plus-tracks. Noah had his guitar plugged in and Pastor Ethan was amazing on his keyboard. But the percussion and the bass parts were rolling in by way of a computerized file and the hotel's massive soundboard, and the songs swelled through the place and out into the lobby. The ticket ladies finally surrendered to the reality that hotel guests were crashing their way into the ballroom, and Ratana waved cheerfully to the newcomers. Noah made some cute jokes about how taking the show on the road now meant Dallas and maybe Disney World in Florida, and our BCS girls squealed their approval.

It was toward the end, after the pop medleys and Beyoncé favorites, when Ratana asked the crowd to quiet down. "We are here for a truly special purpose," she reminded us. "Ladies of Thailand, you are each one chosen. God created you according to a beautiful blueprint. As magnificent as the scenery of Phuket might be, as wonderful and as filled with variety as the fish in the water might be, the beautiful colors in the sunset, even more special and holy . . . is YOU. You, my lovely lady friends, are all daughters of heaven."

She paused, and an expectant hush spread among the BCS girls sitting near to Paloma and me. For a stray moment, I wished Mom could have stayed for this, but she would get to see Pastor Gino's video recording later this summer when she came back over for the wedding and next term.

"And now," Ratana went on, "I want to speak to girls on the other side of trafficking. Someone hurt you; they scarred your heart. They wounded your spirit. You are still here; you are a victor. But what happened hurt you badly. Tonight you can give your hurt away to a strong, tender friend named Jesus."

Pastor Ethan began a familiar hymn on his piano, and when Noah's guitar notes slid into place, I felt my throat tighten up. I had sung this song hundreds of times before, both in America and now at Bangkok's United Christian Church, but somehow the lyrics had such renewed meaning and significance.

All to Jesus I surrender; All to him I freely give.

True, I had surrendered my hatred for those who betrayed me. Standing on the balcony of Orchid Garden Apartments, with Saman singing to me, I had felt a sweet release. But as Ratana sang again, her farewell anthem for her native homeland, I experienced a rush of determination that yes, Jesus, my mighty Rescuer, would absolutely and irrevocably take over my burden.

Thai worshipers seldom embrace the worship idea of uplifted hands, but all at once mine was up. Just my right hand, but as Ratana continued to sing, the accumulated despair of those four months in a brothel seeped away through my uplifted fingertips and up to Jesus.

All to Jesus I surrender, Lord, I give myself to Thee. Fill me with Thy love and power; Let Thy blessing fall on me.

A few of my senior girls saw my emotional state; one eased closer and put a tentative hand on my shoulder. I was able to smile and murmur *kop kuhn*, and as Ratana got to the final chorus, the twin movie screens switched over to Thai and we finished the anthem in unison, Pastor Ethan and Paloma and the other foreigners gamely keeping up the best they could. The applause, when it came, was reverential, and I allowed myself the luxury of weeping into my little sister's shoulder while our BCS friends backed away.

I felt somewhat composed during the scheduled late-night swim fest. The hotel had acquiesced to the organizers' demand of free sodas and fruit punch for all the girls, and we sipped ice-cold Sprites and pineapple slushes while basking in the cool splendor of the pool. Pastor Ethan's boy was a nice-looking kid with longish blond hair, already gaining fluency in Thai, and I could tell he was taking a shine to Paloma.

"I can't believe how well your church did organizing this," I told the pastor. "And the prices are such a bargain."

"I'm really glad," he responded. "And see, to have so many secular young people here from the university is terrific. We hope to snag a ton of email addresses and perhaps begin a campus ministry there. My wife is helping work that part out." He scanned the vast pool, but didn't see her. "For sure I want to introduce you to her before the weekend's up."

The next day's sessions were all brisk, informative events, with a keynote address by a sociology professor who had flown in from Hong Kong. Pastor Ethan's bride served as translator, and she was a charming wonder, adding just the right touch to the stirring seminar. It was obvious that all of Asia was agreed on one thing: *Education! Education! Education!* There is a bright future for females who stay plugged in at school and keep their focus on God's highest callings. I found myself listening more to Vasana than the visiting lecturer, and scribbled down a few notes for my own use.

There was a large easel just on the other side of the main ballroom, and as we all crowded into the hallway for our lunch break, I saw that Pastor Ethan's team had already put up a 2' x 3' poster promoting my address that evening. "New Beginnings: Miss Pranom Daggett." Earlier, Khemkaeng had come by my classroom and posed me for a picture, and now I flushed pleasantly with all the attention. My own students already knew me, of course, but I noticed several of the Christian girls from Chiang Mai and Ubon peering at the poster and then spotting me in the crowd. One pointed and smiled, and I returned her bashful wave.

I was a bit anxious during the dinner buffet, and was already nibbling on my dainty piece of cake when Saman rushed toward our table, almost out of breath. "Sorry," he panted. "The plane was delayed about half an hour, and I was getting nervous. But here we are."

A hello kiss was out of the question in such a public place, but I squeezed his forearm and said how glad I was he was with me. He was eager to meet Pastor Ethan and his new wife, so I towed Saman over to their table and we made small talk for a few minutes. "You should have heard the band last night," I told him, and the pastor grinned appreciatively. "It was fun, wasn't it?"

"It was incredible," I told him.

"We're praying for you tonight," he called out as we walked back to our table, and I felt my fiancé's fingers tightening around my own.

With a month still left in her medical schedule at Mission Hospital, Ratana had flown back to Bangkok earlier this morning. But another packed hotel ballroom was regaled by one of Phuket's own Christian church choirs, and they did a medley of traditional hymns accompanied just by a pianist from the Philippines. Growing up in the funky Daggett household, there were some classics I'd not heard before, and I felt myself growing weepy again as the Christian musicians filled the hall with "Whiter Than Snow."

Khemkaeng got up to introduce me, and managed a bit of whimsical humor. "I attended college in Michigan," he observed. "So there are only a few Thai people like me who truly understand the beauty and purity of snow. Tonight, ladies, we will hear a miracle story for sure. Our good friend Pranom Daggett has shared with some of us, and even though I have heard her experience, it fills my heart with both grief and rejoicing each time." He offered a brief prayer asking God to bless us with heaven's hope and goodness, and then called me to the front.

Earlier today I had ditched my sister and gone for a long walk along the beach, the water from God's mighty ocean lapping at my ankles. Once again, I realized, I needed to forgive those who had so wronged me. Also, I had prayed during my sojourn for the Lord to give me a fresh experience to share, and now as I opened up to these beautiful young girls, the same miraculous flow began to happen within my heart. I remembered conversations, hurtful evenings where one of my sisters in the trade sobbed her heart out while I clutched her hand. Me, a thirteen-year-old comforter.

And then as I moved to the finish, I suddenly had a recollection of just how it felt to be in that go-go bar on the final night and see this bearded American man. "For a moment, I had it in my heart: 'Oh my God! It is Mr. Daggett! How can he be here?' But then in almost the same moment, I came to know something wonderful. He was not there as a tourist. He was not there to use me or to feast on the sight of my uncovered body. No, he was there on a holy mission."

Just saying it now filled me with a wonder and I could hardly go on. "Listen, you guys. Because this is amazing. I just thought of it. But here in our sinful world, what happens in Bangkok and Pattaya and here is not new. There has been prostitution since the first days of our world. In many cultures people make a sad joke about the world's oldest profession. And see, the enemy has made it so. But think of how Jesus came down here. In a way, it was like that on the night when I saw Mr. Daggett. Because Jesus is the holy Son of God. There has never been sin in the heart of Jesus: no lust, no craving, no sexual degeneration. And yet it is like Jesus comes to the bar, right to the place of our deepest despair, and he looks up at us. And he hands us a note saying: 'I love you. I will rescue you. You can have a home where your former agony is a hushed memory only.'"

I knew I faced a cosmopolitan audience, that there were sophisticated young women, bright females enrolled in their master's degree programs at nearby Prince of Songkhla University. So a full-out altar call was inappropriate. But I paused to allow the poignancy of my observation to sink in, and then quietly added: "If any woman here wishes to know more about what a wonderful thing it is to be set free, liberated by a friendship with the Son of God, it is the highest joy of my life to speak of this. There are many, many happy Christians here in this Phuket hotel. Find any Christian and only say: 'Tell me.' They will be glad to do it."

It was time for a closing prayer, and as I bowed my own head and offered a benediction, I could hear footsteps approaching. A moment later a hand seized my own, and I thrilled with the comfort of having Saman by my side where he belonged.

I made my way to the back, and Paloma squeezed me. "That was better than ever," she said loyally, and tears sprang to my eyes. Up front, Khemkaeng took the hotel microphone from its stand and invited Pastor Ethan to join him. "We have many more fine presentations tomorrow," he announced. "Please, ladies, so many of you who are our good friends from Phuket. If you can skip classes and join us, that would be wonderful! If you have jobs, we do not wish to steal you from work. But please come here and worship God with us. And also attend the good workshops still to come. Now, Pastor Ethan, you must please give us the opportunity to pay honor and respect to your helpers who have printed so many meal tickets and who are so proficient in finding bargains from Thai Airways!"

There was general laughter at this, and Pastor Ethan waved away the compliment. "My own contribution has been *nit noi*," he deadpanned. "Very little! But praise God for my brothers and sisters who can organize very beautifully." He motioned to the side door where I saw two women in native Thai garb. They blushed and came forward and I recognized the two guides from the tour buses. "Wow, those dresses are sweet," Paloma said, leaning forward to inspect them.

"And these gentlemen are truly miracle men of God," Pastor Ethan added, gesturing again. There was a clump of students in the way, but I saw another pair of Thai men duck past them and step around the two registration tables. "I can promise you, if we didn't have such gifted friends in the Lord's service, this wonderful time of fellowship would not have taken place."

There was a flurry of perfunctory applause, and

Saman was talking in my ear, telling me how impressed he was with my talk. But all at once I felt all the blood drain from my face. It was there; I was seeing what I was seeing. And now my brain felt like it was locking up, blanking out the vision before me. Standing on the dais of this Phuket ballroom in the Bali Lagoon Hotel was my birth father: Anuman Niratpattanasai. He looked different in a sharp navy blazer and necktie, an engraved tour badge pinned to his lapel. But his gesture as he waved to the gathered crowd of Christians was one I would recognize anywhere. His hair had the same irrepressible droop over his forehead, and he tossed it back with the familiar gesture I'd seen over a thousand dinners as a little girl.

Just to his left was the other half of the brain trust, his apparent partner in this thriving Phuket tour company: my Uncle Viroj.

NO! NO! NO! NO! It was utterly impossible, but he was standing right there. The man who had sold me into sexual servitude was less than fifty meters away, standing shyly in the shadow of his older brother. He wore a charcoal business suit, a white shirt, and a knotted black tie. He looked every inch the prosperous business executive. But polished shoes notwithstanding, Uncle Viroj was the same beast who had thrust me into a hundred seedy hotel rooms, or behind a curtained rectangle containing only a threadbare mattress, condoms in a drawer, and a box of tissues, a lone light bulb casting shadows over the evil scene.

I realized with a shudder that the moment I had so long dreaded and anticipated was abruptly landing on me. Had I honestly forgiven this wicked monster? Did I mean all the ethereal theories I had gratefully breathed up to heaven the evening my sweetheart proposed?

Saman was blissfully unconcerned, his hand still holding mine, but he was leaning closer to say something innocuous to Natty. Paloma dug in her purse for her cell phone; I had this irrational idea she might be getting ready to text Mom and Dad to gush about my well-received testimony. Up on the dais, Khemkaeng and Pastor Ethan were exchanging amiable compliments with the two tour operators; I could see Uncle Viroj nodding and expressing his thanks with a respectful *wai*.

My brain was throbbing, almost banging against the inner cavities of my skull with the shock of this rude interruption, when I suddenly realized something. *No one knows!* My dad and uncle hadn't actually been in the ballroom during my talk. Pranom was a common Thai name, and how would my father know his little girl had been rescued by an American musician who generously offered the protection of his last name?

But what about the poster in the lobby? Hadn't the tour guides prepared all the promo materials? Not in this case, I reminded myself with a flood of relief. Pastor Ethan had texted us for the photo; he'd likely done the poster himself using Microsoft Paint and then emailed the JPEG file to the same Phuket printer his church generally used.

Wow. There actually was an escape route all laid out for me. Even now, I could see a clear path toward the hotel ballroom's west exit. The lobby was emptied out; from my vantage point I could see the two elevators next to the concierge desk. It would be so easy. *Hey, Paloma. I'm kind of tired. Think I'll go back to the room and put my feet up. Maybe we can swim a bit once I catch my breath.* My father and uncle would retreat to their leased offices down by the beach, counting the day's receipts and their generous cut from the hotel for all the business they'd generated. Pastor Ethan had no clue he was dialoguing with my biological uncle. Khemkaeng had never met these men. No one was going to put it all together . . .

Then I caught myself. Hold on. Had I or had I not forgiven the man in the charcoal suit? Was I standing up to my eyeballs in the healing ocean currents of my Savior's forgiveness? Yes or no? And wasn't it the testimony of the entire church that my uncle, a broken and defeated human specimen, had a right to tumble into the depths of grace as well?

Only a few seconds had ticked past as I stood transfixed in my own Armageddon valley. I wanted to sit down, to collapse on the rug, curl up in a ball and think about this hard. Or not. Could I simply walk, one foot in front of the other, and get myself to the elevator? I recalled how Pastor Ethan had boasted about these valued friends, apparently part of his ministry team, who so miraculously created this successful event. Was it possible that my uncle had *become a Christian*? My soul burned over the effrontery of it, and I realized with an inner groan that it didn't matter either way. Absolution was offered in equal portions to the penitent and the pagan.

"So what's up?" Saman tugged at my hand and I forced a plastic smile, but inside a volcano was building up. *Where do my feet take me? To the elevator or to the platform? Oh God oh God oh God.*

There was a noise in my mind now, building up until I could scarcely pick up the jocular bits from my boyfriend and little sister. It felt like a gale storm was blowing through the open front doors of the Bali Lagoon Hotel, buffeting this fragile fort of anonymity where I was cowering in dread. There were nails in the structure protecting me, and as the winds howled and battered my barricade, those metal fasteners trembled in their place. I swallowed hard as I saw streaks of blood rimming the heads of the nails. *Oh my Jesus, these very nails pinned you to the cross. These are the nails that bought our reconciliation. This is what you paid to liberate me, and now I'm afraid to trust in your gift . . .*

And really, that was it. If I retreated to my room, sure, I could survive. I would marry Saman and we would establish our own marital fort in Bangkok, a bustling, anonymous hideout. For the next forty years I would mentally blank out the reality that Dad and Uncle were right down here in nearby Phuket, alive and still making deals and perhaps also sitting in a church pew every weekend opening up God's Word and searching for ways to live up to its high, hard ideals.

The screaming of the wind increased now, and I was but dimly aware that Saman was repeating an endearment over and over. *Hey, babe. Hey, babe.* His voice penetrated, but just barely, and I turned to face him, my soul anxious as those Calvary nails still shuddered in the loosened holes, protecting me from destruction. "Are you okay, honey? You look beat up."

"Um, yeah. I've got to go up to the platform."

"What's up? You forget something?"

"Just come with me, okay." *Jesus, Savior of mine, my Rock, my Fortress, be with me now. I trust you, Jesus my everlasting Protector.*

Paloma must have had a sixth sense about my angst,

because she dropped her cell phone in her purse and followed after us. The college kids had mostly drifted into the lobby, some purchasing snacks at the convenience store by the poolside arcade, and I swallowed hard as my uncle dipped into the inner pocket of his expensive designer suit and handed a business card to Khemkaeng.

Step . . . step . . . step. Now the winds died away and I felt a sudden calm washing over me. The fabric of my dress was dry–I literally reached out with my fingers to touch the silky sleeve–even though I could almost feel the liquid serenity of The Ocean as I stepped up onto the dais. Saman was on my one side and the risen Christ on the other, invisible but oh so wonderfully *there.*

Mr. Anuman Niratpattanasai turned to see this woman, a grown college professor, approaching him. He was confused and disoriented, but before he could collect himself, I cleared my throat and managed just one word.

"Dad?"

TIME STOOD STILL for at least ten seconds before reality hit my father. His lips were working and I could see moisture building up in his eyes. When he spoke, it was all in Thai and a frantic babble. "Pranom? *Nuu?* It's really you? Oh, God! How is this true? I heard you were in America!"

"It's me," I told him. "Yes, I went to live with my new family. But BCS invited me back to teach, and I chose to come." It was hard to get out the next words but I took the initiative, giving him a full hug. "It's wonderful to see you again, Daddy."

Dad's shoulders were literally shaking. Thai men do

not typically show emotions, especially in a public arena like luxury hotels, but he was quite literally overcome. "I'm so sorry," he repeated over and over. "I let you down; I know I did."

"It's all right," I assured him. "I have a wonderful life now. I'm soon to be married; I love being a professor. I became a Christian and am very, very happy."

He seemed nonplussed, and it was with some reluctance that I extricated myself from his embrace. What had to happen next had been scripted two thousand years ago; I knew that. As I turned to face the man in the charcoal suit, yes, I was flanked by Uncle Khemkaeng and Pastor Ethan and Saman and Paloma. But more than that, the entire Body of Christ, yes, the countless generations of the redeemed watching from the bleachers of a packed stadium, rose as one army to their feet in silent support, rejoicing with me that those bloody nails from the crossbeams had held through the storm. I took a step toward my Uncle Viroj, who bit down hard on his lip, wordless and embarrassed. He was about to speak when I raised my hand. "It's all right, Uncle Viroj. Really. Everything is okay. I know you want for me to forgive you, but I already did." I swallowed, and Saman, who was almost white with shock, did manage to put his arm around me. Together we walked into the embrace of this rescued sinner. "I'm so happy our family is reunited," I told my uncle. "If you are willing, I would like to be your niece again."

TWENTY-SEVEN

The Bali Lagoon Hotel's rooftop restaurant floated high above the tropical splendors of Phuket Island, and I guess my dad had unlimited clout with the maître d'. Waiters kept plying us with exotic fruit drinks, and the steaks and dinner salads were first-class.

Saman was with me, and as Dad and Uncle Viroj let their redemptive saga spill forth, we sat and listened in utter amazement. For all his earlier callousness, my uncle was now a rather shy man, and Dad did most of the talking. He had indeed spent the better part of a decade locked up in a Bangkok prison, whiling away his days with tattered Thai novels and listlessly watching soaps and an occasional boxing match if the guards permitted it. Since part of our group spoke little Thai, he managed in a careful English, and I found myself admiring him for his self-taught skills.

"Then you came to us," he said, nodding his head toward Gino. "Do you remember?"

"Um, vaguely. I was only in jail for a few days."

"Yes. But you were talk about God with those two big men. They steal money from lumber company, and know they will be in prison for many years. But you are speaking of Jesus, and since I know some little things from Pranom and her teacher, I think to myself, 'Anuman, this is your good chance. Listen and perhaps God can rescue you.' Then when Mr. Gino is set free very quickly, now I think so even more. Do you remember, Mr. Gino? When you leave, I say to you, 'Maybe I can have your Thai Bible.' And you say okay."

"I should have followed up more," Pastor Gino said apologetically.

"No, no. How could you know all of this story?"

I was anxious about hearing the B side of this album, but my uncle reluctantly shared his own testimony. A decade earlier, during my own scorching experience at the Pussycat Club, he had waited, unconcerned, for me to return from my three-day "long-time date" with a chunky American tourist. When I quite literally vanished from the face of the earth, he carefully approached the go-go bar's resident madam. "But she did not know," he told us. "And I did not know how to inquire. I could not ask police. I could not ask, Pranom, at your old school. Already I felt much shame for what I have done. But as time, it go by, and I think, 'Okay, yes, I hope she has found good new life. Maybe man with much money has taken her to be with him all the time.'" Even now, a decade later, it sounded hollow, and he switched into Thai, apologizing profusely.

He went on to tell us how he left the bars and was able to get a modest job helping one of the hotels organize convention events: driving vans, doing airport pickups, arranging brochure distribution. "I do this work for two years and is okay. But I begin to think: 'Maybe now Anuman is done with prison. I hope so.' And I contact our aunt who live in Bangkok. And she tell me, 'Yes! He has release early because he is do quite well.' So I phone him and am surprise when he tell me: 'Now I am Christian. This is very good for me.' And we begin to think: 'Can we work together and be a good team?'"

Pastor Gino leaned forward, his eyes bright with interest. "So the whole time you men have been down here, you've been active for God?"

My dad nodded eagerly. "Yes, Mr. Gino. We are very happy to serve Jesus. And see? We think, both of us are thinking, 'Okay. If we can do very good work and have good business, but also are in church and serve, maybe a little bit, this can make up for how we both make big mistakes.'"

Uncle Viroj added his own heartfelt agreement. "And we are in such fine church. Soon Pastor Ethan, he come to be with us. Now we are happy to help church all the time. Good programs. Arrange for groups to come to Phuket, and also they can visit church."

Dad abruptly thought of something. "Mr. Gino, I can show you this." He had an expensive valise next to his chair. He undid the clasp and pulled out a tattered blue New Testament, one of those inexpensive side-by-side bilingual Bibles common here in Thailand. "See? This is Bible you give to me. And you write such a nice thing for me to read."

He flipped open the front cover, and Pastor Gino leaned across the table, trying to read his own upside-down handwriting. "'With Jesus Christ in our hearts, we are free even in here.'" Dad managed a shy smile. "I can

read English only a small bit. Not as good as daughter!"
We shared a chuckle over that.

The waiters came back in and set before us a plate
of tempting berry tarts. Also a massive silver bowl filled
with premium vanilla ice cream. My uncle insisted on
serving me first, and I noticed a pleading in his eyes. I
took one bite of the confection and then set down my
spoon. "You guys, I need for all of you to hear something."

Pastor Ethan and Uncle Khemkaeng leaned forward, and I flushed as Saman slipped his arm around my
shoulders. "I just want to say this. What happened to me
a long time ago really hurt. It was wrong, and it hurt, and
sure, I carried around a lot of hate. But since coming
back home to Thailand, and during this year at BCS, I
had a new experience with the Lord. So I want to say
right here, where my dad and uncle can hear me: 'I
forgive both of you. I want for our shared family love to
be pure. Like the snow," I added, remembering the
recent choir song. "When I get married next month, Dad,
I want you and Tommy to walk me down the aisle
together. Uncle Viroj, you're for sure invited too,
because you're my brother in Jesus and now I love you
again. I really do." I reached out and seized his hand,
and his face crumpled. We waited in respectful silence
as he wept, then composed himself.

The restaurant's maître d' eased himself in through
the side door and my dad caught his eye, beckoning for
the bill. It had to be a hefty charge, and I marveled at
how he and my uncle had so bettered themselves
through diligent work. He scribbled his name along the
bottom and, noticing my attention, smiled in my
direction. Then he gave that casual no-big-deal shrug I

remembered from my *Prathom* days. It was such an exquisite memory, bringing my own birth mother back into the scene, that I felt a sharp stab of emotion.

"Look!" Uncle Viroj managed to push away his new shyness as he pointed out the massive picture window. High above the hotel and the surrounding surf, a lone bird was floating with the air currents. The clouds momentarily hid it from view, but then the winged wonder soared through the mist and we watched, agog, as it seemed to hover effortlessly, free and untethered from our world's gravitational tug.

"Very pretty." I felt a sweet lump in my throat, and leaned closer to my redeemed relative. "I am so happy, Uncle, that now you and I have both been set free."

He hesitated, then seized my hand and clutched it. "*Kop kuhn, nuu*," he murmured. "Thank you, child."

MY PARENTS SWEPT into Thailand in high spirits, ready for a gala wedding and a new life at their beloved Bangkok Christian School. We had less than a week to pull it off, but Saman and I had already done most of the legwork, deciding to return to the same Sheraton where other BCS nuptials had come off splendidly.

"Lucky for you the girl's family pays the bill," I teased Saman, shuffling through the hotel's many invoices. "But thank you, sweetie, for your help." His dad had sent us a generous check for 70,000 baht, around two grand in American funds, and that helped a whole lot.

He sighed, glancing over at Tommy, who was scribbling notes to himself about the ceremony's musical lineup. "I feel bad that I got overextended at work. You know, with the loans and all. And then getting the car.

Bad move."

"That nice car kind of melted my heart," I laughed. "So no matter where else we skimp, we're keeping the Mercedes."

To preserve the budget, we opted to have our rehearsal dinner right in the church dining hall, and the UCC cooks put together a delectable feast. Tommy was pouring down the pineapple milkshakes with abandon, and Mom aimed a kick at his shins. "You're not going to fit into your tux," she warned.

"Oh, yeah." He had the grace to look chagrined, and nudged the half-finished treat toward Saman. 'Drink up, son-in-law. It's all yours."

My birth dad had been interrupted by a pair of phone calls, and he suddenly excused himself and dashed down the stairs to the street. A moment later he returned, huffing, and proudly opened up a shipping box. "These are so beautiful," he announced with evident pride, passing around samples of the wedding program. The script was ornate, and I flushed happily as I saw the bride listed at the top: *Pranom Niratpattanasai Daggett.*

Weeks earlier I'd had a heart-to-heart with Tommy about having both fathers walk me down the aisle. And also about using my original birth name in the program. "You're sure you don't mind, Dad?"

"Absolutely not. He gave birth to you, he raised you to be a beautiful princess, and he has a right to share the day."

"You're too much," I had told him. "And you know you'll always be Daddy to me."

"Well, of course."

Now Anuman and my Uncle Viroj motioned, and I followed Saman over to their table. "You must also bring Mommy and Dad. And sister," Anuman encouraged. "We have special surprise for you, Pranom."

Uh oh. I was thankful for my birth father's newfound generosity, but sometimes emotions do get the better of parents, especially when their baby girl's about to walk down the aisle. But nothing in the world could have prepared me for what happened as we gathered around my Thai dad's cell phone.

"Uncle and I have gift for you, Pranom," he said without fanfare. "Please. After your mommy pass away, and also prison, and the shame we bring to family, now God has given a big blessing. More big blessing than we can expect. Business is good. Grow all the time. Now we have eight employees. Everyone work hard. And we think to ourselves: 'There cannot be gift enough to make it okay, what happened to you as child. We are so sorry. So glad God forgive us, and now you forgive us too. What could be a more sweet joy than this?'"

I felt my flesh tingle. What did he have in mind?

"Please look at this many pictures." He began swiping through a series of files, and a nicely appointed house appeared. It had a familiar look to it, and I suddenly suspected it was in the same housing development where Auntie Rachel was raising her kids.

"This house very nice," Dad assured me. "See?" There was a series of photos revealing a spacious kitchen, three bedrooms, a TV entertainment den, bookshelves. The backyard was well manicured. The kitchen table was empty except for a pair of champagne glasses; next to it was an unopened bottle of expensive fruit juice.

"I think I find one more picture," Anuman managed, and I saw a trace of his familiar teasing grin.

"See? Saman, soon my son, you can see okay?"

"I'm looking." We both edged closer, and then the last photo sprang onto the page. The front door of the house had a large banner draped across it. "Home of Saman and Pranom Takuathung."

"What!" I could hardly get my breath. "Dad? What's going on?"

"Daddy and Uncle have small gift for girl we love. We have great pride and joy," my birth dad assured me. "God give us so much blessing. And now, you get married and live here in good home."

Uncle Viroj reached into his coat pocket and pulled loose an embossed envelope. "Please open."

I slid my finger along the crease and tugged loose the sheaf of papers. It was indeed the deed to a lovely new home, and it took only a moment to scan down to the bottom and realize it was ours free and clear.

And I couldn't help it. I burst into tears. Flinging myself into my dad's arms, I wept on his shoulder. Then I hugged my uncle hard, feeling grateful and wonderfully free. "Thank you, Uncle Viroj. Thank you. I love you guys."

Tommy offered high fives all around, grinning from ear to ear. Mom gave me a generous squeeze. "Looks like we better do some real estate shopping in that same neighborhood," she teased. "Not that we want to spy on you kids. But, you know. Just in case grandkids come along."

"Not for years and years and years," I managed loftily, and Paloma cracked up. "I'll bet not. You're going to come back pregnant from the honeymoon."

THE NIGHT BEFORE the grand event, Paloma and I

sat around our cramped kitchen table with our folks, playing Crazy Eights and tossing out escalating insults like in the old Portland days. It felt amazing to be so liberated, and with a sparkling new home about to be ours. Still, as we flipped cards on the table and teased Dad for his miscues, I had that one last nagging *thing* in the back of my mind. Excusing myself for a pretend potty break, I hid in the bathroom and dashed off a nervous text to Saman. *Really need to see you, babe. Just a half hour. Diner?*

He dinged back a yes in less than thirty seconds, and I hit the flush lever to throw my family off the track. We played two more games, and then I leveled with them.

"Listen, you guys, I've got to go downstairs. Just one thing with Saman, and then we can play some more if you like."

One thing I'll say for Mom: she always had perceptive antenna. I think she knew immediately what my agenda's one bullet point had to be. "Are you okay, honey?"

"Yeah. Sure. I think so," I hastily amended.

Saman was waiting for me as I dodged sidewalk traffic and paused at the last corner before the diner. "Want something to eat?"

"Huh uh."

"At least a soda. We'll split it."

We shared a couple of sips and then I just spilled it all. "Sweetie, I just want to talk about tomorrow night. When we're together at last."

He put a hand on my forearm. "You don't have to. I know it's a delicate thing, that you've got scars. But please don't worry. We'll take it slow, we've got fifty years to get it right. As far as I'm concerned, it's our honeymoon night, it's a first for both of us, and the stuff that happened before never did count in heaven's ledger." He smiled at me, and it was the most beautiful thing I'd ever seen. "On top of which, with your birth dad and uncle now back and you forgiving them–which blows my mind, just blows it to heaven and back–I think we're going to have a sweet time tomorrow and a whole million other sweet, explosive bedroom nights following."

"I think so too," I told him, feeling almost swept away with how much in love I was with this special, one-in-seven-billion man. God's eternal gift to me, Pranom Niratpattanasai Daggett.

He leaned across the rickety table, almost spilling our shared soda, and his kiss was pregnant with meaning. "Can't wait to be your husband," he murmured. "Hurry up tomorrow."

Back in the apartment, Mom eyed me knowingly but said nothing. "We'd better get back to the hotel," she announced. "Big day tomorrow. But first, kiddo, come over here and snuggle up with me on the couch."

I rested in her embrace, my head on her still bony shoulder, and it felt just as sweet as a decade ago. "I love you, Mom," I told her. "Thank you again for rescuing me. I don't know why God has given me so many gifts, but I am so, so, so thankful."

"It was always our pleasure," she said, stroking my hair. "And God's beautiful blueprint."

AUNT RACHEL WAS MY main wardrobe lady over at the Sheraton, and by the time we were done with dress, hair, and makeup, both of us were sniffling. "You look like a dream, honey," she said over and over. "And I know you guys will be sublimely happy. I pray for that every day, you know."

"Don't make me cry," I choked. "But thanks, Auntie Rachel."

Left unsaid between us was the miracle of this American lady coming to Bangkok, getting herself cut up in an alleyway, falling in love with a Thai Buddhist, and then becoming my adopted aunt. We shared a bond that outbid blood and DNA, and it was a rush of joy every time I realized I got to be Rachel Marie Chaisurivirat's teaching ally for the next couple decades.

Pastor Gino poked his head in the door and then simply took in the scene. "Oh, my," he breathed. "Pranom, you are . . . just godly. That's what you are. A lovely vision. Saman is a very blessed man."

I thanked him, and he glanced pointedly at his watch. "Are you ready?"

We'd rehearsed the march several times already, and I felt joyous but wistful as I took Dad's arm. Meaning Tommy. Anuman, perfectly contented with how things were, followed us up the aisle, just a respectful few feet behind. At the front of the ballroom, my Uncle Viroj was next to Khemkaeng and a row of our BCS teachers, and we exchanged a meaningful glance. He offered me a silent *wai* that seemed to say, "Thank you again for your forgiveness," and I nodded, relieved that my soul was healed at last.

During Gino's brief homily, he took in the three hundred or so guests, and then set aside his notes. "All my friends here," he added, "Saman and Pranom, when has the kingdom of Thailand ever seen such a waterfall of divine mercy? Heartache has turned into glory. Why?

Because a young girl grew up in the garden of heaven's grace, and she forgave. Weddings are always a story of new beginnings, but never more than in this place and on this day. Pranom, today you are our heroine. Live with Saman in a friendship warmed by grace and nurtured by mercy. You told me once that the ocean of God's forgiveness is always enough; it can never run dry or be depleted by the frailties of our human race. May heaven always shine upon this couple its choicest blessings, its sweetest tunes, its unshakeable faith, its tenderest affections."

We said our vows and then Pastor Gino announced to the eager throng that Saman was now at liberty to kiss his bride. I felt a sweet quiver of electricity pass between us, and out of the corner of my eye, I saw Paloma's smile.

THE FESTIVITIES WERE beginning to wind down when Tommy came over to me. "Thank God it's not a trans-Pacific goodbye," he told us both, and I sense Dad was a little choked up. "Can you guys join Mom and me for just a sec?"

"Sure, Daddy." I knew my parents couldn't top Anuman's wedding present, and hoped they weren't about to offer up some extravagant but foolish gesture. Just Dad dropping his career and coming out to BCS to teach again was a galactic thing.

Most of the young people had gravitated to the makeshift dance floor close to the portable DJ, so the banquet tables in the back were pretty much deserted. The centerpieces each had a pair of candles, all still lit, and the four of us sat together at one off in the corner. Dad was already wrestling with his emotions, and for a moment wasn't able to speak. I leaned my head against his shoulder and just murmured: "Love you, Daddy. I really do."

"I know, kid." He composed himself and then looked directly at both of us. "Look. We all know what happened. And how we're praying that all your honeymoon stuff will be just, you know. Sweet and innocent. Not stained by anything from before."

Saman nodded soberly. "I love your daughter, Mr. Daggett. I swear I'll take good care of her always."

"I know." Dad hesitated, then reached into his pocket and got out a slip of paper. "I've held onto this for ten years, baby. You know what it is."

I didn't, but as I reached out and carefully plucked it from his fingers, all at once I had to bite down hard on my lip. It was the note from the Pussycat Club, the exact same message my adopted father had offered as my rescue. Now I read it again, half-aloud, knowing I might bust out crying.

Tomorrow your BCS family—we will come and save you.

I stared at those ten sacred words, both remembering and rejoicing. This good man had rescued me. My entire future existence with Saman was because he was pure and generous through and through. *We will come and save you.* Okay. But really, it was Dad. His offer, his gift of adoption, everything.

"Sweetie, I thought we'd just take this note, this last trace of Pattaya, and we'd light it on fire and let all that go forever." He pointed toward the candle, its flame wobbly with the currents of the hotel AC. "And then you and this wonderful man can go on your honeymoon and never look back."

364 DAVID B. SMITH

It was such an incredible gesture, so poignant and immeasurable in meaning, that I could scarcely absorb what Dad was saying. And I tried to feel, to anticipate, the release that would come as those ten wrenching words curled up into defeated ashes. Saman and I could head to our honeymoon cottage unencumbered, as free as that soaring bird in the Phuket skies.

But it was my husband who spoke first. "No way," he blurted out. Then catching himself, he repeated it. "No way, Dad. That piece of paper, it's sacred. It's the only reason I got Pranom for my wife." He took my hand, and then picked up the paper and caressed it in his hand. "This never leaves our household. Never."

He excused himself for a moment, and our gazes followed him as he went over to where Pastor Gino was pacing back and forth with little Boonrat, clucking and teasing him. Together they fished in the pastor's familiar satchel, and my husband came back to our table with a brand new Bible. "I didn't really have a decent one of these," he explained to my parents. "But Pastor Gino said he'd get us one."

I watched, my eyes wet, as Saman took that redemptive note and placed it in the back of the Bible, patting it into position and then murmuring a prayer as he set it back down. "There. It stays there forever." His gaze met Tommy's and the two men shook hands. "Thank you, Dad. I'll always be proud to be in your family."

Saman's own parents came out to the front of the Sheraton as a hooting crowd of BCS faculty and students gathered around to say farewell and *kaw hie choke dee*. We still had a ninety-minute drive down to Bangsaen, and I'd already told Saman I really wanted to have a quick walk along the shoreline before heading up to our long-awaited honeymoon. Who knows? Perhaps the tides had finally liberated that stuck-in-place piece of plywood.

SO LET'S SKIP OVER the next, oh, fourteen hours or so. It was a deliciously lazy morning; I awakened in my lover's arms, and we didn't climb out of bed for a while longer. But I knew Mom and Dad and Paloma had a rental car and were coming down just to have breakfast with us in the splendid shoreline buffet restaurant.

Dad was his usual wicked self, trying to curb his teasing impulses. And I could tell both Paloma and Klahan were thinking similar delicious thoughts; I shot my sister a scolding glance, and she busied herself with a glass of apple juice, avoiding my glance.

It was while the guys were over in the made-to-order omelet line that Mom finally had a quiet moment alone with me. "You all right, sweetheart?"

I gave her an innocent shrug. "Yeah. I'm really good."

Mom pursed her lips. "Well, um, I hope you got some rest."

I heaved a theatrical sigh. "Mom, it's okay. I know you love me, and that you're probably wondering how things went. In terms of burning up notes and fresh starts and all that."

"Well, honey, these things do take time."

Dad and the others were still over by the grill; I could hear his characteristic guffaw at something Saman had probably said. I took our shared moment of privacy, and twisted Mom's chair around so she could see out toward the beach. The shore was fairly quiet for a

Monday morning, but quite a ways out into the deep surf, a speedboat was slowly trolling along, the hum of its engine muted by the gentle rumble of the incoming surf. Suspended high above the deep frothing currents was a vacationer floating beneath a red-and-white parasail. He was but a distant dot in the glad, carefree sky, and as the boat slowly churned to the south, the flyer soared even higher until the ski rope was stretched almost taut.

"See that guy, Mom?"

She nodded. "Uh huh. Looks like fun."

I paused. "And how high he is?"

"He's way up there in the clouds."

I allowed that metaphor to sink in. "That's nothing, Mom."

Mom thought this over, and I saw her relieved smile. Then she reached over and gave my hand a squeeze. "I'm glad, baby. After Daddy finishes his omelet, we'll get out of your way."

We sat there on the beach together, me and my American mom. The lingering aromas from the buffet table surrendered now to the cleansing tang of salty air as the ocean waves just kept splashing toward us.

* * *

DEDICATION

When I began writing this story, I chose at random a nice Thai name–Paitoon–for the role of Pranom's new Bangkok boyfriend. Instead, as the story progressed, I felt moved to name him after Saman Kunam, the heroic Navy diver who perished in 2018 while trying to rescue those adorable boys lost in a Thailand cave. God bless the family of this self-sacrificing legend.

NOTE FROM THE AUTHOR

Words fail me. They truly do. This writing project is done, and I am overwhelmed with thankfulness on multiple levels.

First of all, my Lord and Savior Jesus poured these ten Bangkok stories into my soul through his grace and providence. He led my mom and dad to Thailand back in 1957; from the tender age of two, this sweet, tumultuous kingdom was my childhood home. I have never stopped praising heaven for sending my family over the Pacific waves and into this godly and life-changing adventure.

So often as my writing has brought me to the last page of a new manuscript, and I pause over my keyboard, I've had my eyes fill with tears. *Where did this inspiration come from?* I enjoy writing, and it's a pleasant diversion. But I'm not trained in the craft; I was never educated in the art of shaping a novel. These ten testimonies are in my hands and now yours because the Holy Spirit had his way. Thank you, God. Thank you, thank you.

And I thank each of you for picking up these books and absorbing the unfolding of God's will through the lovely characters who walk the *thanons* of Bangkok. I've been deeply appreciative for your words of encouragement, your generous Amazon book reviews, the fact that when you finish one volume, you quickly click on the buy button for the next. It's not yet a massive circle of friends, and I do hope you'll share your enthusiasm with others who might be blessed by the influence of Rachel Marie and Khemkaeng and their BCS community. But at this nice moment of a possible *adieu*, I want you to know of my heartfelt appreciation. Every writer longs to be read and experienced, and to know that the hours at the keyboard have sweetened the life journey of those who board the tour bus.

The last word is this. All ten books are a story of how amazing and good and provident is our God. The saints who populate Bangkok Christian School repeat it over and over: "Jesus is just so awesome! To be his ambassador is sweet adventure." That's my testimony too, my friends.

Kop kuhn mahk. Thank you all.

And DO NOT miss the thrill of hearing these Bangkok love stories unfold in a dramatic audio presentation! Gifted performer Tonya Foster Yancey inhabits the role of Rachel Marie Stone in the gripping debut novel in this series. Be sure to enjoy *Love in a Distant Land* as a full ten-hour presentation.

DISCUSSION QUESTIONS

1.   We immediately encounter Pranom's demons from Pattaya Beach. Besides the awful memories, what other emotions would an unwilling victim of the sex trade experience?

2.   This Thai girl is thankful to have been rescued into a Christian home. But what kinds of faith conflict could we expect such a recovering teenager to feel?

3.   Have you ever held a wrenching secret for long years, not confiding even in a sibling? Was it hard to keep your pain locked away?

4.   Some victims of a scourge like trafficking come out relatively unscathed. Others are scarred for decades. What causes this wide variety of responses?

5.   How have you talked yourself through the valley-of-despair moments when you are tempted to chuck your Christian faith and just walk away?

6.   Several characters in the Rachel Marie series have been tempted with the idea: the guy determines the faith. Pranom nearly succumbs to the reality that a secular life with Saman could be quite wondrous and that if he offers that kind of glittery future, she'll grab it. What's faulty about such a mindset?

7.   When Pranom discovers her boyfriend's treachery, she quite readily forgives Sanam. Would you have broken things off for good? How would you decide if a

special friend's betrayal is a one-time error or an unfixable character flaw?

8.   If a young Christian is facing marriage after the jagged scars of prostitution and her worries about sexual dysfunction, would she be forgiven for carefully experimenting with a new lover just to make sure she's still capable of a physical response?

9.   In terms of Christmas Eve and making out on the edge of the bed, how far is too far? When did Pranom and Sanam cross over a line and into sinful behavior? What earlier mistaken decisions led her into such heartache?

10.   All through this Rachel Marie series, newbies are won to Jesus through the vibrant happiness and the healthy community that is United Christian Church. It's so easy when it's fiction! What are some of the ways where your church is a healing family? Are there tangible ways where you and your family could make more of a difference?

11.   It's a peripheral story, but little sister Paloma is falling in love with a sweet Thai boy. She might relocate to Bangkok, attend a local university, and marry someone from a vastly different culture. If you were Samantha (Mom!), what advice would you give your younger daughter?

12.   If you've read all ten books, do you have a favorite pop-the-question moment? Most of the Rachel Marie characters have a sweet–and often inventive–

engagement celebration. Did your own happy evening live up to your expectations? Is that an important part of courtship?

13. Has your understanding of forgiveness been deepened through your empathy with characters like Samantha and now Pranom? Share with others how the idea of God's ocean of grace has helped you to forgive an enemy when you didn't really feel it.

14. This story deals rather frankly with a couple's hope for sexual compatibility within marriage. What are some ways a husband and wife can help move toward the ideal of giving each other pleasure in the bedroom? How should they deal with issues that threaten to damage such moments?

15. Christian fiction does have the cheerful advantage of "and they lived happily ever after." How convenient that Tommy and Samantha are moving back to Bangkok! What are some favorite Bible promises that can help us cope with the reality that life sometimes has tough detours that go for a really long time?

Made in the USA
Las Vegas, NV
30 April 2022